VILLAGE OF THE LOST GIRLS

VILLAGE OF THE LOST GIRLS

AGUSTÍN MARTÍNEZ

Translated by Frank Wynne

Quercus

First published in the Spanish language
as 'Monteperdido' in 2015 by
Plaza & Janés
Barcelona, Spain

This edition first published in Great Britain in 2019 by
Quercus Editions Ltd
Carmelite House
50 Victoria Embankment
London EC4Y 0DZ

An Hachette UK company

A CIP catalogue record for this book is available
from the British Library

HB ISBN 978 1 78648 843 5
TPB ISBN 978 1 78648 841 1
EBOOK ISBN 978 1 78648 842 8

10 9 8 7 6 5 4 3 2

Typeset by Jouve (UK), Milton Keynes

Printed and bound in Great Britain by Clays Ltd, Elcograf S.p.A.

For Laura, for making sense of everything.

In memory of Gonzalo Martínez Montiel:
Although (I think) I know what he would have
said about this novel, I would have loved to
have heard him say it . . .

The Deer

'Leave the girls to play,' Raquel told her.

Her daughter had climbed up a little hill, plunging her hands into the snow to steady herself as she went. The footprints marking her ascent had transformed into tiny black holes. Having reached the top, she tried to stand up without losing her balance, flinging her arms wide and tottering wildly. It looked as though at any moment she would fall and roll down the snowy slope. She was laughing.

Laughing as though she were being tickled.

Her rubber boots sank up to the ankles, giving her enough purchase to be able to bend and scoop up a handful of snow. Excited as a child on Christmas morning, she giggled as she raced to make a snowball. Ana had just turned eleven.

'They'll end up getting hurt, you'll see,' Montserrat grumbled as she sat down next to Raquel.

At the foot of the snowy hill, Montserrat's daughter hunkered down, waiting for the impact of the snowball Ana was making. The girls were the same age. They were neighbours. They were inseparable.

'There's a lot of snow,' Raquel said. 'If they do fall, they're not going to get hurt. Besides, they've got hard heads.'

That morning, as soon as Ana saw that the storm had passed, she had raced into the kitchen and demanded that her mother take her outside to play. Raquel, who had been preparing breakfast, said that she would, though she would have preferred to have stayed at home in the warmth. After they'd eaten, they popped next door. As soon as Montserrat opened the door, Ana had dashed past her in search of her friend, shrieking, 'Snowball fight!'

A few minutes later, Raquel and Montserrat headed out with their daughters. Wrapped up warm in mittens, woolly hats and puffa jackets (Ana's was pink, Lucía's pale blue), the two girls ran on ahead. Two squealing, furry creatures prancing and zigzagging through the snow, heading for the park.

The little hill Ana had climbed was actually the playground slide, buried beneath a snowdrift. From her perch at the top, Ana launched snowballs, trying to make her voice sound deep; she was playing at being an ogre, a fiendish monster. At the bottom, Lucía hid behind bushes that had been transformed into frozen white parapets.

The sky was cloudless, the sunlight glittered on the soft snow and brought a little warmth to Raquel's face. She closed her eyes and breathed in a lungful of air: cold and clear as a mountain spring. Next to her, Montserrat huddled in her thick coat for warmth.

There was a soft, agreeable murmur. The rustling wind in the trees echoed with their voices and the girls' shrill laughs. Raquel was in no hurry. She was thinking of the scent of bedlinen, the warmth of her husband's skin under the sheets as he took her in his arms.

The river rushed on, invisible beneath a thin sheet of ice.

Silent under the mantle of snow, the pulse of the village continued. Steady, constant.

A deer appeared from among the trees that circled the park. Raquel opened her eyes, as though somehow aware of its presence. Snow hung on its antlers, its coat. It took a few steps towards them, oblivious to the girls, unafraid.

'I can't believe it,' Montserrat whispered, watching as it came closer.

Raquel hissed not to make a sound, not to alert the girls. The deer walked over to where they were seated, hooves sinking into the snow, sunlight making its coat shimmer like copper. It looked taller than any deer they had ever seen before. Huge. When it was only a few metres away, Raquel closed her eyes again. She pictured it passing within inches, pausing for a moment to look at her, to smell her. She could feel its breath. As though it were the breath of this mountain village.

When she opened her eyes again, the deer had vanished.

The girls were laughing and throwing snowballs.

She knew that this image would be forever engraved in her mind. That, in time, she would search for it among her memories, as one might seek out the shelter of home.

Agustín Martínez

MONTEPERDIDO SHOCKED BY DISAPPEARANCE OF TWO ELEVEN-YEAR-OLD GIRLS

Eleven-year-olds Ana M. G. and Lucía C. S. left Valle del Ésera School at 5 p.m. last Monday, 19 October 2009, and set off to walk along their usual route to the neighbourhood of Los Corzos, on the outskirts of the village of Monteperdido, in the province of Huesca. Neither of the girls made it home.

'We are keenly aware that the first 48 hours of an investigation are crucial. We have not been able to do as much as we would have liked, but we will not rest until Ana and Lucía are safely home,' said a police spokesperson, who denied that there had been any evidence of violence at the site where the girls were last seen, which could lead to fears for their safety.

The parents of the girls have not made a public statement, though a spokesperson for the families has said that they are shocked and deeply concerned. Since their daughters were very familiar with the route home, the parents have rejected suggestions that the girls might have become lost, but have no idea who might have taken them. They firmly hope that their daughters will soon be able to give them answers.

A VILLAGE IN SHOCK

Monteperdido is a well-known tourist spot, famed for its spectacular natural setting, ringed as it is by two national

4

parks in the shadow of the highest peaks of the Pyrenees. Ana and Lucía are well known to local villagers. Both are excellent students and, being next-door neighbours, they are inseparable friends.

Although neighbours are doing everything possible to help with the search, there has been a growing impatience at the lack of any concrete results. No witnesses have come forward; it is as though the two girls vanished into thin air. The Guardia Civil has dispatched a number of officers that specialize in abductions of minors to lead the investigation.

'We know that it is difficult, but we would ask that people be patient and respect the privacy of the families during this difficult time,' said one of the recently assigned officers. 'This is a distressing case, but one that we hope to resolve quickly. In order to do so, however, we need the support of the people in the Monteperdido area, and of the media.'

'Of course we want to believe that the girls are safe and well. We're clinging to that hope; it's what is keeping us going,' confessed someone close to the two girls. It is a hope shared by everyone in Monteperdido.

Monteperdido

Five Years Later

1

The Thaw

The glacier was melting in the summer heat. Ice sheets fractured with a soft crack, and a thin trickle of water spurted from the sheer face of the mountain that towered above the village and gave it its name: Monteperdido – the Lost Mountain.

Some way down the slope, at the bottom of a ravine, the front wheels of the crashed car continued to spin. It lay on its roof, the windscreen a spider's web of splintered glass, the whole scene enveloped in a cloud of dust and smoke. It had careered over the edge of the dirt road a hundred metres above. The fall had left a trail of broken trees and rutted earth.

Wind whipped away the smoke to reveal a pool of red inside the car, fed by a constant trickle of blood, like water from a leaky tap. The blood dripped from the forehead of the driver, still strapped into his seat belt, now suspended upside down. His skull had been shattered by the impact.

The only sound was the wind and a faint whimper. A girl dragged herself from the wreck, her arms marbled with innumerable thin slashes, her clothes cut to ribbons, a tangle of golden hair falling over her face. As she crawled through the broken rear wind-screen, shards of glass became buried in her thighs. She was no more than sixteen. She choked back the pain and managed to pull herself free only to collapse, utterly exhausted. She lay on the grass, her breathing ragged, her whole body shuddering with every breath.

The place where the car had crashed was almost inaccessible: a deep gorge between mountains that were still snow-capped in summer.

Along the rim of the canyon, a narrow road wound its way down to the valley. A four-wheel drive had stopped and a man of about thirty was standing on the edge, staring down into the gorge. He took off his sunglasses to check he had not been mistaken: a car had gone off the cliff. He rummaged for his mobile phone in the glove compartment and made a call.

For five years now, the churchyard of Santa María de Laude in Monteperdido had held memorial events for the missing girls. In the early days, it had been the meeting place for the families and their neighbours in the village, for the forest rangers and the jour-nalists. Makeshift shrines were set up next to the church doors, with flowers, stuffed toys, messages . . . Everyone wanted to leave some token of their grief, their anger . . .

Víctor Gamero, a sergeant with the Guardia Civil, remembered that the journalists had been the first to disappear. Although, at the time, he had merely been a junior officer with the force in Monte-perdido, he had been responsible for shielding the families from the milling crowds who came from other villages to take part in the search for Ana and Lucía.

Lucía's father, Joaquín Castán, was angry and frustrated. There were only neighbours from Monteperdido now, and not even all of them. Too much time had passed, the village could not simply grind to a halt every time Joaquín decided to hold another meeting to further the investigation. Two huge photographs of the girls flanked the table at which the parents were sitting. Lucía, with almond eyes and a mischievous smile, looked as though she had been caught in the middle of some private game. Ana, with her mouth open, was flashing a gap-toothed grin. The summer sun had given her skin a golden glow, and her blonde hair was bleached almost white and contrasted with her deep, dark eyes. The girls had been happy when these pictures were taken, yet today, as Lucía's father protested at the scant resources being allocated to the police investigation, the photographs of the girls looked sad.

Sergeant Víctor Gamero felt his phone vibrate and stepped away from the churchyard to take the call. Burgos, one of his officers, explained the situation, tripping over every word. He knew that no one would be happy with the news.

'Why didn't someone alert me? Who gave the order?' Víctor said.

He had a right to be informed. He was the senior officer of the Guardia Civil in Monteperdido, and the only road into the village had just been cordoned off without his permission.

Assistant Inspector Sara Campos gave the officer his orders. He was to stop every vehicle entering or leaving Monteperdido, search the boot of every car, the rear of every van. No one – however well he knew them – was to be waved through. Burgos was irritated by this last suggestion.

'When I wear this uniform, I'm a Guardia Civil to everyone, even my own mother,' he protested.

'Have you alerted the duty sergeant?' she said, ignoring the officer's affronted dignity.

'I just called him. He'll be waiting for you at the petrol station on the outskirts of the village,' Burgos said, still bristling.

Sara turned on her heel and walked back to the car where Santiago was waiting. An icy wind rushed down the mountain, so she pulled on her black fleece jacket, zipped it up and buried her hands in the pockets, her dark brown hair fluttering wildly in the brisk wind.

Inspector Santiago Baín kept the engine idling as he waited for the officers to remove the barriers blocking the road to Monteperdido. He could have spared himself the journey, could have called ahead and told the families to meet him at Barbastro Hospital, but he wanted to observe their reactions in the village, give them the news face to face; he knew that the information he was bringing was not a conclusion, but the first line of a story that was yet to be told.

The passenger seat was piled with papers and case files – it was impossible for Sara to squeeze in – so, careful not to disturb the pile, she set it on the dashboard.

'I just hope he follows orders and checks the boots of the cars,' she said pessimistically. 'I don't think he likes the idea of questioning his neighbours.'

Burgos lifted the barrier and allowed the car to pass. Baín pulled away, heading down the narrow road towards the village. Though it was still early, the sun had already begun to dip behind the mountains. The road ran parallel to the River Ésera, which snaked through a deep ravine between the soaring central Pyrenees, which cast a deep shadow over the whole valley. Though the road climbed steeply uphill, around treacherous hairpin bends, still the mountain peaks towered over the landscape. From time to time, the setting sun flashed through the branches of the trees, staining their vivid green leaves a dusky pink. For a moment, Sara allowed herself to soak up the verdant scene, blossoming with life this 12th July. Standing on a high crag, a deer seemed to be watching the car, then, in an instant, it turned its head and bounded into the trees.

Sara smiled and picked up the mountain of paperwork she had set down on the dashboard.

'Right, so Lucía's parents are Joaquín Castán and Montserrat Grau, forty-seven and forty-three respectively. Aside from Lucía, they have another child, Quim, who would be about nineteen at this stage . . . Joaquín Castán has been the driving force behind the Foundation . . .'

'I think I've seen him on TV a couple of times,' Santiago said, not taking his eyes off the road.

'Ana's mother is Raquel Mur. She's a little younger. Just turned forty.'

'And her father?'

'There is no current address for him on file.' Sara leafed through the documents, desperately looking for the information. 'The whole investigation was a disaster. No wonder the girls were never found. Roadblocks weren't set up until seventy-two hours after their disappearance; no evidence was gathered from the place where they were abducted; by the time forensics were called in, the rain had washed away every trace . . .'

Inspector Baín was not surprised; he was familiar with how Guardia Civil operated in rural villages like Monteperdido. He had worked with them on other cases during his long years in the service – almost thirty-five years. 'So, Ana's parents are separated?' he asked.

'Yes, to all intents and purposes, though they were never legally separated. The father, Álvaro Montrell, was the only person arrested during the whole investigation, and he was only in custody for a couple of days. They clearly had no concrete evidence to hold him. I'm guessing the marriage unravelled after that.'

Sara looked up and saw that Santiago had put on his driving glasses.

'You're really handsome in those glasses,' she mocked.

'As soon as light starts to fade, my eyesight is shot to shit . . . What do you expect me to do? Do they make me look old?'

'No older than you are.'

'One of these days, you'll be my age, and you won't find it remotely amusing when some rookie officer makes fun of your presbyopia.' Santiago Baín smiled.

Sara looked at her boss. His face was lined with wrinkles, but that was not about age. Or at least not entirely. He had had them ever since Sara first met him and, thinking back, she remembered the image that had sprung to mind when she first set eyes on Inspector Baín's wrinkled face: a chickpea.

Both officers fell silent, intimidated by the landscape as the road wound through the foothills of two imposing mountains. The majority of Pyrenean three-thousanders were in this section of the mountain range, which was one of the factors that had made the original investigation so difficult. When she raised her head from the dossiers, it looked to Sara as though they were approaching a dead end; the tarmacked road seemed to stop at the base of the mountain, never reaching the village hidden on the far side. Monte

Albádes and Pico de Paderna towered like colossal statues, like two immortal guards who decided who should pass. As they rounded the last bend, Sara saw the road disappear into Monte Albádes. They took the narrow tunnel that ran through sheer rock like a needle through fabric, and, when they emerged on the other side, what the tourist brochures called the 'Hidden Valley' was spread out before them.

On the horizon, she could just make out the village of Monteperdido. Dark, silent houses were punctured by yellow windows, now that the sun had set. To Sara, the houses looked as though they had not been built by men, but rather had been shaped by nature, by seismic shifts and centuries of erosion, like the sierra all around.

A sign by the roadside gave a name to the stretch of mountain they had just come through: *FALL GORGE*.

'I don't know where I went wrong,' Baín joked. 'The rookie officer usually has to drive.'

'You picked the wrong partner. The day I finally got my licence, I swore I'd never get behind the wheel again.'

'So what will you do when I'm not around?'

'Plod on.'

Up ahead, on the right-hand side of the road, stood the service station – though in fact it was just a single petrol pump. The Guardia Civil four-wheel drive was parked on the forecourt. The headlights were on, picking out the silhouette of someone standing in front of it. By now, it was pitch dark. As Sara was about to get out of the car, Santiago stopped her.

'Just this once, let me do the talking.'

She noted that he was trying to sound offhand, as though this was a throwaway remark, when actually he had been waiting for the right moment to say it.

'Why?' she asked, feeling like she had done something wrong.

'Because I'll want you to deal with the local Guardia Civil from here on. Let them know who's in charge.'

'But you usually like to play bad cop,' she protested meekly.

'I don't have many years left in the service; I'd like to play good cop just once,' Santiago said, trying to make a joke of it.

Santiago clambered out of the car and Sara watched him walk towards the headlights. He did not usually give orders without explanation. And Santiago had never cared about being nice, especially not to people involved in a case. There had to be another reason. It had to be about her. Santiago was trying to spare her having direct contact with those involved in the girls' disappearance.

'Fucking chickpea,' Sara muttered to herself before finally getting out of the car.

Sergeant Víctor Gamero watched as the two officers from the Policía Nacional approached. Five years earlier, specialized officers from the Guardia Civil had led the investigation. He could not understand why the Policía Nacional and the Servicio de Atención a la Familia should get involved now, nor why the road needed to be closed. The officer approaching was an older man wearing a suit. He tucked a pair of glasses into his inside pocket and held out his hand with a warm smile.

'Inspector Santiago Baín of the S.A.F.'

'Víctor Gamero, sergeant in charge of Monteperdido Station. What's going on? If you wanted to close the road, I should have been informed.'

'Actually, we haven't closed it, we've just set up a checkpoint,' Baín explained.

'What for?'

Santiago did not answer but turned to his colleague. She strode across the forecourt, sweeping her hair back into a ponytail. Soft features, not particularly tall, she was wearing jeans and a black sweater that rode up over the gun holstered in her belt.

'This is Assistant Inspector Sara Campos,' Baín said.

Víctor held out his hand and Sara hesitated a moment before proffering hers. She looked at him for only a split second before turning to survey the landscape surrounding the village.

'We need to talk to the families of the two girls,' she said.

'Has something happened?'

'Since we've come all this way, I'd have thought it was obvious that something has happened, wouldn't you?' she said curtly. 'You drive, we'll follow.'

Sara turned and headed back to the car. Víctor choked back his anger as he saw Baín smile; he seemed amused by his pushy fellow-officer.

Víctor drove through the village along Avenida de Posets. In the rear-view mirror, he could see the car carrying the S.A.F. officers. When he came to the crossroads, he took the road leading to the Hotel La Guardia and then headed towards the suburb of Los Corzos. He crossed the bridge over the Ésera. He had already phoned Joaquín Castán, the father of Lucía. The public meeting was over and he was back at home. Immediately afterwards, Víctor had called the *comandante* in Barbastro. Apparently the decision to have the S.A.F. lead the investigation came from high up. All officers were asked to cooperate. Víctor Gamero parked the car outside the parents' houses, at the very edge of the development. To the rear and on the right-hand side, the duplex belonging to Ana's parents was surrounded by pine forest. Lucía's house stood next to it.

Sara got out of the car and looked at the semi-detached houses. Although architecturally they attempted to blend with the style of the traditional houses in Monteperdido, with local stone and slate roofs, they were obviously ersatz. It was a recent housing development. The house on the left had a little shrine next to the garden gate. A photo of Lucía ringed with fresh flowers, three weather-beaten stuffed toys and a slate on which were chalked the words *1,726 DAYS WITHOUT LUCÍA*. The house on the right had nothing to identify it as the one where Ana had lived. The sergeant from the Guardia Civil approached Sara.

'Should I get the two families together?' he said.

Sara saw the door to Lucía's house open. Joaquín Castán appeared on the threshold. She recognized him from photographs in the case file.

'Did you tell him we were coming?' It was not so much a question as an accusation.

'I was asked to track them down,' Víctor said sullenly.

Sara glared at the officer and Víctor realized that this was the first time she had really looked at him.

'We'd like to talk to Ana's mother first,' Sara said.

Then she looked past Víctor, towards the four-wheel drive. He followed her gaze; on the back seat, a dog was clearly visible.

'He's mine,' Víctor said. 'But maybe he's not supposed to know anything either? Because I'm guessing he overheard what we said at the petrol station.'

Sara flashed a half-smile, only to suppress it as quickly as possible. A warning look from Santiago reminded her of her role: this time, she was the bad cop. She quickly turned and headed towards the house of Raquel Mur so that Gamero would not notice her uncertainty. Before they'd arrived, Santiago had asked her to relay the news. This was not the sort of situation where he felt he needed to spare her.

'From now on, any decision that needs to be taken, we'll discuss it first. We need to be on the same page. You understand that, don't you?' Baín said, laying a hand on Víctor Gamero's shoulder. He was young to be a senior sergeant, and Baín felt it would be easy to gain his trust.

Raquel Mur came to the door and, finding Sara there, she clumsily buttoned up her shirt, which showed a little too much cleavage. It was a man's blue, checked shirt that fell to her thighs, revealing her bare legs. It was obvious that she had not been expecting strangers.

'Sara Campos, from the Family Protection Unit. Do you mind if we come in?' She held up her warrant card.

Sara stared at the woman's bare feet as they padded almost fearfully across the parquet floor of the living room. Santiago Baín and Víctor Gamero followed Sara into the house. Raquel was clearly confused; her dark eyes tried frantically to catch Víctor's, waiting for an explanation. Her legs trembled as she slumped on to the sofa. What can she possibly be thinking, this mother who lost her child five years ago? Sara wondered. She had no desire to prolong the woman's anxiety. She sat on a coffee table facing the sofa, took Raquel's hands in hers and smiled.

'It's not often we get to give good news,' she said. 'We've found Ana.'

Raquel Mur felt the air in her lungs congeal, as though her whole body was suddenly crumpling. She gripped the officer's hands tightly.

'She's fine,' said Sara.

Hot tears welled in her eyes. Raquel Mur said nothing, but felt her lips curve into a smile. She brought her hands up to her face and began to sob.

Víctor Gamero led Raquel towards Inspector Baín's car. She was wearing the same jeans and shirt she had worn at the public meeting in the churchyard some hours earlier. She walked nervously, took a few steps back, as though she had forgotten something, then walked on again. Suddenly, she stopped dead, as if remembering what it was she had forgotten. She looked at Montserrat's house and whispered to the sergeant: 'I have to tell Montserrat.'

'The other officer will talk to her,' Víctor Gamero said, gently turning her away.

Montserrat was standing at the window that overlooked the front garden. By now, Lucía's mother must have realized that what was coming was not good news. Joaquín Castán was still standing in the doorway.

Santiago Baín and Sara Campos silently stepped inside, followed by Joaquín. In the living room, Montserrat nervously wiped her hands on a dishcloth, and did not stop until Joaquín gestured for her to sit next to him on the sofa. The walls were a shrine to the memory of their missing daughter: Lucía's smile beamed down from dozens of photographs that charted her childhood from newborn baby to the age of eleven.

'A crashed car was found this morning, about sixty kilometres south of here. It had skidded into a ravine,' Inspector Baín explained. 'When the call came in to the emergency services, they dispatched a helicopter from Barbastro. The site where the car had crashed could not be reached on foot. By the time the helicopter arrived, the driver, a man in his fifties, was already dead. He was almost certainly killed instantly, but we will have to wait for the autopsy results to confirm this. There was a girl there. She was unconscious, but had suffered no other serious injury. She was airlifted to Barbastro Hospital, where attempts were made to identify her. She was carrying no identity papers, but her fingerprints were in the system. It was Ana Montrell. It was at this point that my colleague and I visited the hospital.'

'What about my daughter?' Montserrat murmured.

'There was no one else in the car.'

'Maybe she wandered away from the car. What if she is somewhere nearby?'

'The helicopter scanned the area several times to eliminate that possibility,' Sara said.

'She's dead.' Montserrat began to sob, unable to think of another explanation for Ana's sudden reappearance.

'We have no reason to think that is the case,' Santiago reassured her, gripping her hand tightly. 'I know this is hard, but you shouldn't give up hope. We've been searching for your daughter for a long time, but this is the closest we have come in five years.'

'Who was the driver?' said Joaquín, stiff and motionless on the sofa, listening carefully to every word the officers said.

'We haven't yet been able to identify him. Rescuing the girl was the first priority for the emergency services. At first light tomorrow morning, they will go back to airlift the body and attempt to raise the car . . .'

Joaquín Castán remained silent for a moment. Montserrat was still sobbing quietly. Sara saw Joaquín glance at Baín's hands holding those of his wife, and then he said, 'The driver of the car – is he the man who took our daughter?'

Though the police suspected as much, it had proved impossible to access the body in the tangled metal of the wreck. The car had no licence plates, so Sara would need the chassis number in order to identify the vehicle – something it would be impossible to get until the car had been winched up from the ravine.

'I'm going to drive Ana's mother to the hospital,' Santiago said to Sara as they left the house. 'Ask Sergeant Gamero to take you to the police station and set up an incident room. And see if you can find us somewhere to sleep. We need to be working at 110 per cent tomorrow.'

A hotel called La Renclusa stood at the end of the main street, where the houses of Monteperdido began to peter out and the road rose steeply towards the mountains. The best accommodation in the village, Víctor said as he pulled up outside. The four and five-star hotels were higher up, in Posets, or further still, where the road vanished in the hills. A nervous girl with birdlike features led Sara and Víctor to the second floor. She stumbled through a description of the hotel's facilities, meal times, but Sara was not paying attention. She was staring at this girl, who looked no older than eighteen and seemed as fragile as a porcelain doll that might break at any minute. Her name was Elisa, she said, as she opened the windows that looked out towards the north-east. She talked about the spectacular sunrises over Monte Ármos to be seen from the window. Elisa was pretty, though she wore baggy clothes, as though determined to hide her body.

'Would you like me to get you some dinner?' she asked.

'No, thanks,' Sara said, 'I just need the keys to both rooms.' She looked at Elisa's long-sleeved blouse and the baggy cardigan and smiled. 'Does it get cold up here?'

'It gets a little cooler at night. But it's mid-July, so it never drops below twenty degrees.' The girl was a little confused by the question, then, noticing the way the officer was looking at her clothes, she added nervously, 'I'm a bit sensitive to cold.'

'Wearing XXL clothes won't make you any warmer,' Sara joked.

Inspector Santiago Baín drove in silence, gliding down through the darkness towards Barbastro. Sitting in the passenger seat, Raquel kept her face pressed to the window. She had not said a word since they got into the car. She did not know what to say. Hundreds of memories bustled in her mind, like a crowd of boisterous children trying to pile through a narrow doorway.

As she had taken down the photograph of her daughter in the churchyard only two or three hours ago, and packed it into the boot of Joaquín's truck, Raquel had been thinking that she was sick of these ceremonies. Of being forced, over and over, to relive the pain and the grief. That, if asked what she truly wanted, she would have had to admit she just wanted to move on, to try to overcome the tragedy that had spread like an oil slick over the past five years.

But she had never expressed these feelings aloud. Not even to Ismael, though he had long since realized that she no longer wanted to continue as part of the Foundation. It was something that would need to be discussed with Lucía's parents, something Joaquín would not take well.

You dreamed of finding your daughter's corpse, Raquel was thinking as the car drove on towards Barbastro, towards Ana.

Why had she not had the strength, the courage, of Lucía's parents? It was thanks to them that no one had forgotten their daughters' names. What would have happened had they not been there to support her? Especially in the early days, when the investigation had focused on her husband?'

Other images, other flickering memories of days that seemed blurred, like badly focused images, extracts from a film without a plot: Ana's disappearance, the blind panic that followed, Álvaro being taken into custody. The terror of looking at your husband as though he were a stranger. Of imagining that he could have harmed his own daughter. Since then, in the same way that the tide goes out and leaves the shoreline changed, revealing rocks that were hidden beneath the sand, the accusations against Álvaro had ebbed, but nothing would ever be the same between them.

And now, Ana. Waiting for her in Barbastro hospital. Five years later.

Five years during which Raquel had slowly tried to piece herself together, like a jigsaw puzzle dashed to the floor that has to be carefully reconstructed. Ismael Calella had been instrumental in this task. He had arrived in Monteperdido when the girls' disappearance was still recent – when had she stopped thinking of Ana's abduction as 'recent'? Álvaro had already left, and she had felt unable to go back to work, to the interior design company she had excitedly set up only months before her world had imploded. Ismael had offered to work for her as a carpenter and joiner. He was eight years her junior, he had the drive she lacked. She had managed to get the company on its feet again and, through her work, and Ismael's youth, she had once again found the sense of routine she so desperately needed.

When they had said goodbye outside the church after the meeting, she had whispered, 'I'll be at home waiting for you.' They had slept together for the first time only a few weeks earlier. Sometimes, it seemed obvious to her that what she was looking for in Ismael was the polar opposite of her husband. Why did she still refer to Álvaro as her husband?

It was Ismael she had been expecting when the police came to her door. She had been naked except for one of his shirts, with two glasses of wine poured and waiting in the kitchen, a burning cigarette in the ashtray that she realized only now would have burned away.

She had opened the door and Ana had come back.

She was driving through the darkness, heading to see her.

Víctor drove to the police station in silence. On the back seat, his seven-year-old husky was panting. Next to him, Sara was poring over the pile of paperwork, trying to put it into some sort of order. Víctor glanced at her surreptitiously as she stared into the files as into a bottomless well, her hand deftly pencilling notes. At the petrol station, he had thought she seemed arrogant, but he had been surprised by how she had handled Raquel and, especially, Elisa. A few seconds had been enough for Sara to move beyond first impressions, and get a glimpse of Elisa's personality and forge a bond with her. It was possible she recognized Elisa from the case files, despite the fact that years had passed and Elisa was no longer a teenager.

'I'm guessing you know this area like the back of your hand,' Sara said without looking up, 'but I'd feel a little safer if you looked at the road from time to time.'

Víctor turned and stared through the windscreen; he hoped she did not see him blush. The local Guardia Civil headquarters was new. It had been opened two years earlier on the road leading to the school.

'I didn't catch the name?' Sara said as he parked the car.

'Víctor,' he said, indignantly.

'Not you, the dog.'

'Nieve. Do you like dogs?'

'Not really, to be honest,' Sara said, climbing out of the car, unwilling to admit that her irrational fear of dogs was why she had barely said a word as they drove to the hotel and, from there, to the police station. She could still feel the dog's damp breath on the back of her neck.

She heard Víctor sigh before getting out of the four-wheel drive and opening the back door to let Nieve out. Then they headed towards the station.

'Is it coming with us?' she said, watching as the animal scampered about the place.

'Don't worry. He stays outside.'

Raquel walked nervously along the hospital corridor. Nurses whispered as she passed. A doctor opened one of the doors and ushered them in. Santiago Baín followed her as far as the intensive-care unit where Ana was. As they reached the glass-walled room, Raquel felt her legs give way. Baín reached out and stopped her from falling.

'We've put her under sedation,' the doctor said. 'She suffered slight brain trauma, though we don't think it will be serious. We'll be keeping her in for a few days for observation, just in case there are any complications . . .'

Raquel turned to Baín.

'Can I touch her?'

The inspector glanced at the doctor, who nodded and opened the door to the unit. Raquel went in and took two faltering steps towards the bed. Was this really her? She had thought this moment would never come, had banished it even from her dreams, and so it now seemed curiously unreal. Could it be her? Could it really be Ana?

She stood, staring for a moment, not daring to touch the girl. She was afraid that, if she reached out, she might break the spell and her daughter would vanish, and with her the hospital bed, the room, the inspector. Raquel would wake up in her own bed, sweating, and realize that it had only been a dream. A lie.

But Ana did not vanish as her mother gripped her daughter's hand, as though to stop her escaping. She felt the warmth. Then she ran her fingertips along her daughter's bruised arm to her shoulders, her face. Five years had passed and Ana was no longer a little girl. She was sixteen now. Her face had changed: her features were more delicate, her lips fuller, her skin paler. She was almost a woman.

'Has anyone talked to her? Has she said anything?' Raquel said between sobs.

'Not yet,' said Baín.

Víctor Gamero cleared one of the shelves in the office. The room had been intended for visiting officers, but since they never came to Monteperdido, it had been turned into a storeroom. The sergeant informed Sara that they were expecting four more officers, including the Mountain Rescue Team, led by Chief Sanmartín – though he did not think that Sara should count on much help from them. The M.R.T. barely had the resources to deal with hikers who headed up into the mountains without taking the necessary precautions.

'They'll need to prioritize,' Sara said.

'You're in charge,' Víctor admitted, though he had no intention of taking orders from the S.A.F. unless directly related to the missing girls.

The room was furnished with two desks and a large window. Outside, it was pitch dark, making it impossible to see the road to the school or the forest, the very spot where the girls had disappeared. Sara dropped her pile of paperwork on one of the desks.

'Need anything else?' Víctor asked.

'The keys to the station, and a computer.'

'I'll have a computer set up tomorrow morning,' he said, handing her a set of keys.

'I'll see you in the hotel lobby at six thirty a.m. I need you to take me to the scene where the girl was found.'

'I can get you a car.'

'I'd rather you called by to collect me,' Sara muttered, then she looked up at Víctor. 'If we do this by the book, we'll find Lucía.'

'Around here, we always do things by the book,' Víctor said tensely. 'Can I go now, or do you want me to drop you back to the hotel?'

'I can walk back. There are only four streets in the village; I don't think there's much chance I'll get lost.'

Víctor smiled and left the office. She liked the calm, collected way he moved and spoke, oblivious to her insistence. He reminded her of a sheriff in an old-fashioned western, sitting on his stoop as the sun set over the prairies, rifle in one hand, cigar clamped between his teeth. She moved at a very different tempo, one dictated by the pressure of her investigation; his was dictated by the rhythms of nature itself. Perhaps, in a place like Monteperdido, that was for the best.

Sara was still smiling when Víctor reappeared with a small plate that he set down on the desk. On it was a piece of caramel sponge cake surrounded by a yellowish liquid.

'*Candimus*,' the sergeant explained. 'One of the officers' girl-friends works in a bakery. It's a local speciality in Monteperdido. I asked her to make one when I heard that Ana had been found, so her mother could take her some. But since they're keeping her in hospital for the time being, we might as well eat it, or it will go stale. We can have another made, once she comes home.'

'Thanks,' Sara said, a little disconcerted.

'Caramel and lemon; you'll see – it's delicious.'

After Víctor left, Sara stared at the slice of *candimus*. On top were a few caramel letters from the word that had been iced on the cake: *COM*. Part of *WELCOME*, she guessed.

Sara sighed. Here she was, behaving like an ice queen, while the Guardia Civil in Monteperdido was bringing her cake. She dipped a finger in the custard and brought it to her lips. It was delicious.

★

Santiago Baín watched as the coffee machine in the hospital waiting room dispensed the espresso Raquel had asked for. She had
wanted to stay with her daughter, but the doctor had insisted it was
better to leave her to get some rest. Before heading to the relatives'
room, Santiago had taken the doctor into an empty ward and
spoken to him. He urgently needed to talk to Ana, but the doctor
refused to rush the process.

'You realize that your decision might cost another girl's life?'
Santiago warned.

'Right now, my responsibility is to care for Ana, and I am not
prepared to take any risks.'

It would be a cruel twist of fate if Raquel were to find her daughter, only to lose her again. Baín knew that he had to wait. Ana
would give her statement in due course.

'Who found the car?' Raquel asked as Baín handed her the
coffee.

'A neighbour from Posets. He was driving back from Barbastro
and saw a plume of smoke. At first, he assumed it was a forest fire,
but then he noticed the car.'

'I'd like to thank him . . . If he hadn't spotted it . . .'

'Best not to think about what might have happened. Ana is here
now, and that's all that matters.'

The ensuing silence was broken by the sound of footsteps.
Someone hurried along the corridor, came around the corner and
stopped in the doorway, panting for breath. Raquel looked up,
startled.

'Álvaro? What are you doing here?'

It had been almost four years since she had seen her husband.

★

Sara shifted in the chair and stretched. Her back ached. They had set off from Madrid in the early hours of the morning and had not stopped since. According to the station clock, it was four a.m., and the desk was still covered by a muddle of paperwork: documents full of words circled or underlined. She got to her feet, picked up the keys Víctor Gamero had given her, took the holster she had hung over the back of the chair, clipped it on to her belt and left the station.

A chill wind whipped down the mountain slopes and she wished she had worn something warmer than a jumper. Before heading towards the hotel, she stared at the forest on the far side of the road. She crossed over and, for a second, felt an urge to wander into the woods. It was pitch dark; there was nothing in there that could tell her anything about Lucía.

The girl was her priority. If the man driving the car was the same man who had abducted the girls, it was possible that Lucía was still locked away in unknown conditions, and there was no way of knowing how long she could survive alone.

Monteperdido was hushed. The only sounds were the murmur of the river, the rustle of branches swayed by the breeze and her own footsteps. She knew that she would not get any sleep tonight, but a hot shower and a few hours lying down would be rest enough.

The road wound up towards the bridge that spanned the river; most of the houses in the village were on the far bank. She was walking alongside the forest when she heard a noise. She peered into the trees. The darkness was so viscous it seemed alive. Something was digging in the ground. She tried to force herself to look away, to walk on towards the hotel. She felt for the gun in her holster and released the safety catch, then felt foolish at this sudden

31

wave of panic. It's just exhaustion, she thought. It's this place, thinking about what might have happened to Lucía. That was what was making her feel vulnerable. This is what Santiago tries to spare me from in our investigations.

Suddenly, a shadow darted from the forest and bounded towards her. By the time Sara turned, the animal was almost upon her; instinctively, she drew her gun and fired. Blood sprayed like a red brushstroke painted on the darkness. The dog howled and collapsed on the ground. Still holding the pistol, Sara stared down at the wounded animal. The bullet had opened a gaping wound in its chest. She stepped closer. It was Nieve, Víctor's dog.

Fuck, she thought.

The police officers standing guard at the hospital had orders not to admit anyone – including this man, Lucía's father, Joaquín Castán. After the S.A.F. officers left his house, he had felt like a wild animal pacing in its cage. They had spent years waiting for a miracle, but not this miracle. Though she said nothing, he knew what his wife was thinking: Why Ana? Why not Lucía? Not only had God not healed their wound, now he was pouring salt on it.

'I'm going to the hospital,' Joaquín had said. 'You coming?'

Montserrat barely had the energy to shake her head.

'Do you want me to call your brother?' he asked. 'I could ask Rafael to come over.'

She shook her head again. She just wanted to be alone.

'Will you be OK?' he asked before he left.

'How could I be OK?' Montserrat whispered.

When he was refused entrance to the hospital, Joaquín had called Víctor, but the Guardia Civil could offer no solution. There was nothing he could do; the S.A.F. officers were leading the investigation. Why had he come all this way to Barbastro Hospital? He decided to go back to Monteperdido and wait until morning. Montserrat would be in bed by now, tossing and turning, thinking that the next they would see of Lucía would be her dead body.

From his car, Joaquín saw Raquel emerging from the hospital. She sat down next to the front door and took out a pack of cigarettes, but it was empty. Just then, the S.A.F. inspector who had come to his house emerged, and, behind him, Álvaro. Tall and thin, his long, straight hair had turned grey, though he was still a young man. Joaquín watched as he pushed his fringe off his face, a gesture he had seen so many times. He slammed the car door as he got out; he wanted them to register his presence.

Inspector Baín saw Joaquín Castán and immediately noticed Álvaro's apprehension. Ana's father did not know whether to retreat or stand his ground as Joaquín took long, loping strides towards them. He was tall – at least six foot two – and powerfully built. Despite his age and the clothes he was wearing, it was easy to see he still possessed the swagger of his youth.

'Did they call you?' Joaquín Castán roared as he approached.

'Joaquín, please ...' Raquel got to her feet and tried to intervene.

Santiago stood to one side. He had scanned the case file and there had been no need to read between the lines for him to know there was hostility between the fathers of the missing girls. More than once, Joaquín had called for Álvaro to be arrested.

'Gaizka called me. He was the one who found the car ...' Álvaro said, deciding to stand firm.

'I thought you didn't live round here anymore.'

Álvaro did not answer. His silence was his way of making it clear that he was not about to be bullied. Lucía's father anxiously turned to Inspector Baín.

'What did Ana have to say for herself?' The question sounded like a reproach.

'She's still unconscious, sedated. As soon as we have any news, you'll be the first to know,' the inspector assured him.

'Even though, by then, it might be too late.'

Gradually, Joaquín's rage petered out and gave way to grief.

'Joaquín, if Ana made it back, then Lucía can too,' Álvaro said, and took two steps towards him.

Álvaro laid a hand on Joaquín's shoulder, more as a sign of forgiveness than of aggression, but Joaquín angrily wheeled round and grabbed him by the shirt.

'Don't touch me,' he growled, raising a fist.

Santiago intervened, but he did not need to do any more. Joaquín pushed Álvaro away, took a deep breath and glared at the police officer.

'I hope you're going to keep him well away from the girl.'

'You think I need to?' the inspector asked.

'Ana has to tell the truth. We still don't know what's happened to my daughter.'

'And she will,' Baín said. 'She will tell us everything she knows.'

Joaquín Castán turned on his heel and walked back to his car. He drove out of the hospital car park. Even at night, it took him two hours to make it back to Monteperdido. Two hours during which his jaw was clenched, his teeth gritted. He was not going to fall apart. Not this time.

★

A hospital porter had given Raquel a cigarette. Smoke mingled with her misty breath. It was getting chilly. A few metres away, Baín took a seat on the bench next to Álvaro, who was staring at the ground. Baín had not yet seen him smile. His features were chiselled, his hair white as hoarfrost, his eyes steely.

'Are you OK?' Santiago asked.

'I'm not sure,' Álvaro muttered. 'Yeah, of course I am . . . But it's been so many years, it's hard to believe that the nightmare is finally over.'

Álvaro attempted a smile, but his lips froze. Baín patted his leg, then sighed and leaned back on the bench. He understood the conflicting emotions that Ana's parents were feeling. They could not let themselves feel happy yet; their daughter was still unconscious. What horrors would they discover when she woke up? What stories would she tell?

Baín could not help but think that, in the early hours of the morning, a hospital felt like a funeral vigil.

Víctor was woken by the doorbell. He stumbled out of bed and looked out the window. It was still dark. He turned on the porch light and waited a few seconds to allow his eyes time to adjust. When he opened the door, he found Sara standing there with Nieve in her arms.

'I'm sorry,' she said.

'What happened?'

'He jumped at me as I was walking back to the hotel . . .'

Only then did Víctor notice that Sara's hands were smeared with blood. He took Nieve, who was whimpering in pain.

'What the hell did you do?' he shouted.

'I swear, he came out of nowhere . . . I didn't know what it was . . . I wouldn't have fired if I'd known it was your dog.'

'You shot him?'

'I think he might be all right,' Sara said by way of apology.

Víctor examined the dog, feeling for the bullet wound, muttered, 'Shit,' and took out his mobile phone and called the vet. Sara was still standing in the doorway, hesitating about whether she should go inside. Víctor cradled the dog against his chest; his white T-shirt was already stained red.

'I'm sorry, really I am.'

'Nicolás, sorry for waking you . . . It's Víctor. I need you to get over to my place; Nieve has been shot . . . I'm doing my best to staunch the bleeding, but you need to get here fast.'

As he hung up, Víctor noticed that Sara was still standing on the threshold.

'Fuck off!' he yelled, and slammed the door.

How could she sleep? When she arrived back at the hotel, Sara stopped by the coffee machine in the lobby, put in a coin and waited as her drink was dispensed. On the right, next to the reception desk, were the stairs leading up to the bedrooms. She took the plastic cup, burning her fingers, and headed to the left, where there was a dining room and a small sitting room. Sofas and armchairs were arranged around coffee tables, while, next to the windows, two tables were flanked by straight-backed chairs. Sara walked over to a table in the corner of the room. It was dark, the only light was the faint blue glow of Monteperdido. Her coffee was scalding, almost bubbling. Just looking at it, she felt her stomach spasm, so she set it aside. Even the smell was repulsive. She wanted to cry.

Startled by a sudden creak of leather, she scanned the room. In the darkness, she could just make out a shadowy figure as it shifted on the sofa, embarrassed as though caught *in flagrante delicto*. She heard the deep, hoarse voice, though she could not make out a face.

'Can't sleep?'

The shadow clicked on the table lamp and, as the green glass lampshade flickered into life, Sara saw that the figure on the sofa was a woman. She was about sixty; her dark curly hair was matted on one side and she quickly combed her fingers through it. Her face was curiously rounded, as though made of plasticine. Her eyes seemed to bulge, ringed by the dark shadows cast by the table lamp. Something about her face in the greenish glow reminded Sara of a toad – the sort of wise, kind-hearted frog you'd find in fairy tales.

'Do you mind?' the woman said, nodding towards the chair next to Sara.

The assistant inspector stiffened and picked up her coffee cup, as though making space so that the woman could join her. When she stood up, the woman was scarcely taller than she had been sitting down. Dragging her feet, she walked across the room to Sara's table. Her arms and legs were stubby, as though they had no joints whatsoever. No knees, no elbows. The way she moved, tottering as she walked, simply emphasized this impression. She looked as though she had been squeezed into an old-fashioned diving suit. When she reached the table, she had to hop up on to the chair. Her chubby feet, squeezed into a tiny pair of trainers, dangled in mid-air. She set a bottle down on the table; it was filled with a red liquid Sara could not identify. The woman heaved a sigh, as though the effort of crossing the room had required superhuman effort.

'Insomnia is shit,' she growled with the voice of an incorrigible smoker. 'Every night it's the same. I put on a nightdress, drink a glass of milk, go to bed. I toss and turn until my back hurts, then I get up, pull on a tracksuit and think, Fuck it . . . One more sleepless night. Oh, yeah, sorry – my name is Caridad.'

Sara smiled. She knew exactly what it felt like, to dread going to bed. She noticed that the tracksuit Caridad was wearing was old: a fashion relic from the 1980s, a shapeless mass of pale pink and grey that made her look padded.

'I live across the road,' Caridad said, nodding towards the window. 'Some nights, I walk around the village until dawn, and some nights I come in here; the sofas are comfortable and my back doesn't hurt so much. Elisa doesn't mind; I'm up and out long before the first guests come downstairs. What about you? Aren't you going to introduce yourself? I feel like I'm talking to a ghost, here . . .'

'Yes, of course; sorry . . .' Sara said, a little disconcerted. 'Assistant Inspector Sara Campos.'

'I've got a surname too, you know. Caridad Pissed-Off-With-Insomnia.' She let out a gruff chuckle, like thunder in the silence. 'Sorry,' she said, stifling her laugh. 'It's lack of sleep – it makes me say stupid stuff.'

'Don't worry.' Sara flashed her a smile.

'So, did you murder someone? Or are you the victim?'

Caridad was staring at her jumper, and Sara suddenly remembered the bloodstain across her chest. Nieve's blood.

'No . . . Well, I don't think so,' Sara said, worrying that by now the dog might be dead. 'There was an accident.'

'Are you hurt? Do you want me to take a look? I'm a nurse practitioner. With the Red Cross. And a trained chiropodist, but I'm guessing your feet are fine, yeah?'

'No, I'm fine,' Sara said, touching the bloodstain, which was dried and crusted.

'Should have seen the other guy, is that it?' Caridad's laugh rumbled in the silence. Sara was afraid she would wake someone.

'It was only a dog,' Sara whispered, hoping that this might encourage Caridad to lower her voice.

'Oh, I see . . .' Caridad leaned back in the chair, making no attempt to hide the disdain in her voice. 'Only a dog. So it doesn't matter. I mean, there's nothing like killing a *kan* from time to time — it's good for the soul.'

'I told you, it was an accident,' Sara protested. 'And I don't know whether the dog is dead or not.'

'Why worry? The poor animal is out there somewhere, bleeding to death . . . That's perfectly humane.'

'I brought it back to its master. How else do you think I got blood on my clothes?' Sara was finding it difficult to hide her irritation.

'Don't be like that, Sara Campos. We're just having a little chat, here, until we fall asleep —' Caridad raised her arms in surrender — 'but if you don't want to talk about the dog, we can talk about something else. What brought you here? This thing with the girls? A terrible business, isn't it?'

Sara looked at Caridad in surprise. In a split second, she had shifted from biting sarcasm to warm sincerity.

'I can't talk about the case,' she said.

'So what are we supposed to talk about, then? The *kan*?' Caridad quipped. She leaned forward, pressing her breasts against the table, folding her arms on the table, drumming her fingers irritably. She looked like a bored child.

'I think I'm feeling a little tired,' Sara said, paving the way for her departure.

'Well, fuck that!' Caridad snapped hoarsely, the word echoing around the room. 'No offence,' she added, seeing the look of shock on Sara's face. 'You just toddle off to your *chasilla*, and leave me here.'

'I need to take a shower first,' Sara explained apologetically, as though she had some sort of obligation to keep Caridad company.

'Go on – go.' Caridad waved her hand in the air. 'And don't worry too much about the dog. A bad conscience is like a mother-in-law: once you've got one, you can't get rid of it.' She rummaged in the pocket of her tracksuit and took out her cigarettes. 'Smoke?' She proffered the pack.

'No, thanks,' Sara said, getting to her feet.

'If he hasn't phoned me, Víctor must have the situation under control. Shaving a bunion or saving a dog – it's all the same to me. That's how things work in this village. He's probably with Nicolás Souto.'

Sara had only taken a step when she stopped. Caridad had lit her cigarette and was staring though the window at the deserted streets of Monteperdido.

'How did you know it was Víctor's dog?'

She did not know whether to laugh or be angry.

'It's a small village, hon. You'll find out for yourself.'

'So why ask all those questions, if you knew already?'

'For the sake of talking. Like I said, I don't usually have company in the middle of the night . . .'

From the look on her face, Caridad seemed apologetic. Or was she still toying with her? Sara said goodnight. As she left, she caught a last glimpse of the tiny woman, her legs dangling in the air, sucking on her cigarette in the green glow of the table lamp, and she realized that she would not be at all surprised if Caridad suddenly disappeared in a puff of smoke.

He was sweating so much that his glasses kept slipping down his nose. As he worked, Nicolás Souto had to constantly stop, set down his needle, mop his face and push the glasses back into place, leaving blood on the end of his nose. Víctor could not take his eyes off Nieve, anaesthetized on the table in the kitchen, which now served as a makeshift operating theatre.

'Are you going to arrest her?' Nicolás asked as he sutured the wound. 'I mean, how would the Guardia Civil go about pressing charges against the Policia Nacional? Do you just go to a judge and file a complaint, or do you have to go through Internal Affairs . . .?'

Nicolás set down the needle again, the way someone might set down his knife in the middle of a meal because something else requires his attention. He blinked rapidly. It was a tic, with Nicolás. His glasses had slipped down his nose again. He pushed them back, leaving a spot of blood on the frames.

'How would I know, Nicolás? This is hardly the time . . .' Víctor grunted angrily.

'No, of course,' the vet said shamefacedly, and returned to the task of suturing the dog. 'I mean, filing a complaint in the middle of an investigation would be insane. What with Ana still in hospital and Lucía still missing . . . Madness. And against the officer leading the investigation. That wouldn't make things easy . . .'

Víctor did his utmost to treat the vet's chattering as background noise. He did not want to get angry and blow up at him. He had

had to wait over an hour with his dog. Alone. He had managed to contain the bleeding, but he was afraid the bullet might have nicked one of the vital organs. It had seemed never-ending, a night when dawn refused to break. The vet had finally arrived just before half past five. He had burst into the house, panting, his cheeks flushed, sweat streaming from his face and his armpits. It looked as though, rather than waking him, Víctor had interrupted him while he was running a marathon. Nicolás apologized for the delay and immediately set about examining the dog. Víctor had laid the animal on a cushion, covered him with a blanket and turned on the central heating to keep him warm. At first, Nieve's whimpers had kept him company while he waited for Nicolás. And then the dog had stopped whining. In the silence, Víctor had held his hand in front of Nieve's muzzle to make sure he was still breathing, and he had sat like that, feeling the dog's damp breath on his fingers, until the vet arrived.

'All right. It doesn't look too bad,' was the first thing Nicolás had said when he examined the injury. 'Clear entry and exit wounds. This wasn't done with a hunting rifle. A small-calibre gun, probably a revolver.'

It was at this point that Víctor had told him that it was Sara Campos, the S.A.F. officer who had come to investigate the missing girls, who had shot Nieve. Nicolás had managed not to say another word for half an hour while he sedated the dog, cleaned the wound and sutured the internal injuries. Now that he was closing up, his curiosity knew no bounds.

'Personally, I think you should find some way of paying her back, you know what I'm saying?' Nicolás prattled on. 'I mean, say, during the investigation, you find yourself in a dangerous situation, she's about to fall off a cliff and you're clinging on to her. Then, at the last minute, you say, "This is for Nieve," like that, really dramatic, like, and you let her go and watch her crash on to the rocks below.'

Nicolás cut the last stitch, set the needle on the table and looked at Víctor, beaming from ear to ear.

'So, what do you think?' the vet said proudly.

Víctor bit his tongue. Nicolás had a gift for winding him up. He found the man's absurd gibbering exhausting and unsettling. The events of the evening had been too much for him. But Víctor closed his eyes for a moment, took a deep breath and said, 'Is Nieve going to pull through?'

'The dog is absolutely fine,' Nicolás said, as though this was self-evident. 'He's lost a little blood and he won't be himself for a couple of days. I'm not saying he's not going to die, but, with a bit of luck, he's just going to end up with a bit of a limp. The bullet nicked one of the muscles in his left shoulder . . .'

Víctor smiled. This time he could see the humour in how Nicolás expressed himself. He was a vet who mostly dealt with farmers, treating horses and cows and maybe a few pigs. The only dogs he ever treated were hunting dogs. Their owners did not have the same kind of relationship with their dogs as Víctor had with Nieve. They thought of them as tools. The death of one of their dogs was simply a financial loss. Hence Nicolás's tactlessness in discussing the dog's chances of a complete recovery.

Víctor stroked Nieve, who was still sleeping off the anaesthetic. He brought his face to the animal's muzzle and kissed it. The familiar smell now mingled with the smell of the antiseptic Nicolás had used to sterilize the wound. Nieve had just turned seven. The dog had been a gift from the Cofradía de Santa María. To Víctor, it was as though he had been drowning and someone had thrown him a lifeline. He had clung to Nieve and gradually the dog had brought him back to the shore. He would always be grateful to the dog, and to the whole village, for rescuing him when he did not have the energy to stay afloat.

The dark sky outside the kitchen window was shot through with glimmers of blue. Dawn was breaking. Víctor knew that he should go and collect Sara from the hotel, that he barely had time to shower and change his clothes.

'Don't sweat it,' Nicolás said when Víctor asked if he could stay with the dog. 'I'll stay here until he wakes up.' Then he added, 'But don't go dropping the policewoman off a cliff. Thinking about it, it could land you in trouble. You'll have to come up with a more elegant revenge.'

'You're the writer,' Víctor said, knowing that this was the finest compliment he could pay Nicolás.

Nicolás smiled proudly and promised to come up with some way for Víctor to get even with the cop. Something that would not land him in prison. Víctor went off to shower, thinking about how Nicolás had already transformed him and Sara into characters in one of his crime novels. It was not the first time he had done this. He knew that Nicolás had drawn on him for inspiration before in one of the novels he wrote and never managed to get published. Why did he insist on writing them in *patués*? It was difficult enough to find a publisher; writing his novels in a language spoken by only the most elderly people in the region was stupid. Sometimes he thought that Nicolás's novels did not even exist, that they were simply an excuse to be friends with him, to have something to talk about. And he could not help but feel sorry for this fifty-year-old man who had been born in the village but had never quite fitted in, the man now tending to Nieve in the kitchen, bathed in sweat, with a dot of blood on the end of his nose.

The sun was not yet visible, but shafts of light streamed between the mountaintops and brought a little warmth to the village. The slopes of Monte Albádes on the outskirts of the village were the first to glow green, the trees seeming to rise with the dawn, casting long, slender shadows, like outstretched arms. The black slate roof-tiles, wet with dew, glimmered in the sunlight. The houses were two or three storeys at most, and from their midst the steeple of Santa María soared. With its stone walls and its squat façade surrounded by three mountains – L'Ixeia, Monte Ármos and La Kregüeña – it looked like a toddler standing on tiptoe to reach the grown-ups. Slow and unhurried, the glacier continued to melt, imperceptibly changing from ice to water.

It was 13th July. The slate outside the Castán house read *1,727 DAYS WITHOUT LUCÍA*.

When he had arrived home, Joaquín had found his son sleeping on the sofa. The television was on, with the volume turned down. The room smelled of alcohol. He had gone over and shaken him gently. Quim opened his bloodshot eyes.

'You haven't heard what's happened?' Joaquín said.

His tongue furred from too much drink, Quim could not say anything, but he did not have time to mumble an excuse, anyway, before his father said, 'You stink of booze.'

'Is that all? Open the window, if it bothers you.' Quim lay back on the sofa.

'They've found Ana. She's in hospital in Barbastro, but there's no sign of your sister. Assuming you care.'

Joaquín gave no further information. He climbed the stairs to the bedroom without waiting to see how his son had taken the news. He decided to have a shower and go back to the hospital as quickly as possible.

Sara took a deep breath before leaving the hotel. Through the window, she could see the four-wheel drive parked outside, with Víctor behind the wheel, waiting for her. She walked quickly, keeping her eyes on the ground until she reached the car. She gave a curt, 'Morning,' as she opened the door. He replied without looking at her and, as soon as she climbed in, turned the key in the ignition. Say something, fast, Sara thought.

'How is your dog?' she mumbled as she fastened her seat belt.

'Alive,' Víctor said, looking in the wing mirror and pulling out into the road.

Sara wanted to tell him that she had not been able to sleep. That she hated herself for what she had done. She had been scared, she had not had time to see what was happening, it had been very late and very dark . . . But even as she lined up the excuses in her mind, they crumbled. What difference did it make? It had been her gun, her bullet, and there was nothing she could do to take it back. Reciting a litany of excuses about what had happened suddenly sounded selfish. All the arguments she had spent the night mentally rehearsing seemed futile. She thought about victims' relatives listening to the excuses of rapists, murderers, kidnappers. The commonplace clichés about their traumatic childhood, their inability to control their impulses, their remorse for the pain they had caused. And she knew that such confessions merely served to kindle the hatred of those who had suffered from their actions. Every excuse is a justification, and the last thing someone who has just lost a loved one wants to hear is a justification. There is no excuse that justifies grief. Accepting such excuses would be tantamount to admitting that no one was really responsible. As though the murderer's misfortune were equal to that of his victim.

'This road runs right through the village. A few kilometres uphill, there is a turn-off to Posets. It's smaller than Monteperdido – the population is about three hundred. Most people make a living from tourism,' Víctor said in a professional tone. Seeing Sara's surprised expression, the Guardia Civil explained: 'You're going to be working here, you might as well know the area.'

'No, yes, of course . . .' she said, flustered.

I hope one day you can stop hating me, Sara thought, though she did not say it aloud. She let the sergeant continue his impassive description. To the east, the peaks of Monte Ármos, which Sara could see from her hotel bedroom, and La Kregüeña, behind which hid the village of Posets. They drove along Monteperdido's main street, where the majority of shops, hotels and tourist centres were located. From here, a labyrinth of cobbled alleyways meandered northward. Although the valley was wide, the houses were piled almost on top of each other, as though seeking the shelter of neighbouring walls, huddling together for protection from some outside force. Above the slate roofs soared the summits of Monte Perdido and, to the south, Los Montes Malditos. The River Ésera ran parallel to the main street, spanned by three bridges on its course through the village. Then the road dipped towards Barbastro, although leaving the valley meant driving through Fall Gorge, the narrow mountain pass Sara and Santiago had driven through the night before. Sara noticed that Víctor had told her nothing about the villagers or their customs, only about the lofty crags of rock and ice in the shade of which the village had sprung up, and which defined its boundaries as might pennants on a battlefield. The mountains were all that mattered. They alone would remain when all else had long since vanished.

The four-wheel drive entered the tunnel, and a silence descended. What else did they have to say to each other? Sara felt her eyes well up. The whimper Nieve had made when she fired still reverberated in her mind, an echo that did not seem to fade.

'Do you mind if I put on the radio?' Sara said as she turned the dial.

Víctor noticed Sara turn away and stare out the window, letting the music drown out any sound, but he could tell she was doing her utmost not to sob. He was grateful that she tried to hide her pain. That she did not turn to him for consolation he did not feel able to give.

Sixty kilometres south of Monteperdido, the emergency services had already begun work on winching the car out of the ravine. A crane had been set up near the cliff edge. Several officers from the Mountain Rescue Team were helping with the operation. Víctor Gamero introduced Sara to Sanmartín, the leader of the M.R.T., who gave a brief summary of the situation, peppered with local mountaineering terms – *serac, tuca, arroyo* – like landmines intended to keep her at arm's length. Dressed in an immaculate uniform, hair neatly combed, he reminded Sara of the American G.I.s she had seen in movies – arrogant and faintly ridiculous – but she decided to ignore his attempts at provocation and pretend she knew what the words meant. At that moment, the only thing that interested her was the evidence in the car at the bottom of the ravine, although Sara was aware that it might be days before they could collect it. They would have access to the body of the driver much earlier. The corpse had already been laid on a stretcher next to the wreckage, and it was about to be lifted out by helicopter. Sara would have a chance to do a preliminary examination before it was airlifted to the Coroner's Office for the autopsy. Nervously, she paced the dirt track. Scene-of-crime officers were making casts of the partial tyre tracks. She looked down into the gully. She wished she could climb down and search the car. She needed to put a name to the man whose body had been found with Ana. Her mobile phone rang, startling her. It was Santiago Baín.

'Ana has started having seizures. They're taking her into theatre now.'

The walls were moving, quivering like paper rustled by the wind. Raquel tried to breathe, making a conscious effort to fill her lungs with air, but nothing would come. She could not focus on the bustle and commotion all around: the faces of the nurses, the corridors, the rattle of trolleys, the swish of closing doors. She was tumbling into an abyss so fast that all she could see was a blur of figures. So fast that all she could do was steel herself for the moment when she hit the ground. Finally, she managed to give vent to this wild panic in a harrowing scream, before fainting into the arms of a hospital porter.

'Can someone take her to a side bay?' said the porter.

A nurse came with a sedative. Ismael appeared at the far end of the corridor and saw people milling around Raquel. At first, he could only see her arms, her hands lying on the tiled floor. As the people helping her dispersed, he noticed Raquel's eyes were closed, her face still twisted in a rictus of grief, as though even unconsciousness could not relax her features. A porter lifted her up as someone brought a stretcher trolley. Ismael longed to hug her to him. Longed to tell everyone that he was her partner.

Álvaro Montrell was staring out the window at the expanse of barren land around the hospital. In the distance, he could see the skeletal frames of houses that had never been completed. Five years I've been waiting for this day, and now my daughter might die, he thought, and the idea seemed so cruel that he felt guilty.

'What's happened?' Gaizka stepped out of the lift and moved towards him, elbowing his way past the doctors coming and going along the corridor.

'Ana is in surgery. They're operating now.'

'Is it serious?'

Álvaro had no answer to this, and turned back to the window. Down in the cark park, there were many cars from Monteperdido. He recognized Joaquín's. Rafael Grau and Marcial Nerín had probably come too. They were too far away for him to make out any faces, but he could see the group shuffling nervously down below, unsure whether they should go into the hospital. They looked like wedding guests who had just been told the bride had not shown up.

The treetops shook as the helicopter set down on an area of flat ground beside the ravine. Hunched over to avoid the powerful gust, Sara walked towards the cab. One of the officers from the Mountain Rescue Team jumped out and handed her a bag. The roar of the rotors meant they had to shout in order to be heard.

'This is all there was in the car,' he bellowed above the racket.

'What about the body? I want to see it.'

Sara moved to the rear of the helicopter. She gestured for the officer next to the stretcher to open the body bag.

She did not recognize the face of the corpse: a man of about fifty, the deep gash on his forehead crusted with dried blood. The body had already taken on a yellowish pallor, though the face was livid, the features contorted from the hours the body had spent hanging upside down from the seat belt inside the car. The eyes bulged so much that it was impossible to close the eyelids. The officer slid the zip all the way down so that the body was completely exposed. Like the face, it was chubby but not obese. The khaki trousers and the blue checked shirt were stained with blood. His own blood.

'What about the shoes?' Sara said, seeing his bare feet.

'In the bag.' The officer nodded to the one she was holding. 'They had fallen off.'

She took a last look at the corpse. His skin was suntanned, the arms paler under the short sleeves of his shirt. He had obviously shaved not long before he died. The clothes he was wearing looked new, or at least had not been washed often – information that Sara was not about to attach any significance to, not before the autopsy.

'The pockets?'

'Nothing,' the officer shouted.

Sara gestured for him to close the body bag again. She walked away from the helicopter and it rose into the air, whipping up a sandstorm that forced her to close her eyes and quicken her pace. Víctor's four-wheel drive was parked a few metres away.

Sara set the bag down on the bonnet and opened it.

'Did anyone recognize the body?' Víctor asked.

Sara shook her head, pulling on a pair of latex gloves before touching anything inside the bag.

'We don't know much about the car either. It's a common model around here, no number plates . . . We've taken the chassis number, so maybe we'll get lucky,' Víctor said.

First, the shoes: a pair of brown loafers, size 41. Small feet. There were no socks, and there had been none on the body. An old, printed map and an empty water bottle. A local newspaper published a week earlier: on the front page, a story about prospects for tourism in the region over the summer, predicting ninety per cent hotel occupancy – a success. Nothing Sara found said anything other than that the driver had done his utmost to ensure the car contained no personal information. No licence or registration, obviously; no receipts. No mobile phone.

'There has to be something,' Sara muttered, unable to hide her frustration.

Víctor double-checked every piece of paper after Sara. The bag was empty now. The bonnet was strewn with useless evidence.

'What's this?' The Guardia Civil picked up a small, crumpled receipt caught between the pages of the newspaper.

'La Cruz petrol station,' Sara read.

'That's on the outskirts of Barbastro.'

Sara carefully smoothed out the receipt: thirty euros' worth of petrol, paid by card. A number they could use to identify the corpse.

★

Santiago Baín took a seat in the office as the doctor closed the door.

'What's the prognosis?'

'It's difficult to say. The cerebral oedema is small, but we'll do a craniotomy to relieve the pressure, just to be sure . . . Her blood pressure is very high and—'

'What will Ana be like when she comes round?' Baín interrupted. He needed to be pragmatic. Maybe there was no longer any point in him waiting here for the girl's statement.

'It all depends on the surgery.'

'Amnesia?'

'Very possibly. And there are other possible complications.'

Baín nodded. He took a minute to gather his thoughts before getting to his feet. His primary lead in the investigation had hit a dead end. The answers he needed might well remain trapped in the whorls of Ana's brain. Meanwhile, Lucía was still out there somewhere, waiting. The police were convinced that the other girl was still alive. Her kidnapper had died in the crash. Was there anyone with her? Was there anyone to give her food?

He was seized by an image of a girl locked up somewhere, starving to death while they frantically searched for her. He stood up and tried to shake off this pessimistic scenario.

'Thank you,' he said to the doctor. 'I hope you don't come to regret your decision not to allow me to talk to the girl when I asked.'

Joaquín Castán felt at ease surrounded by his neighbours. At the centre of a group that, over the past year, had begun to crack; some of them had stopped coming to the meetings and the vigils that he organized, others had stayed with him to the bitter end, even if their enthusiasm had waned. At the last meeting, he had seen Nicolás Souto impatiently checking his watch while he had been speaking in the churchyard; he'd seen Rafael, his brother-in-law, shifting his weight from one foot to the other, as though he could not bear to stand a minute longer and was simply waiting for permission to sit down. As he had stood outside the church door, talking about his daughter, those present had looked like a congregation who still attended mass out of a sense of duty, but had long since stopped listening to what the priest had to say.

At least they were still prepared to spend an afternoon outside the church. There were others who were no longer prepared to give him a moment of their time. The journalists, for example. He thought about Virginia Bescos. Where was she now, this woman who, in the early years, had been his staunchest ally? But he dismissed all thought of the reporter. His neighbours were his only army.

He could not blame them for thinking the war was lost. So much time had passed without a glimmer of hope. And yet, today, in the hospital car park, Joaquín noticed a change in their attitude: a renewed restlessness, a sense of urgency, as his neighbours wavered between joy at Ana's sudden reappearance, and fear for Lucía's uncertain future.

As soon as they arrived, they found out that Ana was in surgery and Raquel had had a panic attack. They were like a swarm of flying ants, frantically milling around, unsure what to do. Joaquín looked at them and felt a curious satisfaction. They were once again on his side.

'You know that Álvaro is in there?' Marcial said when he emerged from the hospital.

'You saw him?' Joaquín said.

'Only from a distance. The police have cordoned off the wing where Ana is.'

Marcial Nerín had been in the hospital when Ana was first admitted. His mother regularly came for dialysis and, given her age and the state of her health, things rarely went smoothly enough for them to go back to Monteperdido as soon as the treatment was over.

'I don't know why they let him wander around wherever he likes,' Marcial said, making no attempt to hide his anger.

'Is he with Raquel?' Joaquín asked, taking Marcial's arm and leading him aside.

Marcial shook his head. 'Ismael was there – you know, the carpenter who works for her. One of the nurses said they had had to give Raquel a tranquillizer. Álvaro was with Gaizka, the tour guide from Posets – you know who I mean?'

'He was the one who found the car.'

'Not a tear. His daughter could be dying on the operating table and that son of a bitch Álvaro didn't shed a single tear. *Ve un barbóll,*' he muttered to himself.

'Is it that serious?'

'If she had anything to tell, you can forget about it now, Joaquín.'

Marcial clapped him on the back. He had large hands, gnarled and calloused by years in the sun. Though he was almost seventy, Marcial was probably stronger than many a young man. Even Joaquín felt small standing next to him. He was broad-shouldered and heavyset, with gaunt features, chiselled now by the years. Something untamed, something threatening about him had long ago earned him the nickname 'Wild Boar'.

'I'm sure he's been hanging around the hospital to find out what Ana will say.' Marcial gritted his teeth. 'I bet he's happy about how things have turned out.'

Though many had forgotten, Joaquín and Marcial had not. Álvaro had been cleared during the original investigation, but there had been many questions he could not answer. Montserrat had once told her husband that he was clinging to the notion that Álvaro was guilty because he had been the only suspect. The only target for his hatred. But who would hurt their own child?

'How's your wife taking it?' Marcial said.

Joaquín groped for the right word to describe how Montserrat was feeling.

'She's frightened,' he said.

'We've got a name: Simón Herrera,' Sara said on the other end of the line. 'And we've traced his address. He lives in Ordial. I'm heading there right now.'

'Text me the address.' Baín pulled on his jacket and raced through the hospital, weaving between the staff. 'If you get there before me, call me.'

Sara hung up and immediately dialled another number. Víctor was driving towards Ordial, which was only ten kilometres from where the crashed car had been found.

'Sara Campos, Assistant Inspector with the S.A.F. – I need all the information you can dig up on one Simón Herrera Escolano, national I.D. number 23257552. It's urgent. As soon has you have anything, email it to me.'

Víctor took the next turn-off, crossed the river and, there, at the end of the road, stood the village of Ordial: three narrow streets with a little cluster of stone houses. The road had been resurfaced; the recently refurbished houses were fringed with neatly trimmed lawns; there was not a soul to be seen. It looked as though the village had been built simply as the backdrop for a tourist brochure. A cloudless blue sky provided the finishing touch.

'Do you know where the Camino de Plans is?'

'The other side of the village,' Víctor said as the four-wheel drive moved along the main street.

The petrol station receipt was dated 10th July, two days before Ana was found. The driver might have dropped it as he got into the car. The credit card company had been prompt in providing them with the name and address of the cardholder. From the way he clenched his jaw and kept his eyes fixed on the road, Sara could tell that Víctor was anxious, urged on by the hope that, when the door opened, they would find Lucía. As though the girl was a member of his family.

The road turned into a dirt track, which wound its way up the mountain behind the village. The wheels of their car became stuck in a waterlogged rut and, with a sudden jolt, lurched free.

'Is that it?' Sara said as they rounded a bend.

'There's nothing else still standing around here.'

Simón Herrera's house was surrounded by three crumbling, derelict buildings, the roofs of which would not withstand another winter. Even the stone walls seemed to struggle to remain standing. A tow truck was parked outside. Simón's house looked scarcely better than those around it. A few bedraggled pot plants on the windowsill were the only signs of life in this building that clearly should have been refurbished years ago. The windows were small, the wooden frames warped and cracked, the paint had peeled from the stone walls and a low step was all that prevented the weeds and the mud from overrunning everything.

Sara got out of the four-wheel drive and peered through a ground-floor window before going to the door, where Víctor was already waiting. Sara gave him a sign to knock.

'I didn't see any lights on inside,' she said. 'But there's obviously someone living here. I could see the living room—'

'I heard something,' Víctor said, and knocked again, harder this time.

The door opened and sunlight flooded the murky hallway. A woman stood on the threshold, blinking into the light.

'Hello,' she said, her voice tremulous.

'Sara Campos, Policía Nacional.' She held out her warrant card. 'Can we come in? We'd like a word.'

There was no need to ask the woman whether she knew Simón Herrera, since, when she ushered them into the living room, Sara saw the wedding photographs lined up on a sideboard. There she was, in her white dress, posing next to Simón. Despite the ravages suffered by the corpse, his face was instantly recognizable. Víctor, too, saw the photographs and let out a disappointed sigh.

'I'm afraid we have some bad news. Your husband was involved in a car accident early yesterday morning. He died instantly. We have only just managed to identify him,' Sara said in a rush of words. These preliminaries were necessary, but what she really wanted to talk about was Lucía.

The woman stood, motionless, in the centre of the living room. She looked from Sara to Víctor and back again. She had small, dark eyes, like buttons sewn on to a soft, impassive face. Deadpan, Sara thought. The lines and wrinkles of middle age had gone some way to disguising the subtle signs of disability evident in the wedding photographs: the elongated face, the broad forehead, the wide mouth, permanently hanging open. The room smelled of herbs, of bay leaves and thyme; from the kitchen came the sound of water boiling in a saucepan. They had interrupted her cooking. Sara watched as the woman bit her fingers before saying, 'Are you sure?'

'I'm afraid so,' Víctor said, and he stepped closer, slipping a hand around her waist and gently guiding her to a battered imitation-leather settee with crocheted covers on the armrests.

'I know this must be very difficult for you, but we need to ask a few questions about your husband. You were married, weren't you?' The woman nodded as Sara drew up a chair and sat facing her. 'What's your name?'

'Pilar,' the woman whispered.

'Do you mind if my partner looks around while we have a chat?'

'But everything is such a mess.' Pilar looked up, a flicker of shy embarrassment in her small eyes.

'That doesn't matter,' Víctor reassured her.

'Listen to me,' Sara said, trying to attract her attention, but Pilar's eyes were fixed on Víctor as he left the living room. 'Pilar, listen to me. This is important. There was someone in the car with your husband. A girl.'

'Is she dead too?'

'No, she's not dead, but she is in the hospital. Her name is Ana Montrell – does that name ring a bell?'

Pilar shook her head.

'She's one of two girls who disappeared in Monteperdido five years ago.'

The breakdown began in her hands, which started to tremble

uncontrollably. Pilar's body was shaken by a shudder and she could not stifle a scream. She tried to cover her face, her eyes, as tears began to fall. Her mouth opened in a howl, revealing small teeth and blackened gums. Pilar curled into a ball. Sara went over and sat next to her. She put an arm around her.

'Do you know why this girl was travelling with your husband?'

Pilar shook her head vigorously, like a dog shaking itself dry.

'I don't know what happened all those years ago, but you can do something for those girls now. You have to tell us everything you know. Is the other girl here? Is Lucía in this house?'

'I don't know who they are,' Pilar managed to stammer between sobs. 'Poor Simón . . .'

Sara stroked the woman's hair, which was pinned into a bun. It was coarse and the chestnut brown was streaked with grey. She was swaying back and forth, hugging herself tightly and whispering, over and over, 'My poor Simón.' Sara could see the gulf that had opened up for Pilar. The woman could no longer see her, Sara no longer existed, nor the living room around them. All Pilar could see was a black, bottomless pit. Sara could sense the woman's dizziness.

'I'm just going to take a quick look upstairs,' Víctor said from the doorway.

'You stay with her. I'll go,' said Sara, getting to her feet.

Pilar would need time before she could answer any more questions, and Sara knew that it was best to leave her.

The marital bedroom had twin beds, separated by a nightstand. There was a wardrobe and a dressing table, on which sat a mirror in a wrought-iron frame. All of the furniture was made of stripped wood in various shades, as though the house had been furnished with cast-offs and things found in the street. The floor was laid with terracotta tiles, which were clean, but warped and faded by time. There was no sign of the 'terrible mess' that had embarrassed Pilar. Clothes were neatly stored and everything was in its place.

Sara opened the drawer in the nightstand: a small radio, a mobile-phone charger and a pack of ibuprofen. There was nothing in the dressing table other than clothes; one drawer was Simón's, the others were filled with Pilar's clothes and bedlinen. The contents of the wardrobe suggested a modest, even poor couple: old-fashioned dresses, cheap shirts and trousers.

Sara left the room and crossed the hallway. Directly opposite the stairs was a bathroom. Next to it, another bedroom. She pushed open the door and fumbled for a light switch. The shutters were closed and the room was almost completely dark. A bare bulb flickered on. An improvised table had been made from a panel of timber resting on two trestles. This was Simón's desk: it was covered with piles of paper, bills, publicity brochures, supermarket catalogues. The floor and the bookshelves were filled with cardboard box-files, warped by the damp. Sara opened one of them: car insurance forms. It smelled of must and Pilar's stew.

There was nowhere else to search.

When Inspector Baín arrived, Sara was waiting for him at the front door. She did not need to say a word. From her shrug of disappointment, it was clear that they had found nothing.

'He made his living driving that tow truck,' Sara said as they studied the area around the house. Santiago looked at the truck: it was white and mud-spattered. The tow bar was rusted. 'He had contracts with a number of different insurance companies.'

'What about the wife? Does she know anything?'

'Víctor is with her. She suffers from Williams syndrome . . . It's a developmental disorder . . . She's still trying to process the news that her husband is dead.'

'Have you searched the house?'

'A quick once-over. There's nothing that has any connection to the girls.'

Baín stopped and took a deep breath. He smiled at Sara. 'We're not going to solve this one just by showing up,' he said sarcastically.

'What about Ana?'

'This woman is more likely to give us information than Ana,' Baín said in a defeated tone as he headed back towards the house.

Sara was about to follow when she heard her phone beep. It was an email with details of Simón Herrera's police record.

'Santiago!' she called after him, and he turned. 'Take a look at this.' She held out the phone. 'Simón spent two years banged up in Martutene Prison. Possession of child pornography.'

The tranquillizers had left her with a headache. Raquel sat up in bed, feeling as though her head had been squeezed into a small box and, now released, was swelling to its normal size. Ismael went over to her.

'Do you need anything? A glass of water?'

Raquel shook her head and tried to smile at him; why should Ismael have to walk this path with her? He could spare himself the pain. Why didn't he walk away? Why did he insist on staying with her? Her carpenter. Her partner?

'The doctors want to talk to you,' Ismael said. 'Ana is out of surgery.'

She took a deep breath and struggled to her feet.

Pilar looked at Sara and Santiago as a child might look at someone speaking a foreign language. Though she tried to concentrate, to understand their questions, her thoughts kept coming back to Simón's death, like a moth fluttering against a lightbulb.

'We can't stop now, Pilar. We need you to answer our questions,' Santiago said. 'There is another girl – Lucía. We don't know where she is. The longer it takes us to find her, the less chance she has of surviving . . .'

Death, again. What was death? What was her poor Simón feeling now? God, heaven and the angels – all that Catholic mumbo-jumbo. Be good. Be good, Pilar.

'Did you know your husband had been to prison?' Baín asked, and as he did so, Sara saw Pilar sit bolt upright, as though she had had an electric shock.

'That was a long time ago.'

'And do you know what he was convicted of?' Baín pressed the point. 'Child pornography. He liked sex with children, didn't he? You must have known?'

'No, my Simón wasn't like that.'

'He didn't tell you?'

'That happened before we were married. They tricked him. They planted things that weren't his.'

'Do you think he was capable of hurting a girl?'

'He works. That's all. He drives the tow truck . . .'

'Where was he yesterday morning?'

'On the road, on a job . . .'

'Are you sure?'

'Yes. He didn't lie. Simón would never lie to me.'

Pilar curled into a ball again, whispering, over and over, that Simón was not a liar. Sara began to realize that they would get nothing out of her through intimidation. She glanced at Santiago; why didn't he allow her to conduct the interviews? He seemed to recognize that this aggressive line of questioning was getting them nowhere, and his tone became conciliatory.

'Do you think there is some way we could check? With the company he worked for, maybe?'

'All his papers are upstairs,' Pilar said, as though this would allay all their suspicions.

'Or maybe he spent the day with a friend. Maybe you could give us the names and phone numbers of the people who were close to him . . .'

Santiago opened his notepad. Pilar stared at the blank page and the pen, poised, waiting for her words.

'Our parents are dead,' was all she could say.

'What about friends? Work colleagues?'

'He always drove the truck alone, and I only ever went into Ordial to do the shopping . . . Teresa,' she said, and unexpectedly smiled. 'Teresa knows us.'

'Who's Teresa?'

'She has the shop on the village square. In Ordial.'

'You don't know anyone other than . . . the people who work in the shop?'

'Our parents died,' Pilar said again.

Sara could see that Pilar was trying her best. She smiled at them every time she thought she was giving the answers they wanted. A woman who had spent her life trying to please other people, who was constantly grateful to them for simply allowing her to be present.

'Simón never went out? I don't know . . . to a bar, maybe?' Baín said.

'He didn't like to drink. Just a little drop of wine. And he was always working.'

'Did he spend a lot of time away?' Santiago had noticed Pilar's constant references to her husband's work. He did not want to confuse her; perhaps this was all she knew about Simón's life. 'Working with the tow truck, I mean . . . Maybe even at night, sometimes?'

'Work wasn't going well . . . but he never gave up. He spent all day in the truck. He said it was important to be available. In case anyone called him . . .'

'Did he get home late?'

'The roads around here are terrible, they're worse in winter. They get blocked by snowdrifts and no one does anything to clear them.'

Sara could hear Simón's grumblings in Pilar's words.

'They tax us for everything and no one spends a cent on this village.'

Sara knew that Baín had finished questioning Pilar. Víctor was waiting in the doorway.

'Thank you for everything, Pilar,' Baín said, bending down and taking her hands in his. 'If you need anything, don't hesitate to call us.'

'We'll need to speak to her neighbours in Ordial. This Teresa she mentioned . . .' Sara said to Víctor as they went out.

Walking away from the house, she glanced back and, through the window, she could see Pilar still sitting on the sofa.

'Can you send some of your people over to pick up all the paperwork they can find in the house? I want to go through it, and we need forensics to come and check for prints, though I don't think they'll find anything,' she said to Víctor and, before she got into the car, she took one last look at the house. 'And could you get an officer to stay with her, help her through the process? She hasn't even asked where her husband's body is.'

Baín finished a call on his mobile phone, then came over to the car.

'I'm heading back to the hospital. They've just moved Ana into the recovery unit.'

His sister had disappeared in October. That first Christmas had been sad, and every one since had been morbid. To Quim, it was as though, every December, they were plunged into a horror movie, where the family opens presents surrounded by the mummified corpses of their ancestors. Was he the only one who realized how absurd the whole thing was? How ridiculous and humiliating it was to see a present for Lucía under the Christmas tree?

The boxes, wrapped in bright coloured paper, were still piled on his sister's bed. More than once, Quim had thought about opening them; what do you give to a girl who is missing? They were big presents, expensive, too, probably. Maybe when she turned thirteen their father thought it was time Lucía had her own laptop. How else would she do all her homework for school? This was the sort of logic his family had grown accustomed to.

Quim remembered his father shaking him awake at dawn.

They've found Ana. She's in hospital in Barbastro, but there's no sign of your sister. Assuming you care, he had said.

Then Joaquín had turned and gone upstairs without even waiting for a response. Quim wanted to tell him to fuck off; what did his father know about what he cared about?

In fact, what did his parents know about him at all, now? Little by little, they had pushed him away.

Lucía's absence had taken up all their energy. The memory of his sister seemed more real than Quim's physical presence: he felt like a shadow in his own home – like a ghost his parents did not want to see.

It was almost noon when his mother woke him. Ana's condition had deteriorated, she told him. She was going to the hospital, in case the police needed her for something. Apparently, they had identified a suspect who lived in Ordial. Montserrat could hardly contain her excitement. She told Quim what they had said, and he decided not to tell her what he was thinking: that they were still a long way from finding Lucía. He had spent too many years playing the role of Cassandra.

His uncle, Rafael, showed up at about four o'clock, asked whether he had eaten anything, and left a Tupperware box of rice, in case he was hungry. He had just come back from Ordial, where the villagers had told him Guardia Civil jeeps had been coming and going all day. There was some talk of a married couple who lived up on one of the mountain tracks.

In the late afternoon, Quim smoked his last spliff with Ximena on the outskirts of the forest.

'Do you think they'll find her?' she asked.

Quim shrugged and took a toke. If they do find her, she'll be dead, he thought. But he said nothing.

He walked with Ximena as far as the village shop. Monteperdido was like a vat of bubbling oil.

'Simón Herrera,' the shopkeeper said as she gave him his change. 'He used to drive a tow truck . . . a white Volkswagen; you've probably seen him round here . . . They're saying they were one of those weird couples who never come down from the mountain . . .'

They walked back along the riverbank, avoiding Avenida de Posets. Ximena wanted him to come to her house, but Quim did not feel like it.

'I'll call you later,' he said, and gave her a kiss on the cheek.

He had no dope left. He rummaged through the pockets of the trousers he had been wearing the night before. No money either. His mother always kept a few banknotes in her chest of drawers, next to her underwear. He went into his parents' bedroom: they had left without making the bed, and they hadn't opened the windows. The room smelled of them, and there was no money in the chest of drawers.

Lucía's bedroom no longer smelled of anything except cleaning products. It had been preserved exactly as his sister had left it. His mother swept and hoovered it every day, she dusted what she could without ever moving anything. Even the dolls Lucía had left lying on the floor the morning she disappeared were still there. The only change was the Christmas and birthday presents piled on the bed.

Quim opened his sister's wardrobe. Washed and ironed, the dresses were waiting for her on the hangers. Every now and then, his mother rinsed them so they would still smell of fabric softener. On one of the shelves there was a pink jewellery box. Quim lifted the lid: the earrings she had been given for her first communion lay next to necklaces and bangles – costume jewellery. Quim pocketed the earrings. They were gold, a present from their grandparents. He could sell them down in Barbastro. Who would miss them?

The afternoon was drawing to a close. The incident room in the police station had gradually become a murky den. For some time, Sara had had to squint in order to read. She turned on the light and returned to the boxes of evidence that had been brought from Simón's house. In the middle of the desk was a box file containing the details of the suspect's most recent jobs. Simón had written down the address and the mileage for each job. Their first task had been to check the accuracy of his movements. A few phone calls to local garages were enough to confirm the details. But he had no pick-up on the day that Ana reappeared.

'Any news?' Víctor asked, popping his head round the door.

'Maybe, I'm not sure . . .' Sara looked up and pushed the file towards him.

Víctor came in and glanced over the notes; he could not see what she was getting at.

'The mileage for these jobs has been doctored,' Sara said, then shrugged. 'I'm not sure whether that means anything.'

'How can you tell?' Víctor picked up the file and leafed through the work slips, trying to see how Sara had come to this conclusion.

'It's statistical.' Sara handed him a sheet of paper on which she had scribbled several columns of numbers. 'These are the mileage figures that Simón logged. In this column, I've listed the digits from one to nine and, next to them, how many times each occurs.

The number three appears thirty per cent of the time . . . number seven, five per cent . . .'

Víctor set down the file; he could not make head nor tail of what she was saying.

'It's a mathematical law: in any sequence of numbers, the number one appears as the most significant digit about thirty per cent of the time, while nine appears as the most significant digit less than five per cent of the time – but here it is almost ten per cent. Simón made up these mileage figures.'

Though he tried, Víctor could not suppress a smile as he asked, 'You want some dinner? Pujante is bringing some snacks. I recommend the *chiretas*: sheep's intestines with rice. It's a local speciality in the valley.'

'What's with the smile?'

'Nothing. I'm just surprised . . . how much you know. I guess that's why you guys are leading the investigation.'

'Inspector Baín is more of a specialist in dealing with abductions. That's the first reason,' Sara said coolly. Then she remembered that Baín had insisted that she play bad cop. 'The second is that, over the past five years, the local Guardia Civil have proven their incompetence.'

'And you guys are going to sort things out using a couple of mathematical laws—'

'We are going to sort things out. The rest of that sentence is redundant, Sergeant.'

Sara shifted awkwardly in her chair. She wanted to shut down the conversation as soon as possible. She and Víctor had been working well together all day, at Simón's house and, later, getting witness statements in the village.

'That's all any of us wants,' Víctor said, trying to build bridges.

'Then why don't you help me instead of getting all defensive? You're an officer in the Guardia Civil, not a bank clerk. No one's going to fire you.'

'I think we would be better off going through the witness statements than tinkering around with numbers.'

'You don't think it's significant, that he faked these mileage figures?'

'So, he was conning the insurance companies to make a little extra cash? A major breakthrough in the case, Inspector. Maybe they'll give you a pat on the back.'

'Or maybe he was covering his tracks. Maybe he didn't want anyone to know where he really went when he was on a job.'

Víctor tried to hide his sense of helplessness, like a child forced to bite his tongue in front of the grown-ups. He glanced around the office, looking for an escape route.

'I'll try some of those *chiretas*,' Sara said, 'sample the local cuisine.'

'Are you always going to be like this?' Víctor protested as he turned to leave.

'Only when you're wrong,' Sara said reluctantly. She did not like to gloat when she was right. 'There's a girl's life at stake. We can't afford to make mistakes.'

Víctor nodded and stared at the floor, then left the office. Sara felt a wave of guilt wash over her. What was the point in riling the local officers in Monteperdido? Santiago cold-shouldered them; he had worked with them on other cases. He always treated them like pawns and disregarded their opinions – just as he was doing to her, right now. He was leaving her to deal with the most tedious part of the case: sorting paperwork, sifting evidence. Keeping her from any contact with Ana. He was the one who had led the interview with Simón Herrera's wife. Why? OK, so maybe she was a good desk sergeant, but she was a damn sight better at working directly with witnesses. Baín knew this as well as she did.

When they spoke to Teresa, the owner of the grocery shop, she remembered the Herreras well. She had described Pilar as a poor little thing – 'retarded' was her word. The witness statements from neighbours in Ordial all said the same thing: Pilar was the one who came into the village, did the shopping. People were kind to her, they felt sorry for her because of her disability. The couple had no friends in the area, though they had been living in the valley for years. Their families did not live locally, and Simón was like a shadow – the neighbours' sense of him came more from what Pilar said than from having seen him. It seemed as though he only ever talked to people who needed his tow truck. A man of few words, he was shy rather than sullen, his voice so low that people often had to ask him to repeat himself. This was how they described him. A man who did everything in his power to stay on the outside, on the margin of everyday life. The vehicle in which his body had been found was another anomalous detail; from the chassis number, they had determined it was a car Simón was supposed to have taken to the breaker's yard. Instead, he had kept it. He had tinkered with the engine and removed the licence plates. The perfect mode of transport for an aspiring ghost.

Víctor had been with Sara the whole day. Yet she had not asked about his dog again. And she had bitten her tongue when she could have praised his work – even when he found the petrol-station receipt that had led to everything else.

'Nieve.' Without realizing, she whispered the dog's name aloud.

And, as she did so, she remembered Víctor's shirt, stained with blood as he took his dog from her and cradled it. She wanted to rush out of the office, find Víctor and say, *I'm sorry. I'm really fucking sorry. This is not who I am.*

Then who are you, Sara? she wondered.

'Focus,' she ordered herself. 'Stop letting yourself get side-tracked.' She picked up a pencil and, dismissing all other thoughts, concentrated on the notes she had scribbled on the pad. This is exactly what Baín was afraid of; prove to him you're in control.

When had it all started? When she was a little girl, maybe; sometimes, alone in her bedroom, she would feel her mind racing too fast. Spinning out of control, spitting out images the way a Catherine wheel spits sparks. Images and ideas that piled up too fast for her to make sense of them. She found it suffocating, but did not know how to stop. Until finally she had to scream.

The pencil traced a triangle on the sheet of paper, then, next to it, a square. Sara began shading them in, and geometric shapes began to fill the margin of the report, growing into a seemingly random pattern, a labyrinth of lines in which Sara found something she could cling to, some way of stopping her whirling brain and regaining control of her thoughts.

The hospital car park was empty. As he waited to be allowed to see his daughter, Álvaro Montrell had watched Joaquín Castán talking to Inspector Baín at the main doors to the hospital. It was early afternoon. Then Baín had come to speak to him. He had asked whether the name Simón Herrera rang a bell. Álvaro said no. Baín had shown him a mugshot of a man with a face so ordinary it would have been impossible to remember.

The doctors told him that the operation had gone well. Ana was in recovery, where they planned to keep her overnight while she came around from the anaesthesia. If there were no complications, she would be back on the ward first thing tomorrow morning. He shuddered every time he tried to imagine what his daughter would be like when she woke up, what she would say. A fear that subsided only when he saw Raquel with that bloke – Ismael, they said his name was. What the fuck was this guy doing in the hospital?

Cold. So cold it felt as though there were ice crystals in her bloodstream. Ana curled into a ball and wrapped her arms around herself. She realized she was sobbing, like a child trapped in a nightmare. She could not stop crying, could not stop shivering. Her teeth were chattering. She remembered other nights. The coldest nights. Snow falling through a hole in the roof, icy wind whistling through the smallest cracks while she waited, petrified.

Cautiously, she half-opened her eyes, but the unfamiliar blinding glare forced her to close them again. She saw shadows she could not identify. Five words came back to her: *Earth. Smoke. Dust. Shade. Nothingness.*

'How do you feel, Ana?' a woman's voice said.

She tried to identify the source of the voice. 'Where is Lucía?'

Gradually, the world around her began to take shape: a room with high ceilings and fluorescent lights; a woman in a white coat.

'I'm so cold,' she managed to say.

'That's the anaesthetic,' the voice said reassuringly. 'Sometimes it feels cold, but it will wear off in a little while.'

Then everything fell into place. Like the pieces of a Meccano set tumbling in space and snapping together to create a structure that was her life. A line that had been broken when the car had swerved off the road and plunged into the ravine. She could think back and clearly remember what had happened, but she did not know what had happened afterwards.

'Where am I?' she asked.

'In hospital. You were in an accident, remember?' the nurse said.

Ana smiled at her. She had not noticed yet, but her arms were not so tense now, she no longer felt so cold.

2

The Flood

The floor was like a maze, the gaps between the tiles were avenues and the cracks and crazing were shortcuts that could take you from one place to another in a flash. In the blink of an eye.

Pilar was sitting on her bed. She had not moved all night. Gradually, her tired body had hunched, closing in on itself, while she scanned paths marked out by the lines and cracks in the floor tiles, searching for some way out of her room. But she had not found one.

The silence was broken by the sound of smashing glass.

Her first impulse was to scream, 'Simón!' She heard herself shout his name as she jumped to her feet. She took a few steps, and had just reached the door of the bedroom when she remembered that he was dead.

She heard voices coming from the stairwell. Voices taut as cables about to snap.

It was eight a.m. and, by now, she would usually be in the kitchen preparing lunch. She caught a whiff of celery, chopped leeks, onions. The smell of garlic and onions on her hands. She would prepare everything before going to the bathroom to wash. Then she would get dressed and go down to the village to buy whatever she might need: bread, wine. Simón liked a glass of wine with his meals. But Pilar's routine had been shattered; she felt as though she were using an outdated map on which roads and streets no longer related to the real world. A map that could no longer lead her anywhere.

'Where's Lucía?!'

She clearly heard the bellowing voice, but she could not understand what the words meant. Outside the windows, a group of shadows shifted aimlessly, like flies in a jam jar. In the hallway, at the foot of the stairs, was a large rock, and the floor was strewn with shards of glass that looked like the tail of a comet. A blinding white light burned through the hole the rock had made in the glass.

'You've no right to be here!' she heard someone shout, trying to be heard above the other.

We're out of wine, Pilar thought, and glanced around the room, her small, dark eyes searching for some way she might leave the house and go down to the village.

She remembered the path she used to take home from school as a child, the village where she had been born, her mother's voice telling her to avoid the main square, where old men would be sitting, drinking wine. *Go round the back way. Take the Camino del Porchón,* she would say when she waved her off to school.

Why do they laugh at me? Pilar would ask. *Why do they say rude things?*

Just take the back road, her mother would say.

Simón never said rude things when he drank wine. He would sit at the kitchen table, his cheeks flushed, and eventually he would doze off. She would clear the table and wash the dishes.

'What did you do to those girls?' The shadowy figures showed no sign of going away.

I don't want to talk about it, Simón had said once, before they were married. *And I don't want you asking me again, do you hear me?*

They had told her she was sick. She had said that sick people need someone to take care of them.

Pilar walked away from the stairs and into the room that Simón had used as an office. The police had taken all the papers. The desk and the shelves stood empty, like the discarded skeleton of an animal.

She had seen her mother's corpse. She had kissed her on the cheek; the skin had felt unpleasant, cold and slick like plastic. One of the Guardia Civil officers had told her it would be a few days before she could bury her husband. They had to perform an autopsy.

'Who are these girls they're talking about? What did you do, Simón? They are coming for me and I don't know what to say to them.'

Pilar went over to the window. Through the venetian blinds, she could see the people crowded around her house. Some officers from the Guardia Civil were trying to keep them away from the front door. But there were only three of them. They could not control the crowd. They pushed a few of them away, opening up a gap for others to slip through. She noticed a young boy she was sure she had seen in the village. The boy bent down, picked up a stone and hurled it at the house. He laughed.

The old men on the village square had laughed.

They laughed at her because she was stupid.

They tricked me, Simón had said to her once. *They framed me and I had to go to jail. That's what happens when you trust other people, Pilar. They laugh in your face.*

She felt tears scalding her eyes and trickling in burning rivers down her cheeks. Her legs felt weak and she had to sit down in a corner of the room. Her muscles ached. Still she could hear the voices outside. Still she thought she could hear them laugh.

Laughter.

Old men drinking and shouting that she was a retard.

She had believed Simón.

Simón's hands did not smell of garlic and onions, just acrid sweat. Dirty, viscous, like his body after they had sex. Simón did it quickly, as though it was a unpleasant chore he wanted over quickly. Like clearing a blocked drain.

Other men had used her before. *'Don't you realize? You can't just let men do what they want to you,'* her mother had told her.

Her first period, blood streaming down her thighs. *'Am I dying?'* she had asked her mother.

'Don't wash yourself, don't touch yourself. You have to wait until the bleeding stops.'

'What did you do to those girls?' the voices outside her door screamed.

Pilar wandered deeper and deeper into a maze of memories, feeling guilty and petrified, unable to make sense of what was happening. But these people wanted an explanation. They needed an explanation. She tried to come up with an explanation, but though she racked her brain, she could find nothing. Just narrow alleyways leading from one image to the next, leading to a single conclusion, like a shroud that covered her whole life: *You're a retard. You're a moron. Everybody lies to you. Everybody uses you.*

Under the desk, there was a small toolbox. It was one of the few things the police had not taken away. She dragged it out and opened it. It felt as though she had opened a door, found the exit for which she had been searching.

Joaquín Castán had not got out of his car. He had parked on the side of the mountain track leading to Simón Herrera's house. He could see the Guardia Civil trying to control the situation. Their jeeps were parked to form a cordon outside the house and, now, they were urging the last of the onlookers to leave. He saw Marcial Nerín coming down the hill, livid with anger, panting with every step.

'It's unbelievable!' he said as he opened the car door. 'I don't know what they're waiting for; they need to force her to talk!'

'Are the S.A.F. officers in there?'

'Not a sign of them. There's only Rojas and Telmo and *el niño* there, what's his name?'

'Pujante?'

'That's it. You can see how seriously they're taking it. I can't think what's so important that they're not here.'

Most of the people in the crowd were from Ordial; they had gathered outside the house at first light, as soon as the rumours were confirmed. Simón Herrera was the man who had been in the car with Ana. Some people from Monteperdido had made their way to the village. Simón's wife was in the house. How could she not know something? It had been five years. More than enough time for her to notice something strange, no matter how retarded she was.

'Phone Joaquín,' Montserrat said.

She felt her nerves slither like eels through her chest and around her throat. She looked for somewhere to sit; she could not breathe. Rafael took his sister's arm and led her the few steps to the waiting room.

'Just take a breath, for God's sake! It's good news.'

'I know, I know,' Montserrat said, squeezing her eyes shut.

She tried not to panic about what Ana might say. The operation had gone well; Ana was recovering. She would be soon be transferred back to the ward, one of the nurses had said, though she was still a little groggy. *Lucía is dead.* What if this was what Ana was going to say? *Lucía is dead.* The very thought swept away everything in its path.

'Did you take something? Do you want me to ask them for a tranquillizer?' her brother fretted.

Montserrat shook her head vehemently. She wanted to feel everything, however painful.

'Phone Joaquín,' she said to Rafael again. 'Tell him to get here. Tell him . . .'

The doctor gave them a broad smile. Too broad, Álvaro thought. As though there had been no hope and the result had been a miracle – nothing to do with the surgeon's skill or what had happened in the operating theatre.

'We should thank God,' he said. 'Ana's recovery is significantly better than we had hoped.'

Raquel took a seat. Álvaro remained standing, somewhat aloof. The police officers were listening to the doctor, but Álvaro could not help but notice them glancing at him. What were they doing? Gauging his reactions? If he smiled, if he didn't smile, would they consider it a sign? They were attempting to judge his reactions in relation to a specific profile, but who were they to decide how he felt? They hadn't a fucking clue. There had not been a day in the past five years when he had felt comfortable in his own skin. Álvaro wanted to smile, but he could not. He listened in silence as the consultant explained that the blood clot had been removed, that their daughter had now come round from the anaesthesia and initial test results were very promising. Her reactions and her reflexes were normal. And, although they could not be absolutely certain, they were confident that the surgery would have no side effects.

'What about her memory?' Inspector Baín asked.

Álvaro could not help turning to look when he heard this voice, and found Baín staring back at him. As though the question was not directed at the consultant, but at him.

'We'll have to wait a while. Ana is disorientated, but that is perfectly normal for any patient waking up after anaesthesia—'

'Can we see her?' Raquel said.

'Let's go downstairs and we can—'

'We would like to ask her a few questions.' Santiago interrupted the doctor. 'I'm sure you understand.'

'I insist on being present,' Álvaro said curtly. 'My daughter is a minor.'

'Of course, of course . . .' Santiago Baín's smile did nothing to mask his frustration.

For Álvaro, this was not the end of something, but the beginning. In this very moment, a story was unfolding that he wanted to be part of. He had no intention of simply being a witness, a bystander, someone who could get up and leave at any moment. He was a part of this, and he did not care what the police thought. In other circumstances, Baín's grim smile might have dissuaded him, convinced him to take a step back. But he could not step aside.

On either side, the hospital rooms flashed past, like a landscape seen through the windows of a train. It was a curious sensation, one that Ana had first felt as a little girl on the train to Barcelona. On that occasion, she had been at Huesca Station, leaning back in her seat, and when the train moved off, it did not feel as though she was moving. It felt as though the train carriage was stationary, while everything around was moving backwards: the platform, the station, even the sky.

Lying on the trolley, the strip-lights flickered over her face as they passed.

'Would you like to see your parents?' the porter asked as they came to the door of her hospital room.

Ana remembered her father's hands, gripping her tightly under the arms as he lifted her down from the train when it finally reached Barcelona. She had made a little jump to avoid the gap between train and platform, but at no point had she felt alone. Álvaro's powerful hands guided her through the air.

Pujante looked at the stairs leading up to the first floor.

'Señora? Are you all right?'

There was no answer.

The front door stood open. Outside, Telmo was leaning on the bonnet of a jeep, lighting a cigarette, chatting to Rojas, the other officer from the Guardia Civil. They were laughing, but Pujante could not hear what was being said. There were still a few gawkers hanging around, about a hundred metres from the gate – old people from the village who considered the events something to do with their morning.

'You don't need to worry,' Pujante said as he climbed the stairs. 'They've all gone now, and we're going to stay here with you as long as you need us. Señora? Pilar?'

The beds were neatly made; the room was spick and span – like the kitchen, which he had seen earlier. The floor tiles had been scrubbed. Like the people outside, Pujante could not believe that this woman could be so ignorant. Her husband had been holding the girls prisoner for five years; no one knew what he had done, but it was horrifyingly easy to imagine. His wife had to know something.

But, then, what did his opinion matter? Pujante had only managed to get a transfer to Monteperdido a few months earlier. So far, his fellow officers had done little other than send him on errands, ask him to bring pastries from his wife's bakery, and laugh at the goatee beard he had grown to make himself look older. It did not bother him; he had a job in the village where he had grown up, where his family still lived.

Opposite the bedroom was another room. Pujante crossed the landing, opened the door and stepped inside. Immediately, he noticed the pervasive smell. A smell familiar from his parents' home on days when his father went hunting. He felt a sudden wave of unease. A happy childhood memory had suddenly been transformed into something noxious and unwholesome. The pool of blood had spread across the floor; he was standing in it. Lifting one boot, he saw a viscous thread suspended from the sole. Pilar was lying underneath the desk, her face pressed against the floor.

★

Ana brought a hand up to her head. Until now, she had not realized that they had shaved her head. The skin was smooth and taut. With a flicker of disgust, she warily ran her fingers across her skull, knowing that, at any moment, she might find the scar. In the recovery room, the surgeon had explained that they had had to perform an operation. Then he had asked her one or two questions – her name, her age – and performed a few tests to check that her vision and her reflexes had not been impaired. Ana had been tempted to ask for a mirror, but she had not dared. She worried he might think she was vain, but she could not stop thinking about her hair. The long, beautiful mane of hair she spent hours brushing every day. So many hours.

At the back of her head, near the base of her skull, the incision was covered with a dressing. She glanced to her left; next to the door was a window through which she could see faint shadows moving. Who were they? More doctors, more nurses?

Ever since she had regained consciousness, she had been disconcerted by the sense of movement, as though everything was happening too fast for her to take it in. She longed to be able to put the world on pause, if only to catch her breath, to adjust to the rhythm of events. To concentrate on the people she had seen through the glass who were now trooping into her room. To forget about her hair, about travelling on trains. To focus on what was in front of her. Who were these people?

'Poppet . . .' someone said in a ragged whisper, rushing to hug her. Ana saw tears trickling down the woman's cheeks. 'My poor poppet . . .'

Raquel leaned back so that she could look into Ana's eyes. Little by little, she began to recognize her daughter's features. More defined, more accentuated. Changed, yet recognizable.

85

'You know who I am?' Raquel could not disguise the fear in her voice.

'*Mamá*,' Ana said.

And she saw her mother smile, happy, saw all the muscles in her face relax. This was the expression Ana had spent so many nights dreaming of, the expression that, over the years, had faded and finally disappeared, but now she had found it again. Behind her mother, other figures bustled about. Ana thought she could make out the consultant, a man and a woman who were looking for somewhere to sit and, behind them, her father. Álvaro pushed his way through to the bed. Seeing him, Ana felt as though he were holding her, supporting her with his powerful hands. The hands that now reached out to stroke her face. A shock of white hair fell over his forehead. His eyes were as blue as water.

'My little princess . . .' Álvaro managed to say.

Then he sat on the bed and hugged her; Ana felt his breath against her chest, closed her eyes and finally knew she was once more in control. Her heart was beating at the same rate as everyone else's.

'We need to ask Ana a few questions,' she heard the man she had seen looking for a chair say apologetically. She turned and saw him approach the bed and wait for her father to step aside.

'Can't you wait a minute?' Álvaro said without looking at the man.

'We have already been waiting for some time,' the man said firmly.

'Don't worry, poppet,' her mother said. 'You just answer as much as you can . . .'

Her father stood up and took a step back. It was obvious that he did not like the situation; he looked the way he did when he was about to scold her for leaving her room in a mess again.

'My name is Santiago Baín,' the man said, sitting on the bed. 'I'm a police officer. This is my colleague, Sara Campos.'

Raquel sat down next to her and took her hand. Ana could feel her mother's eyes on her. For a second, she thought that her mother wasn't looking at her, but at her shaved head.

'We want to know how much you remember . . . About how you came to be here, in hospital.'

Ana turned to look at the female police officer. She was pale and she wore her hair pinned up – though, if she untied it, it would probably have fallen over her shoulders. Unlike her colleague, she was not wearing a suit, but jeans and a T-shirt.

'You were in a car accident, do you remember?' Inspector Baín asked, seeing that Ana was not looking at him.

Baín waited for a response and, after a moment, the girl gave a slight nod. Before continuing, he glanced at Sara. She did nothing to hide her annoyance; she wanted to be leading the interview with Ana.

A number of voices filtered in from the hallway.

'Would you mind closing the door?' Sara asked the doctor.

Baín turned back to Ana. 'You're safe, Ana. Your parents are here. Nothing bad is going to happen to you . . . You don't need to be afraid. Can you tell us who you've been with all this time?'

'I don't know,' Ana said quickly, like a schoolgirl doing multiplication tables. Then her eyes sought out Sara. 'With Lucía.'

'Where is Lucía?' Baín asked.

'She's still in the hole.'

'What is "the hole"?'

'The basement. Where the man took us . . .'

'What was he like, this man?'

'I don't know.'

'Was he tall, short? Had you seen him before?'

'I don't know.'

Baín paused. He did not want to pressure her; he needed her to think he was on her side. Sara handed him a file and Baín took out a photograph of Simón Herrera and showed it to Ana.

'Is this the man?' he said.

Ana shook her head. Sara saw her let go of her mother's hand. She sat up in the bed.

'He's not the one who abducted you and Lucía?' Baín said.

'No.'

Álvaro stepped closer to the bed. 'Just tell them what you can remember,' he encouraged her.

'This man is Simón Herrera,' Baín explained. 'He was in the car with you when you crashed.'

'He's the one who saved me,' Ana said.

Sara locked eyes with Baín. This changed everything they had assumed up to this point.

'What do you mean, he saved you?' Baín asked.

'He came into the hut . . . He cut the rope and carried me to the car . . . He said he was taking me home . . .'

'And then what happened?'

'I don't know . . . We were going really fast – in the car, I mean. I was lying on the back seat. I was scared. Then I felt something hitting us from behind . . . The car went off the road, and everything started spinning, and the windows broke . . .'

Ana stopped suddenly. She took her mother's hand again, looked to her for comfort.

'It's OK; you're doing really well . . .' Raquel said.

'Where is Lucía now?' Baín pressed her. He could tell from Álvaro's expression that he would not allow much more questioning.

'In the basement, with him . . . When he went downstairs to be with Lucía, he brought me upstairs and tied me up . . .'

'Do you know where it is, this basement? Had you ever been there before?'

'We were there all the time—'

Víctor came into the room without knocking. 'Santiago, Sara.' He made a gesture to indicate he needed to talk to them outside.

Before she got to her feet, Sara leaned towards Ana and stroked her cheek. 'Your mother is right: you're doing very well.' And then she added, 'And you look really cute as a skinhead. Seriously.'

She followed Baín and Víctor into the hospital corridor. The sergeant stopped a few metres from the room, making sure no one could overhear.

'It's Pilar – Simón Herrera's wife. She's killed herself . . . By the time the ambulance got there, it was too late . . .'

The hospital car park had become a meeting place for the villagers of Monteperdido. Joaquín and Montserrat Castán were there, with Rafael Grau and Marcial Nerín. Ismael joined them as they were discussing what had happened at the Herrera house, how the villagers were still crowded around it because, in a sense, the story of Ana and Lucía was inextricably linked to the villages in the valley.

'Who's talked to Ana? Víctor?' Joaquín asked Ismael, who did not seem to hear. Raquel had left the room without asking him to join her, as though he had suddenly ceased to exist. As though the hours, the years she had spent by his side no longer mattered. And yet he refused to accept this rejection. It was misplaced. 'Ismael?'

Joaquín insisted. 'I asked you if Víctor, the Guardia Civil, was in the girl's hospital room?'

'I think so . . .' Ismael said. 'With the two officers from the S.A.F.'

'If they knew anything, they'd tell us.' Rafael tried to sound reassuring. He could see Joaquín looking blackly at the hospital. His rage was spiralling out of control, dragging Rafael's sister in its wake, like a car hurtling downhill, crushing everything in its path. 'Give them a little time.'

Joaquín was about to say something to his brother-in-law when lights and wailing sirens drowned him out. A police car screeched into the car park, followed by a Guardia Civil jeep. Joaquín felt the urge to stop them, to scream and shout, to demand answers, but he knew it was absurd – like a dog barking at parked cars. He waited a moment or two, until he could summon the strength to look at his wife, then he fished out his mobile phone, muttering, 'They can't treat us like we're nobody . . . like we're dirt.'

'Who are you calling?' Montserrat took a step closer to her husband.

'Víctor.'

Montserrat knew that the sergeant would not answer. No one is in a hurry to be the bearer of bad news, and she was convinced that, whatever they had to say about her daughter, it would not be good.

The onlookers stood to one side as the police cars drove up to Simón Herrera's house. Earlier, they had seen an ambulance arrive. It was still parked outside, next to the jeep. Paramedics and officers from the Guardia Civil were standing around, chatting casually. A paramedic patted one of the officers on the shoulder, trying to comfort him. Rumours were already circulating that Pilar was dead; it would not be long before they reached Monteperdido. 'It's because she knew,' people muttered. 'Why else would she kill herself?'

Sara got out of the car, keeping her eyes fixed on the muddy road, now rutted with tyre tracks from the vehicles coming and going. She stood up straight, resolving to dismiss the regrets that had assailed her as they drove here. Like a couple after an acrimonious argument, she and Baín had not spoken on the way, other than to discuss the route. Platitudes intended to fill the empty space.

As she elbowed her way through the crowd of medics and officers, she glanced at Pujante – the officer who had found Pilar, according to Víctor. He barely looked more than twenty, and from his pallor and his watery eyes, she could tell it was the first dead body he had had to deal with.

Sara saw the broken windows in the hallway, the rock at the foot of the stairs.

'Go up,' Baín ordered.

Reaching the landing, she glanced into the room that Simón Herrera had used as an office. Santiago stepped past her. Pilar's body was exactly as Pujante had found it. The paramedic had laid a thermal blanket over her, but that was all. Inspector Baín hunkered down next to the body of Simón Herrera's wife. Her mouth was open, her face pressed against the floor. A few centimetres from her right hand lay the bloodstained box cutter she had used to slash her wrist.

'I don't understand how she can have done it without screaming . . .' said Sara. 'Have you seen the size of the wound?'

'During the Easter Week processions, you see people walking barefoot, lashing themselves with whips – do you ever hear them scream? They believe that they deserve the pain.'

Baín got to his feet and went over to the window. Down below, Víctor had gathered a number of fellow officers, but further off there was still a group of onlookers. Most were older people, though there were a few teenagers.

'I don't want to clap eyes on that fucking moron again,' Baín said, turning away from the window and stalking out of the room. 'The one who found the body. Or the officers who were supposed to be standing guard, for that matter.'

Sara tried to stifle her rage, but failed.

'You really think this is their fault? We are the ones who could have prevented it.'

Baín stopped in the doorway. He stood with his back to her, and she saw his shoulders slump and his head bow, as though some invisible pressure were weighing on him.

'It was our duty to anticipate what Pilar might do – to station an officer to sit with her,' Sara said.

'Why don't you spare yourself, Sara?' Baín turned back to look at her, his expression not simply weary, but defeated.

'You know I'm right.'

He stood in silence for a moment.

'How important is it to you that we solve this case?' He looked from Sara to the body of Pilar.

'I don't know what you expect me to say to that.'

'Nothing,' Baín said.

'Are you thinking of taking me off the case?' Sara said hesitantly.

'You think you're better than me.'

'It's not that, Santiago. But I know I can be of more help if you let me work on the front line. If you'd let me talk to Pilar—'

'What?' Baín cut her off. 'Her husband had nothing to do with the kidnapping. So tell me, what exactly would you have got out of her?'

'I don't know,' Sara muttered. She did not dare suggest that they might have prevented Pilar's suicide. 'She was terrified. It was as if we'd ripped the ground from under her feet . . . Do you see what I mean?'

'That's enough, Sara.'

He walked over to her and smiled. He brushed the hair from her face and laid his hand on her cheek. Stroked it.

'I don't want to have to watch you fall apart again,' he said.

Sara felt a shudder of shame.

Baín took his hand away. He would have liked to have hugged her. In the end, he simply said goodbye and left the room.

Sara heard his footsteps on the stairs, heard the front door open. Through the window, she watched as he said goodbye to Víctor, gave Pujante an almost paternal hug. She did not wait until he got into the car. She left the office and went into Pilar's bedroom. She imagined the woman sitting on this bed, listening to her neighbours screaming insults, her heart racing as she heard the rock crash through the window. What had she have been thinking? Simón, the only man who had ever loved her, had been transformed into a monster. What did that make her?

Sara went into the bathroom at the top of the stairs. The towels and the bathmat were dry. She opened the cabinet above the washbasin: there were none of the beauty products she might expect to find in any woman's bathroom. Only Simón's razor and various medications. A box of amoxicillin, tubes of antiseptic and hydrocortisone.

'The examining magistrate is here for the removal of the body,' she heard Víctor say.

'We need to go and see the coroner. There's nothing left for us to do here,' Sara said as she went downstairs.

'You mean, leave the place empty?'

Sara did not answer. She walked out and, without a word to the other officers, got into Víctor's jeep. She looked back at the house. Now that Pilar was gone, time would begin to eat away the walls, rain would weaken the roof and, one day, the building would crumble, become a derelict ruin like those that surrounded it. By then, no one would remember the people who had once lived here.

'We need to talk. We need to decide what we're going to do,' Álvaro said.

'What do you mean?' Raquel said, fumbling for her pack of cigarettes.

'When she's discharged. What are we going to tell her?'

Raquel took a few steps from Álvaro. The sun was beginning to set and she realized that she had not eaten. She lit a cigarette and felt her stomach burn as she inhaled the smoke. The doctors had asked them to leave while they dressed Ana's wound. Raquel had needed a cigarette; Álvaro wanted to go with her. The officer taking care of them had also come outside to smoke. She could see him standing about a hundred metres away, talking on his phone and puffing on his cigarette. Raquel assumed he was talking to his wife, telling her he was with the girl who had reappeared, the one they were talking about on the television.

'What do you think we should say?' Raquel asked, walking back towards Álvaro.

'I don't know ... but maybe we don't have to tell her any-thing ... At least not yet. I think that would be best.'

'What about when she comes home and you're not there?'

'I'd like to be there, Raquel.'

Raquel had aged much more than Álvaro in the past five years. She knew that her complexion was no longer radiant, her body no longer as firm as Álvaro remembered. All Ismael's flattering remarks suddenly seemed like lies she had forced herself to believe. Time had not been as kind to her as it had to him, Raquel thought. She tried to imagine undressing in front of her husband again, exposing a body that was five years older, and she knew she could not do it. He had lost weight, the bags under his eyes were more pronounced and his features were sharper: the nose, the cheekbones, the chin. It was as though he no longer had anything to hide, and showed him-self exactly as he was. Those liquid blue eyes she had fallen in love with so long ago were now staring at her with a self-assurance she had forgotten. That same self-assurance she had seen almost twenty years earlier when, for the first time, he had said, *I love you*. Now, Álvaro was asserting his right to be in the house, with her, when Ana came home.

'I don't think it's a good idea,' Raquel said. 'We shouldn't lie to her.'

'I need to be with her,' Álvaro pleaded. 'Tell her we're not together anymore, but don't push me away, please.'

'You're trying to turn me into the bad guy in this scenario.'

'That's not true.'

'So what am I supposed to tell Ana? "I don't want your father to come home"? You're the one who decided to leave. I haven't heard a word from you for nearly four years.'

'This isn't about us, Raquel. I'm not asking to go back to the way things were before. I just want to be close to my daughter.'

'And you will be.'

'Is that a no?'

'Give me time,' Raquel said. 'It's too much to think about . . . I just want to do what's best for Ana . . .'

Álvaro turned and stared abstractedly at the hospital. The Guardia Civil had finished his cigarette and was stubbing it out in the ashtray next to the entrance. He gave them a pointed look before heading back inside.

'It pisses me off that they won't let us be alone with her,' Álvaro muttered angrily as he flicked the hair out of his eyes.

Santiago Baín took the exit a few kilometres outside Barbastro. Signposts indicated a service area ahead. There were a couple of parked trucks and, behind the petrol station, one of those soulless cafeterias that spring up along motorways, like weeds. All the grandeur of the surroundings, the vast sweeping landscape, evaporated next to this tawdry motorway café, the kind of place that might be found in any city. Baín parked and went inside; it was deserted, but for a few elderly customers at the bar. A waitress with backcombed hair wandered over and listlessly asked what he wanted. Baín ordered and hung his jacket on the back of the stool. He could feel his heart hammering in his chest like a tenacious woodpecker building its nest. Twenty-four hours with no sleep and no food was beginning to take its toll.

As he ate, Baín considered how solving a case rarely meant saving the victims. At best, it meant finding the bodies and constructing a story that fitted the evidence. This was not only what his superiors wanted, but what most people involved in abduction cases demanded: a story that would make sense of their pain. This had been his job: giving meaning to apparently inexplicable events.

Sara was right: they were to blame for Pilar's death. Simón Herrera's wife had been unable to deal with suddenly being deprived of the storyline she had shared with her husband. She had died believing the man she loved was a monster, when, in time, Simón might prove to be the hero of the story: he had found Ana, had risked everything to save her, and, though it had cost him his life, he had succeeded.

A man came and sat next to Baín at the counter. They were about the same age, a little over sixty, and, looking at him, Baín felt as though he were looking in a mirror.

'You're one of them cops, aren't you? The ones who've come about them girls that went missing in Monteperdido?'

Baín nodded and smiled. He noticed that his heart had stopped pounding.

The man sighed, as though he understood the difficult position that the police were in. 'It ain't easy finding things in these mountains,' he said. 'They're not made for the likes of men . . . Better left to chamois goats and roe deer . . .'

'We're doing the best we can,' Baín admitted.

'My brother-in-law got lost on the slopes of Ixeia, back before they made that tunnel . . . Never found so much as his shoes.' A smile played on the man's lips. 'Not that anyone much missed him.'

Baín rummaged in his pockets and asked for the bill, then dropped a few coins on to the metal plate and bade the man goodbye.

'The other one . . . the one that didn't show up again . . . She's dead, ain't she?' he called as Baín was leaving.

Víctor stood a little way from the autopsy table. The coroner was reeling off the various factors that had caused the death of Simón Herrera – skull fracture caused when his head hit the dashboard, compound fractures to various bones, subarachnoid haemorrhage – a litany of medical terms that floated amid the smell of bleach and disinfectant, and gradually seemed to fade, as though drowned out by what Sara had told him as they were driving to the Coroner's Office. About how Simón had saved Ana. According to the girl, he had suddenly appeared in the *refugio* – the stone hut – where the man had held them prisoner for five years, and while Lucía was with their captor, down in the basement – what Ana called 'the hole' – Simón had untied her and carried her to the car.

Each of Ana's words was a step along the path that led to answers. *Refugio*, five years, man, hole. Had they been nearby all this time? Who was this man? Was Lucía still trapped in the basement, waiting for them to find her? Was the kidnapper worried that Ana was still alive? What was he doing now, while they were staring at the corpse of Simón Herrera and listening to the coroner's report?

Sara looked at the naked body on the stainless-steel table. She had imagined Simón Herrera as a ghost who made every effort to remain invisible. He had made a mistake once, and it had landed him in jail. Martutene Prison. Since then, Simón had changed: he became cautious, tight-lipped; he hid behind a façade of normality that allowed him to pursue his twisted fantasies. He had been meticulous enough to cover his tracks, to keep the girls imprisoned. The offender profile had seemed simple, logical, and Sara had allowed herself to get carried away.

Now she saw the story differently; perhaps she had arranged the facts to fit her version of things. Simón might have accepted responsibility for his past misdeeds and, ashamed, tried to live a quiet, simple life; perhaps his only sin had been cheating the insurance companies out of a few euros.

Sara looked at Simón's body for the last time, and the phrase that came to mind brought a sad smile to her face: a man without socks. She stared at his feet, which were mottled a purplish black.

'Did he have circulation problems?' she asked the medical examiner.

'Some varicose veins, but nothing serious. The tox screen is clear. Slightly elevated levels of cortisone, but nothing else.'

'I know this isn't easy, but think about Lucía. Do this for her. Try to remember,' Inspector Baín said.

Ana sat up in the bed, leaning against the pillows. Her parents were waiting outside in the hallway; she could see blurred shadows through the glass.

'Give me a minute,' Sara said, and left the room.

Baín saw her approach the parents and, a moment later, the blurred figures behind the glass disappeared. Sara came back into the room and carefully closed the door so that Ana would not be distracted. The girl seemed nervous, even frightened. Sara noticed that she had a nervous tic, constantly picking at the skin on her fingers, her nails digging into the flesh as though trying to bury something. The small red scars around her fingernails indicated that it was a tic she had developed while in captivity. A way of dealing with her vulnerability, her fear.

'I don't know what to say,' Ana mumbled.

'We just want to talk about the hole, about the mountain hut. What does it look like?' Baín said, sitting on the bed next to her.

Sara took out a tape recorder and set it on the nightstand; Ana looked at the flashing red light before she spoke.

'It's a ruin. One side of the roof has fallen in. And part of one of the walls too.'

'Is it a stone building?' Baín asked, and she nodded almost imperceptibly. 'What could you see around the building?'

'Mountains. Trees and mountains.'

'Try to describe them. What did they look like? Do you know what kind of trees they were? We need to find this place and you're the only person who can help.'

'We never went outside . . . When he went down to the basement, he left me upstairs . . .'

'He left you tied up, alone for hours,' Baín said. 'One of the walls had collapsed. It must have been very cold.'

'Very cold,' Ana said.

'What could you see through the hole in the wall?'

'The mountains, though most of the year everything was covered in snow. When it was windy, the snow would blow in. And it came through the roof too . . . I had a blanket, but some nights it was so cold I couldn't sleep.'

'But it's summer now,' Baín tried to guide her. 'There wouldn't be any snow now, would there?'

Every time she thought back, Ana seemed to lose her way. 'Only at the very top,' she said.

'Could you see anything else? A river, maybe? Another building? A road?'

Ana shook her head. 'Only the mountains. Now that it's summer, there are lots of leaves on the trees . . . I don't know what kind of trees they are . . . The trunks are not very fat, and the leaves are . . .'

'Long? Round?'

'Like hearts . . . Little green hearts, that's what they looked like to me . . . I called them fibbers, the trees . . .' Ana smiled as she remembered this private joke. 'Sometimes they'd make me think it was raining, but it was just the wind rustling the leaves . . . It really sounded like rain, though.'

Baín paused. He glanced at the tape recorder, where the numbers on the digital display ticked silently. Second after second. And still Baín could not find a way into Ana's memory, a way to picture this place where they had been held.

'Some nights, you slept upstairs, yeah? Could you see the sunset from where you were?'

'No. The light gradually faded. In winter, it was weird; it would be pitch dark, but the snow still twinkled . . . all by itself . . . like it was electric or something . . .' Ana had briefly allowed herself to get caught up in her story, but then withdrew into herself again. 'That's just silly . . .'

'It's not silly.' Sara spoke for the first time. 'Everything you tell us is useful, Ana.'

'We know you can't give us a complete description. No one could,' Baín said. 'We just want you to tell us what it looked like to you.'

'A hole,' Ana said confidently. 'It didn't matter whether you were in the basement or upstairs . . . It was like the whole place had sunk into a hole. Sometimes it looked like the mountains and the trees would fall on top of us . . .'

'When it rained heavily, did it flood?' Baín asked.

'A couple of times, and the water would bring in tree branches and stuff like that . . . There were leaks in the basement . . . We used to pretend we were in a submarine and . . .' The sudden smile drained from Ana's face, as though the thought that she might fondly remember a single minute of her ordeal was grotesque.

'And the man who kept you captive, he must have been a strong man; he could have fixed the walls or the roof.'

'I don't know if he was that strong.'

'If he dragged you up from the basement and you were struggling, he must have been strong—'

'I didn't struggle . . . Why would I do that?'

Baín took a breath, and softened his approach. 'It would be normal that, after such a long time, you would become friendly. It's nothing to be ashamed of . . . What else could you do?'

'He wasn't my friend. I never spoke to him.'

'Ana, it's been five years; how could you not have spoken to him?' Baín stared coldly at Ana. He was no longer playing at being caring and compassionate. He needed to make it clear to her that his patience was wearing thin. 'Why are you lying to us?'

'I'm not lying, honestly.'

Ana looked to Sara for sympathy, but Baín gently took her chin and turned her face, so she was forced to look at him.

'Who is he?' Baín asked. 'We'll be here to support you. No one is going to hurt you, I promise. But, please, enough of this nonsense. Or don't you care what happens to Lucía? You're here, you're safe with your parents, soon you'll be going home . . . but unless you help us, by the time we find Lucía, she will be dead. Is that what you want?'

Ana's face trembled as Baín held it. She was a little girl, chilled to the bone, alone in the night. Tears welled in her eyes, trickled down her cheeks to where Baín's hand still held her firmly. It was the first time they had seen her cry.

'He wore a mask . . . He wore it all the time . . .' she managed to whimper.

Baín reached for a tissue, dried her eyes and looked at her, his face kind and compassionate once more.

'I'm sorry, Ana, but we have to do these things.'

She lay back on the bed. She wanted the police to leave; she wanted to curl up under the sheets and go to sleep. To forget, until all of this was over. To be dust, shade, nothingness.

Gaizka came back from the cafeteria with some snacks wrapped in cling film, and two drinks cans. Álvaro was staring at the far end of the corridor where Raquel and Ismael were talking. She did not look Ismael in the eye; she kept her arms wrapped around herself, as though defending her space, as though reluctant to reveal the closeness between them – a closeness that was obvious to Álvaro.

'Dinner!' Gaizka announced, and Álvaro abruptly turned towards him, trying to hide his mistrust with a poker face. 'If you like, I'll go get coffee later. The stuff from the machine doesn't keep you awake, it just fucks up your stomach.'

'You don't have to hang around,' Álvaro said. 'Go home. I'll call you tomorrow and you can drive me to the station.'

'Don't sweat it; I'm used to going without sleep,' Gaizka joked. 'One more night isn't going to kill me . . .'

'Seriously, there's nothing for you to do here,' Álvaro insisted.

'Eat your dinner,' Gaizka said. 'We'll worry about the rest of it later.'

It was ten p.m. In a couple of hours, Gaizka could be back at home in Posets. He would collapse on the sofa, he thought, roll a spliff and let dope and exhaustion lull him to sleep. It had been a long couple of days.

When he had first seen the plume of smoke rising from the ravine, he had been tempted to turn his car around and get the hell out of there. His legs had felt as heavy as though lead were coursing through his veins. He could feel the first jolts in the back of his neck, the warning signs of an impending migraine. He knew that if he called the Guardia Civil in Monteperdido, they would only pass on the information, since they did not have a helicopter, so he had called the Mountain Rescue Team in Barbastro. He described what he had seen — a wrecked car at the bottom of a ravine — and gave them his precise location. Then he had searched the glove compartment of his car for some ibuprofen to ease the pounding in his brain, the stabbing pains that were part of the comedown from the drugs. There was no ibuprofen, and he had had to wait until he was at the police station making a statement to ask an officer for some painkillers. He remembered that his first thought then was the same as it was now: go home, smoke a couple of joints and fall asleep. They identified Ana, and asked him not to leave; they might need him to make a further statement. He had gone to the toilet and called Álvaro. *You need to get here, now,* he had said. *It's your daughter. They've found her. She's alive.* After that, he had sat and dozed on an uncomfortable bench, ignoring the clamour of police officers, telephones and slamming doors. By the time they let him leave, after he had repeated his statement to the S.A.F. officers, it was late evening. He had not thought about Álvaro's reaction until late that night, when he was at the hospital. Only then did Gaizka remember the silence that had greeted his words: *They've found her. She's alive.* Since he could not see Álvaro's face, and could hear no sound on the other end of the line, Gaizka had said, *Are you still there?* Álvaro had hesitated a few seconds longer before saying, *Where is she?* Gaizka told him, and said, *Congratulations,* but Álvaro had already hung up.

'Maybe I will go home for a bit, if only to take a shower,' Gaizka said.

Álvaro swigged from the can. 'Get some sleep. I'll be fine.'

'Do you want me to bring you anything from the shop?'

'Tomorrow. They have to run some more tests before they discharge her . . . Another M.R.I. scan . . . I'll go up with her.'

'I'll call and come down to collect you.'

Álvaro slapped Gaizka's leg and muttered, 'Thanks.' Then he bit hungrily into the sandwich.

Gaizka had expected to come face to face with a changed man. After the years of pressure, after all the things that had been said about Álvaro, the tension would finally be relieved. He had always believed that this tension was the reason Álvaro could never relax, why he was constantly wary and alert. Even when they got drunk together, Álvaro never lost control. But when Gaizka had seen Álvaro in the corridor and hugged him, he had still been the same block of ice.

The pine forest where the girls had disappeared was across the road from the school, opposite the police station. Looking at the tall pine trees, Sara was reminded of a platoon of soldiers, standing to attention, ready for inspection. Only a faint glow of moonlight pierced the treetops.

Sara needed to be alone. This was not the first time that she had felt so lost. Work was how she managed to stave off the feelings of helplessness, of emptiness. The lives of missing persons and their families were part of her life too. If she didn't have that, what was left?

She was a vampire, feeding on the lives of others. Although their blood was bitter, it was sweeter than her own.

She knew that this was precisely what Baín felt needed to change. He wanted her to stop becoming emotionally involved in investigations and take a long, hard look at herself, to heal her open wounds, learn to control the fears that made her so vulnerable.

She thought about home. About the apartment in Almería where she had lived as a child. The bedroom plastered with posters. The bed where she curled up and tried to sleep, more miserable that afraid, searching for an explanation for the way her parents behaved, wondering how she could be better, why they looked at her the way they did, what she needed to change to be the daughter they longed for. She thought of the long afternoons when her mind would spin out of control, spewing millions of ideas, millions of different versions of herself: a girl who would not make mistakes. But none of the versions she tried out was ever the Sara that her parents wanted. And just when she thought she had found the right version, she lost them forever. She became like Gretel, abandoned in the middle of a forest.

'Sara Campos?' The sound of her name brought her back to reality. 'Taking a stroll or looking for evidence?'

Caridad came towards her, crossing the dirt track that wound between the trees, with that stiff gait that made it look as though her limbs had no joints. She was wearing the same pink and grey tracksuit she had been wearing when they first met in the hotel lobby.

'Looking for evidence, obviously.' Caridad answered her own question. 'This is where Ana and Lucía disappeared. One of the girls' schoolbags was found lying just over there.' She pointed to a tree; at the base of its trunk was a gnarled, warty clump of mushrooms. 'Marcial wanted to transplant it. Does that sound normal to you? I don't know how much they were planning to spend, uprooting that tree and replanting it in front of the church. Like it was a memorial to the girls . . . The Foundation even collected money,' Caridad went on, sitting at the base of the tree, 'but apparently the roots are diseased – some rare fungus or something, I don't know. I don't know shit about trees . . . But, anyway, if they tried to move it, the tree would die.'

'So what did they spend the money on?' Sara asked with a smile.

'New football strips for the local team.' Caridad gave a loud cackle. 'You see, there's more to life than tears and tragedy. There's football.'

Sara leaned against the tree opposite Caridad, who was still carrying her bottle of red liquid. Caridad opened the bottle, took a long swig and set it down at her feet. Then she fumbled for her pouch of tobacco.

'There must be something else people in the village are interested in, other than football,' Sara said.

'Shooting guns in the mountains,' Caridad muttered. 'By the way, have you had any news about the *kan*?'

'I know it's alive.'

'But he's going to be lame, isn't he?'

'It sounds like you know more about it than I do.'

'There's not much to do in Monteperdido except gossip. I ran into Nicolás, the vet, in the shop; he told me. You should talk to him sometime; apparently he writes books about cops.'

'What's his surname? Maybe I'll buy one.'

Caridad let out one of the thunderous laughs that shook her whole body. Nicolás had never managed to publish any of his books – and, besides, he wrote in *patués*.

'The man's boring enough, without reading his stories,' she mocked. 'Forget what I just said; give him a wide berth.'

'Maybe you should make a list of the villagers I should talk to and those I should avoid.' Sara laughed.

'A list?' Caridad fell silent for a moment and stared pensively into the trees, as though she thought this might be a good idea. 'Joaquín's family, now, you know them? Have you talked to Lucía's grandparents?'

'Not yet.'

'Joaquín's mother, Aína, is one of those grannies who thinks it's indecent to take off your socks and show people your feet. And his father . . . Arrogant twit. They breed cattle, and they've got lots of land. They own half the valley, by my reckoning, but they're tight-fisted bastards. Wouldn't give their son a cent. People say they never forgave him for not taking over the family business. Cattle rearing – *bakada*, we call it in *patués*.'

'Joaquín has a haulage company,' Sara said, remembering the case file.

'Transportes Castán: four battered old trucks that are falling apart. Started out well enough. But ever since this thing with his daughter, he hasn't been near the business. And just look at it now.'

'It hasn't gone bankrupt, as far as I know.'

'Rafael – Montserrat's brother – he took it over. The poor schmuck is a truck driver; he doesn't know shit about running a business. Breaks out in a rash just thinking about the fact that the whole family now depends on him.'

Caridad took a long drag on her cigarette. Sara thought about going back to the police station.

'What have you found?' Caridad asked; then, noticing that Sara had not heard the question, added, 'In the *piná*, what evidence have you found?'

'Nothing. It's been too long for any forensic evidence to survive.'

'So what are you doing here?'

'I could ask you the same question.'

'Stretching my legs. I walk for an hour every day before I head home. Try to tire myself out so maybe I'll get some sleep.'

'Does it work?'

'You want the truth? Nope. I just end up with insomnia *and* stiff joints.'

Sara walked a few paces away. She could see the dirt path by which she had come, and, some distance away, the main road.

'Sara Campos,' Caridad said. 'You're happy to talk about other people, but what about you? I know nothing about you – except that you've got an itchy trigger finger.' Still sitting at the base of the tree, she pointed a gnarled finger at Sara and winked, as though she had discovered her secret.

'Oh, I'm not very important,' Sara said, feeling as though this little woman was mocking her. It was as difficult to guess her intentions now as it had been that first night. She said goodbye to Caridad and set off down the path towards the main road. Before disappearing into the trees, she glanced back, but the woman was gone. All that remained was the sickly tree, the trunk ringed with rare fungus.

Sara was aware that Baín would not approve of her decision, but she had resolved that, from now on, she was done with pretending. If there was a price to pay for doing her job, she was happy to pay it.

'Right now, all that we can say for certain is that Lucía was still with Ana up until Ana escaped. And she was fine.'

Santiago Baín had decided to visit Joaquín Castán before heading back to the hotel. Lucía's father had been on the phone to the police station all day, and he had been calling Víctor Gamero, demanding information. Sitting on the sofa, they listened attentively to Baín's story. It bothered Baín to have to do this. Though he tried to avoid it, he knew he was opening doors of hope that might slam shut tomorrow. He could see that hope in the eyes of Montserrat; Joaquín, on the other hand, tried to assume a professional, almost official coldness. As though Lucía were not his daughter.

'Have you any idea what it's like, this place where they were kept?' he asked.

'Ana's description is very vague . . . It's not far from here. In the mountains. We don't know anything more—'

'These mountains have been searched a million times. By the Guardia Civil, the M.R.T . . . Fingertip searches, helicopters . . .

The Cofradía have been through it with a fine-tooth comb. There's not a square centimetre that we haven't scoured ...' Joaquín protested.

There was a creak on the stairs and Baín turned to look. Quim had appeared in the middle of Joaquín's speech and was standing on the bottom stair, staring oddly at his parents.

'Did Simón Herrera see the kidnapper?' Joaquín asked, ignoring his son.

'No. He found Ana tied up. He didn't see Lucía. He probably didn't even know that she was there.'

When Santiago looked at the stairs again, Quim was gone. Montserrat muttered something unintelligible. Baín turned and asked her to repeat the question. But Montserrat hesitated. Joaquín put an arm around her and said what his wife could not bring herself to say: 'It's possible that, if this guy knows Ana has escaped, he might decide to hurt Lucía . . . He might already have hurt her . . .'

'We can't be certain of anything,' Baín admitted, 'but it is certainly a risk. We're trying to work as quickly as we can, and we're only too aware that time is against us.'

He got to his feet. He was tempted to say more: Joaquín's constant appeals for information, and his sudden appearance outside Simón Herrera's house, were an unnecessary obstruction. Dealing with him meant wasting vital minutes. Lost opportunities for finding his daughter. But, in the end, the inspector merely said his goodbyes and hugged them both. He asked how their son was taking the news. Joaquín said, 'Fine,' but his voice was flat, as though he was papering over the cracks. Baín surmised that Joaquín had not spoken to his son. He could have no idea what was going on in the mind of the teenager who had holed himself up in his room.

'If you need anything, you know where to find us,' Baín said as he walked out.

It was the third time that Víctor and Sara had listened to the tape of Ana's most recent interview: she gave a bleak description of the *refugio*. Víctor forced himself to pay attention to the girl's words, trying to ignore Bain's questions – some of them aggressive, as though Ana was capable of anything. But he understood why Baín had acted that way. The chances of finding Lucía alive faded with every passing hour, assuming the man in the mask had not killed her already.

Sara had pinned a map of the valley to the office wall. 'The Secret Valley', as tourists called it. The outline of the village reminded her of a birch leaf, orientated towards the west, the point of the leaf at Fall Gorge, where the tunnel through Monte Albádes emerged into the valley, then fanning gradually eastward to the Hotel La Renclusa, where the village ended and a narrow trail wound up the slopes of Monte Albádes and on past La Kregüeña to the village of Posets, where it came to an end at La Maladeta National Park and the Hotel La Guardia, the highest inhabited point in the region.

The ravine where Ana and Simón had been found was further south, before the mountain pass, on the road to Barbastro. Sara marked the spot with a yellow drawing pin.

'Which mountain was Ana talking about on the tape?' she asked, without looking around.

'It could be any of them,' Víctor said wearily.

The road wound along the banks of the River Ésera, dotted here and there with tiny hamlets like Ordial and Val de Sacs; on the map, they looked like a trail of breadcrumbs, dropped so someone might find their way home. Off the main road, there were a multitude of paths and mountain trails, like a network of veins covering the mountain slopes. Not all appeared on the map – there was no sign of the Camino a Francia, the road that led to Ixeia, where work had begun on a tunnel that would connect Monteperdido to the other side of the Pyrenees and the French border. A tunnel that had never been completed, and was now simply a black hole in the mountainside.

Víctor rewound the interview to the beginning.

'It's a ruin. One side of the roof has fallen in. And part of one of the walls too.'

As he listened, his thoughts drifted from the case to Nuria – the woman with whom he had planned a life – the way a wave brings to shore the flotsam from a shipwreck.

'How many huts like this are there in the mountains?' Sara's question brought his thoughts back to the room.

'I don't know . . . A lot.' He could not hide the irritation in his voice, not at Sara's question, but because he had allowed himself to be distracted from the case. 'Some are derelict, more or less ruins . . . The ones along the hiking trails that people don't use anymore . . .'

'Is there anyone in the village who knows these mountains better than you do?'

'I don't think so,' Víctor said, petulantly.

'Listen to me – I don't have time for wounded pride. If there's anyone who knows every last *refugio*, I want them brought here, now.'

Víctor got up, went over to the map and, as he spoke, began to illustrate what he was saying with a red marker, as though to underline his words:

'The trees Ana mentioned are called trembling aspens – around here, we call them *trémols*. They grow at altitudes above eighteen hundred metres. There are a lot of them in the national park, but they don't stray much further. If we take the ravine where the car crashed as our starting point, we can reach five separate forests of *trémols*. The leaves are exactly as she described: they look like little hearts . . . and, when they're rustled by the wind, it sounds like rain. As for the mountain, it seems obvious that it must be to the north-east, since the sun does not set behind it, but it still catches the glow of sunset. That's almost certainly what she meant when she talked about the snow twinkling . . . At the point where the car crashed, the range runs this way, and the highest peak is Ixeia, but that's not necessarily the mountain Ana saw. At the foot of the mountain, there are a number of valleys – that would explain why the *refugio* got flooded. But we're talking about five thousand hectares; access is very difficult, even where there are trails . . . It would take a week, maybe more, to search it . . .'

Víctor turned to Sara and tossed the marker on the desk, where it rolled and stopped next to a case file.

Sara stared at him. 'What are you waiting for?' she said. 'A round of applause? A lollipop?' Seeing the colour drain from Víctor's face, she tried and failed to stifle a giggle that turned into a nervous laugh, making her blink rapidly.

'I'm sorry,' she said. 'It's just . . . I'm exhausted. Everything you've said is brilliant – really. It's fucking amazing.' Still she could not stop giggling.

Víctor looked at her, bewildered, but her laugh was infectious and he struggled not to laugh himself. 'I'll take that as a compliment,' he said after a moment, turning away from Sara so that she would not see his smile.

'I'm serious. This is good information. We need to find some way to speed up the search . . . You just caught me off guard,' she said, all serious again.

'I think, in future, you should get more sleep,' Víctor said as he picked up his notes. 'You want me to pick you up at the hotel first thing tomorrow?'

'Please,' she said, trying to regain her composure.

Sara's cheeks were bright red and, as she stood up, it seemed to Víctor that she was more relaxed; her earlier stiffness had disappeared, as though she had been released from invisible chains and could finally move freely.

'See you in the morning,' he said.

Nieve was lying on his cushion. The dog looked as though he had barely moved since the last time Víctor had seen him. He sat down and scratched the dog's neck. On each of his brief visits during the day, he had been terrified that he would find Nieve cold and lifeless. But, though weak, Nieve was still fighting. Before taking a shower, Víctor cleaned the wound and changed the dressing. Nicolás Souto would be back to check on the dog tomorrow; the vet now had a spare set of keys so he could come and go as needed. Víctor was tired, and felt the urge to lie down next to Nieve and close his eyes; instead, he got up, went into the kitchen and tidied away the dressings and antiseptic. An image came to him: Simón Herrera's wife lying dead in a pool of blood. Lucía. He closed his eyes and tried to calm himself, to regain control. He was the senior sergeant of the local Guardia Civil. He could not let fear get the better of him.

★

Santiago Baín saw a crack of light under Sara's door. She was still awake. The girl at the reception desk had given him his key, but, before going to his own room, he decided to knock on Sara's door. She appeared in the doorway, still wearing the same jeans and grey T-shirt she'd been in all day. Behind her, the bed was strewn with papers.

'How did it go with Lucía's parents?' she asked, stepping aside and ushering him in.

'They're going to be tough to manage, especially the father,' Baín said, then he surveyed the bed and asked, 'Are you planning to sleep under the case files?'

'I just wanted to look over them one last time,' Sara said, a little awkwardly, and began to tidy them away.

'Go to bed. Get some sleep. You can't think clearly if you're not rested.'

With a sigh, Baín slumped into the armchair next to the little table. Aside from the bed, these were the only pieces of furniture in the room.

'*Refugios* don't normally have basements.' Sara gave up on sorting the documents and simply piled them into a mountain on the table. 'He prepared everything in advance. God knows how long it took him. Months, probably.' She sat down on the edge of the bed, facing Baín. 'Víctor has marked out a search area on a map. The best thing would be to stage a reconstruction with Ana, but I don't think she's in any fit state ... We need to talk to her again first thing tomorrow.'

'Have you had dinner?' Baín asked.

'No.'

'You hungry?'

Sara shrugged.

'Well, I'm hungry. All I've had was that limp service-station sandwich, and that feels like hours ago. You think they'll send something up, or is it too late?'

'We can always call reception and ask.'

'I bet they've already closed the kitchen.' Baín waved a hand, dismissing the idea, and wearily sat up in the armchair.

'I know what you're trying to do, Santiago,' Sara said appreciatively, 'but you don't need to protect me. Let me talk to the girl.'

'Are you telling me I don't know how to conduct an interview?' Santiago said ironically, sidestepping the subject.

'Play the fool all you like; I know you love me really,' Sara said. 'And you're afraid I'll get too emotionally involved. Trust me. I can handle it.' She did her best to sound convincing.

Santiago awkwardly got to his feet. How long had they known each other? Twenty years? More? He remembered the first time Sara had walked into the station. A gawky adolescent, skinny as a toothpick, feigning a self-confidence that was mostly sadness and fear. He remembered ushering her into his office and hearing her voice for the first time. *I'm Sara Campos. They're looking for me,* she had said to Baín. And how she had struggled to stop those green eyes shattering into a million pieces when he said, *No one is looking for you.*

Baín always remained aloof from the cases he worked on, but he could not distance himself from this lost little girl. Reluctantly, he'd found himself taking Sara under his wing. He'd found himself calling her a dozen times a day to ask how she was. To wish her a happy birthday. Advising her about what courses to study. Inviting her to live at his place.

He knew her weaknesses better that anyone. They were what had made her a great police officer.

'One day, I won't be around to pick up the pieces,' he warned.

'But that day is a long way off,' Sara said with a smile. She knew that, despite the warning, he had agreed to her request. 'Let's see if we can get them to make you *chiretas*. You'll love them.'

A nurse came with the breakfast, but at a signal from Sara, the officer standing guard stopped him entering and closed the door. Baín had shaved and his skin glowed, as though he had just slept for twelve hours straight. Sara, on the other hand, could not hide the fact that she had not had a wink of sleep.

They'd swapped roles. Now it was Baín who sat, listening, at the other end of the room, while Sara asked the questions. The doctors had told them that Ana had had a bad night. Her scar was bothering her and she had been woken several times by nightmares. She was still a little groggy. It was not easy to piece together, from her disjointed memories, the route that Simón Herrera had taken.

'We know you can't tell us exactly which way you went. But any details you can remember would be really useful. What could you feel? Were you going uphill or down?' Sara said cautiously, as though starting out on an unfamiliar case.

Ana tried to come up with the answers they wanted, but her memories from the point at which they left the hole to the moment when the car crashed were a confusion of noise and images. At once brief and endless.

'Don't worry about being logical, honey,' Sara said, sitting on the edge of the bed and taking Ana's hand. 'I just want to be in the car with you. If there are answers, it's up to me to find them.'

The assistant inspector's words made Ana feel more relaxed. She opened the windows of memory so that Sara could peer inside. She remembered lying on the back seat, one hand braced against the driver's seat so that the hairpin bends did not throw her on to the floor of the car.

In front, Simón Herrera was gripping the steering wheel hard.

The trees were a blurred streak outside the windows.

The fear of being free.

And then, suddenly, something was ramming the back of the car. The free fall into the ravine. The shattering glass and the panic that this might prevent her escape.

'Let's go back to before all this happened.' Sara tried to guide her. 'When you were in the mountain hut. When Simón appeared.'

Through the gap in the broken wall, she could see a patch of sky and mountain. The trembling aspens were doing their imitation of rain. Fibbers. The pain in her joints was no longer bothering her; she was used to being tied to the beam.

'Don't scream,' Simón's voice whispered in Ana's memory. 'Don't scream. I'm going to get you out of here.'

The routine of her captivity was suddenly shattered; she frantically looked around to see where this man could have come from, but he was already cutting the ropes binding her. When she tried to stand, her legs gave way, more from shock than weakness. He was dragging her out of the stone hut and Ana was hesitating between calling to Lucía or running like hell.

The trapdoor, in the middle of the floor, staring at her like an accusation. Simón pulling at her, the noise from down below like a roar from the belly of the building.

She let herself be led. The infinite landscape all around made her dizzy. Too much space, too much distance. She was terrified of losing her balance, of falling, but the man took her by the arm. 'Let's go,' he said.

The trees pressed in on her, there were sounds. They had to climb over a low wall and she slipped. She felt the cold hard shock of stone against her elbow, and then the hot rush of blood.

They kept running.

He went on ahead, glancing behind occasionally to make sure she was still following.

Once they had cleared the wall and run into the forest, the *refugio* disappeared. The sound of rustling leaves was deafening. This was not rain; it was a gigantic swarm of bees buzzing around her.

Simón opened the back door of the car. 'Get in,' he said. She was grateful to be in a cramped, enclosed space once more, a place where she could reach out and touch the boundaries, not the vast emptiness she had just traversed. He started the car, then turned and said something that she didn't hear.

Too much noise.

When he keyed the ignition, the radio had come on at full blast. She buried her face in the back seat. Someone was singing, a girl, but she could not make out the lyrics. After five years in the hole, the whispered conversations with Lucía, the endless, numbing routine: waiting for the trapdoor to open, the shadow of the man coming down the stairs, the black mask, the Tupperware boxes of food, the gifts for Lucía, the latrine where they had to relieve themselves, and their promises not to look when one of them had to go, the bottled water, the books and the dolls, the nights when the man dragged her upstairs and tied her to the beam, the stars in the pitch-black sky, while he stayed in the cellar with Lucía. Five years, the same thing, over and over, and now, suddenly, an explosion of unfamiliar stimuli: the speeding car, the blaring music. The open space that felt almost painful.

'You were very brave to leave the hole,' Sara said. As Ana had remembered, she'd gripped Sara's hand more tightly. For her, the most difficult thing had been braving the outside world, breaking the barrier. Sara looked at Ana's fingernails, which were bitten to the quick. 'Now I want you to think about a different moment. Later on. After the car fell into the ravine.'

She opened her eyes and saw a thin trickle of blood dripping from Simón's head. She put her hand out to support herself, and felt slivers of glass dig into her palm. Her hair had fallen over her face.

'Was the radio still playing?' Sara asked.

There was a whine inside her head. A shrill whistling sound that drowned out the music on the radio. The same girl, singing in a language she did not understand, then the voice of an announcer, chirpy and casual; it grated on her nerves.

'Thank you, Ana,' Sara said.

'I'm sorry, but . . . I can't remember anything else,' Ana said apologetically.

'I think we have enough information for the moment,' Sara reassured her, then got up from the bed. Santiago looked at her worriedly and Sara forced a smile, not wanting him to see that Ana's agoraphobia weighed on her so much it physically hurt. She had got what she was looking for. That was all that mattered.

A crane lifted the car out of the ravine. The workers below stood aside as the steel cable attached to the tow bar began to raise the vehicle. Not far from where the men were working on the car,

Víctor Gamero was organizing a search. He divided his officers into groups that were to focus on the areas where there were aspen groves. Sara pulled up in a jeep driven by a Guardia Civil officer and beckoned Víctor over. Getting out, she spread a map of the mountains across the bonnet.

'When Ana got into the car, there was a song playing on the radio,' Sara explained when Víctor was in earshot. 'When the car plunged into the ravine, the same song was playing for at least a few seconds. We can't be sure whether she heard it from the beginning, but, if we say that, on average, a song lasts three minutes, we can calculate that she would have been in the car for two and a half minutes, maybe a little more. On roads like this, a car driving at sixty kilometres an hour would feel like it was going very fast. Based on these figures, we're looking at a distance of two and a half to three kilometres . . . Are there any aspen trees within that radius?'

Víctor jabbed at a small green patch on the map.

The road snaked its way up the mountain along a narrow gorge that grew deeper as they ascended. From time to time, the wheels of the jeep sank into potholes; Sara clung to the door handle. Víctor drove confidently. Two Guardia Civil cars followed behind. Sara called Baín to let him know. He had just left the hospital. He had stayed with Ana, trying to unearth other memories before the doctors performed further tests.

Arriving at the area marked on the map, Víctor got out and scanned the area furiously. The last bend had swerved away from the gorge and into a wooded area, where the trees quivered in the wind, making a sound like rain. Sara stared at them and thought they seemed more alive than any tree she had ever seen. As though they were aware of the sound made by their leaves.

'Now what?' Víctor spread his arms wide, as though to take in everything around them.

The track continued into the woods and forked a few metres ahead. The mountain hut had to be nearby. Víctor tried to keep calm, but from the moment he had climbed behind the steering wheel, he had been unable to shake off the image of Lucía, trapped in that hole. She was waiting for them. He stubbornly believed that she was still alive.

He saw Sara wandering around, looking for a path through the trees that might tell them which way to go. The other cars pulled up behind them. Pujante got out and headed towards Víctor.

'Which way?' he said.

Víctor brusquely motioned for him to shut up. He looked around for Sara, waiting for her to say something. She had disappeared into a clump of aspens, only to reappear muttering, 'Shit,' as she stared at her mobile phone.

'No signal.' She glanced at Víctor. 'Have you got any?'

Víctor fished out his mobile phone. In the mountains, most people used satellite phones. None of the networks had coverage this high up.

Sara grabbed the phone from him. 'I need the number of the duty doctor in Ordial . . . Do you know it?'

After a short conversation, during which she had to repeat herself and shout a lot due to the bad connection, Sara handed the phone back to Víctor. She peered into the trees, at the base of their trunks: there were no flowers.

'What is "bear's ear"?'

'It's a plant,' Víctor said, puzzled.

'I know that! I mean, what does it look like? Where does it grow?'

Víctor waved for her to follow him, and Sara explained as they walked into the grove of aspens.

'Simón's doctor says he might have been allergic to this plant . . . and probably others, too, but this is the one most commonly found in the valley . . . You remember his feet were covered with eczema? It was as though he had recently been in contact with it. It's possible he was walking around a place where it grew—'

'It grows on bare rock,' Víctor said, striding ahead. The other officers followed, a few metres behind.

Emerging from the grove of trees, they found themselves facing a rock wall. Small purple flowers grew between the cracks. Thick fleshy stalks, covered with downy hair.

'That's what you're looking for,' Víctor said.

Sara began to climb the rock wall. She remembered Ana saying that she had slipped and hurt her elbow just before she came to the thicket of *trémols*. Sara had to feel for handholds. Her left foot slipped, a shower of rocks tumbled away, and she gripped the thick stem of one of the plants, which held out just long enough for her to recover her balance.

The wall was not very high and, reaching the top, Sara could see a little valley at the foot of the mountains. There, in a hollow, stood the *refugio*. Four stone walls, barely able to hold up a crumbling roof.

As soon as Víctor reached the top of the wall, he sent his officers to form a semicircle around the stone hut. There was not a sound, other than the steady pitter-patter of rain from the aspen trees. Sara drew her gun, but, as she approached the building, she lowered her arm and let it swing by her side, marking time, like a pendulum.

'We're too fucking late,' she swore.

Behind her, Víctor relaxed and stood up from his crouching position. The north-east wall of the stone hut had partly collapsed, the stones long since ground into gravel. Inside, the floor was blackened and strewn with a few charred pieces of wood. Sara stopped by the entrance, looked down at the ground: the fire had been stamped out before it reached the dry grass, so that only a few stray blades had been singed. Inside, it was a different story. The floor of the hut had partially collapsed and the 'hole' where Lucía and Ana had been imprisoned looked like a blackened cauldron.

'He's burned everything,' Sara said as Víctor came and stood next to her. The beams that had propped up the roof of the basement, broken and splintered when the floor collapsed, rose up like stakes between the mass of stone, soil and charred timber. The twisted metal of what might once have been a bed was buried beneath the rubble.

'Please, God, don't let Lucía be in there,' Víctor whispered as he stepped inside. 'Don't come in.' He held out a warning hand to Sara. 'We need to secure the building. The rest of the floor might collapse . . .'

The leaves of the *trémols* went on rustling, tireless, insistent, fluttering in the breeze, mimicking the sound of rain in an open field.

'I don't know how the noise didn't drive her insane,' Santiago Baín said, staring at the trees.

'There's no sign of Lucía,' Sara informed him.

'When did he burn the place?'

'We will have to wait for forensics, but my guess is he did it in the last twenty-four hours.'

'While we were still focused on Simón,' Baín muttered. He looked back at the mountain hut. Buttresses had been brought to prop up the soil so they could go down into the basement. A forensics team were photographing the scene. What could they possibly find in this pile of charred rubble? There would be no fingerprints, no fibres . . . It had all been burned away, Baín thought. 'What do you think he's done with her?'

Sara looked down at the men working in the 'the hole'.

'She's alive,' Sara said confidently. 'If he'd wanted to kill her, he would have let her burn with everything here.'

Baín wanted to believe her. He turned away from the stone hut and wandered into the little valley. 'The man who held them captive always wore a black helmet with a plastic visor. The visor must have been polarized, because they couldn't see his face through it.'

'Like a motorcycle helmet?'

'Something like that . . .' Baín scanned the range of mountains. To the east was the snow-capped peak of Ixeia, where Ana had seen the reflection of the sunset. Despite the wind, it was not cold. The place felt sheltered, hidden. By contrast, the sweeping, soaring landscape made you feel vulnerable.

All this time, they had been so close . . .

Álvaro Montrell slumped, fully clothed, on to his bed. He stared at the ceiling, at the crack that sometimes reminded him of the jagged mountain peaks. The tests had gone well. One more day and Ana would be allowed to come home. What was his role to be? Why did he have to accept the conditions laid down by his wife, as if their daughter were her personal property and every time he was allowed near her was a gesture of goodwill? Ana belonged to him, too. It was not possession that he felt, but belonging.

He was being unfair, he thought. He was pushing things too fast. He had to try to put himself in Raquel's position. While he had always known where she was, Raquel had come to think of Álvaro as a distant memory, and perhaps she'd thought he was guilty. It was almost four years since he had walked away. There are reasons; there are always reasons and guilty parties. It's something we all need, he thought, even if our version of events bears no relation to anyone else's.

When he had first seen her again, standing, petrified, in the hospital corridor, Raquel had seemed more beautiful than she had the day he left. She had the cold beauty of a wounded woman, like the glacial mountains that ringed their world: Infiernos and Tempestades, twin cirques at the peak of Monte Ármos, carved by glacial erosion into a vast amphitheatre, the soaring walls of which looked down on the valley. The heat of summer and the thaw revealed gaping wounds on the mountain slopes, cruel scars they bore, not with shame, but pride. Just as Raquel, with her dark eyes and her mane of dark hair, looked down on others, making no attempt to hide the scars inflicted by the past five years.

He opened the wardrobe, dressed in some clean clothes and went out of the room. His burrow, Gaizka called it. Up here, in the village of Posets, Álvaro had hidden away like a frightened animal, in the storeroom of Gaizka's tour company. It was little more than a barn, on the outskirts of the village, where Gaizka kept the equipment he used for mountain tours: sledges, abseiling lines, canoes, paintballing gear. In return for this makeshift accommodation,

Álvaro took charge of keeping the tackle in order, preparing it for the guides who took tourists into the gorges and the tarns.

It was ridiculous, this idea that he needed to give Raquel time. Hadn't they wasted enough time already? He did not want to wait. He was not prepared to be separated from Ana, he thought as he walked through the storeroom.

There were no witnesses to Álvaro's decision. Only a row of paintballing helmets along the wall. Hanging from metal hooks, the black helmets looked down at him in silence, like the heads of sacrificed animals.

3

The Dance of Men

'We'd had a fight . . .' Ana began.

The hospital manager had offered a room where the police could interview her. She had been discharged and Raquel was insisting on taking her home. The police could not stop her, though they would keep Ana under observation during these first days. Even her parents were not allowed to be alone with her.

'Was this in the pine forest?' Sara asked, and Ana shook her head.

She cast her mind back to a past that she had long since buried; now, guided by Sara, she began to unearth old memories, as though scrabbling to dig up old bones. Ximena Souto – the daughter of Nicolás, the vet – what had become of her? 'The Colombian', they'd called her. The third girl.

'Just do your best,' Sara said.

The story of my life, Ana thought, and decided to try.

Ximena was the same age as Lucía and Ana, but the bond between the two girls was a barrier to her. Although 'la colombiana' lived nearby, opposite the semi-detached houses of the other two, and although she clamoured for their attention, their friendship, every day, she never quite succeeded in getting it. Her frustration meant that, when they were thrown together, it often ended in a fight.

They were heading home from school, their satchels slung over their shoulders, the chill October wind whipping their faces. Ximena was talking about Quim, Lucía's older brother. She had just seen him in the hallway at school; he had had his hair cut. 'Why did he have it cut? He looked so cute with long hair.'

'My mother made him,' Lucía said, and as Ximena continued to talk about Quim, the other two girls started to tease her. It was something Ana and Lucía often did, though it embarrassed Ximena.

'*La colombiana* is in love! Do you want my brother to kiss you?' Lucía taunted as the girl's cheeks flushed crimson. 'I can ask him for you, if you like.'

This was the point on the road where they usually went their separate ways. Ana and Ximena headed into the village, where they took piano lessons. Lucía would set off on her own, taking the path through the pine forest to the suburb where she lived.

I hate the piano, Ana had been thinking, just as Ximena, angry at being mocked, pushed Lucía hard. She fell to the ground. Ana did not get a chance to help her to her feet. While still on the ground, Lucía picked up a stone and hurled it at Ximena. All Ana could see was Ximena screaming, her hands covering her face. Was she bleeding?

Ximena ran back towards the school. 'You'll pay for this!' she shrieked.

Lucía scrambled to her feet and fled, probably afraid of being told off by a teacher. Torn between the two of them, Ana did not know what to do. In the end, she decided to run after Lucía.

'Lucía!' she called, but Ana's cry was lost among the silent trees.

How long had she searched for her friend? In her memory, time seemed to expand and contract. A few heavy raindrops began to fall. She was afraid of getting lost in the woods if she left the path; she caught the damp metallic smell of an approaching thunderstorm. 'Lucía!' Ana called again, but there came no reply. In the October afternoon, there was little light among the trees.

Mamá is going to be furious if I'm late for my piano lesson, Ana was thinking when she saw a grey four-wheel drive – or was it brown? The tyres and the bodywork were spattered with mud, that she remembered clearly.

What on earth are you doing, Lucía? She did not say the words, she simply thought them as she saw her friend sitting in the passenger seat, her face pressed against the window, her eyes closed. Is she asleep? Ana wondered.

As Ana approached the car, she suddenly felt a hand over her mouth, a sharp prick in the side of her neck; there was a bitter taste in the back of her throat. The effect was instantaneous. Everything around her became blurred. The dirt and the leaves seemed to part and a bottomless black hole opened up. She felt herself falling.

'When I opened my eyes again, I was in the hole,' Ana said.

She breathed slowly, taking several seconds to fill her lungs, as though slowing her breathing might stop time. Sara could feel her fear, but she would go with her.

'There was no light,' Ana said. 'At first, I thought I was dead . . .' And she continued with her story.

In the darkness, Ana managed to make out a figure lying on a mattress. Lucía. She crawled over and put her arms around her friend, and, feeling her breathe, Ana felt calmer. Lucía was sobbing.

It was cold. Bitterly cold. The walls and the floor were damp. Is it a cave? she wondered. How did we get here? Something strange was still coursing through her body, like a tiny snake slithering through her veins. She felt as though she might throw up, but managed not to. She was beginning to feel claustrophobic. The walls looked as though they might fall in at any moment. Lucía went on sobbing in silence.

A rectangle of light appeared in the ceiling and something fell down – a ladder? Someone was coming down, blocking the light from the trapdoor. Ana looked around for a way out, but all she could do was curl up, shivering, in a corner. Leaning against the walls made her clothes damp, and she felt a shudder run down her spine. She could not see a face, only a silhouette that was coming towards her, growing larger. Huge. Why me? she thought. He forced her to stand up and put something over her head. A burlap sack.

The world went dark again.

He carried her out of the basement. She was disorientated and could see nothing inside the sack, which swelled and deflated with every breath. She was gasping now. Panicked. She felt as if she was suffocating, as though the air in her lungs was thinner, warmer, stale.

As he set her down, she felt a brush of metal then heard a dull thud. Every sound was suddenly muffled. She could feel an engine thrum. The space was too cramped to stretch her arms or her legs.

She could not remember how long it was before the engine stopped. This time, after a metallic click, she could taste cold fresh air coming through the burlap sack over her head. The man forced her to get out and stand up. She could not keep her balance; her legs refused to obey her. She collapsed on the ground and fell, mud between her fingers. He dragged her to her feet.

The man ripped off the sack. Ana opened her mouth, like someone pulled from a deep lake, gasping for air. It took her eyes a moment to adjust to the darkness. He was standing in front of her. He was wearing a black helmet and carrying a hunting rifle. She thought about making a run for it, but her legs were still trembling; she fell to her knees. The man cocked the rifle and pressed the mouth of the barrel against Ana's forehead.

What is the threshold of an eleven-year-old girl? How much pain, how much panic can she endure? Sara saw the world through Ana's eyes so she could feel her terror, try to find some clue as to the identity of the man who had dragged her to this hell. Would Sara be able to endure this? The innocence of childhood was the best shield; she knew this from bitter personal experience. As they grow into adults, people inevitably learn to anticipate what will come next. Blows. Rape. Death. But a child's imagination is rooted in the present.

'He stood like that for a long time, with the rifle against my head. I squeezed my eyes so tight it hurt,' Ana said. 'I peed myself, and I felt really ashamed.' She looked at the officers. 'I told him I was sorry, that I couldn't help it.'

'Did he say anything?' Sara asked.

'"One day, I'll kill you." That's what he said. "When you're least expecting it, I'll kill you." Then he lowered the rifle and put the sack over my head again.'

It was then that Sara felt Ana distance herself from her memories.

'Trust me,' Sara said, feeling her pull away. 'All we want is to find the man who hurt you.'

Ana had not stopped talking, but now it was as though she was giving a swift tour of a gallery, not stopping at any of the paintings. Before Sara could ask her for details, she had moved on to the next room.

Her description of the man who held them captive was inconsistent. There were no salient characteristics that they could use to start a search. The helmet covered his whole head. She could not tell what his hair was like, or even the colour of his skin, or whether he had a beard. Sometimes, Ana remembered him as being very tall; at other times, he was about her height. Sometimes he was stocky, sometimes overweight. The man was a shifting creature; Ana had transformed him into an imaginary beast that could take on different forms, but was always the same. A fantastical figure, so she could convince herself that what she experienced was not real. The only solid evidence they had was the helmet Ana had described, no trace of which had been found among the charred remains of the mountain hut.

'After the thing with the rifle, he didn't come back to the hole for a few days. Nothing much happened. He put the sack over my head again and took me upstairs, but this time he didn't take me anywhere. He tied me to a beam and left me there for so long I fell asleep. When he untied me and brought me back down to the basement, Lucía told me he had been with her all the time.'

'Did she tell you what he did to her?'

'I wouldn't have understood,' Ana said sadly. 'We were too young. Lucía looked older, but there were only a couple of months between us.'

'Why are you using the past tense?' Sara said, startled. 'What changed?'

'Now she's the one who seems younger than me,' Ana whispered.

As though the five years had simply been a few days, Ana talked only about this routine: every so often, the man would come down into the basement, take Ana upstairs and stay alone with Lucía. Sometimes, there were long periods when he did not come. Or when he only opened the trapdoor to give them Tupperware containers of food. Ana's explanation was that he had had an argument with Lucía, that he was sulking and this was his way of showing it.

It smelled terrible down in the hole. Especially at first. After a while, they became accustomed to the dank, musty smell, since the only ventilation was the trapdoor. The walls were cold stone, the floor of rough, untreated timber. There was a mattress, on which Ana and Lucía slept with their arms around each other, and, later, a bed frame. Days without sunlight felt never-ending but hazy, and seemed to run together.

Sara focused on the detail. The half-naked doll lying on the floor; Lucía sitting on the bed, hugging her knees, staring into a corner and dreaming aloud about having a television. *We could put it over there. We could watch cartoons.* Ana, standing a few feet from her friend, holding a tattered old book from which – out of sheer boredom – she had learned some poems by heart.

Before your gilded age shall fade
not to silver or to withered violet
but to Earth. To Smoke. To Dust. To Shade. To Nothingness.

And, afterwards, she danced with no music, to the rhythm of a tune playing in her head.

'Who is he?' Ana had asked Lucía.

'It's better if you don't know,' Lucía said, and quickly jumped down from the bed and knelt beside the doll; she had drawn a huge smile on her using red marker. 'Señorita, you are very late for your appointment,' Lucía said in a silly voice, pretending to be the doll.

'What does he do to you?' Ana had asked, and since her friend said nothing, only concentrating on the doll, she went back to her dancing.

'Did he have sexual relations with you?' Sara asked.

Ana shook her head and then looked at Baín, who was still sitting at the far side of the room. It was a pointed stare, as though she had noticed that he doubted her words.

Sara stroked Ana's hand, the bitten skin around the fingernails almost red raw. She felt disappointed. She had expected more from this interview.

'You must be tired,' Baín said, getting to his feet and smiling broadly to allay her suspicions. 'That's enough for now. Would you like to go home?'

'Of course,' Ana said with a forced smile.

Baín opened the door of the room. Outside stood the Guardia Civil who was to go with Ana and her mother. As soon as they were alone, Baín went over to the window and stared out at the barren ground that surrounded the hospital.

'She's lying to us,' he said.

'I don't think it's that . . .' Sara said thoughtfully. 'I think she is trying to keep us out . . . I'm not sure whether she is scared or whether she can't bring herself to remember.'

Baín felt guilty for having allowed Sara to lead the investigation. The empathy that made her a good officer was precisely what fed her insecurities.

'I'll drive Ana home. You go back to the station and arrange to have the witness statements collected.'

The story had made the lead in every media outlet. It was impossible to avoid the scrum of reporters in Monteperdido, the expert criminologists offering opinions on television. Quim could picture them drinking coffee in their ultra-modern kitchens, booking a luxury holiday online. A weekend in Bali, that was what Ana's reappearance meant to them. All they needed was a couple of minutes on every chat show, talking about offender profiles, post-traumatic stress and all that shit. Then the story would lose steam, and the TV stations would stop calling. But by then the criminologists would be getting drunk in Bali.

Quim had woken up late, and then only because his father had turned up the volume on the news bulletin. He drank a glass of milk and sat playing games on his computer with his headphones on. The explosions and gunfire from the game echoed inside his head. He did not want to know anything, but from time to time he could not help but think about the journalists, about the questions the villagers would start asking him again. Is there any news about your sister? Do you think she's still alive? He decided not to answer, to give them a wide berth rather than tell them all to fuck off. He kept firing; he was no longer really aiming at anything, just emptying the clip. He always played online, and his nickname was 'Disappeared2009'. He knew that if his father found out he used that name, he would not find it funny, but Quim did.

Now they want to talk to me, Joaquín Castán thought, looking through the list of unanswered calls on his phone. Everybody wants to talk to me now. Barely three days earlier, no one would return his calls. No one wanted to come to the ceremony in memory of the girls. There was no point being proud. What good would it do? He knew that the media were necessary to keep hope alive. On his phone, there was a text message from Virginia Bescos. The reporter was staying in a hotel near Val de Sacs and wanted to meet up with him. After almost two years, she wanted to see him again.

Ana had stared out of the car window all the way home.

Barely a word was spoken. Raquel sat next to Ana and gently held her left hand. She could see Ana's reflection in the glass. She still found it difficult to recognize this new face as her daughter. Ana had changed, and the flicker of disappointment she felt that her daughter was no longer the little girl she had lost made Raquel feel guilty and selfish.

'Are you OK? Nervous?' Baín asked from behind the steering wheel. 'Would you like me to drive slower?'

Ana tried to remember driving with her parents to Barbastro to buy clothes, or simply, as her father put it, to have a break from Monteperdido. *We're like three soldiers on furlough,* Álvaro would joke. But the woods did not look the same as they had then. The bends in the road were not as sharp. She wished she could recognize something: a tree, a mountain peak framed against the blue sky, the softness of her mother's hands. Something that would make her feel that she was coming home.

'How much longer?' Ana asked.

'It's not far. Twenty minutes and we'll be home,' Raquel reassured her.

'What about Papá?'

*

138

The mobile phone had woken him. Gaizka took a quick shower and got into his car. The radio instantly came on, the volume so loud it aggravated his hangover. He switched it off and drove to the meeting point. The tour group and the guide were already waiting for him. He had tried phoning Álvaro, but his phone was switched off and he did not want to insist. Gaizka knew that he could not count on him right now. The sun slanting between the peaks and the glittering summit of La Kregüeña straight ahead forced him to squint. He had barely had two hours' sleep. He could still taste gin in the back of his throat. He lit a cigarette and rolled down the car window. To the left of the road was the gorge known as Oscuros de Balced. This was where the tourists would be heading. He glanced at his reflection in the rear-view mirror: his skin was pale and yellowish, as were his eyes; his damp, dark hair was a rat's nest of curls – he needed to get it cut someday. He needed a shave.

As soon as he arrived, he apologized.

'Didn't you tell Álvaro we had a tour today?' Noguera, the guide, asked.

Gaizka shot him an irritated look as he searched for the keys to the storeroom. Noguera knew nothing about Álvaro. He lived in Huesca for most of the year, and only came up to Monteperdido for the summer season, when it was possible to do abseiling tours in the canyons. He rented a room in a mountain lodge close to the office in Posets, and had no idea what went on in the village. As far as Noguera was concerned, Álvaro was just some junkie who lived here and looked after the equipment for Gaizka. The only conversation they ever had was small talk about the weather or the tours. Gaizka thought Noguera was a moron, but he had discovered, over the years, that this was a common trait in guides. It did not matter whether they were from the mountains or the valleys – all guides seemed to be born with the stupid gene.

'I called him, like, twenty times, but he didn't pick up,' Noguera complained. 'He must have his phone switched off.'

'And it took you twenty attempts to work that out?' Gaizka went inside and turned on the lights. The storeroom was behind a little counter. Noguera followed him into the back to get the equipment he needed for the tour.

'You're not the one who's had to listen to these bastards whingeing for the past half-hour.' Noguera jerked his chin towards the door, where the five tourists who had booked the tour were waiting.

'You don't think that, maybe, being the boss gives me the right *not* to have to deal with these jerks?'

'If they keep up this shit, I'll leave one of them at the bottom of the ravine,' Noguera muttered as he left.

Gaizka felt relieved to be rid of him. He went back into the storeroom, opened a wardrobe and wondered where Álvaro kept his painkillers; his headache was screaming for a sedative. Why did he never have one on him when he got a headache? The wardrobe was empty. At the back of the storeroom was a door that led to the room, three and a half metres by three and a half metres, where Álvaro had been living.

Gaizka had been in there on other occasions. In Álvaro's burrow. In that uncomfortable bed surrounded by bare walls. Álvaro never brought any personal items into the room. Everything was temporary, from Gaizka's offer to stay there for a few days, to his later offer of a job. Everything could come to an end at any moment. Gaizka had never imagined that the end would be Ana's return. To tell the truth, he had always assumed that one day Álvaro would grow tired of waiting in that cramped little room; he would realize that he was simply throwing his life away, and one morning Gaizka would arrive and he would be gone.

Gaizka sat on the bed and rolled a cigarette. Before sealing it, he took out a small phial and mixed a thin line of cocaine with the tobacco. Then he lit it and blew out smoke. He fell back on the bed and closed his eyes. Fuck sedatives, he thought.

He had always been an outsider in this valley. Just as Álvaro was, although the locals pretended that he was part of the community: he gave art history lessons at the school; Ana had practically been born here; Raquel had set up a business here; they had been invited to the dinners at the Cofradía de Santa María de Laude. They had even been awarded a fucking badge emblazoned with the Cofradía's coat of arms. But, after the girls' disappearance, Monteperdido needed a fall guy. It was at this point that Álvaro once again became an outsider: the stranger whom no one really knows.

'In this village, if they don't know your grandfather's name and how he took his coffee, it's like you're a stranger. They love people who come, spend a wad of cash in Monteperdido and leave again. But they have a problem dealing with the ones who come and stay,' Gaizka remembered saying to Álvaro one night over a bottle of gin.

'Because they haven't a fucking clue who your grandfather was.'

'Yeah, I mean, it's not like they can say, "There goes Gaizka, old Sebastián's grandson," or whatever.'

Álvaro had laughed, but refused to join in the game. He preferred not to talk about Monteperdido or the people who lived there. Sometimes, Gaizka thought, he seemed to feel some sort of guilt about the disappearance of his daughter, that the villagers' condemnation had been warranted.

'I think I'm going to fire Noguera,' he had told Álvaro another night.

'Doesn't matter. Whatever guide you hire to replace him will be just as stupid.'

'Why *do* they have to be so fucking dumb?' Gaizka had laughed. 'Why can't there be a single normal guide in the world? Maybe I should import a Sherpa from the Himalayas . . . If he can't speak Spanish, he won't be able to give us so much lip . . .'

'I think it's something about the profession . . . about being a "guide", you know. It's like, "I know where I'm going".' Álvaro mimicked Noguera's voice.

'I don't know about you, but I'm going to have another glass of gin.'

Gaizka left Álvaro's room, feeling the rush of the coke. In the space of two minutes, he had gone from crippling hangover to floating again. Straight ahead, the paintball helmets hung from the shelf. A long line of black masks. Some were spattered with red from the game. The translucent plastic visors stared down at him, as though waiting for an answer that only he could give.

'If you want to know something, ask a fucking guide,' he muttered.

Sara scanned the open-plan area of the police station. Burgos was sitting at one of the desks.

'He can take the first shift,' Víctor said.

Burgos was short and chubby. He had a bushy moustache that

completely hid his upper lip, and, when he talked, he looked like a ventriloquist's dummy.

'What experience has he got?'

'He was regional clay-pigeon shooting champion about ten years ago. I don't know if that's what you're looking for on a C.V.'

'Are you having a laugh?'

'I'm being honest. I thought you wanted us to collaborate?' Víctor smiled.

'I need him to guard a witness, not shoot pigeons,' Sara half-heartedly protested.

They were interrupted by whistling and clapping. Sara tilted her head and saw Pujante arriving in the squad room, carrying two trays of pastries.

'They're the cakes for Ana,' he explained, seeing that Sara did not understand what was going on. He set one of the trays down on the desk and gestured for everyone to gather round. 'My wife made a *candimus* for us,' he said proudly.

Víctor could guess what Sara was thinking, but before she could protest, he said, 'We've got something to celebrate. We've spent five years looking for those girls, and today Ana finally went home.'

Sara nodded for him to go and join them. 'Five minutes,' she said, 'then we need to head over to Ana's house.'

'You sure you won't join us?' Víctor said.

Sara shook her head. 'It's your celebration.'

She pretended to go back to the paperwork, but in fact she was focused on the officers eating cake and sipping plastic cups of wine, laughing and joking with each other. Víctor was part of that family.

How could she allay the suspicions of a group that was so united?

Everyone living in Monteperdido was somehow connected. They were godparents to each other's children, had sat next to each other at school, thrown parties together, and spent winters cut off, with no electricity – with no company other than the neighbours, the mountains and the animals that lived in them. The deer, the wild boar, the roebucks. Víctor had mention them. There were a few foxes in the woods on the slopes of Monte Ármos and of Ixeia. Simultaneously loved and hunted. Men, women and animals, their lives inescapably intertwined to become a single life: Monteperdido.

One of these men had donned a black helmet and abducted the two girls.

Sara was convinced that, unlike five years ago, they had reacted in time. They had cordoned off the access roads, carefully managed Ana's reappearance. They had arrived too late at the site where the girls had been held captive, but it was unlikely that the perpetrator had had time to get out of the cordoned area. This was why they urgently needed to get witness statements from all the neighbours. Cross-check alibis for the period during which Ana made her escape. The work was back-breaking, and could seem futile, but it was the very foundation of the investigation.

Víctor clearly did not feel comfortable questioning his neighbours. Nor did the other officers. Sara could tell that every interview would begin with an apology: *Sorry; these are the officers from the Family Protection Unit; if it were up to me, they wouldn't be questioning you.*

Sara was aimlessly doodling on the cover of a case file. Looking down and seeing the maze of geometric figures, she remembered something a psychologist had once said about her doodles. Santiago Baín had insisted she see someone when he found out about her night terrors. *It represents your need to shut yourself in,* the shrink had said. *It represents my need to protect myself,* Sara had thought of saying. But she had not.

Remembering the symbolism, she could not help but wonder why Ana had not told them everything that had happened.

When you're least expecting it, I'll kill you, the kidnapper had said.

She must not be left alone. The kidnapper could not know whether she had been able to give them a clue about his identity. Surely he would do something to try to stop her.

Sara tried to put herself in his position: terrified that the police were closing in, trying to get Lucía to a new hideout and all the while wandering around Monteperdido pretending to be normal.

What would his next move be?

Ximena Souto imagined the coast of Almería as a paradise within easy reach. She could picture herself under the blazing sun, skinny-dipping on one of the nudist beaches she had heard about from Montserrat's brother, Rafael Grau, feeling her skin grow taut as the salt water dried.

All she knew of Almería was this fantasy, and though she had never visited the beaches she dreamed of, she felt more at home there than she did in the valley encircled by mountains where she lived.

In Monteperdido, she was an extraterrestrial.

Her skin was a deep caramel brown and she had to struggle every day to straighten her frizzy hair, something she had inherited from her mother – like her lips, and her eyes. She could see herself in the few photographs she still had of her mother. The ones that Nicolás had taken before she left. No one ever used her mother's name, she was simply '*la colombiana*', and Ximena had inherited the nickname too.

In Monteperdido, she was the Colombian.

Quim was one of the few people who called her Ximena.

She got dressed in a miniskirt and a crop top that revealed her navel, and put on a pair of leather boots. In the living room, Nicolás was sleeping on the sofa in front of the television. Mouth open, glasses askew, he was drooling on a cushion.

Life really dealt me a shit hand, thought Ximena.

She walked through the housing estate as far as the pine forest, then took the path that led to the school. Downstream there were a few houses, but the village had really blossomed to the north, where Rafael had a modest house.

When Ana and Lucía were kidnapped, Ximena had experienced a mixture of conflicting feelings that it took her some time to digest. On the one hand, she could not help but feel a certain childish glee. The girls who had rejected her friendship had been punished. On the other hand, in her heart of hearts, she was disappointed that she had not been kidnapped too. This was the ultimate rejection.

She went into Rafael's house without bothering to knock. He and Quim were in the kitchen and it smelled of coffee and toast. The cleaning lady, Concepción, was hoovering in the living room. The windows were wide open; there was a cool breeze. Rafael asked her to close the kitchen door so they would not be bothered by the noise of the hoover.

Why hadn't her mother chosen him instead of Nicolás?

She knew the answer: Nicolás was an idiot. That much had been obvious to her every day of her life. Ridiculous, nervous – the village idiot. Who else would have taken on the child of a complete stranger? In a sense, her mother had been thinking about Ximena before she left.

Quim pulled up an extra stool and she sat down as Rafael put toast on the table.

Rafael was a man of few words, unlike Nicolás, who, once he got started – especially on the subject of his novels – was impossible to shut up. Did he never get tired of the sound of his own voice? Ximena often wondered, when she saw Nicolás boring someone else with his interminable stories.

He thought of himself as a writer. His current novel was entitled *El follét del albarósa*. In *patués*, like all the others. Ximena had always refused to learn a word of that stupid yokel language.

Rafael asked them to load the dishwasher when they finished breakfast. He had to go to work. Ximena would have liked him to stay a little longer, tell her about his travels. Some anecdote from the days when he had been a globetrotter, sitting behind the steering wheel of his truck. He had been to all the places she wanted to visit. He talked to them about Scandinavia, about Asia. For a while, he had lived in Latin America, visiting every country, from north to south. When he returned to Spain, he worked for Quim's father at Transportes Castán.

Ximena felt Quim's hand on her bare thigh. He slipped it under her miniskirt as he took a bite of toast. She checked his advance, but gave him a smile. She knew he, more than anyone, was finding Ana's sudden reappearance difficult. And she knew how hellish his home life was.

They had planned to run away together someday. Ximena had talked to him about the coast of Almería. Quim did not care where they went, as long as it was far away from the mountains.

Rafael slipped on a jacket, left forty euros on the table and asked them to give it to the cleaning lady when she had finished. He tousled Quim's hair as he left. 'Don't do anything I wouldn't do,' he said to Ximena with melodramatic solemnity.

'So, what are we going to do?' Quim asked as soon as they were alone.

Ximena shrugged. She knew he needed distracting from all the stuff about Ana. She was about to ask whether he had seen her, but instead suggested that they watch a movie online. Lie on the sofa in Rafael's living room. He was happy for them to treat the place like their own.

Ximena had only been a little girl when it all happened. But she had grown up quickly. She had sought out Quim, and finally got what she had always desired. Two years after her friends disappeared, when she was about to turn thirteen and Quim was sixteen, he had kissed her.

It was summer, and they had gone swimming in the Ésera. The water was cold and they had laughed and tried to see who could stay in longest. Quim had pushed her under, and when she had come back to the surface, Ximena had clung to him so he could not do it again. She remembered how his body had pressed against hers. What she'd felt was not sexual, but protective. Quim had kissed her, and that night Ximena had not been able to sleep.

They never talked about what this was. Sweethearts. Lovers. Friends. Ximena sometimes felt that he was not as committed as she was, but she was not about to let him get away. She tried to convince herself that, every time he stood her up, his sudden distance was about his home life. About his relationship with his parents.

But the increasing fear that one day Quim would no longer be there by her side was tangible.

The police car pulled up in front of the house. Montserrat saw the officers standing in the street, waiting for Raquel and Ana to get out. The Guardia Civil had cordoned off the nearby streets to stop journalists accessing the housing development. They were in quarantine, as though they were contagious. A strange silence hung over the village. A silence that reminded her of the days following her daughter's disappearance. And that silence was becoming deafening. Montserrat did not need anyone to tell her, just as she had not needed anyone to tell her back then. She knew what was going on in their minds, at the Hunting Society and the Cofradía de Santa María de Laude. Lucía is dead: this is what they were thinking. Once Ana had managed to escape, the kidnapper would not have hesitated. He would have got rid of her daughter. Montserrat did her best to dismiss the idea. She had spent five years doing so, but it simply became harder with time.

Ana's shaven head gave her a hard look, utterly unlike the innocence of her little-girl fringe. She was as tall as her mother now and, beneath the baggy clothes, she had the curves of a woman. But she did not seem weak; Montserrat had imagined she would be like an invalid. She walked confidently, not clinging to her mother's arm. Seeing her face, those black eyes, flanked by police officers as she walked to the house, Montserrat felt a shudder run through her. She thought she could see Ana smile, and she sobbed, wondering what Lucía looked like wherever she was right now.

She closed the curtains and leaned against the wall.

Joaquín came over and hugged her. 'You want to talk to her?' he asked.

Montserrat nervously shook her head. She broke from her husband's embrace and went upstairs. Ever since losing Lucía, she had allowed herself to be swept along. As though she had fallen into one of the rivers in the valley and was simply letting the water carry her down the mountain. But now the raging torrent seemed about to dash her against the rocks, the spiralling eddies driving her insane.

At first light that morning, before the streets were cordoned off, Álvaro Montrell had been prowling around the outside of the house like a thief. He had avoided Joaquín's house, afraid his neighbour might be peering through the curtains, watching the street.

His key no longer opened the door. Álvaro tried to let himself in, but Raquel had changed the locks. Not because she was afraid of him, probably, but simply because she was afraid. The devil had come into their lives one day, why would he not do so again? Álvaro knew it; he had seen the panic in Raquel's face the day he came to pick up his clothes. He had not been thinking about her. In that moment, he was thinking only about himself. The whole village had turned on him. He was a marked man. He felt besieged, surrounded, like an exhausted fox that had spent days running from the pack of baying hounds. The hunters were closing in. At any moment, someone would shoot. They had accused him of child abuse, called him a liar. *What did you do to our daughters at that school? What did you do to your own daughter?* He had had the chance to escape, and he had taken it. When he had climbed into the car, he had not looked in the rear-view mirror. He did not want to see the streets of Monteperdido, his house, his wife receding into the distance as he drove away.

He had let himself in through the patio door. Raquel had left it unlocked. He imagined how nervous, how confused his wife must have felt when the police arrived. The terrible fear that it might be a mistake, until she could get to the hospital, see Ana, touch her. Now, here they were, coming up the front path. He had heard the cars arriving. The sound of the front door opening. Álvaro waited in what had once been his room, the blinds closed. Now, finally, his liquid blue eyes shed a tear.

Ana climbed the stairs, trying to recognize something familiar in the smell of the walls. She stopped halfway up and looked down at her mother and the Guardia Civil assigned to protect them. She was sniffing the air like a lost pet looking for a familiar scent, trying to find its way home. But nothing she could smell was familiar: the perfume Raquel wore these days was new; the cooking smells coming from the kitchen were for a meal she'd never had as a child; the cleaning products had wiped away the sweet smell she remembered in her home. When she reached the landing, she smiled. Her pounding heart began to calm. Beneath all these alien smells there was a faint scent that she recognized, one that had refused to fade, despite the years. It smelled of bicycles, of sweat after play, of long lie-ins in the dead of winter. She glanced at her bedroom door, but did not yet feel brave enough to open it.

'Don't you realize that all you're doing is making us waste out time?' Sara exploded at Joaquín Castán. 'I thought I made it clear when I said that, if there was any news, you'd be the first to know—'

'You've been talking to her all morning; are you really saying you've got nothing to tell me?' Lucía's father pressed her.

He had met them on the threshold of Raquel's house. Víctor had tried to intervene, to calm Joaquín down, but he could not persuade him to lower his voice. Powerful and wound up, like a man accustomed to having his own way, he paid no heed to the Guardia Civil. Joaquín wanted answers from Baín and Sara.

'You're not the first officers to work on this case,' he growled. 'I've seen them come and go. We're the only ones who are still here – the families.'

Baín came out of the house to try to calm the situation. 'Ana is unable to identify the man who abducted them,' he conceded at length, 'but we are following other lines of inquiry.'

'What do you mean she's "unable"?'

'Joaquín, we have to be careful how we manage the evidence in this case,' Sara said, though she looked away from him and at Burgos and Raquel, who were also now coming out of the house.

'So this is police diligence? It's not worth shit. Why isn't my daughter's picture all over every television screen? Or are you saying that Ana may have something to say about Lucía?'

By now, Sara had turned away from Joaquín, whose voice was fading as she approached Burgos.

'Where's Ana?' she said, alarmed.

'She's inside,' Burgos said, a casual smile visible behind his thick moustache.

'She'd like to be alone for a minute,' Raquel explained.

Sara raced inside, calling Ana's name, but was met with silence. She took the stairs, three at a time. Víctor and Baín stepped inside, wondering what was going on. Ana's name echoed around the house, but there came no answer. ('Dust. Shade. Nothingness', Sara thought.) The walls and furniture stared back silently, mute witnesses to what had happened in the seconds when the girl had been left on her own. What was the point of assigning an officer? On the landing, Sara threw open the door to the bathroom, the office . . . She had stopped calling Ana's name.

'Relax.'

Sara reached for her gun as she whipped round. Álvaro raised his hands as though trying to calm her, and he smiled; despite the tears that streaked his face, he seemed serene.

'Where is she?' Sara said, still gripping the pistol by her side, though she did not raise it.

Álvaro stepped away from the bedroom door and gestured for her to look inside.

Sara took a couple of steps forward and then, leaning over the banister, she called down. 'It's fine. She's fine.' She holstered the pistol and looked at Ana, sitting on the edge of her parents' bed. 'You are fine, aren't you?'

Ana nodded, letting her head fall forward. Álvaro excused himself and went to the bathroom. Sara could hear footsteps – Raquel and the others. Sitting on the bed, hands resting in her lap, completely calm, Ana waited for them. Looking at her as she sat in this dark room with the blinds closed, Sara knew she was building a dam that would keep everything that was in the past at bay. She wanted to begin again from zero. She was a woman now, she had shed all her weaknesses along the way and, beneath her skin, she had an armour made of steel. Indestructible.

Santiago Baín cut the meat into smaller and smaller pieces. Elisa, the girl at the Hotel La Renclusa, had recommended the dish: *ixarso*. It was a stew made from mountain goat – *sarrio*, they called it around here – cooked with thyme, rosemary, garlic and bay leaves.

Sara pushed her plate aside to make room for her notebook. On the way back to the hotel, they had talked about next moves. While forensics finished processing the evidence from the mountain hut – which they firmly expected would turn up nothing, given the state of the charred debris – they would have to do what Joaquín Castán had suggested. They had already requested that a police-sketch artist be dispatched to Monteperdido. Hopefully, Ana's description would be enough to create a picture of what Lucía looked like now. But Baín was reluctant to send the image to the media.

'We have to remember that she's still with him. We've no idea how he might react,' he said.

For five years, this man had felt free. Now, everything had changed. One of the girls had escaped. The police could not stand by and do nothing, but if they put pressure on him, released an identikit image of Lucía, he might panic. He had chosen not to kill her in the mountain hut. He had taken her somewhere else. But if her face became a threat, Lucía would be a burden. And the most logical thing would be to get rid of her.

Elisa came over with a basket of bread and said, 'Everything all right? Are you not enjoying the *ixarso*?'

Sara looked at her plate, still untouched, and said that she was not very hungry. Looking up at Elisa, she saw the girl trying to avoid her gaze, her eyes like little birds flitting from branch to branch. She had her hair pinned back with a velvet hair slide.

'That's really pretty,' Sara said, nodding to it.

'Thanks. I make them myself.' Elisa blushed.

'Maybe you could make me one someday.'

'Of course.'

Elisa stood there for a moment longer, as though she had something else to say, but changed her mind. Timidly, she turned and walked off.

The hotel dining room was unassuming. Eight or nine tables, surrounded by stone walls decorated with local knick-knacks – traditional snowshoes and old hunting rifles. A picture of the Virgin Mary hung from the pillar in the middle of the room. Apart from an elderly French couple on holiday, they were the only diners.

'That's what I'd like to be like,' Santiago Baín said, nodding towards the French couple.

'I hope you're not thinking about your retirement already.'

'Why? I'm not far off it now. I've mastered the quirks of an old codger –' he gestured to his plate of food – 'and the attitude. In fact, I probably look like an old man who's blown his pension on a pretty young girl.' He pointed his fork at her.

Sara distractedly picked up a bread roll. Her stomach was in knots. Santiago brought a forkful of *ixarso* to his mouth. 'It's very tender,' he said, encouraging her to eat. She knew what Santiago was trying to say: sometimes, the job was exhausting. Not because of the hours put in, the constant travelling, having to infiltrate the families of missing persons like impostors. It was the human condition itself that was depressing, that really took it its toll.

'Why did she lie to us?' Sara asked, gazing out the window.

Baín hesitated a few seconds before replying. He poured himself some more wine and said, 'Shame, is my guess. I can't think of any other reason.'

At the hospital, Ana had told them that the man had not touched her. That, in the years she had been captive, he had treated her with contempt, as though she were a burden, an inconvenience. But the medical reports had revealed something very different. Ana had had sex; though it was impossible to tell how often, it was clear that she had lost her virginity at least two years earlier.

'Do you think she's lying about never having seen his face?' Sara asked.

Now, her entire statement seemed flimsy. It was possible to imagine countless reasons for her lies, from embarrassment to repressed memories; perhaps her mind had blocked out those things it could not bear. They had seen similar reactions in other cases. But this case was different from all the others: Ana had not been alone, and while she had managed to escape and could try to deal with her past, Lucía was still being held captive. Every lie Ana told to protect herself was a handful of earth on Lucía's grave.

'I know this might sound crazy, but . . . what if Ana doesn't want us to find Lucía?'

'Eat your dinner, and stop scribbling in that notebook,' Baín ordered. 'You can't throw good meat like this in the bin.'

Sara looked at her notebook, geometric figures spread across the margins like a spider's web. Reluctantly, she ate another mouthful of *ixarso*.

'Lucía and Ana lived together for five years in a space that was – what? – twenty square metres? They're not friends, they're sisters. They were a family. And you know as well as I do that families breed grudges as much as they breed love,' Baín said.

'Can I interview Ana again?'

'Let me do it this time,' Baín said.

Sara looked at him sulkily. He gave her a broad smile, his eyes all but disappearing beneath the mountainous wrinkles on his forehead.

'What about you? What's your grudge with me?' he asked.

'That you're not my father, Chickpea,' Sara taunted.

'Screw you. Sara, there are times when you're so soft-hearted it scares me. I don't know why I don't just find a partner with balls.'

Santiago Baín got up and left the dining room. Sara saw him cross the road and stroll casually down the main street of Monteperdido. She found it funny, being affectionate to this man who pretended he loathed all forms of sentimentality. Calling him 'Chickpea' drove him insane. We all bear our scars, and he was no exception. Just as he tried to heal hers, so Sara hoped that one day she might be allowed to help heal his.

Locked in the bathroom, leaning on the washbasin, Raquel broke down and sobbed; she hated Ismael. Why did you have to get close to me? Why did you have to make me think there might be a different future for me? She clamped her hand over her mouth; she did not want anyone to hear her cry, least of all Álvaro. She felt dizzy. She sat on the toilet and put her head in her hands, but the feeling refused to go. In the darkness, behind her veil of hair, she tried to control her breathing.

Before leaving, the police had informed them that Officer Burgos would be staying with them. Another officer would take the night shift. Álvaro was clearly uncomfortable with this idea; he could not understand why they should sacrifice their privacy. Would it not be enough to have a police car parked outside? But Sara had been insistent. The only alternative would be for Ana to come to the police station. That way, they could have the privacy they wanted, she said. Raquel stood by, feeling as though she had no part in these conversations. As though the speakers were shadowgraphs projected on a wall. She looked at her daughter, at her husband, and she was afraid to catch her reflection in the hall mirror. Why did she feel this way? she wondered. Surely she should be blissfully happy? Why all these sudden cracks?

She had been in the kitchen getting a glass of water when she heard Álvaro and Ana go back upstairs. They were engrossed in a conversation she could not hear. Her fears drowned out every sound. It is impossible to live without a future, without some idea of tomorrow. People thought she had lost that tomorrow on the day Ana disappeared. But that was not true. It had happened later, when her faith in Álvaro had faltered. She had tried to turn a deaf ear to the rumours, to the gossip about what he had done to Elisa, but when he had been arrested, she could not carry on. Was it possible that her husband had kidnapped the girls?

After he was released, Álvaro had left. Raquel had been unable to keep him. It had been a long and painful process. She had needed to blot out everything she had felt for Álvaro so that she could find a path that might take her somewhere else.

Suddenly, she'd snapped out of these thoughts, the glass had slipped from her fingers and shattered in the sink, the bright shards glittering against the aluminium. She raced up the stairs. Burgos, who was stationed on the landing, had looked away when he saw her, unable to hide what he thought of her in that moment. Álvaro and Ana were standing in the doorway of Ana's room. The girl turned to her mother, her tone ingenuous.

'You cleared out my room?'

Raquel looked at the desk and the shelves that she and Ismael had bought in Barbastro one Saturday morning. Why did I let you persuade me to do it, Ismael?

'Where are my things? Did you throw them out?' Ana said, stepping into the room and looking through the office equipment for some trace of her childhood.

'I . . . No, of course not . . . They're in boxes in the basement,' Raquel stammered.

Ana looked at her mother and, in her eyes, Raquel thought she could see a question: Am I a burden? Did you hope I would never come back?

'It's been years, Ana,' Álvaro interrupted. 'It's a miracle that you're here now, when we'd almost given up hope . . . You do understand, don't you? Just because your things aren't here, it doesn't mean we forgot you. Not even for a second.'

Álvaro had taken his daughter's face in his hands and looked into her eyes as he spoke. The way he had when, as a little girl, she would wake up, terrified, from a nightmare. *It was just a bad dream,* he would say. He had always been able to find the words that seemed to elude Raquel.

Raquel had felt her chest shudder, as though it was about to explode into a thousand pieces. This was why she had locked herself in the bathroom. Why did you let Ismael sweep you off your feet? Why did you take all your daughter's possessions and give them to charity?

There was a knock at the door, and Raquel stood up. She combed her fingers through her hair and dried her tears.

'I'll be out in a second,' she said when she felt confident she could sound self-assured.

'It's Álvaro. Can we talk for a minute?'

Raquel glanced in the mirror and then half-opened the door. She needed a little more time to pretend that she was fine.

'I'll just be a second, honestly. Tell Ana I'm fine. It's just the excitement at having her home again . . .'

'Can I come in?' Álvaro insisted. 'Please.'

Raquel hid behind the door before opening it wide.

Álvaro stepped into the bathroom and, as he closed the door, caught Burgos's attention. 'Keep an eye on my daughter. That's what you're here for,' Álvaro said as the officer tried to hide the fact that they were the ones he was keeping an eye on.

Álvaro looked around for somewhere to sit. The bathroom was tiny. Raquel was leaning against the towel rail. In the end, he sat on the edge of the bath and, as he did, he smiled. Raquel looked at him, almost offended.

'Sorry,' Álvaro said. 'I was just remembering . . . Never mind . . . It's stupid.'

'Remembering what?'

'The weekend we went to visit your parents in Barcelona.'

Raquel could not work out what he was getting at.

'You don't remember? We locked ourselves in their bathroom so we could fuck . . . But it was impossible. The bathroom was even smaller than this one . . . And, if that wasn't bad enough, when we finally found a comfortable position, your mother started banging on the door . . .'

Álvaro laid the memory at her feet, the way a cat brings the bird it has killed to its master. It was strange, but pleasant. Raquel smiled, remembering how they had hurriedly turned on the shower in order to fool her mother. They had been like two teenagers, although she was already pregnant with Ana, Álvaro's hair was already white as snow, and they were already planning their move to Monteperdido. As though sliding down an embankment, Raquel came back from that day in her parents' house to today, in this bathroom.

'You have no reason to feel guilty,' Álvaro said. 'When you've had to go through what we went through, who's to say what's right and what's wrong?'

'I should never have thrown out her things, but I needed space for the business, and . . .'

'Honestly, Raquel, you don't have to justify yourself. Not to me,' Álvaro said. 'You daughter is out there. It doesn't matter what happened in the past five years. All she wants is for you to hug her.'

Raquel wanted to go to him, to let him put his arms around her. Instead, she offered a reproach: 'Why did you never let me know where you were?'

'I didn't think you'd want to know. Maybe I made a mistake too.' He looked sadly at Raquel. 'Can I stay the night?'

'There's a sofa bed in the living room . . . I'll bring you down some sheets.'

Víctor brought her the old case files: four boxes gathering dust in the basement of the police station. Then he drove her back to La Renclusa. Sara wanted all the files so that she could check whether there were any inconsistencies with those she already had.

They drove back to the hotel in silence. Sara, lost in her thoughts as she stared out at the darkling mountains that surrounded the village and ushered in the night, as though swathing the houses in a black sheet. Víctor, ill at ease, still brooding over the argument with Sara about allowing Burgos to keep an eye on Ana. *That's how things go, in this village. No one forgets to make cake, only how to do their jobs,* Sara had said finally. What the hell does she know about this village? Víctor was thinking as he pulled up outside the hotel and they coldly said their goodbyes.

Sara was setting the boxes of files on the bed when she heard laughter. She popped her head out into the corridor. At the far end, near the stairwell, the door of one of the rooms opened. She heard a few words in French she could not understand, and then she saw Elisa emerge. Hands pulled at her, trying to bring her back into the room, but the girl laughed and shrugged them off. 'That's enough.' There was more than one man in the room: a group of lads she had seen at breakfast. Elisa adjusted her blouse, covering her bared shoulder, and pinned her hair back with the velvet hair slide. 'You're troublemakers, you are,' she said. She was like a joyful insect fluttering around a flower, playful and preening – until the door closed and she turned away and once more stared down at the carpet, her shoulders hunched, as though she suddenly felt cold. She padded soundlessly downstairs.

Night gathered in Monteperdido. Ana could no longer hear the rain in the trees, those phantom raindrops that had been the soundtrack to so many nights. Tonight, her mother's breathing kept time. Raquel was sitting in an armchair in the corner of the room, having persuaded Ana to take her bed. She'd also insisted on leaving the light on; Ana did not want to contradict her. The truth was that she was used to the dark; it was the light that frightened her. She tried to close her eyes.

The bathroom window looked out on to the back garden. On the lawn, there was a yellow rectangle of light from Raquel's bedroom. Montserrat stared at that luminous rectangle the way a homeless person might stare at a house filled with Christmas lights; she felt dirty, she hated herself. She closed the window and hunted through the bathroom cabinet. It was full of boxes of medicines that she might never need, but that was the way in Monteperdido. In winter, when snow blocked the roads, it was impossible to get to the pharmacy in Barbastro, and the little village shop stocked very little. Most people in the village made trips to Andorra to stock up on medications for the winter – pills and syrups that were long out of date before anybody used them. Montserrat could feel a black rage welling in her chest and frantically searched for some tranquillizers. She remembered hearing Raquel's moans of ecstasy. She had known for some time that there was something going on between Raquel and Ismael Calella, the carpenter who had helped her get her business off the ground. Then, a few weeks earlier, while she was tidying Lucía's room, Montserrat had heard them making love. Now she could not get Raquel's happiness out of her head.

Víctor cleaned Nieve's wound, changed the dressing and got the dog to drink a little water. He was much better, though not yet strong enough to support his head, so Víctor had to hold his muzzle while he lapped from the bowl. Then he stroked the dog and watched him fall asleep, as though just back from a trip to the summit of Ixeia. The little chest rose and fell with the ragged breaths, and Víctor could not help but remember . . . Nuria in her hospital bed. Him, sitting in the uncomfortable plastic chair, waiting for her to wake up. The machines forcing her lungs to keep breathing.

He did not want to stay in the house looking at Nieve and remembering. He needed to talk to someone, needed the noise of conversation to stop him from thinking. He picked up his keys and, before heading out, went over to the table, where he had left the report he had slipped out of the case files. He had not been able to stop thinking about it as he drove Sara to the hotel, picturing the papers in the boot of the car. It was better that she did not read it.

When Víctor arrived, the Hunting Society was heaving. His brother, Román, was bustling between the bar and the tables, and barely had time to give him a wave as he came in.

'You see the news?' Marcial asked from where he sat playing dominoes. 'They say it's going to rain.'

Víctor had not had time. He felt as though he were a ripped net, unable to catch a single fish.

'I'll have a look first thing,' he said apologetically.

'No big deal. Thunderstorms, but not too serious,' Marcial said, turning back to his game, looking at the tiles he had just been dealt. Then he looked at his opponent. 'Hey, Nicolás? Are we ready?'

'We're ready, Marcial. We're ready.' Nicolás had trouble disguising his nervousness. He pushed his glasses up the bridge of his nose and smiled awkwardly: the weird kid who had just been picked for the football team for the first time.

Víctor turned away from the table as Román came over.

'A Coke?' he asked, as he uncapped the bottle.

'Did you see the news?' The threatening rain went round in Víctor's head like a fly buzzing around a room.

'Don't sweat it. It's more likely to rain up in Posets. You've got enough to worry about here.'

'I haven't had a minute to myself.'

'That policewoman seems like a bitch.'

Víctor simply smiled, saying nothing about Sara, but then again he would not have known what to say. Sometimes he was irritated by the way she was leading the investigation, but at other times she seemed like a woman who needed more help than he could give. He took a swig of his Coke.

'Why the fuck are they asking us all where we were when the girl reappeared?'

'It's routine, Román. Don't make it into something serious.'

'Pujante came and asked me. I told him to fuck off. And if he asks again, I'll smack the guy.'

'Don't go doing that; the poor bastard has to report to the S.A.F., not to me. You'll just get yourself in trouble.'

'Well, where do you think I was? I was at the Cofradía with half the village, preparing stuff for Joaquín's memorial thing. Pujante saw me there himself, asked me if there were many boars around this year ... Whether I was planning to take the dogs out hunting.'

'Would it have been so hard just to tell him that?'

'The guy winds me up, Víctor. We've had enough shit in this village without a bunch of wise guys coming here and treating us like criminals ... '

Román was pushing seven years his brother's senior – about to turn fifty, something Víctor found hard to believe. Just as he found it hard to believe that he was over forty himself. He remembered when they were kids, running around the wilds of Monteperdido, looking for new trails, for places no one had ever been. Román was always in front, stubborn, single-minded; even when their explorations led to a dead end, he insisted on carrying on. Víctor, dragged along by his big brother, had never felt as strong a connection to every stone, every tree. It was as though it was a part of Román, this world of valleys and mountains, glaciers and lakes, of animals skulking in the forests. If Víctor had chosen Monteperdido, it was not because he loved the village or the landscape, but because he had loved Nuria.

He had been in love with her. They were going to be married. What would their life have been like? Víctor often wondered, but the roaring torrent of the River Ésera had swept away the answer. It had been seven years since the flood, since the river burst its banks, leaving the village, and his life, in ruins. All his plans had been reduced to mud and mire. Seven people had died. Nuria had been one of them. For a long time, he had wished the waters would come back and take him.

As he watched Román casually moving among the tables, serving drinks and chatting briefly with the customers, Víctor admired his brother's assurance. The ease with which he sailed through life. He had hardly ever set foot outside Monteperdido, but he had never really felt the need. He had started working at a young age; his feel for the land and for the animals made him one of the finest guides in the village. Román was the person who organized the battues for the boar hunts – there would be one in mid-August – and that was how he had come to be Hunt Master at the Cofradía. He was the one who led the bay dogs on leashes – white Andalusian Manetos that could sniff out a boar's nest anywhere in the forest. Nor had it taken him long to marry Ondina; they were hitched before he turned twenty-six. Shortly afterwards, with the money he inherited from their parents, he had set up the Hunting Society; it was a bar, but mostly it was a private club open only to people from the village. Víctor remembered saying he thought it was stupid to alienate the tourists who came to the village: *That's where the money is.* Or that was what Víctor had thought. Time had proved him wrong. The people of Monteperdido needed to protect themselves from interlopers. They wanted a place where they could meet. A place filled with familiar faces. Román had rented a building in the centre of the village, walls panelled with exotic hardwoods. Hunting trophies hung all around the bar, with pride of place given to the first animal he had ever killed: a stag, which greeted people as they entered. The taxidermist had managed to preserve the look of defiance Román said the animal had the day he shot it.

'I don't know why I bother playing, I always end up getting fleeced,' Nicolás Souto said, coming to join Víctor at the bar.

'Is the game finished?' The Guardia Civil seemed surprised.

'I can't count. I start out well, but then I get confused about how many fives there are on the table . . . Marcial gives me a funny look and I start sweating . . .'

From the table, they heard Marcial's voice: 'I told you, Nicolás: they've got the five. How many times . . .? It's like you're brain-dead.'

Nicolás nodded; all he wanted was for Marcial to shut up so he could order a gin and tonic.

'When will you realize that dominoes is a serious business?' Víctor teased.

'They were one man short, so . . .' Nicolás trailed off. He ordered his drink from Román, pushed his glasses up his nose, blinked once or twice and then said, 'How's Nieve?'

'I cleaned the wound. I think he seems a lot better.'

'I'll swing by tomorrow and take a look . . . But you need to keep an eye on that fever.'

'I can't be with him all day.'

'Do you want me to take him to the animal hospital in Barbastro?'

Víctor did not want to be separated from his dog. He preferred to take what time he could during the day to check that Nieve was all right. He did not want him to die somewhere else. Who would want to die far from home?

'I suppose you don't have much time, these days,' Nicolás said awkwardly, his eyes darting around behind his glasses, giving him away. He was trying to seem sympathetic, but actually he wanted to wheedle details of the investigation from Víctor. 'At least you'll have got a lot of evidence from that place where the girls were being held . . .'

'Not really, to be honest.'

'The guy eliminated his tracks, did he? Someone said he burned the place.'

'You know I can't talk about the case.'

Nicolás leaned back on his stool and threw up his hands, as though he had no intention of asking anything more. He feigned indifference, only to immediately betray himself with a crafty smile.

'You don't need to name names . . . but you must have a couple of suspects in mind. Because it's pretty clear that this Simón guy had nothing to do with it . . .'

Víctor gave him a curt glance – something anyone else would recognize as a sign that the conversation was at an end, but not Nicolás.

'Álvaro? You don't have to say anything, just give me a sign. Take a swig of your Coke if I'm on the right track—'

'I came in here for a drink, not to talk to you about the case.'

'If it is Álvaro, it would be pretty weird. With the daughter back in the house . . . Do you know if he's back with Raquel?'

'Nicolás, please . . . Do I really need to tell you to piss off?'

Víctor had raised his voice and several people turned to look at them. He was beginning to think it had been a bad idea to come to the Hunting Society, and took a swig of Coke.

'You took a drink – that means something, doesn't it?' Nicolás whispered in his ear.

Víctor sighed; he had known Nicolás since he was a child, had dealt with him a lot, given that he was the only vet in Monteperdido, but the guy still drove him crazy.

'How are things going with the policewoman?' Nicolás asked. 'I've been worrying about that whole affair.'

'Well, you can stop worrying,' Víctor said.

'She shoots your dog and you're just going to let her get away with it?' Nicolás was indignant. 'Did she apologize?'

'More or less.'

Nicolás leaned closer and lowered his voice. '*El follét del albarósa*,' he said in a confiding tone. 'What do you think?'

'What do I think of what?' Víctor said, confused. 'What is it?'

'The title of the novel I'm writing,' Nicolás explained.

'I don't know. I don't really understand much *patués*.'

'You know that *alborósa* means a birch grove, don't you?' The vet was beginning to sound irritated.

'Oh, yes, that's right. But what is *el follét*?'

Nicolás proudly sat up straight, pushing his glasses back up his nose; this was what he had wanted to tell Víctor from the beginning.

'*El follét* is an imp, a malign spirit that lives in the forest and some-times hides in the manes of horses and drives them insane. Makes them rear and buck. They're more mischievous than evil. Has no one ever told you stories about the *follét*?'

'Seems to me you're the only one in Monteperdido who knows these stories.'

'Someone has to keep the traditions alive,' Nicolás said proudly. 'But, in my novels, it's a play on words. *El follét*, the forest sprite, but it's also the *patués* word for a roe deer. And the novel opens with a dead deer.'

'And – don't tell me – two missing girls and a policewoman who shoots a dog?'

'Something like that,' Nicolás admitted.

'If you wrote it in Spanish, at least there would be some chance I might read it one day,' said Víctor, getting to his feet and setting some money down on the bar.

'There's another way of reading the title,' Nicolás said as Víctor was on his way out the door. '*El follét* is Ken Follet. In other words, me. I'm the Ken Follet of the birch grove.' And Nicolás laughed so hard at his own joke that, to Víctor, it sounded more like a cry for help.

She went downstairs to look for her. Sara could not sleep and, as she was tossing and turning, she thought about Caridad. Would she be in the hotel lobby about now? She pretended to be getting her-self a coffee as she glanced at the sofas and the armchairs in the next room.

Caridad's voice came from the shadows. 'I'm here, *filla*. I'm here.'

It was then that Sara saw her face as she sat up on the sofa.

'For me, every night is the same.'

Sara and Caridad sat at the same table where they had first spoken. Sara with her scalding coffee, Caridad arriving a moment later, with her stiff-legged walk and a bottle of red liquid.

'Blood,' she said, when Sara asked what she was drinking. 'I've got a load of kids in the basement of my house and I bleed them a little every day. That's how I stay so young.' Caridad smiled and pulled her skin into a parody of a facelift. 'I hope you're not going to arrest me.'

'I'll think about it.'

Caridad rummaged in the pockets of her tracksuit and took out a deck of cards, dexterously shuffled them, slapped them on the table, cut the pack and said, 'A quick hand of *brisca*?'

Before Sara could answer, she had already started dealing the cards.

'Cups are trumps.' Caridad studied her three cards carefully and said, without looking up, 'You start.'

'Were you walking around the pine forest again today?' Sara said, laying the four of coins on the table.

'For a couple of hours. Then I walked around the village.' Caridad played the knave of coins and took the trick. 'People are strange.'

Stranger than you? Sara thought, but bit her tongue and played the two of clubs on Caridad's six.

'Ana has gone home, but we still don't know anything about Lucía,' Sara said, trying to show that she felt sympathetic towards the people of the village.

'Dumb fucking cop,' Caridad muttered, playing the three of swords. 'How do you know my niece isn't a journalist? Imagine getting up tomorrow and seeing the headline in the papers: *WE DON'T KNOW ANYTHING.*'

'Is your niece a journalist?' Sara asked, playing a card and picking up two points.

'Don't have a niece.' Caridad looked at her suspiciously. 'What's going on? Have you been checking my police record?'

'I don't think you've made the list of suspects just yet.'

'Don't worry; you'll find suspects enough in Monteperdido.'

Sara picked up a few more points in the last hand and Caridad looked at her, piqued.

'You're winding me up so you can win.'

'I might be a dumb fucking cop, but I can hold my own playing *brisca*.' Sara laid the ace of cups on the table.

'All yours.' Caridad admitted defeat.

Sara's pile of cards continued to grow, while Caridad's dwindled. The woman grabbed at the cards every time she had to pick one up, and snorted when she looked at it.

'You think there are that many suspects in the village?' Sara said.

'Everyone thinks it was Álvaro Montrell. But then, they don't think much, in this town. Or they think what everyone else thinks. The people in the Cofradía, for example.'

'What's the Cofradía?'

'A bunch of sanctimonious prigs with more power than the mayor.' Caridad finally played a winning card and took the trick. She smiled triumphantly at Sara, then immediately became suspicious. 'Are you letting me win?'

'I just got dealt a bad hand,' Sara said apologetically.

'Let's see . . . Show me . . .' Caridad leaned across the table and tried to look at Sara's cards, but she hid them.

'Keep playing, and tell me more about this Cofradía,' Sara said.

'It's, like, a billion years old. In the beginning, it was this religious thing, but it hasn't had anything to do with the Church now for a long time. They organize street parties, clear the roads when it snows . . . that sort of stuff,' Caridad said quickly. She was winning and she did not want to break her rhythm.

'So who's in it?'

'The whole village. The prior, that's what they call the leader, is Marcial Nerín, Elisa's father. Have you met him? He has a gunsmith's shop on Plaza del Ayuntamiento.'

'Not yet.'

'What are you waiting for, child? Marcial is the one who pulls the strings round here. Personally, I think he's no saint; he's a scandalmonger. Always poking his nose into other people's lives. Need someone to clear the snow from your driveway? Here comes Marcial and his Cofradía. Short on the mortgage this month? Let us lend you money. Depressed? Here, have a dog – that'll cheer you up.'

'There's obviously a lot going on in this Cofradía.'

'I'm whipping your arse, now,' Caridad said gleefully, as she picked up another trick. 'Did no one tell you that they run everything round here?'

Sara looked at her cards. She could win the last hand, but something that Caridad had said was nagging her. She set down her cards.

'Víctor's dog. Did the Cofradía give it to him?'

'Round here, we help each other out; it's no big deal. Poor bastard was going through a rough patch. His fiancée died in the flood, seven years ago. He couldn't catch a break. Besides, he had a tendency to . . .

um . . .' Caridad made an exaggerated drinking gesture. 'The dog was good for him. It was a bit of responsibility. He had to take it for walks, feed it . . . Well, up until you shot it, obviously.'

'Thanks for reminding me,' Sara said irritably.

'It's not something you should forget,' Caridad said, then her expression changed. 'Although, now I think about it, he has to clean the wound and change the dressing so the dog doesn't die. That's even more responsibility.'

Sara tossed her last card on the table. Caridad won the trick. Her chubby little fingers began to count the cards so she could tot up the points.

'Seventy-two. Don't bother counting yours,' she said. 'Why don't you go over to his place and say you're sorry?' Caridad slipped the deck of cards back into her pocket. 'Worst case scenario, maybe he gives you a slap. Maybe not. But, if it's what you want to do, what the fuck do you care what he thinks?'

In a way, Caridad reminded Sara of herself. Argumentative, hard-hitting, this woman seemed to be able to read her mind. What did she care what he thought? She had spent her life worrying about what other people thought. She remembered sitting at the kitchen table as a little girl when her mother, who was poking the fire, turned and looked at her. What was it she had seen in her mother's eyes? Shame? Hatred? Was she upset that her daughter had to see her like that? She'd quickly turned away, her face black and blue from the beatings.

'What's up with you?' Caridad said with a curious smile. 'What are you thinking about?'

'I'm thinking you should enrol in the Cofradía. If they really are gossips, they'd be right up your street.'

'I've been treasurer for the past eight years,' Caridad said, taking a swig of the red liquid.

He knelt in the last pew in the church. Inspector Santiago Baín could not remember how it had started, this habit he had of visiting the churches wherever he went in his investigations. The church in Monteperdido was Romanesque in origin, a vestige of the past glory of a village that, thanks to tourism, was enjoying a renaissance. Centuries of cold and snow had passed between the two eras. The first began when a handful of gentlemen chose the spot – probably because of its proximity to the border – and built palaces and churches, enchanted by the magic of these mountains that also served as a fortress. Perhaps they imagined there were gods, up here, near the peaks of La Kregüeña and the Accursed Mountains. Amid the perpetual snows. Wrathful gods, who unleashed violent thunderstorms. Who gave you permission to trample our paradise? Baín could almost picture the first inhabitants of Monteperdido sitting on these wooden pews, seeking refuge behind the stone walls of the church, praying to a more merciful God. And to a Virgin, the one depicted in the chapel fresco, in the midst of her Assumption, her face upturned as she pierced the clouds, surrounded by angels.

He made the sign of the cross and got to his feet. His footsteps on the flagstones rang out. The morning light streamed through a rose window, illuminating the fresco. To either side of the nave, small gloomy chapels lined the transepts. In one of them, he saw a carved wooden image of the Virgen de Laude, dressed in a white cloak trimmed with gold, holding the Christ child in her arms, both of them crowned with gilded haloes. At the foot of the statue, candles

cast equal amounts of shadow and light: a flickering flame, a protective warmth. An old woman dressed in widow's weeds moved
among the shadows, arranging flowers. She must have heard his
footsteps, because she turned to him, and Santiago Baín smiled at
her. The woman scarcely glanced at him for a second before returning to her flowers.

Inspector Baín looked up towards the cupola. It was cold, here in
the church. The stonework prevented the warmth of July from
entering, as though it had to prove that it was not simply passing
through, but would stay for the summer. Baín buttoned his jacket
and went out.

Sara was waiting for him, leaning on a wall in the churchyard,
bored, tracing the cracks between the flagstones with the toe of her
shoe.

'Have you recited all the prayers you can remember?' she said,
heading towards the gate. Baín followed her. 'I don't know how
you can set foot inside a church, after all the things we've seen.'

Baín smiled to himself. Indeed, the Church had not played an
edifying role in the cases of child abuse they had worked on. Nor
was he about to defend it. He shuddered as he felt the summer
warmth, so different from the chill inside.

'I believe in God, not in man,' he said.

'And you think God is going to help us?' Sara said, expecting no
response.

The wall that surrounded the church created a large courtyard.
The whole village seemed to have been built in the same manner,
turning its back on the world, on the mountains, on outsiders. They
took the cobbled lane leading to Avenida de Posets, the only street
where there was two-way traffic.

'You know the problem with people of your generation?' Baín said. 'You don't believe in anything. Just look at people your age. They're all having panic attacks by the time they turn forty.'

'Maybe that's because we take our work seriously,' Sara said defensively.

'Or maybe it's because you don't believe in anything. Trust me; agnosticism will be the undoing of this world,' Santiago said as they crossed the avenue.

On the other side, various narrow, twisting streets burrowed into the most populous area of Monteperdido. There were almost a thousand inhabitants here, according to the census. Some of the houses looked as though they had been converted into bed and breakfasts. Tourists took over the streets in family groupings. They were not difficult to recognize; they constantly gazed in wonder at the natural world all around, surprised to find new vistas open up at every junction, while the villagers, inured to such wonders, went about their business, going to work, doing the shopping, playing with their children.

The alley they had chosen led to the plaza dominated by the town hall, flanked on both sides by colonnades with several shops: Nerín's Gunsmith's, a grocery shop, a clothes shop. This was also where the Hunting Society bar was located. They decided to grab a coffee.

As they entered, they were greeted by the desiccated head of a stag. The reddish pelt, the antlers and the waxen eyes gave an alarmingly vivid appearance of defiance. Hanging in the hallway that led to the Hunting Society, the stag's head was the villagers' victory over nature, tamed and turned into a trophy. Baín and Sara noticed that everyone fell silent as they entered, and the eyes of the few customers present turned to look at them. The interior was infused with ochre and earth colours, the windows of tawny glass made it almost impossible to see outside. On the bar, there was a chocolate sponge cake with a candle in the middle, which Víctor Gamero had just lit.

'I hope we're not interrupting anything,' Baín said. 'We just wanted to get a coffee.'

'The Society is for village residents only,' a heavyset man in his forties said with affected cordiality. He was standing behind the bar and seemed to be the owner.

'I'm sure they can have a coffee, Román,' Víctor intervened. 'This is my brother, and this is Inspector Santiago Baín and Assistant Inspector Sara Campos.' His sweeping gesture took in all those in the Society.

'What are you celebrating?' Baín nodded at the cake as he settled himself on a stool.

'It's Rafael's birthday.' Víctor pointed to the table where Rafael was sitting, hands in his lap, waiting for his birthday cake; like all those present, he was over forty. His head hung down on his chest, making it impossible to see his neck – if indeed he had one. Had he blushed, or was it simply the light from the coloured glass?

Joaquín Castán laid a hand on Rafael's shoulder and gave the officers a terse, 'Hello,' that made it clear they were not welcome.

'Rafael is Montserrat's brother,' Víctor explained, setting the cake down in front of him.

'My wife made the cake,' Joaquín said.

A slim man with a nervous disposition pulled up a stool next to the officers. 'Nicolás Souto,' he said, shaking Baín's hand. 'I'm the local vet.' Then he tilted his head like a curious animal and peered at Sara over Baín's shoulder. 'How are you finding the village?' he said with a smile, and pushed his glasses up his nose.

'It's a beautiful spot,' Sara said.

'And the mountains? I hear you've already been on a little tour.'

'I wouldn't call it a tour,' Baín said with a smile.

Román set two coffees on the bar. The espresso cups quivered on their porcelain saucers. Inspector Baín turned his around to look at the design: an eight-pointed star.

'It's the symbol of Santa María de Laude, the patron saint of the village. And the Cofradía,' the owner explained.

'The Cofradía is like a neighbourhood association,' Víctor added. With a sweep of his hand, he indicated the members who were present: his brother Román Gamero, Joaquín Castán, Rafael Grau and Nicolás Souto.

'Marcial Nerín is prior of the Cofradía,' he said, beckoning Marcial over. 'He owns the gunsmith's on the other side of the plaza.'

Marcial was older than the others, certainly older than sixty, although the extensive web of fine wrinkles over his face made it difficult to guess his age. He held out a thick, powerful hand. There was something aggressive about the shape of his face: the jutting chin, the snub nose, the beady eyes half-hidden beneath a prominent forehead. As he shook the man's hand, Baín was reminded of an animal, as wary and as dangerous as any of the beasts that lined the walls of the Hunting Society had been, before they became stuffed trophies.

'Surely you must have better things to do than drink coffee?' Marcial said.

'We've picked up the disgraceful habit of eating and drinking.' Baín's smile did not waver.

Sara saw the candle on the cake was burning away. Wax dripped and began to spread.

Nicolás Souto got down from the stool where he had been sitting. 'When all this is over, you should take a tour up to the Accursed Mountains,' he said, as though trying to defuse the situation. 'Or Thunder Peak cirque. It's spectacular at this time of year.'

'I'm not sure they sound terribly inviting, with names like that,' Baín joked.

Nicolás wandered over to the table where Rafael Grau was waiting to blow out his candle. He sat next to him and encouraged everyone to sing 'Happy Birthday'. Only Víctor joined in, and the singing quickly trailed off in scattered applause. Rafael blew out the candle with a sigh of relief and embarrassment. His small eyes stared down at the stone floor while he listened to his friends' congratulations. Baín and Sara went over and wished him all the best.

'Forty-five,' he said, when they asked how old he was. 'Two years older than my sister.'

Joaquín Castán stuck a knife into the cake and began cutting; the strawberry jam that smeared on the blade looked like blood. Víctor's brother brought some plates and spoons from behind the bar, but Santiago and Sara politely declined a piece.

'*No fe kuérpo ta nósa*,' Marcial Nerín muttered.

Baín saw him walk towards the door. *I don't have the stomach for a party*, was what he had said, but Baín pretended he had not understood. He said his goodbyes and he and Sara left the Hunting Society.

Outside, dazzled by the glare, he fumbled in his pocket for his sunglasses. In Monteperdido, they spoke a curious language all their own; it was based on the *patués* common throughout the region, and contained elements of Catalan, Basque, Spanish and French, but it was a distinct language. Cut off from the rest of the world, the people of Monteperdido had ended up speaking a dialect only they could understand, just as they had grown up listening to legends familiar to few others. These towering peaks swirled with myths and maledictions that attested to the villagers' dread of the cruelties of nature – like the ice giant that lived at the summit of La Kregüeña and came down into the valley to steal animals and food.

An ice giant who was still holding Lucía captive, Bain thought as they arrived at the station and saw La Kregüeña to the north, framed against a bright summer sky that stubbornly professed that all was well.

Ana was wearing new clothes.

'They're mine,' Raquel explained. 'We're almost the same size.'

But she did not mention that it had been Álvaro's idea. When she'd woken this morning, her body aching from a night spent sleeping in the armchair, she had found her daughter and her husband in the kitchen. There was a plain-clothes officer with them; he had a notepad on which he had sketched the outline of a face – the rest was blank, waiting for Ana's description. Álvaro said that he had to go out, he had a couple of things to do, and must have noticed how alarmed Raquel was at the prospect of being alone with Ana, because he added, 'Why don't you see whether some of your clothes fit her? Otherwise, we'll need to go shopping.' Even Officer Burgos had thought this was a good idea.

'I'd like to speak to her alone,' Baín said to Raquel, taking a chair from the office into the bedroom, and sitting facing Ana, who was seated on the bed. 'You don't mind, do you?'

Raquel took a deep breath before answering, but it was useless, the words would not come; she simply left the room and closed the door.

'Do you think the composite image looks the way Lucía looks now?'

'The artist is drawing what I'm describing . . .'

'That doesn't answer my question.'

'Yes, of course it looks like her,' Ana said self-consciously.

Baín leaned back in the chair and looked at her. Ana's reticence was beginning to bother him. He had worked on many abduction cases and, although the victims could be unreliable, it was rare to come across an account as composed and yet as evasive and contradictory as Ana's. Five years in captivity must surely have left more of a mark.

'You're not afraid that he'll come for you?' he asked abruptly, gauging Ana's reaction.

'I don't know; should I be?'

'Of course not. That's why we're here – to protect you,' Baín reassured her, seeing the genuine terror on her face.

In Ana's account, the sense of time passing was confused. Having been locked in a basement for long periods, deprived of any light, subjected to an unvarying routine, it was understandable that she would have trouble establishing a chronology of the years of her confinement. Baín steered the conversation, trying to find some memory that might indicate a day, a season. But Ana found it difficult. She admitted that there were times when she had been surprised, thinking it was summer only to be brought up from the cellar by her captor and see the mountains covered in snow.

At such times, she felt as though she had slept for months in a sort of stupor.

'Can you remember the last time you heard it rain, or snow, while you were being held at the *refugio*?'

'I don't know,' she said, flustered. Though she seemed to be making a genuine effort to remember, it was as though she were feeling her way in a dark room.

'Did you see any animals near the hut? Do you remember if it was very windy?'

To each of Baín's questions, she shook her head. Then her face tensed for a moment, as though she had glimpsed a faint light in the darkness.

'Maybe this sounds silly,' she said, 'but I remember a night, it was a while ago now . . . It wasn't cold. I was only wearing a cardigan, but I didn't feel cold. I was upstairs. He was down in the basement, with Lucía.'

'OK. What else happened that night?'

'When he left me upstairs, I usually tried to face away from the hole in the roof, because the wind blew in. But, that night, the sky was clear and it was warm.'

'Go on,' Baín encouraged. He placed the tape recorder in his lap so it would pick up Ana's voice clearly. 'Did you see the moon?'

'No, I couldn't see it from where I was . . . But I saw some shooting stars. Before . . . Papá and I used to lie out in the garden and stare up at the sky; he said, if we saw a shooting star, we could make a wish.'

Baín leaned back again, trying to hide his frustration. He hoped that Ana would say something more than that she'd missed being with her father.

'I made a million wishes . . . but I never wished to get out of there.' Ana looked at him, her dark eyes like black holes. 'I didn't think that would ever happen.'

Baín smiled. With Ana, he fluctuated between affection and suspicion; there were moments when she seemed so confident, and others when she was as vulnerable as a wounded animal.

'Why are you lying to us?' he asked. 'Are you trying to protect him?'

Ana stroked her shaved head; the scar left by the operation was no longer covered. A zigzag line of sutures held together the scalp where the incision had been. Her dark eyes contrasted with the paleness of her skin, which had not seen the sun in many years. Baín did not look away from those deep, dark holes. He wanted to know what was hidden inside, to light a torch that would illuminate her true story.

'Why would you say that?' Ana whispered, with a shiver.

'Right now, I think it's because you're scared. You're ashamed to remember what happened there. Please, don't lie to me anymore.'

'I'm trying to remember everything . . . Maybe the stuff about the shooting stars is stupid, but it happened . . .'

'I don't care about the stars, Ana. I'm talking about him.'

'I told you, I never saw his face. The helmet—'

'You also told me he never touched you.'

Instinctively, Ana hugged herself. Her mother's jumper was still a little too big for her, and her body seemed to be hiding inside. Nervously, she looked down at the floor, as though at any moment a monster might appear from under the bed.

'Maybe you don't realize,' Baín went on, 'but the tests they did at the hospital . . . You remember? Those tests can tell us a lot of things. For example, they tell us that you have had sex.'

As he said this, Baín remembered that Ana had been an eleven-year-old girl when she was abducted. What had she experienced since then? What had she learned? What things seemed strange to her that would seem normal to anyone else? At first, her answer came as an inaudible whisper. Baín had to ask her to repeat what she had said.

'It was just once.'

'Are you sure?' Baín pressed her.

The tears made it impossible for her to say more. Baín knew she would have felt more comfortable with Sara, but this was precisely why he had decided to conduct the interview. He did not want Ana to be wrapped in cotton wool; he needed to see how she reacted when there was no compassion, no sympathy.

'I know that this is difficult. You're scared, you're crying . . . But you're safe, Ana. But Lucía hasn't been so lucky. Maybe that's the way you want it—'

'That's not true!' Ana screamed. She looked up and glared at Santiago Baín. 'It was just once. A long time ago.'

The door flew open and a panicked Raquel rushed in. 'Are you all right?' she asked, and turned to Baín. 'What's going on here?'

'Please . . .' Baín said.

He gestured for Burgos, who was standing on the threshold, to take Raquel out of the room and close the door. When Burgos took her arm, Raquel struggled.

'Why is she crying?' Raquel said as the officer led her out. The door closed and their voices became muffled.

Ana was sobbing. Her cheeks were wet. A teardrop hung from her lips, but there was still that confidence in her expression. When Baín turned towards her, she was looking straight at him.

'He got angry with Lucía. That's why, one day, he made her go upstairs and he stayed in the basement with me. He didn't like being with me. He couldn't stand me. He was only interested in Lucía. He only did it to hurt her. He threw me on the bed. He told me to take my clothes off. At first, he didn't touch me. He wanted me to touch myself, to stroke myself . . . all over. But then he took his clothes off too . . . He made me kneel with my back to him. I wanted to get out of there . . . to be anywhere except on that bed. I was afraid and I was ashamed; it felt like lots of people were watching me . . . and it was all my fault. I knew this was something I would never be able to forget.'

Baín listened without interrupting. Her story had brought her to a precipice, and here she hesitated.

'He hurt me,' she said, staring blankly into space.

'And it never happened again?'

'No. When he left and Lucía came back down . . . she begged me to forgive her. She begged me. She said she was sorry, that it would never happen again . . .'

'Did you notice anything about him physically? When it happened, I mean.'

'I closed my eyes. When he made me get on my knees, I closed my eyes.'

Baín realized that he believed her. 'I'm sorry . . .' he said. 'This must be . . . I know it must be very hard to talk about this. But I need to know.'

Ana did not say anything, but she seemed calmer, her body and her face relaxed. Baín got up to go.

'Are you going to tell my father?' Ana asked as he left the room.

The charred basement of the mountain hut was like a wound in the earth. A savage bite.

Summer had brought a lush green to Monteperdido, which for most of the year was buried under a white mantle of snow. Only for a few months was this burgeoning life on display. Trees and plants brought forth blazing colours, animals gambolled beneath the trees, among the brambles, on the mountain slopes. Roe deer and wild boar. Hundreds of species of birds. Silent witnesses to what had happened, Sara thought. They knew the brute who had sunk his teeth into the ground here.

His prints were somewhere in that hole, which had now been taped off by the forensics team searching it for trace evidence. The flames had reached high temperatures as they burned away the wooden beams, causing the roof of the basement to collapse, and the rush of fresh oxygen had made it burn even hotter. The stone walls of the shelter had contained the blaze, acting like a fire pit, preventing it from spreading to the nearby trees. But everything inside had been gutted. Reduced to ashes that made it impossible to know what had happened in that hole. Five years had been utterly wiped out. This was the gist of the preliminary forensic report.

Sara pictured a cremated body. Family members on a hill, opening the urn and scattering ashes to the four winds. The physical remains of the dead person vanishing into the air. Ashes could no longer tell a tale, whereas a corpse contained the story of a life. The delicate grooves on the bones, notches that marked out every fracture. Skin and internal organs held details of diet and habits. Everything was written on the mortal remains, written in a secret language that only science could decode. Six feet under, the corpse was still waiting to tell its story. When the time came, Sara thought, she wanted to burn. To disappear completely, to rub out her own story.

She had woken with a bitter taste in her throat. She could not remember how many coffees she had drunk during the night, while she reread the original case files of Monteperdido's Guardia Civil. Too many. When Víctor came to the hotel to collect her, she had felt lightheaded. As though she were sleepwalking. She had barely had an hour's sleep. It was not lack of sleep that made her miserable, though, but lack of adrenaline. Víctor had given her the witness statements his officers had been gathering and she'd read them as they drove up to the hut. They were depressingly humdrum.

'Are you likely to be long? I can come back and collect you,' Víctor said, after they had been at the mountain hut for almost an hour.

Sara gave a last look at the hole and then headed back towards Víctor's jeep. 'Could you drive me up to Posets?' she asked as she climbed in.

Most of the files Víctor had given her related to Álvaro Montrell. For months, he had been the prime suspect in the investigation, and the media had taken it for granted that he would be charged with his daughter's murder, even though Ana's body had not been found and there was no physical evidence linking Álvaro to the abduction. Only a pile of circumstantial details that merely proved he had lied to the police in his first statement.

He'd stated that he had been in his office at Valle del Ésera Secondary School when Ana disappeared. He had lied. Why? It was possible that, at first, he had assumed this was just a prank, and Ana would show up at any moment. But Álvaro Montrell stuck to his lie. During the first reconstruction, the police spoke to Ximena, whom everyone in the village called 'the Colombian'. She recounted the argument with Lucía, who had apparently teased her for being in love with her older brother, Quim. They had fought. Lucía threw a stone that hit Ximena on the head. Furious, she'd raced back to the school. Her anger was directed as much at Ana, who had done nothing to defend her. She ran to Álvaro's office, but he was not there. The school janitor had calmed her down, cleaned the slight graze on her forehead and taken her home.

When the police confronted him with Ximena's statement, Álvaro tried to brazen out the lie. He had gone for a walk and come back, he claimed, but he had not seen Ximena. That day, he had arrived home later than usual. By the time he'd parked his car and gone inside, Raquel had already called the police. She'd tried to phone Álvaro, but he had not answered his mobile. He claimed to have left it at school.

No one believed him. For the period between five p.m., when the girls left school, and ten p.m., when he arrived home, Álvaro Montrell had no alibi. It was then that Raquel began to doubt her husband. She told one of the officers that Álvaro had been in a strange mood when he arrived home. Tense. He had told her he didn't want dinner, had taken a shower and gone to bed. He had barely listened to what Raquel was saying: Ana had disappeared. Later, when he realized that Ana was not simply late home, he too had been scared. Or so Raquel thought. But still the doubts crept in.

While investigating him, the police had tried to get a sense of his relationship with his daughter and with Lucía. The girls were neighbours, best friends. Everything seemed normal. Álvaro got along well with his daughter; no one had noticed anything unusual in his behaviour towards Lucía. They had intended to arrest him and take him in for more serious questioning, but, checking his phone records, they discovered that, shortly before five p.m. that day, he had received a call. It had been brief, barely a minute. They identified the phone that had made the call: it belonged to Elisa Nerín.

Sara remembered that, reading the files in her room in La Renclusa, she had tried to picture Elisa, the shy girl who worked at the reception desk, when she was five years younger – when she was just sixteen. Turning the page in the file, she had found a photograph. It was Elisa, and yet it was a different person. People change as they grow up, Sara thought; their personalities become more apparent in their features. With Elisa, the reverse seemed to have happened. The sixteen-year-old girl in the photograph had a mischievous, almost provocative look about her – a smug half-smile. She was very sure of herself. But, with the passing years, her face had become less distinct; now she was the timid girl who worked on the reception desk. Sara had seen only a flicker of that earlier self-assurance, when Elisa had come out of the room where the French boys were staying.

From the moment people knew about the phone call from Elisa, all eyes turned to Álvaro. Not just those of the police, but everyone in the village. The file mentioned that, on several occasions, Joaquín

Castán had demanded that Álvaro be arrested. Elisa's statement –
which she had given at Monteperdido police station, accompanied
by her father, Marcial Nerín – buried Álvaro a little deeper still.
Sara found a transcript of the police interview with Elisa among the
papers Víctor had given her.

'Were you with Álvaro that afternoon?'
'No, I phoned him, but he didn't come to see me.'
'Elisa, you're not to blame for any of this. You've done nothing
    wrong. We just need you to tell us the truth.'

Sara could not suppress a shudder of disgust as she read the statement. The officer conducting the interview exonerated Elisa, but
he took it for granted that Álvaro had committed a crime – 'done
something wrong'. He was leading the witness, not trying to get to
the truth. Further on in the transcript, she read:

'What was the nature of your relationship with Álvaro?'
'He teaches me History of Art.'
'Anything else?'
'For the tape: the witness has not answered.'
'Let me put it another way: did he ever see you outside school?'
'Yes.'
'And he was nice to you, wasn't he?'
'Álvaro is a nice guy.'
'He can't hurt you now, Elisa. What are you afraid of? Your father
    is here with you, and you know me. Are you OK?'
'Yes.'
'Then tell us about your relationship with Álvaro.'

'We were in love.'

'Is that what he told you?'

'Yes.'

'Did the two of you ever have sex?'

Elsewhere in the file, there was a medical report confirming that Elisa had had sexual relations. Sara could not help but regret the wasted opportunity the interview had been. Elisa was confessing to a romantic relationship with her teacher, in front of her father, guided by a police officer, who – reading between the lines – was simply trying to confirm that Álvaro had harmed Ana and Lucía. What was the value of Elisa's statement? No greater than if it had been written by the police officer himself.

From this point in the interview, Elisa's father constantly interrupted:

'Why don't you go arrest that son of a bitch? If you leave him walking around out there, I swear, I won't be responsible for my actions.'

'Marcial, please, let us finish.'

'What more evidence do you need?'

'If you're having trouble dealing with this, you can wait outside.'

The prior of the Cofradía, Marcial Nerín. Sara remembered seeing him earlier that day at the Hunting Society. In one of his reports, Pujante had said he was hanging around outside Simón Herrera's house. He had been one of the people who had triggered Pilar's suicide.

Five years earlier, when the police were questioning his daughter, his presence had led to the interview breaking down and her statement remaining incomplete. The girl had mentioned, however, that her family had a property further down the valley, in Val de Sacs, a village that was little more than a string of dilapidated houses on the road between Monteperdido and Barbastro. This was a place that had seen little benefit from the rise of tourism in the area. No one ever used the house, and Álvaro and Elisa had turned it into a love nest for their furtive trysts.

On the day the girls disappeared, Elisa had called Álvaro from the house. She had bunked school and caught the morning bus to Val de Sacs. She had waited for him all afternoon until, sometime around eight p.m., deciding that Álvaro was not coming, she left to catch the last bus home. Elisa's account left Álvaro Montrell without an alibi. It left a gap of fours hours in which no one had seen or spoken to him. Four hours during which he could have done anything with the girls.

He had been arrested. Interrogated. He had tried to change his initial statement, claiming that he had been with Elisa, but had not mentioned it earlier because the girl had been drunk, in no fit state to go home, and was terrified that her father would be angry. He had tried to protect his pupil. This was how he always referred to her: 'my pupil', as though, with these words, he could distance himself from her. The officer who conducted the interview did not believe him. Nor did he believe Álvaro when he said he had not had sex with Elisa. Álvaro spent several days in the cells.

However, there was not enough evidence to charge him. No footprints or D.N.A. had been recovered from the area of the pine forest where the girls had disappeared. The police had no choice but to release him, at which point Monteperdido rose up like a wounded animal and lashed out at the person it believed to be guilty: Álvaro

Montrell. According to the case files, less than three days after his release, Álvaro reported an assault to the Guardia Civil. Joaquín Castán had confronted Álvaro, had beaten him and threatened to kill him. If he had not carried out this threat, it was only because both their wives had intervened. But the situation was untenable. Raquel had requested a meeting with the officer leading the investigation, during which she asked him to swear to her that Álvaro had not hurt Ana or Lucía. The officer could not do so. He was frustrated that he could not find the evidence that would allow him to take Álvaro into custody. He suggested to Raquel that it might be better if she did not continue to live with Álvaro in the same house.

A few days later, Álvaro was fired from his job at the school, and shortly afterwards he left the village. When, some months later, the officer leading the investigation was replaced, his successor noticed that all efforts had been focused on Ana's father, ignoring all other lines of inquiry. A theory was gaining ground that the culprit might have been a stranger. Someone from outside the valley, possibly associated with a criminal network. It was a less painful theory, Sara thought. The wolf comes from without; the wolf is not family.

'Why was Álvaro Montrell never charged with child abuse?' Sara asked Víctor as they drove up to Posets.

'You mean because of Elisa Nerín?'

'Did he have relationships with other girls?'

'No, just Elisa. The school launched an investigation, but—'

'Let me guess. None of the other girls had been given special treatment. Just Elisa.'

Monteperdido was far behind them now, as they drove up the steep, twisting road. Víctor slowed the jeep as the road grew steeper.

To the right, a narrow ravine dropped away into darkness. The mountain peaks that previously seemed to soar into the heavens were now so close it seemed possible to reach out and touch them. But this narrow gorge running alongside the road reminded them just how high they were. Sara felt as though she were on a floating island. A vast slab of land and mountain, floating in the air.

'This ravine is called Oscuros de Balced,' Víctor explained, seeing her peer into the dark, narrow gorge. 'In summer, a lot of tourists come to do abseiling here . . . At the bottom, there is a river that flows into the Ésera . . .'

Sara found Víctor's explanation comforting; it connected this place with a place she already knew: the valley and the river.

'Although, this summer has been a little weird; a lot of the hotel reservations have been cancelled,' Víctor went on. 'I suppose what's going on hardly makes for good publicity . . .' He took a narrow bridge across the river. 'We'll be in Posets in about ten minutes. The office of Gaizka's tour company is just outside the village.'

The trees had disappeared. The green mantle that covered both sides of the road was like the skin of a chameleon, trying to camouflage its true nature. At this altitude, the ground was cold and flinty and hostile to life.

'Elisa Nerín had a breakdown,' Víctor said as they turned off the road on to a dirt track. 'I don't know whether you've had a chance to talk to her at the hotel. But it really affected her. She dropped out of school, she never graduated. Her father was afraid of making things worse – that's why he spared her the ordeal of a trial.'

'Maybe there wasn't enough evidence to convict Álvaro.'

'Or maybe he did what was best for his daughter,' Víctor said.

He stopped the jeep. They had arrived at Gaizka's tour office. It was a small wooden prefab. A faded sign, pinned to the roof, read, *Adventures In Posets.*

'I need to get back to Monteperdido,' Víctor said. 'Do you want me to send someone to pick you up?'

'Please. In a couple of hours.'

The cold, clean air coursed through her lungs, so pure it felt as though it might be dangerous. She heard the crunch of tyres on gravel as Víctor drove off. There was another car parked outside the office: a Nissan four-wheel drive pickup. Even the windows were spattered with mud. What was visible of the bodywork was a greenish brown, but the driver's door was white – probably stolen from a breaker's yard to replace the original. Gaizka's office was open. Sara went inside.

When Álvaro Montrell left Monteperdido, he also severed all contact with everyone who lived there. Among the many complaints Joaquín Castán lodged with the Guardia Civil was the fact that the only suspect was missing without trace. Now they knew that he had never been far away. Like the girls.

Stepping into the tour office, she saw a boy packing a rucksack. The counter was strewn with helmets, ropes and roaming rings. He looked as though he had packed and emptied the rucksack a hundred times and still could not find a way to make everything fit. Hearing Sara's footsteps, he looked up for a second and then went back to his task.

'Looking for someone? I'm just saying, because the office is actually closed,' he explained.

'I'm a police officer.' Sara showed him her warrant card.

He did not bother to look, but simply nodded and carried on trying to stuff a safety harness into the rucksack. 'Good for you,' he said as he continued to struggle. 'Listen, I've got to run, OK? I'm meeting a tour group in, like, ten minutes, and I'm already late . . .'

He was like a hermit, or a lone lumberjack living in the forest, with long hair that tangled with his thick beard. Noguera was not even thirty and he was working as an abseiling guide for Gaizka. Only for the summer, he explained. 'The rest of the year they can go fuck themselves,' were his precise words. He seemed keen to badmouth Gaizka, and Sara sat down and listened.

'The guy's a wanker and one of these days he's going to get us in deep shit. Have you seen the equipment?' he said, lifting up the ropes. 'These are, like, a hundred years old. I don't know how many times we've repaired them. As for the karabiners . . . Jesus fuck . . . You can't even trust the clasps—'

'Why don't you say something to him?'

'Might as well piss in the wind. Anyway, the guy doesn't know shit about canyons and abseiling,' he sneered.

'Maybe you should just quit. If anything happens, you'd be responsible.'

'You bet your life. You can call him all you like, he never comes. He shows up whenever it suits. Even then, you'd better cross your fingers that he's sober. And if there's a problem with a customer, he's never around.' Noguera dropped a snap hook on the counter and snorted. 'I don't know how the fuck Álvaro gets everything into these fucking rucksacks.'

'So he's not around?'

A mischievous smile appeared in Noguera's thick beard. He looked at Sara like a little boy who had just worked out the secret to a magician's trick.

'You're here to see him?' he whispered.

Sara pretended that he had found her out. She lowered her voice to a confidential tone. 'I don't have a search warrant or anything. Do you mind if I take a look around inside?'

'He's one weird dude, Álvaro. I've never seen him outside this place,' Noguera muttered. 'There is a red thread that connects those who are destined to meet . . .' He raised an eyebrow as though this made his intentions clear. Then he slung the rucksack over his shoulder and stuffed everything that would not fit into a bag. 'If you show up here and the door is open, it's not my problem,' he said as he walked out.

Sara waited until the guide had left. There were people who hated the police, who despised them for no reason, and others who liked to be on the sidelines of an investigation, as though hoping that something they said or did might provide the key to unravelling a mystery. *I often saw him take out two, sometimes three rubbish bags at a time,* an elderly lady had told Sara during an investigation many years ago. Like Noguera, she too had raised one eyebrow and dropped her voice to a whisper. On another case, involving a missing teenage girl, a man had hissed, *My niece says he used to do these strange drawings. Sort of satanic, like.* Stupidity did not bother Sara Campos, but she had no time for those eager to badmouth others.

Noguera was probably trying to get even with Gaizka for something or other, Sara thought as she stepped behind the counter. What are you expecting to find, Sara? A side door that led into the equipment store. She flicked the light switch. Fluorescent striplights glared down on old canoes, rock-climbing equipment; in one corner, there was a pile of muddy bobsleighs. At the back was a door, through which it was possible to see the end of a bed. Sara assumed that this was the room where Álvaro had been living. She walked through the storeroom. On the opposite wall, a long line of black helmets hung from metal hooks.

'Get out of my house!' Montserrat screamed.

Raquel took a step backwards, tripped on the doorstep and almost fell. She could feel her ears burning with embarrassment.

'What are you doing here?' Montserrat was still screaming as Joaquín held her in his arms, trying to restrain her.

Raquel attempted to explain that she just wanted to know how they were, but the only sound that came from her mouth was an incomprehensible stuttering. Burgos was standing outside in the garden, hesitating as to whether he should stay here or follow Ana, who had gone home.

'Tell her to talk!' Montserrat howled, managing to wrench one of her arms from her husband's grip and pointing it towards where Ana had been standing.

Stupid, Raquel thought. How did you expect them to react? She had thought that it would do Montserrat good to talk to Ana. As though her daughter could be a comfort to her, just as Montserrat had been to Raquel for so long. *We're your family,* Montserrat had said to her when times were tough. Looking at her now, she seemed like a stranger. Raquel was no longer listening to the words, which were little more than a wail. Joaquín held his wife in his arms and pleaded with Raquel to leave them alone.

'You know he's not supposed to be here, don't you?' he said.

Raquel could not find the words to explain how she felt. Something was broken. A trust in how others saw her. A sense of seeing herself reflected through their eyes. All that was gone. She heard the telephone ring in her house.

'You want me to answer that?' Burgos asked from the doorway.

Raquel shook her head. The phone seemed to ring louder.

'You know it wasn't supposed to be you,' she heard as she reached the garden gate.

A selfish, ungrateful woman: this was what Raquel had seen in Montserrat's eyes. Why the sudden change? How could Raquel be blamed for what was down to fate? But she did not delude herself. She had seen the signs before Ana reappeared – when she had started to spend more time with Ismael, when she had stepped back from the Foundation. It was as though Montserrat resented her for wanting to live.

'Are you all right?' Burgos asked as he came into the house.

'Fine,' she said, and only then realized that the telephone had stopped ringing. 'Where's Ana?'

'Upstairs,' Burgos said as he headed up.

The police-sketch officer appeared from the kitchen. 'I was just getting a glass of water. Hope you don't mind,' he said as he collected his things from the living room.

Raquel saw his sketchpad on the hall table. He had created a portrait of Lucía based on Ana's description. And yet, to Raquel, it was the face of a complete stranger. The sketch – a tracery of pencil lines attempting to define the curve of the chin, the slant of the eyes, the facial expression – had a ghostly quality about it. More an apparition than a real person. She took out her mobile phone and snapped a picture. The sketch artist was still in the living room when the phone rang again.

Quim no longer knew where to go to find peace. The shouts followed him like tongues of fire. He closed the door to his room, but still he could hear them. His mother was sobbing. His father was making promises – about what? It didn't matter. Quim tried not to listen. They were sick – addicted to tragedy and drama. He was convinced they were happy that Ana was the one who had reappeared. This way, they could wallow in their tears, like pigs in shit. He opened the bedroom window. The roof of the back porch was less than a metre away. He jumped across and then climbed down to the ground. This was his emergency exit. For some time, he had been using it as a way to go out without anyone knowing. Not that anyone bothered to look for him now. He did not need to worry that his parents would come up to his room. They wouldn't.

'What an acrobat!'

Quim was startled by the voice. He looked around, but could see no one.

'You're getting colder,' the voice teased, and this time he realized it was coming from the first floor. Ana was leaning out of her window and smiling at him as she stroked her shaved head.

He felt himself tremble. Just nerves, he thought, angry with himself. Why did he feel this way? Why did he have to feel anything? He didn't care that she was home. Sorry, he thought. I don't care that you're back from the dead. But he said nothing. He turned around and walked away, slowly, despite the terrible urge to run.

Ana stayed at the window for a moment longer and watched as Quim turned left at the gate. She watched his shadow flickering in the gaps of the wooden fence, and then he disappeared. She did not want to look away from the window. She knew the officer would be standing guard at the door. And she wondered whether her life had really changed. The wail of the police sirens forced her to turn around.

Gaizka's face was puffy, his bloodshot eyes floating above the dark bags beneath. His skin was taut over his cheekbones, but elsewhere it was slack and flabby. He was famished. His arms hung from the short-sleeved shirt like dried branches. He reeled and staggered as though he might collapse at any moment. Though he had only recently turned thirty, he looked older. Payback for too many nights like last night, Sara thought. This morning, having been in his office, she had tracked him down and brought him back here. He did not smell of alcohol. Only of stale smoke.

'Are you OK? Can you answer a few questions for me?' Sara said, ushering him inside.

Gaizka leaned both hands on the counter, like a castaway who had finally reached dry land. 'Yeah, sure . . .' he muttered, looking up and giving her a fatuous smile. He must have realized how ridiculous he looked, because he burst out laughing. 'Sorry . . . It's just . . . I should probably get some sleep . . . or take a shower . . . Do I stink?'

'This will only take a minute. Can we go into the stockroom?'

'If we have to.' He tried to stand up straight and follow Sara, but the cocaine was still buzzing in his brain.

'Who's in charge of the stockroom?' he heard Sara ask.

'Álvaro . . . Though, obviously . . . Well, now . . . I think he's probably quit.' He laughed at his own joke. What did he care about Álvaro now?

'When I arrived, the door was open, and, while I was looking for you, I noticed these helmets . . .'

Gaizka followed Sara's finger. The helmets had always looked to him like severed heads. 'We use them for paintballing . . . You know, grown men running round with splatter guns . . .' Gaizka explained.

'How long have you had them?'

'I don't know . . . Since we opened . . . It was one of the first activities we offered. Paintballing and sledging . . . but then I realized that I had to feed the huskies all summer, so I gave up the sledging.'

Sara scribbled something on her notepad and left the stockroom. Gaizka felt a breeze as she passed, a faint whiff of perfume. And, suddenly, he felt weak. Alone. He looked at the officer in alarm.

'We're done here, for the moment. We may need to conduct a more thorough search,' Sara said without looking at him.

Álvaro had spent the morning wandering around Monteperdido. He stared at the ground, imagining his feet stepping into those same tracks they had left here four years earlier. He remembered how, as a boy, he would spend summers in a village in Castellón. Every September, when he went back to Zaragoza, he would go into his house and everything would seem both strange and yet familiar: the hall, the kitchen, his bedroom. He knew that he was home, even though everything seemed strange. It was this same sense of security, of being where he belonged, that he felt now, as he wandered around Monteperdido. He bought some croissants in the bakery on Avenida de Posets and, without realizing, found himself whistling – the same song he had whistled the first time he'd walked around this village in the snow: 'Fox in the Snow' by Belle and Sebastian. How many times had he felt like that? Starving, like a fox in the snow, prepared to do anything to avoid starvation, to avoid freezing to death.

He wandered away from the church and crossed the old bridge. The Ésera flowed serenely from the mountains. He was reclaiming control. Not only of the situation, but of his life. And this time he would not lose it. Until now, he had not lived in the moment. When he was young, he had been obsessed with the future; later, he had been preoccupied by the past. Always starving. 'Today' was something that had never existed for him.

He strolled away from the village. The road leading to his house was crawling with journalists, so he decided to go via the forest path where Ana had disappeared, a shortcut he had used ever since Ana was at school. He was eager to be home with Raquel and Ana, sitting around the kitchen table, sharing the warm croissants. The light beneath the branches was dappled with green. He looked up at the sky obscured by the treetops. It was beautiful, he thought, this forest.

By the time Sara arrived at the police station, Baín had already begun the interrogation. Before entering the interview room, she saw Álvaro Montrell through the two-way mirror. He looked tense, but not overwhelmed. On the table were photos of the paintball helmets and a drawing the sketch artist had made from Ana's description of the kidnapper. They were identical. Víctor was sitting next to her, watching through the two-way mirror. He was the one who had handcuffed Álvaro outside his front door. On the table in front of him was a bag of croissants.

'Has he admitted anything?'

'Nothing,' Víctor said, his eyes still fixed on what was happening next door.

Sara entered the interview room and sat next to Baín. Álvaro did not even look at her. He was staring at some indeterminate spot in the room, as though trying to work out what he was going to say next.

'This will go much easier if you help us out,' Baín said. 'Your daughter is safe, but we don't know where Lucía is. Or how she is.'

'I'm not the only person who has access to these helmets,' Álvaro said, as though for the hundredth time.

'You are in charge of the stockroom. Have you ever noticed one missing?'

'I only started working there four years ago. By that time, who-ever did this would already have had the helmet—'

'But you had been to Gaizka's place before then,' Sara inter-rupted. 'You were friends.'

'What does it matter what I say?' This time Álvaro looked Sara in the eye. 'Seems like you've already decided that I'm guilty—'

'Seems like you're not doing much to prove otherwise,' Baín cut him off. 'Why don't you tell us where you were the day your daugh-ter reappeared?'

'In my room. In Posets. There were no tours that day. No one called by. Perfect, isn't it? My alibi is a piece of shit.' Álvaro's frus-tration was beginning to get the better of him.

'How did you know she was in Barbastro hospital?'

'Gaizka phoned me.'

'Why didn't you tell anyone you were still living in the valley?'

'Do I really have to explain? Everyone was convinced that I'd kidnapped the girls. It's not like I had any friends left . . .'

'So why didn't you leave?'

Álvaro looked at Santiago Baín, and took a deep breath. 'I couldn't . . .' he muttered. 'Because of Ana.'

'Let's go back five years . . .' Baín said, searching for a file among the papers on the table. 'To the day of the abduction. You had no explanation for where you were then, either. You claimed you were with a pupil, Elisa Nerín . . . However—'

'She made up a whole pile of shit,' Álvaro interrupted Baín. 'Do we have to go over all this again?'

'Do you have any idea of the position you're in?' Baín pushed the files aside. 'You are unable to give a satisfactory account of your whereabouts on the day of the abduction, or on the day that Ana reappeared. You had access to the helmets . . . You might want to stop playing the injured party, otherwise I don't see you getting out of here.'

'I did go to see Elisa that day,' Álvaro stated. 'She'd been out all night at a party. She'd taken pills and she was still off her face . . . She was terrified of her father seeing her like that. I don't know if you've met Marcial . . . I was just trying to protect her.'

'Because of your relationship?'

'This whole thing about us having a relationship – she made it up,' Álvaro sneered.

Sara allowed Baín to lead the interview. Under the table, she was holding a bag. Waiting for the right moment.

'Why would she make up a story about you abusing her?' Baín asked. 'It hardly seems very clever, given her father was so strict.'

'Who said people always do the clever thing?'

'So, in your opinion, Elisa was trying to hurt you?'

'It's possible.'

'So, we should should just disregard Elisa's statement. She was lying when she said she was having a relationship with you, and that she didn't see you on the day the girls disappeared.'

'That's right.' Álvaro looked at the officers; they seemed to believe him. Was somebody finally going to listen to his version of events?

'You never had a relationship with Elisa Nerín. Not then, and not since,' Sara said, as though keen to get past the subject.

'Of course not,' Álvaro said emphatically, and he felt himself begin to relax.

'In that case, why did I find this in your room in Posets?'

Sara laid the sealed evidence bag on the table. Inside was a hair slide decorated with a purple velvet bird. She pushed the bag towards Álvaro.

'Elisa makes hair slides like this. Pretty, don't you think?' she said as she gauged his reaction.

'A while back . . .' Álvaro stammered. 'Maybe a year ago . . . Elisa came to the tour office. I don't know how she found out I was there . . . We talked for a bit. I told her I didn't want to see her again . . . When she left, I noticed the hair slide. Maybe she dropped it . . . I don't know.'

'And, during this conversation, did she apologize for lying about you in her statement?'

'Yes.' Álvaro was aware of how delicate the situation seemed.

'How convenient.' Sara smiled. 'Then there won't be any problem; we'll just have a word with her. If she confirms your story, you've got your alibi.'

Álvaro tensed. He was tired of this intimidation. The same suspicions, the same cynicism he had faced five years ago. Accusations like arrows in his side.

'Are you going to keep me in custody?' he asked.

★

Raquel collapsed on to the sofa and stared at the floor. She felt an emptiness in her stomach that made her dizzy. Officer Burgos came over and took her hand. Raquel wanted to jerk her hand away, but she did not have the strength. She was like a threadbare rag doll. The police sirens still echoed in her head. She knew she should go into the kitchen, be with her daughter. Why did she not dare to ask Ana straight out? Was it your father who hurt you?

Ana angrily got up, knocking her plate off the table. A slice of *candimus* skidded across the floor, leaving a trail of cream in its wake. The china plate danced over the tiles, making a shrill screech, before finally coming to a stop.

'This is how they go about finding Lucía?' she yelled. 'By arresting Papá?'

Burgos followed the girl as she ran upstairs. 'They just need to ask him a few questions, Ana,' he said. 'He hasn't been charged with anything.'

'But they won't let him see me!' she screamed. She went into the bathroom and slammed the door.

Burgos stood outside.

'Give me room to breathe!'

He almost went off the road. The tyres screeched on the side of the road. On the right, behind the barrier, was a deep ravine. Gaizka tried to focus on his driving. He had to stop panicking. There was no traffic. The police cordon had stopped the usual flow of tourists. Most of them had found places to stay lower down the valley, in Ordial or Val de Sacs. Only a few had honoured their reservations in Monteperdido. Business had fallen steeply compared to the previous summer. Noguera had called him to complain; he worked on commission. Fuck him, Gaizka thought as he pulled in to the Hotel La Guardia. The road narrowed as it climbed the steep slopes towards the peak of La Kregüeña. Rounding the bend, the hotel appeared on the left and the road trailed off into a dirt track. It was the highest inhabited spot in the valley. A former waypoint for pilgrims, it had been bought by a man called Vicente Serna who converted the building into a luxury hotel.

Gaizka found Serna at the lookout tower. Two hundred metres from the hotel, a cleft in the mountain offered the most spectacular aerial view of the valley. Far below, like beads on a rosary, lay the villages of Posets, Monteperdido and Ordial, connected by the winding silver thread of the River Ésera.

'The police are going house to house. I have to do something,' Gaizka said by way of a greeting.

Serna looked at him in surprise.

'I haven't got time for pleasantries about how beautiful the fucking valley looks from here, Serna.'

'So, what do you want me to do?'

'I need to get out of the valley. Just until this blows over. You've got a couple of industrial units down in Barbastro . . . Let me use one of them—'

'You've always been a fuck-up when it comes to business, Gaizka,' Serna grunted. 'It's at times like this that I wonder what I ever get for helping you out . . . Why should I give a shit that you're in trouble?'

Gaizka leaned on the parapet of the tower. The view made him feel powerful. As though he could reach out and crush everyone in the valley with his fist.

★

'I think you lost this,' Sara said, pushing the evidence bag containing the hair slide across the hotel reception desk.

Elisa looked at the purple bird, its eyes as big as eggs, its wings outstretched, its pink beak. She made to open the bag, but Sara stopped her.

'I can't give it back to you just yet.'

'Why not?' Elisa asked. She glanced nervously over Sara's shoulder, as though someone might come into the hotel lobby and see them.

'How long had you known that Álvaro Montrell was living in Posets?'

Elisa shrugged, shoved her hands into the pockets of her cardigan and glanced around, looking for some way out.

'I've got nothing to do with him.'

'Relax, Elisa,' Sara said, taking the girl's hand. 'I just want to know if you went to see him.'

She was like a reed whipped by the wind, Sara thought: always about to break, but always able to bend. Able to withstand sudden reversals.

'Some tourists who went on a day trip up there mentioned him. Must have been a year ago. They didn't know who he was,' Elisa said. 'I went up one night to see him.'

'Why?'

'You know what he did to me?' Elisa's fretful eyes met Sara's. There was no anger there, only self-assurance.

'What happened up there?'

'I told him to leave the valley. Told him that, if he didn't, I'd tell everyone where he was.'

'But you didn't. Why not?'

'I was scared.'

She was fragile once again. Sara had the impression that, beneath Elisa's skin, there were two different women. Mostly, she was a meek, shy girl. But from time to time there was a glimpse of another Elisa. Though she appeared only in flashes, she seemed to be in charge, to be able to steer the timid, docile Elisa as she pleased.

'What about now? Are you scared now?' Sara asked.

Nerín's Gunsmith's occupied the ground floor of a three-storey building on the corner of Plaza del Ayuntamiento. The peal of the bells hanging on the door echoed through the shop as Santiago Baín entered. The gun display cases in the window blocked all natural light, so the place appeared murky but for the yellowing strip-light over the counter.

'Hello?' Baín said, approaching the counter. He waited for a response, but none came.

He looked around and quickly noticed that the business was obviously on its last legs. The guns and accessories on the shelves looked as though they had recently been salvaged from an old trunk; the shop seemed more like a pawnbroker's. Suddenly, he felt uncomfortable; from the far end of the counter, an old woman in a wheelchair was staring at him. Baín smiled nervously.

'Hello. Is Marcial Nerín around?'

The woman did not answer. Her eyes continued to bore into him, though he was beginning to think that she was looking through him, at some distant point. He took a step to one side, out of the woman's line of vision, and she did not react: she sat motionless in her chair. Baín wondered whether she might be blind.

'She doesn't really understand what's going on,' Marcial Nerín said as he came through from the back office. 'Alzheimer's. She's had it for three years. Within months, she started to forget things, she didn't recognize people . . . This is how she is now. She still makes the *disná* . . .'

'Every mother likes to feed her kids,' Baín said. 'I'm sorry. She is your mother, isn't she?'

Marcial nodded, a little uneasy to discover that Baín understood *patués*.

'*Charré prou mal el patués*,' the inspector said. 'It's easier for me if we speak Spanish.'

Marcial Nerín went over to his mother and laid a blanket over her knees. The way he moved reminded Baín of an animal, a boar wandering through the forest. He treated his mother with great tenderness, like a brute beast trying not to harm a baby with its clumsy paws.

'We're asking routine questions of all the neighbours, as I'm sure you know.'

Marcial nodded and gave him a wary look, as though struggling not to say what he thought of this particular decision by the police.

'It's just protocol. If you can remember, can you tell me where you were the day the girls disappeared? And also on the day that Ana was found?'

'I told the officers who came here five years ago where I was.'

'Would you mind telling me?'

'I was here, in the shop. I was working.'

Baín made a note on his pad and smiled, as though none of this had any importance. 'Is there much game around Monteperdido?'

'Red deer, roe deer, chamois goat, boar . . . Can't complain.'

'It must bring a lot of money to the village. Hunting licences, shotguns . . .' Baín gestured to the display cases.

Marcial knew exactly what the officer meant, and as he packed away a box of cartridges lying on the counter, he was forced to admit that he did not particularly benefit from the popularity of hunting. Most hunters bought their equipment in the city, in specialist shops that he could not compete with.

'Soon as I find a buyer, I'm selling the place,' Marcial said. 'I've been doing this too many years.'

'Your daughter isn't interested in taking over the business?' Baín met Marcial's suspicious expression with a smile intended to signal that this was just small talk. 'My partner and I are staying at La Renclusa . . . where Elisa works . . . I'm sure running this place would be better than cleaning hotel rooms.'

'Children seem to want to do anything except what their parents do,' Marcial said curtly.

'My father was a lawyer, and I can tell you that the last thing I wanted to be was a lawyer,' Baín joked, and then, without dropping his friendly tone, he added, 'Though he never beat me just for not following in his footsteps—'

'They were different times,' Marcial cut him short. He stopped tidying away the things on the counter and stared hard at Baín. Serious, as though daring the inspector to ask the question on his lips.

'It can't have been easy, bringing up a daughter on your own.'

'Bringing up a daughter is never easy.'

Baín nodded sympathetically. He cleared his throat, as though he found it difficult to broach the subject, when in fact it was not.

'We've been going through the old case files of the investigation, including those detailing the relationship between your daughter and Álvaro Montrell.'

'That bastard took advantage of my daughter. I don't know what else I can say. I don't like seeing him back here in the village; I don't suppose any father would, who'd been through what I went through.'

'But there was insufficient evidence to press charges: there was no proof of the relationship.'

'Laws are one thing, life is something different. Don't tell me you don't know that.'

'Oh, I do,' Baín conceded. 'That's why we're here: so that laws can reflect life.'

'I'll believe that when I see Álvaro Montrell sitting in a cell.'

Baín could hardly blame the man for being bitter. It was something he had often witnessed: fathers watching helplessly while the monsters who hurt their children were set free because of some judicial loophole. By his silence, Baín conceded the point to Marcial, but before he left, he added, 'Oh, I forgot: I also need to know where you were the day we found Ana.'

'I was in Barbastro. In the hospital. My mother is on dialysis and I have to take her there a couple of days a week.'

Santiago Baín looked at Marcial's mother, eaten up by illness, confined to a wheelchair, defying death the way a guilty man insists on his innocence when all the evidence is against him.

Her mobile phone rang, but she ignored it. Montserrat was still swept up in a maelstrom of feelings that she loathed, yet could not put behind her: the envy, the bitterness, the rage . . . and a feeling of superiority she longed to shake off. Joaquín was constantly on the phone. He had called the police station and, when no one answered, he'd dialled the personal numbers of every officer, one by one, until he found out that Álvaro had been released. Montserrat picked up her phone and headed upstairs to bed. She used the phone as an alarm clock. She was on the stairs when she saw she had a message. She assumed it was an apology from Raquel. She hesitated before opening it. A picture appeared on the screen. A pencil drawing. *This is your daughter,* Raquel had written. *I feel sure you'll be able to hug her soon.*

At first, Montserrat was unable to reconcile the lines of the portrait. They seemed random, disconnected. A mane of long straight hair fell over the shoulders, as though imprisoning the face. Almond eyes, turned down slightly at the corners; a strong nose that reminded her of Joaquín's; the lips curved into a gentle smile, which she assumed was artistic licence – what reason did Lucía have to smile? Montserrat gripped the banister as things whirled in her head and she tried to make sense of them.

'Joaquín!' she called down. 'It's Lucía.'

She quickly forwarded the message to his phone so he could see it.

The walls of the house were covered with pictures of Lucía, her dreams were filled with them; how could she replace that image of her daughter with this ghostly pencil sketch?

It was getting dark. Quim was sitting on the riverbank, dangling his feet in the water. The current tickled his bare skin. He took a toke on the spliff and passed it to Ximena.

'Have you seen her?' she asked, after inhaling deeply.

'In passing,' Quim said, still staring at the water.

'What does she look like?'

He shrugged. He thought of Ana at her bedroom window. *What an acrobat!* she had said. Remembering the word made him smile. Acrobat. Who said that? It was a ridiculous word for a girl who had been kidnapped at the age of eleven to know. How had she come across it? Perhaps he had expected her to be a little savage. A child, with a thick mane of matted hair, who spoke only in grunts, was covered in mud and ate with her hands. A woodland creature.

'Hey!' Ximena said, elbowing him. 'You're off your face, aren't you?' She smiled.

'Jesus – it's this hash. I don't know where Gaizka got it, but it's serious shit . . .'

'So, what is Ana like?'

'I don't know. Normal.'

Ximena giggled.

Quim looked at her, confused about why she was laughing.

'She gets kidnapped, spends five years locked up somewhere, and comes out normal . . .' Ximena managed to say when she finally stopped laughing.

The hotel lobby was empty. He rang the bell several times and it trilled through La Renclusa like an electrical current. He waited until he heard footsteps on the stairs. Elisa stood in the doorway.

'Álvaro,' she said. 'What are you doing here?'

'They won't let me go home. I need a room.'

You're in control, Álvaro thought to himself. This time, no one is going to take away what belongs to you. In a hunt, the prey has two choices: to run, or to kill the hunter. He had tried the first option and realized that it was futile. If you run, then you have to keep running forever. He felt safer here in Monteperdido. He knew the habits of the native animals. He could fight them.

They went up to the second floor in silence. Elisa walked ahead. Álvaro had a small rucksack of clothes slung over his shoulder. He waited for Elisa to open the door.

'Which floor are the police on?' he asked.

'The third,' Elisa said, avoiding his eyes. 'Breakfast is from eight a.m. to—'

'Why don't you come in?' Álvaro said, taking her by the arm. 'I'd like to talk to you.'

Elisa trembled. The pressure of Álvaro's hand sent a wave of heat coursing through her whole body. She felt dirty when she realized she was aroused.

'Come on . . .' Álvaro wheedled.

He gently pushed her into the room. He followed behind, closed the door and did not turn on the lamp. The only light was the yellowing glow from a moon obscured by clouds.

'The police have been asking about us,' he said.

'They've spoken to me too,' Elisa whispered.

Álvaro stepped closer; she could feel his warm breath.

'And what did you tell them?'

'I told them I'm scared of you.'

Elisa looked up and stared at Álvaro – at those blue eyes and the snow-white fringe that tumbled over his forehead like sea spray. Then she smiled.

'And it's true,' she said.

'You have to tell them the truth.' Álvaro hoped it did not sound like he was begging.

'And what is the truth?'

'Elisa, please. Don't you think this game has gone on long enough?'

'I still find it entertaining.'

Álvaro took a few steps away, bowed his head and sat on the bed.

'They won't let me near Ana,' he said, burying his face in his hands. 'I'm not allowed to hold my daughter, to talk to her. And she needs me, don't you see?'

When he looked up again, Álvaro's eyes were brimming with tears and Elisa thought about how summer thawed the mountain glaciers.

'Don't cry, please . . .' It pained her to see him like this. She went over and crouched down next to him, her hands on his knees.

'It's such a fucking mess,' Álvaro blubbed, and tried to wipe away his tears. 'Help me.'

She stroked his face; he laid his hand on hers. Gently, he guided it to his chest. When he let go, Elisa let her hand slide down his stomach. He took her chin and raised her head, brought his lips close to hers. He could feel her ragged breathing as he kissed her. She was trembling like a frightened child. When he drew back, he saw that she was crying.

'Are you scared?' he asked.

'I'm happy,' she said.

Álvaro laid her back on the bed. Never taking his eyes from hers, he unbuttoned her cardigan and took off her blouse and her bra. He kissed the skin under her breasts. She sighed. A light drizzle flecked the windowpane. A soundless rain.

The windscreen wipers flicked intermittently. It had been raining all night – a fine mist that left the windows and the ground damp, but was barely noticeable when you went outside. Sara had become aware of Víctor's decision that morning when Telmo came to collect her from the hotel.

'He's upriver with some people from the Cofradía,' the officer had said.

Staring through the windscreen, Telmo was explaining why Víctor had summoned all the officers of the Guardia Civil to dredge the river. Although the rain was barely noticeable now, there were storms forecast for the coming days.

'And the Guardia Civil are the only people who can do it?' Sara asked.

'The Cofradía are helping out. Around these parts, we all pitch in,' he said proudly.

They passed the turn-off to Posets and continued up the mountain until they came to a dirt road that brought them close to the riverbank. They drove through the birch grove.

'Right now, everything looks lovely and green, but you can't imagine what it's like living here in winter. We get two, sometimes three metres of snow. The roads are cut off. There are times you can't even open your own front door . . . Either someone helps you, or you're in big trouble.'

He pulled up next to the river's edge. A little higher up, some thirty people were working, on both banks. As they got closer, the noise of the dredgers became deafening. Rubbish bags, filled with branches and twigs, were piled up next to a van belonging to the Cofradía. There was a crest painted on the side: an eight-pointed star with the inscription *SANTA MARÍA DE LAUDE*. Sara remembered it from the design on the saucers at the Hunting Society. A moment later, she saw Víctor's jeep. Marcial Nerín was working with a group of men taking stones out of the river. In the shelter of the trees, the only sign of rain was the stippling of raindrops on the water. She had to shout to make herself heard. Marcial pointed further upstream, where the river narrowed under the weight of vegetation. 'Víctor's up there,' he said. She saw Rafael Grau, Montserrat's brother, and there were other faces familiar from the case files. Víctor was clearing the bank and did not hide his surprise when he saw her.

'You've come to lend a hand?' he said with a half-smile.

'I've been phoning you,' Sara said.

Víctor said nothing, but simply returned to his task. He waded into the river, the water up to his waist.

'If this needs to be cleaned up, fine, great,' Sara said, trying to remain calm. 'Call in a task force from SEPRONA, or whoever is responsible for rivers and waterways. But you can't reassign every single officer in the station.'

'Burgos is still looking after Ana,' Víctor corrected, hauling rocks on to the bank.

Sara had been determined not to aggravate the situation, but she was finding it difficult to contain her anger. Until now, they had managed to keep the village under a tight cordon. Now, all that work was wasted because of a few drops of rain.

'Get your men out of here. I need them down in the village collecting witness statements and processing evidence from the hut. Who's manning the roadblock?'

'Right now, nobody,' he said.

'What are you playing at, Víctor? You can't really be that stupid, can you? Do you want me to suspend you, is that it?'

Víctor carried on calmly, his oilskin coat so wet it was almost black. Then he looked downstream. 'You've no idea how much damage this river can do. What might seem stupid to you, is what keeps people in this valley alive.'

He clambered on to the bank, splashing water everywhere.

'What about Lucía?' Sara said. 'Do you realize that, thanks to you, we might never find her?'

'What none of us wants is to find her dead. The rains are going to get heavier. If we don't dredge the river, it will burst its banks. Everyone around here knows what that means. And we don't want it to happen again. Call your superiors, if you want. Call the Ministry of Defence. I don't care. I'm not leaving here until the village is safe.'

Without waiting for a reply, Víctor walked off and joined the rest of the Guardia Civil and the Cofradía. There were not many women, but Sara recognized Caridad. Seeing her surrounded by the people of the village was surprising at first, and then reassuring. She had begun to think the tiny little woman she had conversations with at night was a ghost. And now, here she was, diligently working alongside everyone else, as though she were just one more busy bee in the hive.

When Sara got back to the station, Elisa was in her office, sitting with her back to the door. She was toying with a pen, drumming it on the desk, and Sara wondered which face she would be wearing today.

'Elisa?' she said as she stepped into the room.

'Sorry; I just came in . . .' Elisa said. 'There was no one in the station.'

'It doesn't matter.' Sara glanced at her desk. Given the muddle of paperwork, it was impossible to know whether the girl had touched anything. 'Has something happened?'

'I've come to tell the truth,' Elisa said.

Sara plumped into her chair and feigned a surprised smile. 'You mean you haven't already?'

'Everything I said about Álvaro was a pack of lies.'

'Do you mind?' Sara said, turning on the digital recorder.

Elisa stared at the device for a second. 'No, of course not,' she said, shaking herself out of her thoughts.

She was wearing a tight top, her hair pinned up with one of her handmade slides. Her face was clear, her eyes dark; there was no longer any trace of self-doubt. Elisa had take over from Elisa.

'Where would you like to start?' Sara asked.

'When Ana and Lucía were kidnapped, Álvaro was with me,' she said, without a flicker of hesitation.

Sara remained silent for a moment. Waiting it out. She wanted to put Elisa's new-found confidence to the test.

'That is not what you told me as recently as yesterday.'

'You made me realize that I can't carry on like this.'

'Thanks, but I don't think I deserve much credit.'

'It's true. I owe it to you.'

'So, can you tell me what *did* happen that day?'

'I'd been out the night before – in Monteperdido – and, later on, I went down to Val de Sacs. I'd been drinking and I popped a couple of pills. Two or three, I think. I was still partying at dawn, and I just carried on. At about three in the afternoon, I started to freak out. I was still tripping. My father had spent the night in Barbastro, that was the only reason I could go out . . . but by then he should have been back in Monteperdido. And so should I. I was scared to go home. I was completely off my face . . . That's why I called

Álvaro. So he could come and pick me up from Val de Sacs and help me get myself straight.'

'And, according to this version, he did come?'

'He stayed with me for a couple of hours. Then we had an argument. He dropped me off at the bus stop and he left.'

'What happened during that couple of hours?'

Elisa Nerín looked down, but this was not shame at having to relate something embarrassing; it was the mischievous look of a teenage girl relishing her lies.

'I wanted to sleep with him,' she said finally. 'I'd been in love with Álvaro ever since I started going to that school. I couldn't get him out of my head. What with everything I'd taken the night before, I forgot about boundaries . . . I was pretty pushy . . . Eventually, he got really angry and took me to the bus stop.'

'You never slept with him?'

'I wish!' Her eyes glittered at this impossible dream. 'When I found out he was still in the valley, in Posets, I went up to see him . . . I said I was sorry for all the lies I'd told. I just wanted him to love me . . . But . . . after what I'd done, I thought he hated me. So I didn't go back.'

'You really hurt him.'

Elisa shrugged. She was sitting up straight, studying the papers on the table as though already bored with this conversation.

'I was angry when he brushed me off . . . and I thought, I'll show you. I was just a kid . . .' But even she did not believe this excuse.

'That's fine. You were just a kid,' Sara said. 'And maybe things went further than you planned. But when the girls didn't show up, and everyone turned against Álvaro . . . didn't you think about telling the truth?'

'Have you met my father?' Elisa said, turning to look at Sara again. 'I couldn't change my story.'

'Are you still in love with Álvaro?'

'What does it matter?'

Sara remained silent. She had noticed that, when Elisa was like this, self-assured and brazen, she was troubled by periods of silence.

'Yes . . . I still love him. I suppose I always will,' she said quickly, to fill the void.

Sara got up and went over to the window. From here, she could see the forest where the girls had been abducted. The rain was falling harder now. There were puddles on the ground outside the station. If it did not stop soon, it would be a quagmire.

'Can I go?' Elisa asked. 'I need to get back to the hotel.'

'Of course,' Sara said, without turning to look at the girl. She felt a sudden wave of revulsion. As though she were handling something dirty, putrid. She walked Elisa to the door. 'Thank you for telling me all this.'

'I didn't want Álvaro to have to go through all that again,' Elisa said.

'You were right to come to me, but I'm not sure it will be enough.'

Elisa stopped on the threshold. Sara's hand on her back urged her on, but she resisted.

'What do you mean, not enough?'

'You change your testimony after five years. That's a long time. Suddenly, it tallies exactly with the statement given by Álvaro. The man you're in love with. How can we be sure that what you're telling me now isn't a lie? I mean, I believe you, but I'm not the only one working on this investigation—'

'Ask Gaizka. He'll tell you.'

'What has he got to do with it? He gave Álvaro a job, but that was a year later—'

'That night . . . I was with him. With Gaizka. He left just before Álvaro came and picked me up, but he knew he was coming . . . Then I saw that his car was still parked outside the house. So he must have seen Álvaro.'

The rain was now a white sheet that shrouded Monteperdido, giving the village the spectral glow of night, though the sun had not yet set. Further down the valley, Joaquín Castán was staring out the window of the guest house, as raindrops bounced off the bonnet of his car. He could imagine the sound, but here in the room, there was only silence.

'Would you like a drink?' Virginia Bescos asked, opening the minibar. 'There's no wine. Only gin and whisky.'

'No, thanks,' Joaquín said, without looking away from the window. 'I need to drive home.'

She had put on weight, although she was still a slim woman. Virginia had bleached her hair blonde, perhaps in an attempt to cling on to her youth, but the dark roots were obvious. She used to be much more vain, Joaquín thought.

'How long has it been?' Joaquín said. 'Two years?'

'Are we really going to waste our time trading blame?' she said, sitting down on the bed.

'What else have we got to say to each other?'

'You tell me,' said the journalist. 'I sent you the message, but I didn't think you'd agree to see me.'

'You let me down.'

'You're not the centre of the universe, Joaquín,' she said. 'Bad things happen to other people too.'

'Have you ever lost a daughter?' he said heatedly.

'No. Only my job,' Virginia said. 'There were a bunch of layoffs at the newspaper. We got shit-canned, tossed out on the street with a pathetic severance package. I've spent the past two years breaking my back just to pay the mortgage . . . OK, maybe I should have called, but what could I offer you?'

Two years since their last meeting, but it had taken its toll on her. For a moment, Joaquín thought about the physical damage of five years spent searching for his daughter. Had he, too, become a different person?

'It's been two years since I published an article. I'm forty-six. If print journalism is a complete disaster right now, just imagine what it's like for someone my age . . .'

A long time ago, when Joaquín realized that police work would not be enough to track down Lucía, he had turned to the media. He had given interviews, invited reporters into his home, published photographs of the family. This was when he had met Virginia Bescos. She was working for a newspaper, but she had friends in television. She had been the one who got him into the studios, encouraged him to set up the Foundation, to make his daughter's name a banner of every missing girl.

'What about television?' Joaquín asked.

'They probably think I look too old. They don't want a reporter with saggy tits . . .'

It had been a strange time. For two years, Joaquín had been somebody. He was invited to meetings, debates – even politicians sat down with him. He was the voice of grief that everyone understood. His personal tragedy authorized him to offer an opinion. Virginia had been by his side, she had almost been his agent. She advised him which functions to attend, which interviews to accept. She managed his career as though he were an artist. They would often meet up in hotel rooms in cities where Joaquín was touring, and sometimes he would forget why he had started this crusade. There were times when he was happy. But he quickly realized that, like any manufactured star, he was simply a passing fad. There was no specific moment, no particular day or hour. He simply ceased to be the focus of round-table discussions and found himself pushed to the sidelines. Fewer people were involved in the Foundation. And, one day, he discovered that he had to call the television station if he wanted to be invited, because they had stopped calling him.

At first, Virginia had stuck with him. She regularly wrote articles about the missing girls, although the newspaper relegated them to the inside pages and edited them down to brief columns designed to fill pages.

'Why did you come?' Joaquín asked. 'It's obviously not out of friendship.'

'Now I'm the one who needs to ask you for a favour,' Virginia said, sounding like someone forced to visit a soup kitchen for the first time.

She had stopped answering his calls. Joaquín had been loath to write her off as one of the opportunists who had clustered around him for a while. Virginia was not like that, he thought. But her continued absence said otherwise.

'I don't know why I should do you any favours,' Joaquín said, thinking about that period.

'Nobody is forcing you,' she said. 'Just think about it, please. Give me something – an interview, a photo of Ana – something I can get into one of the nationals. I need the money.'

Joaquín looked at Virginia and understood why she was holed up in a grubby guest house in Val de Sacs. She could not afford a room in Ordial or Monteperdido. Certainly not at the Hotel La Guardia, where she had always stayed when she came to see him before.

'Will you do it?' she pleaded. 'Will you think about it?'

Joaquín slipped a hand into his pocket and ran his fingers over his mobile phone. He thought about the police sketch of his daughter, lying waiting on the memory card.

The day had slipped away as stealthily as a gatecrasher at a party – by the back door, without saying goodbye – making way for the night. Sara turned on the desk lamp so she could go on working on the reports. Baín had bought some *bocadillos* and, although she had not touched hers, he was already finishing his, encouraging her to eat before it got cold. He sat facing Sara, with his feet up on a chair.

'First thing tomorrow, I'm going to talk to Gaizka,' Sara muttered, scribbling something in a margin.

'How can you even work like this?' Baín said, gesturing to the piles of files, half-eaten food and photographs. 'What you need to do is sort out this desk.'

'I know exactly where everything is,' Sara said, spreading her arms wide to claim the desk as her territory.

'I'm telling you, you need to sort it out,' Baín said paternally. He had finished eating. He crumpled the paper from his *bocadillo* into a ball and tossed it at Sara.

'And this is your way of helping me?' Sara smiled, but Santiago Baín was already leaning back in his chair, eyes closed.

The rain continued. The smell of damp earth invaded the police station. After her conversation with Elisa, Sara had reread the statements that Álvaro had made. At his insistence, the Guardia Civil had felt compelled to check his alibi. Five years ago, no one had seen him near the house in Val de Sacs. However, several witnesses had mentioned a brown-grey Nissan pickup with a dent in the driver's door. Reading the file, Sara immediately realized that the description matched the car Gaizka still drove, except the passenger door had been replaced. It was absurd to maintain the restrictions on Álvaro's movements. She spoke to Raquel and told her they no longer considered her husband a suspect. Then she had personally called Álvaro and told him he could go home, while Baín had paid another visit to Marcial at the gunsmith's.

Lying back in his chair, Santiago Baín's breathing was slow and shallow; he looked like some petrified giant, in the shadows. With him beside her, Sara felt safe. When life became unfathomable, a few words from him could make sense of it. He had a way of understanding the illogical, suicidal, selfish behaviour that set the rhythm of their investigations. Like the charade that Raquel and Álvaro performed for the sake of their daughter. Like the self-destructive atmosphere that reigned in Lucía's house. The ties that bound family members to each other were often unhealthy.

The most dangerous man is a solitary man, because even he does not know who he is. This was a maxim Santiago Baín liked to repeat. *Because there is no one to tell him his story.*

Sara could not help but wonder who there was to tell her story.

Who are you when no one is looking? Baín would say. *No one, or whomever you want to be.*

Sara was aware that, when Baín offered this worldview, he was also offering her a justification for her own life choices. He was saying, *Use it, make it your own. Stop feeling guilty.*

That night, Sara left earlier than Baín. She walked back to La Renclusa in the driving rain. She took a shower and, still wet, spread a towel on the bed and lay down naked. She was tired.

She thought she had managed to fall asleep, but moments later she opened her eyes again. This was something she had not experienced for months and, at first, she could not believe it was happening. She was lying motionless on the bed, looking around her, but unable to move a muscle. It was as though her body no longer belonged to her, as though she were hiding inside a suit of armour, peering out. She tried to move her arm, her leg, but it was futile.

She knew that someone had come into the room. A shadow fell across the bed. She had to get up. She had to grab her gun from the nightstand. But she lay there, paralysed.

She could not hear footsteps, but she knew the figure was approaching.

Then she remembered that she was naked. She wanted to cover herself, but still her body refused to budge.

A man was standing at the foot of the bed. He was naked too. At first, she thought it was simply the way the shadows fell, but, when he sat down on the bed, she saw that his face had no features. No eyes, no nose, no mouth. Nothing but a tiny hole in the centre of a blank expanse of smooth skin.

She was terrified. She tried to scream. To leap up from the bed.

Somewhere, a telephone began to ring, and she made a super-human effort, screaming to herself: 'Wake up!'

Rain lashed against the office window. Víctor Gamero, exhausted after a day spent dredging the river, hoped that their efforts would be enough. The river was already rising as the rain mingled with water from the melting glacier, threatening to burst its banks.

Someone knocked at the door, although it was open. He turned and saw Santiago Baín.

'You look like a scared dog in a thunderstorm,' Baín said.

'I didn't realize you were still here.' Víctor went to the window and unhooked his oilskins. 'I'm heading home,' he said. 'Can I give you a lift to the hotel?'

'I want to go through a few more files.'

As Víctor reached the doorway, Baín put out an arm to stop him.

'Is there anything you haven't told me?'

'That I'm exhausted?' Víctor said sarcastically.

'Sometimes I think that the people in this village are more interested in protecting their own than in finding Lucía.'

'We're a family. Nothing is more important to us than finding that girl.'

'Then why did you reassign so many officers today? You know the rain isn't heavy enough to flood the river. You've seen the forecast.'

'Around here, nature has a tendency to do whatever the hell it likes. It doesn't pay much heed to weather forecasts.' Víctor angrily pushed Baín's arm aside and walked out.

★

His nose was burning. Gaizka had snorted two lines of coke before getting in the car and driving down to Monteperdido. On the passenger seat was a rucksack with the rest of Álvaro's things. It was difficult to see the road for the driving rain against which the windscreen wipers were little help. Without realizing, he had turned the music up too loud. Drum and bass, pulsing and repetitive. Gaizka sniffed hard and rubbed his nose. He was convinced there were flecks of white powder on his face. The car shuddered as he pulled over and stopped. Let's do this. Gaizka got out, bent double against the downpour. The raindrops were like needles stabbing into his back. Álvaro came out into the garden to meet him. Gaizka was panting, agitated.

'Here's your clothes,' he said.

Álvaro punched him. Gaizka fell back on the lawn.

'Have you lost your fucking mind?' he shouted, sprawled on the grass.

Álvaro kicked him, then knelt down and grabbed him by the shirt. 'You saw me with Elisa!'

Gaizka felt his head hit the ground as Álvaro shoved him away, though he could feel no pain. The roar of the cloudburst clashed with the music blaring from the car. He had left the door open.

'You fucking bastard!' Álvaro screamed, lashing out with another kick. 'There I was, going out of my mind – and you said nothing!'

Gaizka writhed on the ground, turning on to his stomach, the taste of grass in his mouth.

'Four fucking years I spent grovelling and thanking you.' Álvaro's voice was barely audible above the rain and the music. The same song, going on and on.

Álvaro raised his leg to give another kick, but Gaizka rolled over, grabbed his foot and knocked him off balance. He scrabbled on top of Álvaro, one hand gripping his throat, choking him, the other a raised fist, coming down again and again.

'Leave me alone!' Gaizka howled, his fist still pounding Álvaro's face.

He heard the crack as Álvaro's nose broke. The blood washed away in the rain. He panted. He had no intention of stopping. Again and again the fist came down. All the excuses he had never given rang in his head: he had fucked Elisa, a minor; if he had spoken up, he would have gone to prison; he'd been banged up before and had no intention of going back; he'd given Álvaro a job, a place to live; he'd spent nights drinking gin and tonic with him into the early hours.

Something roughly jerked him backwards. Gaizka fell.

'Leave him.' He heard the voice, and then he saw Burgos.

He got to his feet. The officer tried to grab him, but Gaizka dodged and, while Burgos was helping Álvaro to his feet, he got into his car and turned the key in the ignition. Was this still the same song? The wing mirrors were misted; he did not see Álvaro break away from Burgos, refusing to go back into the house. By the time he ran after him, Gaizka was far away. His heart was pounding. He knew he would still have to deal with the Guardia Civil. Tomorrow, he thought. If I can just make it until tomorrow.

Elisa was in the back seat. Her father insisted that she sit next to her grandmother, although Elisa found it revolting. Every time she accidentally brushed against her, it felt like touching a corpse. Usually, when her father took his mother to Barbastro, Elisa stayed in the house on her own. She enjoyed these days when she could wander around the house naked. She would smoke in bed and watch television until she fell asleep. Her father always left in the late afternoon and spent the night in Barbastro. He took his mother for dialysis the following morning and arrived back that afternoon. Elisa did her best to arrange her days off from the hotel to coincide with those days when she had the house to herself. But, today, Marcial had refused to let her stay behind.

'Shut up and get in the car,' was all he said.

He had heard about Elisa's statement to the police, but she did not care. There was a time when she would have cried all the way to Barbastro. She knew he would give her a beating. 'Hit me, if you like,' she muttered to herself in the back seat.

The rainstorm had turned the road into a dark tunnel; only the blurred road markings were visible. Just before they passed Ordial, Marcial had jerked the steering wheel and turned on to a dirt track. Elisa could feel the wheels juddering over the potholes.

'Where are we going?' she said.

She could see her father's face in the rear-view mirror; his teeth were clenched. His rotting teeth.

'The rain is too heavy; the river is likely to burst its banks,' Marcial said. 'I know a place where we can wait out the storm . . . before we go back.'

Elisa felt reassured. She looked at her grandmother, who swayed with the motion of the car like a rag doll. The seat belt was all that stopped her from falling over. She barely had the strength to hold her head up.

The headlights illuminated the narrow track weaving between the trees, until finally they arrived at a patch of open ground. Straight ahead of them, Ixeia soared into the clouds, and here, at its base, like a yawning black mouth, was the tunnel to France. It was something Monteperdido had dreamed of for years: a road that would cut through the Pyrenees and put an end to the isolation, the poverty. But work was never completed. The planned tunnel was nothing more than a dark cave in the mountainside.

Marcial stopped the car, got out and opened the back door.

'Help me with your grandmother,' he said, shouting over the rain. 'We're high up, here; if the Ésera does flood, we'll be safe . . .'

Elisa unfastened her seat belt and, as she climbed out, she stared into the mouth of the abandoned tunnel. It was overgrown. Shrubs and trees grew over the vaulted arch; the ground was a twisted mass of roots and wild grass. It seemed as though nature were trying to heal this gaping wound in its flank.

'I thought the river had been dredged?' Elisa said, putting her grandmother's limp arm around her shoulder.

'Get the wheelchair out of the boot,' her father said.

While Marcial helped his mother into the tunnel, Elisa opened the boot and took out the folding wheelchair. The lashing rain had turned the ground to mud. The wheels of the chair got stuck and would not move, no matter how hard she pushed. Mud spattered her clothes. She was drenched. She realized that the only way to move the chair was to carry it. Marcial re-emerged from the dark tunnel to help his daughter. Elisa, exhausted, dropped the chair.

'What are you doing?' Marcial roared, picking up the muddy chair with one hand. He looked at his daughter as she stood in the rain, her dress clinging to her body. She was not wearing a bra, and the cold made her nipples visible.

'You make me ashamed.'

This was the only thing Marcial said before he lashed out. Elisa did not have time to protect herself, and caught the blow full in the face. She fell to the ground. Marcial set down the wheelchair and took a step towards her. Elisa buried her hands in the mud, trying to get to her feet.

'If you're a frustrated slut, it's not my doing.'

She knew this meant more blows. She did not care. Marcial grabbed her arm and dragged her to her feet.

'What am I going to do with you?' he said, pressing his face to hers.

Elisa spat at him. Her saliva mingled with the rainwater. Disgusted, Marcial wiped his lips with the back of his hand. She kneed him in the stomach and he doubled up in pain and let go of his daughter's arm. She broke into a run, heading for a thicket of trees further up the mountain, slipping on the wet stones. Marcial plodded after her; he knew he would catch her. Elisa was already lost among the trees. He did not care that she'd had a head start. He knew these woods better than anyone. Before he started to run, he looked into the black hole – the cave where he had left his mother.

Sara met with the forensics officer in the hotel lobby. When would this rain stop? she wondered. Sara got herself a coffee from the machine and sat down at the same table where she and Caridad had played cards. She was still trying to shake off her nightmare. Outside, it was dark. The street lights were blurred yellow moons. The forensics officer laid an evidence bag on the table.

'We found it while we were processing the scene. It's gold. That's why it survived. It withstood the heat of the flames.'

Sara picked up the bag and peered at what was inside.

'Any idea what it might be?' the officer asked.

It was a small badge; the pin had twisted in the heat. It was in the form of an eight-pointed star – the emblem of the Cofradía of Santa María de Laude. Sara's mobile phone rang before she could reply.

'Santiago,' she said, 'we've got something.'

'Get over to Ana's house.' Baín's voice crackled on the line. Sara could hear the storm. 'Can you hear me? I had a call from Burgos. He says they can't find Ana . . . she's left the house . . .'

'Where are you now?' Sara asked, clapping a hand over her other ear.

'I think you're right. We've got something.'

Quim took the shortcut home. He had spent the afternoon with Ximena. Her father, Nicolás, had not been able to drive home from the farm he was visiting, because of the rain. They had fucked and, afterwards, Quim had fallen asleep. By the time he woke up, it was dark. From the living-room window, he could see the flashing lights of a Guardia Civil car. Ximena lent him one of her father's anoraks and he left by the back door. He would avoid the roads, take the shortcut through the pine forest and get in by the kitchen door. He staggered forward against the lashing rain. Fucking rain. By the time it stopped, the village would be a disaster area, the streets ankle-deep in mud, the river spewing all the shit it swept down the mountain. The true face of Monteperdido, Quim thought. Like in the film, *The Shining*, when the mad guy is hugging a beautiful woman who has just stepped out of the bath, and then sees her reflected in the mirror, a rotting corpse.

A clearing opened up ahead. And there she was. Her arms spread wide, her face turned up, her mouth open. Rainwater spilled over her lips. Her sodden blouse was pasted to her skin. Was she laughing? Quim stopped a few metres away. He stood, watching her, as though he had just stumbled on some timorous nocturnal animal. He felt as though he should not intervene. Who was he to interrupt her? He could see her breasts rise and fall with her breath, as though she were trying to suck in the night itself, to contain it within her lungs.

'Ana,' he said, finally.

She turned towards him, a little shy, as though he had found her naked in the river. Water streamed down her face like a cataract, glowing in wide meanders around her dark eyes.

'I'll bet there's a shitload of officers out looking for you.' Quim approached her warily. 'You snuck out without saying anything, am I right?'

Ana looked up at the sky again before answering.

'Do you know how long it's been since I got drenched by the rain?'

Marcial's mother was sitting on a rock in the middle of the hole in the mountain. Rain whipped the trees at the entrance to the cave, a constant pitter-patter, like machine-gun fire. Her hands were in her lap, her head slightly tilted, as though looking at something curiously. But her eyes were not looking at anything; they were lost in an abyss, where there was no light.

Something moved amid the shadows at the back of the tunnel, where the granite rock face of Ixeia was still intact. A rat, maybe, or an animal sheltering from the rain. Marcial's mother was oblivious to the sounds and the movements deep in the darkness. Meanwhile, someone was trying to escape, unaware that there was no need to be careful.

There was a sound of footsteps from behind. The darkness seemed to gather to form a silhouette – the figure of a man coming towards her. He walked quietly across the stone floor. She was not aware of the shadowy figure behind her. Then the figure raised a rifle and pressed the barrel against the back of her neck. Still the old woman did not move. A heart pumping blood. A pair of lungs. She was no more than a machine made of flesh and blood. What was left of this woman underneath her skin? The figure cocked the rifle.

'Don't do it. She doesn't even know you're there.' The voice was a whisper, as though she were afraid of making a mistake. A second figure stepped from the shadows, from the bowels of the mountain.

'She saw you,' the man said.

Lucía stood in front of Marcial's mother. Her hair fell halfway down her back. She had a knitted blue cardigan pulled tightly around her. It was too big, and emphasized her slim figure. Lucía tilted her head, like a reflection of Marcial's mother. Their eyes met. But the old woman's eyes were glassy. Lifeless.

Lucía, here in the mountain, like the mountain spirit of Ixeia, hidden in this tunnel that men had drilled into the rock, the shadowy burrow of Monteperdido. Lucía was not a pencilled ghost, nor was she a little girl, lost in the forest. She was ice and fear. A glacier, cracked and fractured by five years in captivity. Pale as the snow, as the windswept peaks. An abandoned doll.

The man shouldered the rifle, finger on the trigger.

'Don't shoot!' Lucía rushed over and pushed the barrel away from Marcial's mother. The man lashed out, cracking her with the rifle butt. She fell to the floor, a thread of blood trickling from her lower lip.

'I'm sorry,' he said, ashamed.

She touched the blood with her fingertip, surprised that, somewhere inside her, there was still this living thing: blood. She felt the sting of the wound. Lucía got to her feet, crouched down next to Señora Nerín and took her hand.

'You're a good man,' she said, looking into the old woman's eyes, as dark as the tunnel where they had been hiding. 'She can't do us any harm.'

Seeing the woman sitting motionless on the rock, the man thought of the wax museums he had been to. Then he reached out his hand to help Lucía up.

'We need to get out of here,' he said.

As they left, a cold gust of wind whipped the old woman's face, but still she did not move. Frozen, detached from reality, her head tilted to one side, her eyes blank, alone in the tunnel. The right hand in her lap clenched. A drop of blood trickled between her fingers as she formed a fist, as though to hold Lucía back.

On the outskirts of Monteperdido, just past the petrol station, there was a side road that led to Joaquín's haulage business. There was no fence around the unit. Inspector Baín parked his car and walked under the awning to shelter from the rain.

He tried to focus on what he had come to find, but something was going round and round in his head.

He was sure that this was best for Sara.

He counted four trucks. Through the rain, he saw the glow of a torch behind the last of the trucks and assumed that this was him.

Every investigation progresses by cutting new paths, trails that lead off the main road. Some of them you have to abandon for fear of getting lost. At other times, trails that seem to lead nowhere turn out to be the main road, and you have to retrace your steps, go back so you can find the right way.

'Hey!' Santiago Baín called out.

He thought he could see feet moving under the trucks. The torchlight he had been following flickered off. He walked around the truck, but did not have time to see it coming. The shot rang out, like the pop of a champagne cork. It hit him square in the chest, knocking him to the ground. It was no ordinary bullet. He had suffered gunshot wounds before, but this was different. The hollow-point bullet pierced his chest, shattered his ribs and then expanded. A scorching wave flamed through his heart, his lungs. He could not move. Could not feel his legs, his arms. The heat was followed by a bitter cold. His last thought was of the undernourished Sara who had shown up in his office so many years ago. The gawky teenage girl whom he'd had to tell, *No one is looking for you.* Santiago's eyes were open, gazing up to the inky sky over Monteperdido. And the rain was falling on him.

By the time Gaizka approached, Inspector Baín was already dead. The pale skin contrasted with the bloody crater that had once been his chest. The rifle trembled in Gaizka's hands. He saw a light come on in a nearby house. Had someone heard the gunshot?

Despite the cold rain, he was sweating.

4

The Dark Canyon

Sara felt an intense pressure inside her head. The same pain she had felt when, as a teenager, she'd first travelled by plane: that invisible force that slowly moved through her ears as the plane soared, threatening to burst her eardrums. She had clutched her head in her hands as wave after wave of pain shot through her brain. She'd felt like she was about to pass out and, as they glided over the grey ocean far below, she convinced herself that it would never stop. This invisible hand squeezing on her skull would be with her for the rest of her life, until one day it forced its way through the soft grey tissue and her brain exploded, like an overripe plum, dark juice oozing everywhere. There would be no end to the pain and, at the same time, it panicked her to think that it might end. What would be left of her if that happened?

What will there be when you're gone, Santiago? she wondered.

Chickpea, she wanted to say, *I love you.*

Here in Monteperdido, rain was still falling on his body. The blood – deep red, almost black – thinned to a watery pink pool beneath his corpse.

*

She could hear voices. Perhaps it was Víctor talking to her, but she could not tear her eyes away from the crater in what had been Santiago's chest. Nor could the rain dull the vivid, fleshy red at the edges of the wound. It looked as though it was spewing lava.

She felt Víctor's warm hand on her shoulder, but she did not turn to look at him.

Her body was no longer responding. Her mind scrabbled to escape the pain. Silently, she screamed to herself, *Get moving, Sara. Cordon off the area. Issue an arrest warrant for Marcial Nerín.* But the screams were faint and came from far away, from the bottomless pit where she was building dams against the grief. Against this pressure that was crushing her.

The lights of the Guardia Civil vehicles flashed hazily through the dark curtain of rain. Officers moved away the onlookers who had gathered around Transportes Castán. Pujante, half hidden by his green oilskin, muttered rather than spoke, pushing the small crowd back to clear a space around the body of Santiago Baín. He and the other officers were all overwhelmed by the situation; they moved heavily, dragging their feet, like sleepwalkers.

Gaizka was frozen stiff. Soaking wet, he had taken refuge under an umbrella belonging to one of the bystanders. There were fifteen, maybe twenty of them. He huddled among the group of rubber-neckers drawn here by the sirens of the ambulance and the police cars. He was shivering and finding it difficult to see straight. He laid an icy hand on the shoulder of the man holding the umbrella.

'You all right?' the man said, seeing his ashen face and feverish eyes.

Who is he? Gaizka wondered. The man looked familiar. He had

a square face, his forehead and jutting chin forming perfect right angles, the sides so straight they looked as if they'd been traced with a ruler. Gaizka was sure he had seen him around the village, maybe even spoken to him once or twice, but he quickly forgot about the man and his attention returned to the officers bustling around the corpse. Behind them stood the line of trucks. Mute witnesses to what had happened.

He had been shot with a hunting rifle. With a Remington Core-Lokt 30-06 Springfield 150-grain round-nose bullet that peels back into four 'petals' on impact. It had destroyed his lungs and heart. It was the most common calibre in the area. Perfect for hunting boar and deer. Even at a hundred metres, it could pierce the skin and the thick layer of subcutaneous fat.

Sara gestured for them to cover the body with a thermal blanket. The smell of rain and mud masked the stench of death. Behind her, the onlookers had fanned out in a semicircle, like spectators jostling for position in a stadium. *What the fuck are you looking at?* she wanted to scream.

'Track down Marcial,' she ordered Víctor.

I think you're right. We've got something. These had been Baín's last words on the phone.

What have we got? Sara wondered. What did you come here for?

And the questions instantly became a reproach.

Why did you have to come here?

She squeezed her eyes shut. The pain in her ears was excruciating. Her eyes were dry. Rain whipped her face. The drops were too thick, too viscous; they felt not as though they had fallen from the sky, but as though they had spurted from an open drain. Still the pressure built up, crushing her brain.

What will you do when I'm not around? Santiago had once asked her.
'Plod on,' Sara had answered.
Plod on. But to where?

Seeing the Guardia Civil jeep coming out of his unit, Joaquín
turned on to the road he had tarmacked himself and resurfaced
every spring when it cracked during the winter cold. On the
forecourt, where he parked his trucks, a crowd of people had
gathered. He could not see how many; they were hidden beneath a
sea of black umbrellas. Beyond was an ambulance and three police
cars.

He pulled up outside the unit and got out.

'Joaquín!' someone called to him. 'We've been looking for you.'

He took out his mobile phone and saw he had no missed calls.
Looking for me where? he thought.

Behind the police tape, officers were moving in slow motion, not
out of tiredness, but desperation. Pujante, the youngest officer in
the station, was leaning against the bonnet of a jeep, staring down
at his muddy boots. He seemed paralysed, as though the mud were
holding him in place and he did not know how to break free. He
stroked his beard. Then Joaquín saw Sara Campos. She had no raincoat, no oilskin. Her wet black hair was plastered against her cheeks.
In the flashing lights that whirled soundlessly, her face was streaked
with shadows, now blue, now orange.

A pair of dirty, blood-smeared shoes stuck out from beneath the
thermal blanket.

'The cop's been murdered,' someone said.

He could see Sara trembling, about to collapse. Víctor quickly
strode over and caught her in his arms before she fell.

Now you know what it feels like, Joaquín thought. Now you understand suffering.

Hidden in the pool of shadow beneath the umbrellas, the faces of the onlookers whirled around her. In the darkness, she saw dozens of pairs of eyes glittering. Time was suddenly a broken jigsaw puzzle, with pieces strewn everywhere.

Sara remembered the night she arrived in Monteperdido, the houses springing up like geographical accidents as they passed. She imagined the eyes watching from behind the curtains, trying to work out what the police car was doing there. Faces she had not known at the time. Now, here they were, witnesses to her pain. Who exactly was here? Who had come to Transportes Castán to see the spectacle? Were they laughing and whispering to each other?

Sara saw Joaquín. He was standing at the cordon marked by the police tape, beckoning to Pujante to let him pass. Who the fuck did he think he was?

Víctor took her arm, keeping his other hand around her waist so that she could stand. 'Can I take you back to the hotel?' he seemed to be saying. Staring into the blue-black rain, she thought she saw his dog bleeding, floating in the air. Like a scarlet bird.

Gaizka was here too. Drenched, despite the fact that he was standing under an umbrella. His eyes flickered red from the flashing police lights, or were they simply bloodshot?

Only a few hours earlier, Santiago had been sleeping in a chair in the police station. Now that seemed like an eternity ago.

They're looking for me, Sara had said, the first time they met, and Baín had replied, *No one is looking for you.*

She had turned away from the body and was reluctant to turn

again and look at it. She did not need to. The image of Santiago Baín's body, lying in the mud, his chest an open wound, his arms flung wide, his eyes staring blankly at the black sky over Monteperdido, was engraved on her memory.

Víctor led Sara towards the offices of Transportes Castán. Her body slipped from his arms, partly because of the rain, partly because she did not have the strength to stand upright.

'Come on, Sara,' he tried to encourage her; at the same time, it felt as though she were not really there, inside her skin.

He managed to get them out of the rain, into the shelter of the awning.

Sara leaned against the wall. 'Just give me a minute,' she said, and slowly her legs buckled until she was sitting on the sodden ground.

The feel of the wet concrete reminded Sara of the river where she had seen Víctor working. The dredgers clearing weeds and shrubs. The villagers working together as the rain began to fall.

The first drops of the storm that was to come.

The symbol of the Cofradía emblazoned on one of the vans parked by the river. An eight-pointed star. The same symbol that was on the badge the forensics officer had found among the scorched ruins of the mountain hut.

Sitting on the ground, Sara looked up at Víctor.

'Have they tracked down Marcial Nerín?'

He said he would go and ask.

The tree where the girls had disappeared. The tree whose diseased roots meant that it would die if it were transplanted.

Sara felt her stomach heave as she pictured those putrefied roots snaking beneath Monteperdido, a few inches from where she was sitting, running under the feet of the onlookers. She imagined the roots beneath Santiago's body, waiting to embrace him when he was buried.

She looked up at the sky. It was still raining, and suddenly she realized that this was the only sound she could hear: the rain drumming on the ground, on the bonnets of the jeeps, on the branches of the pine trees encircling the forecourt. It was as though the rain were a predator and other sounds had fled, like frightened animals.

Officers from the Guardia Civil were lifting the body into the ambulance. Gaizka mingled with the crowd and waited for his moment.

The sound of the gunshot was still ringing inside his head, like an echo trapped in a bottle. The warmth of the trigger against his index finger. He stuffed his right hand into his pocket, as if afraid it might betray him.

Too many people. Too many police.

After it happened, he had put the torch in the boot of his car, then he had driven down to the petrol station and filled the tank, even though it was almost full.

He did not know whether he might need to make a long journey.

He had waited for the ambulance and the Guardia Civil to arrive. He had seen a few of the villagers show up – some in cars, others on foot – to see what was happening. Only then did he get out of his car and walk back up to Joaquín's hangar.

As soon as he got there, he saw someone talking to Víctor – a man of about sixty, with a plastic rain hat pulled down to his eyebrows. Old people and their fucking insomnia, he thought. Under the dark green oilskin that fell to his thighs, Gaizka could see the man was still wearing blue and red checked pyjamas. Gaizka did not take his eyes off this man. He was making a statement, and pointing to a house about a hundred metres further up the hill.

Gaizka did not need to hear to know what he was saying. He had been woken by the rifle shot, then he had put on his rain hat and oilskin and had gone outside. It was hardly likely to be a hunter, given the rain and the time of night. When he had arrived at the hangar, he had found the policeman's corpse behind one of the trucks.

He had seen nothing else. Tell him you didn't see anything else, fucker, Gaizka was thinking, his teeth clenched, his eyes boring into the old man.

From the casual way Víctor walked away from the witness, it was clear that he had not revealed anything important.

If I hadn't been such a fucking idiot! Gaizka thought.

He was not looking to excuse what he had done. It was not the murder that bothered him, but how he had reacted afterwards. Panicky, almost hysterical. He'd walked around and around the cop's body, stopping to watch the arteries pulsing blood. All the while, he had still been clutching the rifle.

He had taken too much coke, so, instead of worrying about an alibi, his brain had immediately started devising absurd plans. He thought about dismembering the body and placing the pieces in the hills around the village, so that, seen on Google Earth, they would form a gigantic question mark.

He had even laughed at the idea.

Meanwhile, time ticked on. Time was closing in on him.

He considered putting the body in the car, driving to Oscuros de Balced and tossing it into the canyon, so it would smash on the jagged rocks of the River Grist. Dumping it at the foot of Monte Ármos, leaving it for the wild boar, in the hope that they would devour every last bone.

Was he really coming up with these ideas, or was he borrowing them from movies he had seen?

And then time had run out. He had heard the voice of the man who had later given Víctor a statement. The neighbour who had been woken by the shot. 'Anyone there?' he had called.

Crouching under one of the trucks, Gaizka had seen the man's shadow grow longer until he could almost touch it. He could almost see the pyjama bottoms tucked into the rubber boots.

He had looked down at his hands. In his left, the torch; in his right, the rifle, giving off a wisp of steam as it cooled in the rain. He had made decisions – bad ones, probably, but at least they might give him a chance.

He had jammed the rifle above the rear axle of one of the trucks. Who was going to look for it there?

Quickly and soundlessly, he had gone around the back of the hangar and cut through the pine forest to his car, which he had parked out of sight of the road. It was unlikely that anyone would have noticed it.

After leaving the torch in the boot, he had crouched behind a tree, waiting for the neighbour to leave the forecourt and go back home to fetch his pistol. But the old fucker had a mobile phone. He had called the Guardia Civil and stayed with the body until they arrived.

Now the officers were clearing a path through the crowd for the ambulance to leave. Gaizka looked at the truck where he had stashed the rifle. A battered blue Pegaso, bleached almost white by the years. He felt like putting his finger to his lips and saying, *Shhh! Wait until everyone has gone.*

Quim was in the bathroom, a towel wrapped around him. The room was full of steam from the scalding shower. He could hardly see his reflection in the misted mirror. He had not said much to his mother when he arrived home, except that he had forgotten to take an umbrella, and that, on his way home, he had run into Ana in the middle of the forest and had lent her his raincoat.

Montserrat had followed him upstairs. She wanted to know how Ana was. The police had been searching for her. Why had she run off without saying anything to anyone? But Quim did not have the energy to answer, and said simply, 'I don't know.' Then he'd locked himself in the bathroom and turned on the shower.

Stepping, naked, under the hot spray, he remembered Ana's body. Soaked as though she had stepped out of a mountain lake. Her mouth open, drinking the water falling from the sky, as he was doing now, in the shower, the water brimming over his lips, trickling down his neck, his chest.

She had smiled when she saw him. *Do you know how long it's been since I got drenched by the rain?*

Quim knew what she meant: *Do you know how long it's been since I felt alive?*

As he showered, he smiled too. Ana's happiness was contagious. For the first time in a long time, Quim had seen something that he wished he possessed: this lust for life.

★

Montserrat left the house, keeping her eyes fixed on the ground. She could feel the rain pounding on her head, her back, as she walked to the Montrells' front door. She hoped Raquel herself would answer, but, when the door opened, it was Burgos. The officer was talking on his mobile, and he gave her a quizzical look, as if to ask what it was she wanted.

Montserrat overheard snatches of his conversation: 'Should I stay here? . . . How is she holding up? . . . I was worried when she disappeared . . . It's fine, everything's under control here.'

Burgos looked at her again and Montserrat had to say something.

'I just wanted to know if Ana's all right.'

'Yes. Don't worry. It was nothing serious,' Burgos said.

Montserrat glanced inside. In the living room, Ana was sitting on the sofa, wearing a bathrobe. Her mother was drying her hair with a towel. Then their eyes met. Montserrat was afraid Raquel would look away, after the way she had behaved earlier, screaming abuse, hysterical. Instead, Raquel smiled. Montserrat mouthed the words, *Thank you*, but by then Burgos had closed the door.

How could she have been so stupid? Blaming her friend because it had been her daughter and not Lucía who had reappeared? How could anyone be to blame for fate?

Montserrat was walking back to her house when she heard Raquel's door open.

'Say thanks to Quim for me,' her friend called after her. 'For bringing Ana home.'

Montserrat turned around. 'Raquel . . .' she began, but suddenly words seemed inadequate to express her remorse. 'You didn't have to send me a photo of the sketch . . . I was . . . I don't know how to apologize . . .' she stammered.

'Come round to the house someday, Monte. Talk to Ana, let her tell you about Lucía.'

Montserrat nodded. Raquel was right; the police sketch had given her a glimpse of something she had thought she would never see: her daughter's face as a sixteen-year-old.

Until that moment, Lucía had remained frozen in her memory as a girl of eleven. Now she knew Lucía had grown up, that she was still alive. If Ana could talk to her about Lucía, tell her things her daughter had said, it would be like giving the sketch a voice. A life.

So you're the one who's going to find my daughter, Joaquín thought, as he watched Víctor lead Sara to the car. She was limp as a rag doll. For a moment, she looked at him, at the villagers who had come to gawp, at the sky and the incessant rain. It did not matter where she looked, she saw nothing. The image of her partner lying dead in the mud was burned on to her retinas, blotting out everything else.

Was the grisly game of musical chairs about to begin again? New officers coming to take over the investigation. Poring over the same case files, the same reports, the same interviews with the families. They could go back and start from square one whenever they liked. For Joaquín, it was impossible. Getting here had been a long journey, and he could not believe that the path would not lead him somewhere.

'Is Rafael around?' he asked Pujante.

'We called him a while ago. He should get here soon,' Pujante said. He was deathly pale; too young for what he had just witnessed.

They could not turn back now, Joaquín thought. He looked around at Transportes Castán, at the forecourt and the trucks, at this business that, a few years ago, had seemed too small. He remembered the plans he had made, the money he had invested, the Saturday nights when they all went for dinner in Barbastro and talked about the future, he and Montserrat and Quim and Lucía. He remembered the long summer evenings. *Papá is going to buy a hundred trucks,* his daughter would say, with a mouth full of hamburger. A luminous summer he could never go back to. The last he had experienced before his life fell apart, and all he could do was blindly forge ahead.

'Where have you been?' Raquel asked as she came into the kitchen. 'You need to get someone to take a look at that nose.'

Álvaro shook his head and slumped at the kitchen table. He was exhausted. His hair was still dripping from the rain, his shoes oozing muddy water. Propping himself on his elbows, he pushed the mane of sopping hair off his face. His nose was caked in dried blood, the bridge was swollen. The livid bruises around his eyes looked worse in the glare of the halogens. He looked as though he had been crying.

'Get those wet clothes off,' she ordered.

He gestured for her to wait a minute, holding a palm up to her, like a patient who had just been sick and needed time to catch his breath. Then he looked at his wife. Or should he call her his ex-wife? Raquel was wearing a grey cotton T-shirt and loose cotton slacks. She had let down her hair and it fell around her shoulders. It was a rich brown that, depending on the light, could look like honey. Random images popped into his head: blazing logs in a fireplace, a blanket, the warmth of Raquel's breath. Not for the first time, he told himself he had been a fool. Five years he had spent holed up in that burrow in the mountains. His supposed saviour had been his jailer. Now he knew that, with a word, Gaizka could have given him back his home, his wife. Was it too late?

Raquel insisted that he take a shower. She went upstairs with him. Ana was asleep, she said. Burgos had left and another officer was watching over their daughter. She decided not to tell him that Ana had run away just after his fight with Gaizka. She knew what Álvaro would say: that their daughter had escaped from one prison only to find herself in another. That, after all she had been through, she needed her freedom.

They went into the bathroom. Álvaro sat on the edge of the bath. Raquel leaned across and turned on the shower. He noticed that she was wearing no perfume. There was nothing artificial about her, just the smell he remembered from all those nights spent sleeping beside her; he secretly preferred it when she did not mask this smell with artificial scents. Suddenly, the memory of her naked body pressed against his was as vivid as though they had made love only minutes ago. Her skin, her lips.

Steam from the shower filled the room. For a second, Álvaro felt selfish. He should be thinking about Ana, about how to help his daughter readjust to normal life. But then he thought that, as her parents, they needed to be a part of that normal life. They had a duty to resolve their problems. What had happened to the guy he had seen Raquel with at the hospital? Ismael? Gaizka had told him that he worked for Raquel as a carpenter. Remembering the conversation with Gaizka, he felt a wave of fury at the man he had thought of as his friend. He wished he could punch him again; how much of their friendship had been real, and how much pretence?

Raquel crouched down next to Álvaro. 'You know something?' she said. 'I don't care how we got here. All that matters to me is that we're here now.'

Álvaro hesitated a moment. 'I love you.'

Instinctively, Raquel looked away, as embarrassed as a teenage girl. Álvaro guessed that she was blushing. Her hands were on his knees and, without thinking, he parted them.

'I need to fuck you,' she heard Álvaro say, but she did not dare look up.

He took her wrist, got to his feet and helped her up. He pressed himself to her, pinning her against the washbasin. Her blouse was wet from his sodden clothes. A torrent of images cascaded through her mind: from the moment she had watched Álvaro's car drive away four years ago, to the night she had first slept with Ismael. What had her life been in the interim? She wanted to run out of the bathroom, and, at the same time, she wanted to stay, take off her clothes and feel Álvaro inside her.

She needed to feel pleasure.

Álvaro laid a hand on her neck and she leaned her head towards it, like a cat being stroked. Water thrummed in the bath, a metallic drumming that seemed to match the rhythm of her heartbeat.

She was the one who pulled Álvaro closer, pressing his crotch against her own. She opened her mouth and kissed him.

Outside the car window, the trees and the mountains scrolled past, like a backdrop wound by an invisible hand, distorted by the darkness, the rain, the smudged glass. Sara had refused to go back to the hotel. As they got into the car, someone – possibly another Guardia Civil officer – had told them that Marcial Nerín was in Barbastro.

One of the villagers had seen him leave with his mother. 'She'll be at the hospital,' Víctor had said. 'She's on dialysis.' Sara wanted to talk to Marcial as soon as possible. Had Víctor said that she was in no fit state to be on duty? What did he know? She had asked him to call La Renclusa to find out whether Elisa was working. It was supposed to be Marcial's daughter's day off, but no one had seen her.

They drove down the valley and into the tunnel at Fall Gorge. For a few minutes, the pounding rain stopped and they were enveloped in darkness.

Some kilometres in front of them, the ambulance carrying the remains of Santiago Baín would be following the same route.

Sara and Víctor drove in silence. She had her face pressed to the window, though she did not really see what was on the other side. She was here, in the car, heading for Barbastro, and at the same time she was far away.

In a different time, a different place.

There was the room where Santiago Baín had taken her shortly after she'd first met him at the police station. Sara had turned up at his office, convinced that her parents were looking for her; in fact, all they had felt when she ran away was relief. Santiago had taken pity on her – although, at first, Sara had mistaken it for desire. She was a pretty young girl; he was a single man in his fifties. He had taken her number and called her a few days later. He wanted to know how things were going, how she was managing to get by. They met up in a café and Sara had told him she was living on the streets. He had taken her home. Bought her new clothes. Fed her. As in a fairy tale, Sara waited for the moment when this charming older man would be transformed into a demon.

The transformation never happened.

Sara had stayed, living in his apartment.

Shortly after moving in, she had a nightmare – one that hovered between wakefulness and sleep, where she felt trapped in her body, unable to move. She was staring at the walls of a room to which she was not yet accustomed, and from the shadows came the familiar parade of strange creatures. They did not touch her, did not speak to her. They simply sat the foot of the bed and stared at her. Men and women without faces, like the husks of human beings, watching her.

That night, she had felt a hand. A hand on her shoulder, shaking her awake. The creatures vanished and Sara regained control of her body. Sitting next to her, she recognized Santiago, his round face covered in an impossible tracery of wrinkles. 'You were trembling,' he said. She could not find the words to explain. Santiago did not insist; he simply hugged her.

There, in that bed, feeling Santiago Baín's protective warmth, was where she wanted to be.

She had never wanted to think about the fact that Santiago would die one day.

Never again wanted to feel the loneliness she had been drowning in before she met him.

Dawn was breaking as they reached Barbastro. The sun rose into a clear sky. The clouds had disappeared and, as they got out of the car, there was only a spattering of rain. A grey mist shrouded the façade of the hospital, and the workers beginning their shifts were moving warily, still tailing the last wisps of sleep. Everything was muffled: the sound of the cars, the conversations of the relatives stretching their legs after an uncomfortable night sitting with patients. It was as though she had her hands over her ears.

As they entered the hospital, Sara struggled to come back to reality. But she needed to, if she was to catch the man who had murdered Santiago.

The onlookers had lost interest. Most of them headed home at dawn. Only those who lived nearby were still hanging around Transportes Castán, though by now they were talking about things that had nothing to do with what had happened. Whipped by the wind, the police tape trailed in the mud. After the removal of the body, most of the Guardia Civil officers had left; only two remained, like the last customers in a bar, refusing to go home even after the lights are turned on. Pujante and Telmo, hollow-eyed, lost for words, staring blankly at the depression left by Baín's body. And the earth streaked red with blood.

Hey! Don't you get it? They've rolled down the shutters and turned off the music, Gaizka wanted to shout at them. But, instead, he let himself be led away, afraid that his continued presence might attract attention. He left with the old man who had raised the alarm. Moisén, he said his name was. As they walked up to his house, Gaizka noticed that his pyjama bottoms had come out of his rubber boots. The cuffs were stained with mud that looked like shit.

Moisén ushered him into the kitchen, while he went to change his clothes. His wife, a plump woman wearing a purple towelling bathrobe, offered Gaizka coffee and he accepted. He sat next to the window, from where he could see the forecourt of Transportes Castán. He stared fixedly at the truck where he had hidden the rifle, oblivious to Moisén's wife as she bustled about making coffee and grumbling – 'What on earth is this village coming to? Mother of God, who knows what tragedy we'll see next.'

Nor did he hear Moisén when he reappeared, wearing a pair of overalls – 'I was lying awake, worrying about the gutters; they always get clogged with pine needles when there's heavy rain. That's when I heard the shot.' Now that he had taken off his plastic rain hat, Gaizka could see the greasy shock of black curls plastered to Moisén's head.

He excused himself and asked the way to the bathroom. He flushed the toilet to drown out the sound as he vomited. He was terrified that, when he opened the bathroom door, there would be officers waiting to arrest him. He felt his forehead and noticed it was feverish.

Going back into the kitchen, he saw from the window that the forecourt was now deserted except for the two officers on guard. Without even touching his coffee, he said goodbye to Moisén and his wife and went out on to the road, trying to appear normal. He walked up towards the village until he came to the pine forest. Checking to make sure there was no one on the road, he ducked into the trees, taking the same route he had the night before, when he had run away from Joaquín's forecourt.

The previous night seemed remote now. Like a memory from a million years ago.

The ground was peppered with puddles and rainwater dripped from the branches of the pine trees. The dawn light filtered through the dense canopy, giving it a greenish tinge. Of the officers still guarding the forecourt, Gaizka only knew Pujante. He was somewhat younger and, before he had joined the force, they had spent a few nights drinking together. Gaizka remembered one particular binge, in a bar in Posets, maybe, when they had put their arms around each other's shoulders, singing at the top of their lungs to whatever was playing. Pujante had given up partying once he got his stripes. Or had he got married? Doesn't matter, Gaizka thought.

Creeping to the edge of the forest and hiding behind the trunk of a tree, Gaizka could see them. The other officer was trying to make conversation with Pujante, who was leaning against the bonnet of the jeep. They were probably talking about football. Or the hunting season. Whatever the subject, it did little to change the grim expression on Pujante's face. He smiled reluctantly when he spoke. From time to time, he looked at the muddy imprint where Santiago Baín's body had been.

Gaizka did not want to think about the cop, or the black hole he had opened in his chest with the rifle. He tried to be positive: he had managed to get out of a difficult situation. He was like an actor in a comedy, constantly teetering and about to fall, but always managing to regain his balance at the last minute.

He took out his mobile phone, looked through his contacts and dialled the number for Transportes Castán. Immediately, the phone in the office started to ring. The officers did not hear it at first, but then Pujante glanced behind him; the office door was open and the ringtone floated on the breeze. He took a couple of steps, intending to answer it, but the other officer obviously said that he would deal with it. Gaizka saw him walk towards the hangar. Pujante moved around to the back of the jeep, so all that was visible was his cap.

The truck was a few metres away. A faded blue Pegaso that, in the light of day, looked clapped out. Gaizka crouched down, but, from where he was, he could not see the rifle jammed into the chassis. He hung up, waited for a few seconds, then dialled again.

He could tell that the Guardia Civil officer was still inside the office, and Pujante could not see him creep out of the forest from where he was standing, since the jeep blocked his view. Gaizka took a breath and, hunched over, he scurried towards the truck. He felt ridiculous. Like a character in a bad spy movie. He reached the cab of the truck and, peering underneath, he could see two pairs of feet: Pujante and the other officer, who had obviously re-emerged from the office. He was surprised that he could clearly hear what they were saying: 'There's no one there,' and then, 'Hello? Hello?' Suddenly, Gaizka realized that the sound was coming from his own phone; he had forgotten to hang up. He stuffed a hand into his pocket and ended the call. He felt panic rising in his chest and tried to slow his breathing.

It was now or never.

He dropped to the ground and saw the Browning rifle lodged above the axle. He crawled towards it.

The sound of an approaching engine froze him to the spot. He could see a car driving into the forecourt and stopping next to the police tape. The two officers went over to talk to the driver. Gaizka grabbed the oak butt of the rifle.

Someone got out of the car wearing rubber boots and jeans that were rucked up over them. Gaizka's heart was beating so hard it was physically painful. All of a sudden, he was afraid he would have an aneurysm from all the coke he'd had. How was he supposed to get out of here now? Who was the guy who had just arrived?

He thought it might be a forensics officer. What if he had brought sniffer dogs? One of the officers lifted the tape to allow the man to pass, and he walked towards the truck. Gaizka shouldered the rifle and aimed it towards them. Who should he shoot first? Pujante, he thought. Then he remembered him drunk, singing, back when they used to hang out together in bars. What was it they had been singing?

Keep a cool head, he told himself.

First, shoot the new guy. Pujante is a mess, anyway. With a bit of luck, he'll do a runner.

The three men stopped a few metres from the truck. Gaizka could hear a murmur of voices, but could not make out what was being said.

He crawled back behind one of the wheels. He edged his head out, trying to see who had just arrived.

When he saw it was only Joaquín's brother-in-law, Rafael, he relaxed. He was waving his arms, pointing to the hangar, explaining something or other. Then he turned and walked towards the office. The officers followed him.

As soon as their backs were turned, Gaizka bolted.

He scrabbled from under the truck and ran until he was, once more, lost among the trees. He looked at the rifle in his hands and laughed as he tried to catch his breath. They had nothing on him now.

Sara sat next to Marcial's mother. The old woman was reclining in a chair that was too big for her. Her left arm, palm up, was lying on the wide armrest. Two I.V. tubes snaked into her arm. Blood came out, and, once it had been purified, flowed back into her body. The woman stared into space, completely detached from the procedure, which seemed to cause her no discomfort. Her mouth hung open, her lower lip slack.

Víctor had gone to find Marcial Nerín. One of the nurses had said that he left after bringing his mother in. He had been there first thing that morning, just before they had arrived at the hospital. It was likely that he had gone back to the apartment he rented in Barbastro. They had tried to phone him, but he was not answering.

Víctor did not understand Sara's urgent need to talk to Marcial. She had told him about the eight-pointed star that forensics had found in the mountain hut, the gold Cofradía pin that had survived the fire. Marcial Nerín was prior of the Cofradía. But Víctor had said, 'So what? Everyone in the village is a member of the Cofradía. Even I've got one of those.'

Sara knew precisely what was bothering Víctor: the discovery of the pin definitively ruled out the possibility that the kidnapping had been the work of an outsider. Or even someone from one of the neighbouring villages.

The man who had abducted the girls was from Monteperdido.

A friend, a neighbour. Someone Víctor probably bumped into every day, someone he smiled at and said hello to. Someone who had worked shoulder to shoulder with him dredging the River Ésera. They were bound to have shared coffee and cake at the Cofradía meetings next to the church. *How are things?* Víctor might have said, receiving the reply, *Oh, you know. Getting by.*

He was not angry with Sara; he was angry with reality.

While she waited for Víctor to come back, Sara watched the blood flowing from Marcial's mother, through the tubes, into the dialysis machine. Bubbling, almost black.

She would have liked to have taken care of Santiago when he was an old man. When his body no longer did as he wanted. She would have sat next to him in a hospital room somewhere, talking about stories from the newspapers. Killing time. Easing his pain.

Marcial's mother was wearing a black dress that looked more

like a housecoat. A hospital blanket covered her lap, and, below, her scrawny legs dangled in the air, not reaching the ground. Her grey, slightly greasy hair made Sara realize that Marcial had not taken her to the hairdresser for some time.

Once the façade crumbled, who cared what went on behind the scenes? In the eyes of everyone else, this woman was already past recovery. Her body had ceased to be habitable.

The nurse came back to check the dialysis machine.

'She has Alzheimer's,' she said when Sara asked, something Santiago had mentioned to her. 'And kidney failure, obviously.'

Sara would have liked to have asked the old woman where she had been the night before, from the time she left Monteperdido to the time she arrived at the hospital. The journey had taken much too long, even allowing for the rain. They had left the village at ten o'clock and she had not been admitted to the hospital until this morning.

Who could tell her what had happened?

The night of the storm had thrown up shadows that Sara needed to shed light on: not just Marcial's journey, but also where Elisa might be. And Santiago. Especially Santiago.

Why had he gone to Joaquín's workplace? What was he doing at Transportes Castán?

Joaquín's business was barely staying afloat. Some months earlier, Rafael had stopped paying his security company, so the footage from the C.C.T.V. cameras in the office and the hangar were no longer being transmitted anywhere. The night watchman had also been laid off; they had been struggling to pay him for almost a year. The trucks, which barely left the hangar most days, were getting older and increasingly unreliable.

I think you're right. We've got something, Santiago had said.

The nurse moved the pillow Marcial's mother was leaning against. The old woman limply allowed herself to be manhandled.

When the nurse removed the blanket in order to straighten it, Sara saw the old woman's right arm, which had been hidden in her lap. Her hand was clenched in a fist.

'Does it hurt?' Sara asked, and, seeing the nurse's puzzled look, explained, 'The dialysis – does it cause her any pain?'

'I don't think so,' the nurse said, smoothing the blanket. 'Well, no more than an ordinary blood test.'

'Does this mean something?' Sara said, lifting the blanket to reveal the old woman's clenched fist.

'No, it doesn't mean anything,' the nurse reassured her.

Víctor came into the room.

'Marcial Nerín is outside. Do you want to talk to him?'

Sara re-covered the old woman's lap and followed Víctor down the corridor to a side room, where Marcial was standing by the window. A Guardia Civil officer waved them in, then closed the door.

'What's all this about?' Marcial said when he saw her, struggling not to raise his voice. 'Coming to my home like I was some sort of criminal—'

'Where were you last night?' Sara cut him short. 'From ten o'clock, when you left Monteperdido, until you reached the hospital, first thing this morning.'

'On the road . . .' Marcial replied. 'You dragged me out of bed for this?'

'It must have been a very long drive,' Sara pressed, though she was aware she was having trouble focusing on the conversation. Her brain had started going in a different direction.

'Marcial, why don't we just cut the bullshit?' Víctor said curtly. 'You've been asked a straight question, why not just give a straight answer? And don't tell me it took you nine hours to drive to Barbastro.'

Marcial gave Víctor a confused look. The Guardia Civil had been brusque, as though frustrated at having to talk to an imbecile. He raised his head and gave the sergeant a contemptuous look.

'Are you going to start with this nonsense too?' he said disdainfully.

'Fuck,' Víctor muttered. He heaved a sigh and then grabbed Marcial by the collar and slammed him against the wall. 'A police officer was murdered last night. Are you going to stand there and waste my time? Are you serious?'

The look of surprise on Marcial's face seemed genuine. Stammering, he asked who had been killed. Was it someone from the village? And he could not hide his relief when he was told that the murdered officer was Inspector Baín. Víctor steered him back to the previous night. To this apparently endless drive.

'It was raining heavily,' Marcial began. 'I was worried the river would flood. You know as well as I do that we didn't have time to dredge it properly. I turned off the main road, on to the Carretera de Francia. The Ixeia tunnel seemed a safe place to wait. There's a section inside the tunnel where you can shelter from the rain, so I waited there with my mother until the storm eased off.'

Sara turned away from Marcial; an idea was taking shape in her head. A nebulous idea based on gut feelings and hunches. She tried to shape it into something she could express, but the pieces would not quite fit.

'When I got to Barbastro, I dropped by the apartment,' Marcial carried on. 'Ask the neighbours. I'm sure one of them heard us arrive. I cleaned my mother up before bringing her here to the hospital.'

Víctor let the man go; he knew there was nothing else he could add. He looked to Sara for an order about how to proceed.

'Where is Elisa?' Sara said, without looking at Marcial.

'I don't know. At home, I suppose.' But the answer came too quickly, and his tone was hesitant.

'She left Monteperdido with you,' Sara insisted, suddenly realizing that this must be true. 'Where is she now?'

Marcial looked to Víctor for protection, but the sergeant refused to give it. He was as eager for the response as Sara. Marcial smoothed the shirt Víctor had just creased, then ran his hand over his bald head.

'We had an argument.' Once again, Marcial look to Víctor for support. 'You know what she's like. She never got over . . . Anyway, now it turns out she's made a statement supporting Álvaro. How am I supposed to take that? This is the same bastard who ruined her life—'

'Where's Elisa?' Víctor snapped.

'I told you, I don't know!' Marcial roared in frustration. There was a helplessness about his gestures as he seemed to become aware of his mistakes. 'We had a fight and she set off back to the village . . . She's either at home or . . . What do I know? In bed with some tourist, probably.'

Víctor choked back his anger. Everyone in the village knew how things were between Marcial and his daughter; it was like one of those truths that, if never said aloud, people hoped would disappear. What had Monteperdido ever done for Elisa? Looked the other way, turned a blind eye while she wasted away with Marcial. No one had wanted to know the truth. And suddenly Víctor acknowledged something that had been staring him in the face, something that he had chosen to ignore: the village had invented a narrative when the two girls disappeared. A story that began by blaming Álvaro and, later on, some random outsider: anyone who was not from around here. A story that allowed them to feel virtuous. Innocent.

This was how Monteperdido had behaved towards Elisa; no one was prepared to admit that they knew what was going on between Elisa and her father. Víctor felt a vicious twinge of shame in his gut. He thought about the looks people had given Elisa when she had turned to them for help. The looks that told her she was unbalanced, a girl whose cards were marked because of her relationship with Álvaro. And Elisa could find no comfort.

Suddenly, Sara broke the silence, leaving the room and slamming the door behind her. She raced down the corridor, quickly followed by Víctor, who asked what was going on; she did not answer. She went into the room where Marcial's mother was receiving dialysis. As she did so, Víctor stopped to answer his phone; it was a call from the station and he thought it better to take it in the hallway.

In the hospital room, Sara went over to the old woman. She was still attached to the I.V. Sara lifted the blanket from her lap. She gently took the woman's clenched fist, looked into her lost, bewildered eyes and said, 'What are you hiding?'

Somewhere in the old woman's mind, there was a spark, a flicker of consciousness sending signals from the darkness. One finger after another, Sara unravelled the fist, as though it were a knot, until she could see the woman's palm. There were traces of dirt and a murky stain. Dark red. Blood.

'Has she got any injuries?' Sara asked the nurse.

'Not that I know of.'

'I need this blood analysed. If it's not hers . . .' Sara trailed off, leaving the words hanging in the air as she mentally completed the sentence: . . . *then whose is it?*

Víctor came into the room. He was hanging up his phone call as Sara barked orders at an officer she had just summoned.

'I need you to get it cross-matched against a blood sample from Elisa, or, failing that, from Marcial,' she was saying, then, seeing Víctor arrive, she paused. 'Has something happened?'

'Rafael told Pujante that one of the trucks is missing. It left just before Inspector Baín arrived at Transportes Castán. It's headed to Barcelona. It's a refrigerated truck carrying a consignment of veal. They talked to the driver and he said he hadn't noticed anything.'

'But . . .' Sara said, stepping towards him. 'Because there is a "but", isn't there?'

'The driver said that, before he left, he was with Gaizka, who had asked him to take a couple of boxes to be stored in an industrial estate, here in Barbastro. I've told all officers that our first priority now has to be to track down Gaizka.'

'Where's the industrial estate?' Sara asked. Although she tried to concentrate on the fact that they had a suspect, something about it made her suspicious. As though the door that had suddenly opened in the maze might be a trap, something to lure her away from the right path.

Despite this feeling, Sara knew that, until she crossed the threshold, she could never be certain.

★

Avenida de Posets, which led through the village, was almost deserted, which was strange for a weekday in July. Ordinarily, there would be rental cars driven by tourists, a bottleneck at the traffic lights outside the church, a coach of day trippers. Gaizka drummed his fingers on the steering wheel and stared at the speedometer, careful to keep it hovering around fifty kilometres an hour.

A bizarre summer. The police presence had shooed away the tourists like a hand swatting flies. Business was bad.

The rifle was in the boot of the car. What should he do with it?

He eased up on the accelerator as he drove through a puddle and felt the front tyre sink into a pothole.

Outside a clothes shop, the owner was smoking a cigarette and looking bored. Through the windows of the Corza Blanca café, on the corner of the road leading to the school, he could see empty tables. A waitress was leaning on the counter, idly leafing through a magazine.

Monteperdido looked like a village overwhelmed by some tragedy that had robbed its inhabitants of the strength to go outdoors.

He should dismantle the rifle and bury the parts in various locations in the mountains. At the foot of La Kregüeña. This was a possibility worth considering.

Did he still have a stash of coke at his place? He thought so. He decided to go home before he did anything. The desperate need for a quick line clouded his brain and made it impossible to think logically.

He noticed that his left foot was twitching wildly in the footwell. He gripped his thigh and tried to stop it.

Tossing the rifle into the river was another possibility.

Or maybe drive to the Hotel La Guardia, climb up the lookout tower, drop it and let it shatter on the rocks below.

The end was just around the corner. He knew that the police would find his lock-up in the industrial estate, but so what? The truck driver – what was his name again? – anyway, there was nothing he could say that Gaizka could not explain away.

He felt a surge of bravado. Come and have a go, if you think you're hard enough.

But he needed to calm down, and, for that, he needed a quick toot. Maybe two.

Leaving Monteperdido behind, he continued on his way up to Posets.

Montserrat was waiting in Raquel's back garden.

A cloudless day had dawned after the fierce night of rain. The oilskin she was wearing was too hot and hardly necessary. Or perhaps she was simply feeling nervous.

What was she expecting from this conversation? She could not answer. But she knew instinctively that it had to happen, like a mother, waking in the middle of the night, knows that she has to check on her children to make sure they are all right. That they are still breathing.

Ana followed her mother out into the garden. She was wearing a black baseball cap, the visor of which hid her eyes. The flower-print dress she was wearing accentuated the whiteness of her skin. Montserrat launched into an apology that Raquel immediately cut short.

'It's all forgotten.'

The three women sat down at the teak table that Raquel brought into the garden when the weather was fine. Montserrat smiled and refused Raquel's offer of coffee. Where should she start? What should be her first question? She suppressed the urge to ask whether Lucía had often talked about her. Not that it was a selfish question; she simply needed to know that the link that bound her to her daughter was mutual. Did Lucía miss her mother as much as she was missed?

'Lucía was always telling me things about you,' Ana said, as though reading her thoughts. 'About the chocolate cakes filled with strawberry jam you used to make on Sundays, how she loved being in the kitchen in the warm glow of the oven when it was snowing outside.'

Montserrat felt her lower lip quiver as she smiled. She had promised herself she would not cry, or at least not too much, but now she sensed it would not be easy to hold back her tears.

'And the songs you used to sing to her,' Ana went on. 'In the early days, before we went to sleep, she'd always hum a lullaby that you taught her – do you remember?'

Montserrat remembered the tune, and the nights she had spent sitting on her daughter's bed, stroking her hair until she fell asleep:

Close your eyes, go to sleep
mister sandman is waiting
just to guide you on your way
with his basket full of dreams.

'I don't know what to ask,' Montserrat confessed. How was it possible to recreate her daughter's life with only a handful of questions?

'Whatever you like,' Ana said.

'Why don't you tell us what you and Lucía used to do?' Raquel suggested. 'How did you spend your days?'

Ana shrugged, and turned to look at the pine forest behind the house. 'That's complicated,' she explained, with the childlike worry of a little girl facing an exam. 'We'd make up songs. Listen to the radio. For a while, we even had a T.V. – a little one, about this big.' Ana held out her hands, indicating a size no bigger than a book. 'We could hardly see anything. Lucía really liked *Hannah Montana*. It's a series—'

'It's pretty famous,' Montserrat said.

'And we would read. Well, I would, mostly. He would bring second-hand books and Lucía liked me to read them aloud. Sometimes, she'd fall asleep and then, if I carried on reading, I'd have to go back to the last bit she remembered . . .'

'What was her favourite book?' Montserrat asked.

'Well, we didn't really have much choice. She never liked the one with poems in. She thought they were boring.' Ana raised her chin and sunlight shimmered on her skin, glinted on her dark eyes that had been hidden under her cap. '*The Hunger Games*. She loved that.' Then, pretending to complain, Ana said, 'Sometimes she'd make fun of me. She'd put on a silly voice and say, "This quiet roof, where doles of doves assemble / Between the pines, the gravestones, seems to tremble". It's a poem I learned by heart.' Then, almost with a laugh, she added, 'It drove her crazy, me learning poems.'

'You learned poems?' Raquel said with a smile, and, for a second, she had to stop herself from remarking how difficult it had been to get the girls to read when they were at school. Better to say nothing. The sense of normality that had returned to their house was still new to Montserrat.

A cloud passed over the sun, throwing a shadow across the garden as Ana carried on telling trite anecdotes. The first months began to merge into the long period when they had assumed that they would be imprisoned for the rest of their lives. For them, the phase most adolescents spend in anxious excitement had been like a stagnant pool in which they were submerged for five years. Montserrat pulled her coat tighter, as a breeze brought a chill wind from the mountain. She looked up at the sky – *where doles of doves assemble*, she thought – watching the red-tinged cloud that masked the sun begin to disperse, even as it still cast a shadow on them.

'What Lucía liked most was Barbie dolls,' Ana remembered. 'She spent ages and ages playing with them, dressing them, making up silly games . . . Sometimes, she'd take a red marker and draw faces on them – smiles and tears and pink cheeks . . . He brought her more dolls and more clothes . . . In the end, she must have had about twenty . . .'

He brought her . . . Like a stranger arriving on tiptoe, the man had slipped into Ana's memory. Montserrat pictured her daughter in the mountain hut, kneeling on the timber floor, moving the dolls and imitating their voices – and, behind her, the figure of this monster. Relishing the torture.

At the weight of this thought, Montserrat lowered her eyes, as though an invisible hand had grabbed her by the neck and forced her to bow her head. She felt Raquel gently take her hand and hold it, trying to stop her from once again erupting in an outpouring of rage and fear. Her daughter was alive. That was all that mattered. She could sense her life in Ana's words.

'Until, one day, she got bored with the dolls,' Ana said. 'Lucía was like that. She could be a bit . . .' She hesitated for a moment, searching for the right word. 'A bit fickle. She'd get obsessed with something and spend her whole time doing it, and then she'd suddenly get bored with it.'

Montserrat did not think of Ana's description as a criticism. She did not hear the gentle reproach that had crept in, like a sneaky thief. She recognized Lucía in this trait. This was the same girl who had followed her around the house, begging for a pair of roller skates, only to abandon them at the bottom of the wardrobe as soon as she got them. The girl who would grab Joaquín's finger when they were in the toyshop and point out this and this and this. All the things she wanted and almost always got.

Rather than worrying her, the memory of her daughter's flaws made her seem closer. She felt that if, one day, she held Lucía in her arms again, she would be the same little girl who had got lost in the forest. A little spoiled. But whose fault was that? Her parents'. But she had also been smiley and eager to play, cuddly and affectionate as a baby – although, by the time she disappeared, she had begun to grow up. Stubborn and demanding, never prepared to take 'no' for an answer. Physically, she took after her mother – the dark hair, the almond eyes, the bronzed complexion, the same thin lips that Montserrat had always hated in herself – but what she had inherited from Joaquín was like a flag planted in foreign soil: her strong, aquiline nose. Her character.

Ana had spent all morning talking about Lucía, with Raquel or Montserrat interrupting only rarely, but now she seemed tired. Montserrat was first to get up; she went over and hugged Ana.

'Thank you. I really mean that,' she whispered.

Raquel walked her to the door.

Before saying goodbye, Montserrat said that she wanted to straighten things out. 'With Álvaro, too,' she said. 'I know that we really hurt him.'

'We have time,' Raquel said.

Montserrat went home. Joaquín was waiting in the living room. She had forgotten all about him. When she went over to see Ana, she had been afraid that, at any minute, she would be found out; but, as she had listened to Ana, as she had begun to see her daughter more clearly, it had gone out of her head. Now, she felt guilty. Like a spy.

'Give it to me,' Joaquín said. 'Let's hear the recording.'

Montserrat rummaged in her bag, took out her mobile phone and unlocked it. The voice recorder she had switched on while gazing at her own house and waiting for Ana to come out into the garden was still running.

'This isn't right, Joaquín,' she said.

'You've seen how the police are handling things. Do you really think they're going to get anywhere? Baín was the one leading the investigation. What do you expect me to do? Sit here with my arms folded until they send some other inspector?'

'They invited me into their home . . . and we . . . I should have at least told her first.'

'So that Álvaro could have vetoed it?' Joaquín took the phone and pressed *stop*. He played it from the beginning to check that everything Ana had said had been recorded. 'Darling, if we don't do something, no one will.' He kissed her cheek — a brief, half-hearted kiss — then he went out.

Montserrat stared at the living-room walls. The photographs of Lucía as a little girl were like a shrine to the dead, and for the first time she wanted to tear them down. Lucía was not dead. She was alive, she was nearby. She still played and laughed, she still got angry and wrinkled up her nose the way she had always done when she was scolded. She was not a corpse.

★

Sara and Víctor followed the security guard down the long corridors of La Portellada, the vast storage complex in the industrial estate off the Huesca Road, south of Barbastro. On either side were lines of private lock-ups, each with a metal shutter. A yellowish light filtered through the frosted skylights, giving the guard's pale complexion a sickly, cirrhotic hue. He had been waiting on a motorcycle outside the industrial estate, and had led them to the storage complex where the truck driver from Transportes Castán had dropped boxes off the previous evening. The security guard had only just come on shift.

'It's number thirty-seven,' he said, searching the keys on the huge ring hanging from his belt for the one that would open the lock-up.

Víctor took a step forward, wondering what lay behind the metal shutter. Sara allowed herself to be led by the logic of the investigation, though she still had a nagging feeling, like a knot in her stomach, that they had taken a wrong turn. But, even if that were true, which way should they go? At what point should they turn? She looked around the hangar at the rows of locked storage units. Which one should they open?

The security guard crouched, and his trousers slipped down, revealing an arse crack as pale as his face. Zacarías – that was how he had introduced himself. Víctor behaved with an affected familiarity, the way you might with someone whose name you have forgotten or maybe never bothered to remember. Zacarías called the sergeant by his first name, and wanted to know what they were looking for in 'his kingdom'. This was how he had referred to the industrial estate, with an idiotic grin.

Zacarías rolled up the shutter. It made a metallic screech that echoed around the hangar. Like a human scream. Víctor stepped inside and immediately saw the wooden boxes that the driver had left. He looked for something with which to crowbar the lids, which were nailed shut.

'I'm not sure this is legal,' the security guard said, though he did not seem to care one way or the other. He took a crumpled pouch of tobacco from his pocket and lit a cigarette. 'What has all this got to do with those missing girls?' he asked.

Víctor shot him an angry look and went back to opening the first crate.

What *did* it have to do with the girls? Sara was wondering. Could Gaizka have been the one who abducted them? What was in these crates?

Zacarías covered his mouth as he let out a burp, though it did little to mask his rumbling belly.

Víctor lifted off the lid of the crate, tossed it on the ground, plunged his hand inside and brought out a black helmet spattered with red and yellow paint. He could not hide his disappointment. What had he expected to find?

Sara walked over and looked into the crate. Nothing but piles of paintball helmets. She knew the contents of the other crate would be the same.

'What the fuck is that?' Zacarías said, exhaling a long plume of smoke.

Víctor dropped the helmet on the ground, picked up the crowbar and opened the other one.

'Did you see the truck driver unload the crates?' Sara asked Zacarías.

'I had to do it myself,' he said. 'Juan, the driver, he's got a hernia, so he's not allowed to lift anything . . .'

The second crate, like the first, was filled with paintballing helmets.

'Whose name is on the lease for this storage unit?' Sara asked.

For the first time since they'd met him, the security guard looked nervous. He mumbled something about not being allowed to divulge that information. He tossed his cigarette on the floor and ground it to shreds, hiking up his trousers as they slipped beneath his considerable paunch.

Víctor leaned on the edge of the crate and said that, if he preferred, they could all wait here until someone arrived with a warrant.

'It belongs to Vicente Serna,' Zacarías finally admitted. 'Not just this one, the whole hangar.'

Sara looked to Víctor to shed light on this name.

The sergeant stood up and kicked at the dusty floor. He smoothed his uniform and shrugged as though the name was of no importance. Picking up the helmet and lobbing it into the crate, he said, 'He's the owner of the Hotel La Guardia. Up in the mountains, where the road runs out.'

His mobile phone rang. On the screen, he saw it was Noguera, the fucking abseiling guide. He rejected the call and, knowing that Noguera would immediately call back, set his phone to mute. In the pocket of a pair of jeans at the foot of his bed, he had found a baggy containing just over a gram. He cut himself a couple of lines on the glass table. His gums went numb and he was starting to feel a little calmer. He had made a decision. He picked up the car keys and took a last look around the house.

Gaizka owned a small apartment in Posets, about seventy square metres. He liked to feel frugal. He kept his money piled in shoe-boxes in his wardrobe. This was the only thing about which he was organized. The rest of the house was a pigsty. Dirty clothes were strewn all over the bed and the floor, and the smell of sweat and socks pervaded every corner. In the kitchen, the pile of dirty dishes in the sink looked as though it would topple over. He opened the living-room window and a blast of fresh air rushed into the house.

Maybe the time had come to quit. To shut up shop and leave the valley.

How much money had he saved? Enough to start again some-where. He could live for years without having to work. Sometimes, he imagined himself as an ascetic, a monk leading a life devoted to meditation and austerity in the mountains.

A monk with a coke habit, he thought, and laughed.

He left the house, got into his car and turned the key in the igni-tion. The rifle was still sleeping in the boot.

He intended to drive to the bridge, then take a right and head up the mountain as far as the Hotel La Guardia. He would drop the rifle from the lookout tower. The ravine below was inaccessible, and one of the first to get snow in winter. His secret would be safe.

He would have to wait a couple of days. Then he would pack the money into the boot of his car and leave the valley.

As he drove, he fantasized about where he might go. He was sick and tired of the cold, of endless snowy winters. He would go some-place warm. The Canary Islands, maybe.

He drove past the road leading to his tour company, Adventures In Posets. Some adventure, he thought. He crossed the river, the car juddering on the cobbled bridge. When he got to the main road in Monteperdido, he turned right. There was still some way to go before he reached the Hotel La Guardia, high in the mountains. If there was anyone Gaizka admired, it was Serna. King of an inhospitable territory, happy with his lot. Confident as a stag leaping between perilous crags.

The flashing lights of a Guardia Civil vehicle flickered in his rear-view mirror. He had not seen it coming. An officer was signalling for him to pull over.

He felt his throat tighten, leaving only a narrow opening for him to breathe. He considered flooring the accelerator and driving off, but stopped himself. What did they have on him? Nothing. He had an answer prepared for every question. Besides, where would he go? He was driving up a road that came to a dead end a few kilometres ahead. There was no way out.

He'd hesitated too long before braking; he realized this when the officer turned on the siren.

Gaizka shifted into first gear, turned on his hazard warning lights and pulled to a stop at the side of the road. To his right, beyond the crash barrier, the mountain fell away steeply into yet another gorge. For the first time, he thought of this place as a face lined with scars. He watched as the jeep pulled up behind him. In the wing mirror, he saw Pujante get out of the car. Gaizka rolled down his window.

Just breathe, he told himself.

'Sorry. I was miles away; I didn't see the lights,' he apologized, as Pujante drew alongside.

'How are things, Gaizka? Listen, I need to take you down to the station. Víctor wants a word with you.'

'Does it have to be right now?' Gaizka said.

'Yes. Right now.' Pujante tried to sound firm.

Gaizka felt himself smile nervously, and tried to keep a straight face. He rubbed his nose – a gesture that had long since become a tic. 'OK, fine. I'll follow you,' he said. 'Any idea what it's about?'

'No, sorry.' Pujante turned and walked back to the jeep.

Gaizka looked at the road leading to the Hotel La Guardia. He jerked the steering wheel. Pujante stood in the middle of the road to ensure there were no cars coming as Gaizka turned his car to face downhill, towards Monteperdido. He had been so close to getting things sorted; every minor delay since the moment he recovered the rifle now tolled inside his head like a reproach: the need to stop for a quick line of coke, the seconds he had spent looking at the messy apartment before he left. Had he avoided just one of those moments, Pujante would not have caught him.

As he was about to head back towards Monteperdido, he remembered the phone call. He pulled alongside the Guardia Civil jeep as Pujante was making a U-turn. Two kilometres away, just past Posets bridge, was the canyon called Oscuros de Balced. Gaizka leaned his head out the window.

'Pujante!' he called. The officer looked over. 'Do you mind if we stop at Oscuros de Balced on the way? I've just had a call from Noguera. He's with a tour group, and I need to give him some stuff I left in the car . . . They need it for the abseil.'

Pujante thought for a moment, and then said, 'OK.'

Álvaro took the morning to visit a doctor in Monteperdido, who realigned his deviated septum and bandaged his nose. The bruising under his eyes had become more visible. And the pain was excruciating, like needles stabbing from his nose to the back of his eyes. But, generally, he felt fine.

Agustín Martínez

He did not notice that the streets were half-empty. Nor that she was following him.

The river was high, the waters muddy from the rains, but the current had eased and the surface was smooth and calm.

There were still one or two T.V. vans parked outside the housing development, but most of the journalists had left.

Today's headline news was the death of Inspector Baín.

How long before they completely forgot his daughter?

It felt cynical to think that his daughter's peace of mind depended on more death, more terrible tragedy. What would it take for the last of the reporters to pack up their things and leave the valley in search of something more newsworthy?

He crossed the bridge next to the police station and, at the far end of the road, he recognized the silhouette of the school. He knew he would not go back to work there, but he was no longer worried about the future. He had spent his whole life looking forward or looking back, fretting about the past and the future, oblivious to where he was: the present.

She called to him as he was crossing the road to go into the pine forest. Álvaro turned in surprise when he heard his name. He had not recognized her voice. Elisa rushed over and tried to hug him. Álvaro felt her face pressed against his chest. Disgusted, he shoved her away.

'What the hell do you think you're doing?' he said, making no attempt to hide his disdain.

Elisa looked at him, bewildered. Her face was drawn, as though she had not slept all night. Her clothes, dirty and spattered with dried mud, clung to her body. She no longer knew what to do with her hands, her arms, now that Álvaro would not let her hold him.

'I've had such a shitty night −' her voice was pleading − 'I just need you to hug me. No one can see us here.'

'I don't care if the whole village can see.' Álvaro jabbed a finger at her. 'I don't want you anywhere near me, ever again.'

'What did I do wrong?' Elisa whispered.

'You're a crazy fucking bitch.'

She took two steps back, as though his words had physically pushed her. Álvaro turned away and set off into the forest.

'Álvaro, don't turn your back on me,' she whimpered. 'I love you.'

But he carried on walking, receding into the distance.

Elisa could feel the sting of his rejection in the lacerations on her back. It felt as though all the wounds had opened and were bleeding.

'I saved you, you bastard!' she howled through her tears. 'I'll go to the police again; I'll tell them it was all lies. I'll tell them you're a pervert − I'll say you raped me!'

Álvaro turned before disappearing into the trees. 'Do what you like. No one believes a word you say anymore.' And he carried on walking home.

A flock of blackbirds took to the wing, vanishing into the sky like specks of ash carried on the wind.

They were driving back to Monteperdido when his telephone rang. Víctor pushed the hands-free button to take the call. At first, Pujante's voice was unintelligible. Sara wound up her window to eliminate the background noise.

'I'm with Gaizka,' Pujante's voice crackled over the speaker.

'We'll see you at the station,' Víctor said. 'Can you hear me?'

'Yeah, at the station,' Pujante said. 'We've just stopped for a minute at Oscuros de Balced because Gaizka had to give something to the tour guide. We'll be there in ten minutes.'

Víctor hung up. Sara turned and looked at the mountains as they slowly closed in on the road: Monte Albádes and Pico de Paderna. She thought of the first time she and Santiago had driven along this road.

'How do you know the security guard?' she asked Víctor.

'Zacarías? I think he worked at Joaquín's place for a while.'

The car sped on through the funnel created by the mountains, towards the tunnel that led to the Hidden Valley. Sara felt lightheaded; she could not seem to focus. Ever since Santiago's death, everything around her had taken on a dreamlike quality.

She remembered the guide. Noguera, he had said his name was. She could picture him, irritably trying to pack a rucksack with the equipment he needed for an abseiling tour. Leaving the door open for her, so that she might find something to incriminate Gaizka.

She felt her ears pop; they were inside the tunnel.

You can call him all you like, he never comes, Noguera had told her.

They emerged from the tunnel and the beauty of the summer scene upset her; she wished it was winter, not this glorious July day. Every patch of colour, every leaf, every animal felt like an affront to Santiago. She wanted to see bare branches, life buried beneath a mantle of snow.

'Call him,' Sara said. Then, more insistently, 'Call Pujante back. Tell him not to let Gaizka out of his sight, even for a second. We're heading to that canyon.'

Víctor accelerated, as though the urgency of Sara's words had pushed his foot down on the pedal. He did not ask questions. He was beginning to understand her and he knew that, once she had her ideas in order, she would tell him.

Gaizka opened the boot of the car. The rifle was hidden under a threadbare red blanket. He wrapped the blanket around it, then carefully popped his head up. Pujante was casually walking in circles, chatting on his mobile phone. Gaizka had the impression the officer was watching him out of the corner of his eye.

Behind Gaizka was the Oscuros de Balced canyon.

Pujante had followed him to the Posets crossroads and they had turned down the dirt track that led to the ravine. The crack in the earth began as a thin line, like a shadow drawn on the ground, and gradually broadened out as it headed east, revealing its true depths. The rock face plummeted a hundred metres to where the River Grist rushed to join the Ésera. The roar of the waters echoed on canyon walls worn by erosion until they were as smooth as a baby's skin – sheer limestone, shot through with veins of startling green and turquoise reflected from the river and the sun.

Noguera was forty metres away, preparing for the descent. Five French tourists were laughing and waiting for the moment to begin. From where they were standing, they could hear the river, though they could not see it, since the walls of the canyon curved as they plunged into the shadows. Noguera favoured this route, since, halfway down, climbers could jump into the deep pools formed by the River Grist. He might be an idiot, but Noguera knew this area like the back of his hand; he knew the places where the water hid jagged rocks that could kill a climber, and he knew the exact moment when the canyon walls became a rainbow of limestone.

The tourists peered into the dark canyon as though they were explorers heading into uncharted territory.

Monteperdido seemed to be a place of secrets. Tourists roamed the environs feeling as though they might discover something new, might uncover a place where no man had ever trod.

Like this river, as it wound its way through the shadowy ravine.

The secrets of Monteperdido had all come to light long ago. It was those living in the valley who cultivated the air of mystery.

As soon as he'd got out of his car, Gaizka had gone over to Noguera and, in a whisper, asked him not to make a fuss. The guide assumed he was bringing new harnesses. He had refused to carry on working with the old equipment and, though he was surprised that Gaizka had responded to his call, he was not about to pass up an opportunity to reiterate his demands.

'That's fine,' Gaizka said. 'I'll go and look in the boot; I think I might have some.'

The car was parked facing the Guardia Civil jeep. When Gaizka opened the boot, Pujante could not see him. He peered at the officer one last time, and saw him opening the door of the jeep and connecting his phone to the charger.

Gaizka lifted the rifle wrapped in the blanket with the wariness of someone handling something extremely fragile. He left the boot open as a screen to hide his movements. The canyon was directly in front of him. He glanced behind and saw the officer's boots moving towards the car, towards him.

'Gaizka,' Pujante said, 'I'm going to have to ask you to wait in the squad car until Víctor gets here.'

The canyon was barely two metres away. In a few steps, he could reach the edge and drop the rifle; the walls of the ravine would catch it, like a dog catching a bone.

'Is that the harnesses?' Noguera shouted, seeing him holding something wrapped in a blanket.

Gaizka would have liked to have shot him. Blown his arrogant head off.

'No . . .' he called to Noguera. Gaizka felt himself run out of words. 'It's . . . rubbish.'

Why hadn't he got rid of the rifle earlier?

'What have you got there?' Pujante said. He could see Gaizka standing like an idiot, facing the canyon, holding something in a red blanket.

Gaizka turned and gave a nervous grin. Then he took another step towards the lip of Oscuros de Balced. What if he just threw it from here? The chasm seemed to be calling to him.

'Don't be such a pig,' Noguera shouted. 'You can't chuck rubbish into the canyon.'

God, he longed to see that man's head explode into a thousand pieces!

The laughter of the French tourists echoed around the mountains. Gaizka stared at them, at those grinning mouths. Were they mocking him? What the fuck were they laughing at?

He knew that, at this point, he had only one option: run.

He pulled at the blanket and the rifle fell to the ground.

'Stay right where you are,' Pujante barked, but Gaizka did not even turn to look.

He saw Noguera's idiotic expression.

Gaizka bent down and picked up the rifle, released the safety catch and, without aiming, squeezed the trigger.

Amplified by the canyon, the shot sounded like a canon blast.

The French tourists stopped laughing and started to flitter aimlessly, like startled bees.

Noguera put his hands behind his head and ran for cover.

The gunshot was still echoing when Gaizka dropped the rifle into the ravine. He watched it ricochet off the rock. He knew it wouldn't reach the bottom, but he did not have time to see where it did land.

He rushed to his car and wrenched open the door; he saw Pujante ducking behind the jeep for cover as he fumbled for the gun in his belt.

Gaizka pulled away, the car hurtling along the dirt track and juddering on to the main road. The bridge over the Ésera was a hundred metres away. When he came to the crossroads, there was only one way out: down the valley, through Monteperdido.

In the rear-view mirror, Noguera, the tourists and Pujante had vanished.

Víctor did not turn off the siren when he reached the outskirts of the village. He had driven hell for leather through Monteperdido, to worried looks from neighbours and puzzled glances from journalists.

The road up to Posets was deserted.

Sara was staring through the windscreen as the car devoured the black ribbon of road, scraping against a crash barrier that seemed a vain defence against the vertiginous drop on their right.

Pujante's voice over the police radio told them that Gaizka had absconded.

'We'll catch him,' Víctor said, with a calm that surprised Sara.

She closed her eyes. *The most dangerous man is a solitary man.*

Though she could see nothing but the black curtain of her eyelids, still the sensation of speed persisted.

Víctor took a steep curve too fast. The metallic shriek of the bodywork against the barrier was like a shrill, unending wail.

Still she did not open her eyes.

The darkness was dotted by flashes of colour: green, red.

She pictured Marcial's mother's clenched fist, opening like the petals of a flower, the bloodstain on her palm.

The abstract notion that had been brewing in her mind all day was beginning to take shape.

As they rounded another hairpin bend, she opened her eyes. Ahead was a straight stretch of road that dipped in the middle. Gaizka's car careered out of the dip, like a soldier appearing from a trench. It was heading straight for them.

To the right, a sheer drop; to the left, the steep slope of Monte Ármos. There was no hard shoulder, only two lanes, barely wide enough for cars to pass.

Gaizka did not slow down.

Sara saw Víctor put a hand on the gearstick, never taking his eyes off the road. She curled up in her seat, steeling herself for the impact.

Víctor braked hard and wrenched the steering wheel, spinning the jeep so the driver's side was exposed to Gaizka's oncoming vehicle. He shifted into reverse, put his hands behind his head and turned his back to the side window.

Gaizka did not have time to change course. He swerved right, hoping that his car would fit through the narrow gap between Víctor's jeep and the precipitous rock face.

The bonnet of Gaizka's car slammed into the back door of the jeep and was deflected into the mountainside. The Guardia Civil jeep spun around with the force of the impact, while Gaizka's car scaled the slope of Monte Ármos until the front wheels were spinning in mid-air, then it fell sideways on to the road in a deafening crash of metal and shattering glass.

Sara felt Víctor's body fall across hers. She was tempted to grab him, but realized that might make it worse. The back of the jeep scraped along the crash barrier. She could picture the rain of sparks.

The canyon, the road, the mountain – then they flashed past again – the canyon, the road . . . everything whirling like a demented fairground carousel.

For a split second, she hoped that it would never stop.

Or maybe that they would crash through the flimsy barrier separating them from the canyon, and fall.

A clean fall into the void.

But, gradually, the jeep came to a standstill. The pressure eased.

Víctor had banged his forehead and a thin streak of blood trickled slowly between his eyes and his nose. Like tears of blood.

Sara was relieved when she heard him say, 'You OK?'

His parents' house was half an hour from Monteperdido, on the far side of Fall Gorge, down a dirt track that wound through the foothills of Ixeia: far from everyone and everything. By the time the Castán family home came into view, it was possible to hear the roaring waterfall at Forau de Aigualluts. Joaquín had not visited his parents for almost a year. Nor had they come into the village. They treated the encircling mountains like a fortress they had to defend. As he got out of the car, the thunder of Aigualluts grew louder, carried on the north wind, though from the house it was impossible to see the waterfall. Aigualluts was one of the most visited tourist attractions in the area. Joaquín had never liked it.

As the glacier melted, the water became a cascade that disappeared into El Forau – a deep chasm that might more accurately be called an open drain. A cesspit. The water flowed on through underground channels and into the Ésera.

Joaquín had spent his childhood growing up next to a sewer.

His parents felt tied to this land: two elderly people dragging their sense of superiority around the grounds of their mansion, scornful of the village, of its inhabitants, of their own son.

When Lucía had disappeared, they had tried to take over his life, insisting that Christmas and birthdays be celebrated at their mansion in the mountains. In the first two years after Lucía's abduction, Joaquín had not known how to refuse, and so it was here that they had celebrated their daughter's birthday.

Why did his parents have to drag them all the way out here? Why could they not understand that they wanted to be in their own house, close to their own things, to the room where Lucía had slept?

They had used their granddaughter's disappearance as a way of tightening the bonds it had taken him years to unpick. His parents' selfishness was just one of the minor misfortunes he had felt compelled to endure during that period.

Joaquín racked up the concessions, the favours, the debts, hoping that one day he would have the courage to confront them.

Rafael was another debt. Montserrat's older brother had given up his globetrotting lifestyle to manage Transportes Castán. Joaquín knew that Rafael would rather be behind the wheel of a truck, eating up the road, with nothing to hold him back, but he had come to help out for a couple of months after Lucía went missing.

No one had asked him to stay. Rafael had taken over Joaquín's responsibilities with the blasé air of someone lifting a weight without admitting they cannot carry it. He took charge of keeping the business afloat when Joaquín could not bear to spend a moment there, and he came around every night to ask if there was anything they needed. Rafael's affection had been a refuge for Montserrat at a time when Joaquín was travelling the country, trying to keep their daughter's case in the news.

But Rafael did not have the skill to run the business as Joaquín had; over time, he lost clients; they were hit hard by the financial crisis and had been forced to sell off some of the trucks. Joaquín no longer dreamed of expanding the business. He no longer dreamed of anything. Surviving was enough.

Money. Worries about fucking money had started to eat into his thoughts, destroying minutes and hours, like cancer spreading through a body.

The debts, and the need to fund the Foundation, had forced Joaquín to turn for help to the very people he loathed: the elderly couple who lived next to the sewer, in the mansion, in the shadows of Ixeia. His parents.

When he'd realized that he could not pay his bills, he had gone to see them. He thought he'd seen his mother smile when he confessed that he needed their help to get by.

Only Montserrat understood how much it had pained him to swallow his pride and ask his parents for money. Money that they well knew how to turn into charity.

Today, his mother, Aína, was sitting outside the stable that housed her favourite horse: a white mare she lavished with more affection than Joaquín had ever seen her expend on a human being – not his father, not him, not even her grandchildren.

He waved to her from a distance, and his mother barely turned her head. As he walked towards the stable, he remembered the day Aína had asked her grandchildren to name the filly she had just bought. *Estela,* Lucía had said. Quim had shouted, *Izazu,* or something like that. Aína had looked at them, not bothering to hide her disappointment, and had announced, *I will call her Verónica.* Seeing the frustration in his children's eyes, Joaquín had been furious. He would have liked to have said something to his mother, but he was rarely able to summon the courage or the words.

'What have the police said?' his mother asked, still looking at the mare.

'Not much. You heard what happened last night? The inspector leading the investigation was murdered.'

'I saw something on the television,' she said offhandedly.

Joaquín looked around him at the place where he had grown up. This vast stone house, twelve bedrooms, the gabled slate roof, the hardwood furnishings, the leather armchairs. The smell of cattle and manure that even the roaring fire in the hearth could not dissipate. The constant moan of the wind and the thunder of the waterfall when the thaw set in.

'Where's *Pare*?' he asked.

'He's gone down to see to the cattle. I've told him a hundred times we have people who are paid to do that, but will he listen? He still gets up every morning at five.'

This conversation would have been no easier with his father, who had always held on to his money as though, at any moment, the rightful owner might show up and reclaim it. Any time that Joaquín had needed financial help, his father had refused to give him cash. He would ask how much he owed, and to whom, then he would go to the bank or to the shop and settle the debts.

'I need money,' Joaquín said to his mother. 'As much as you can afford. Say, twenty thousand euros.'

'Why do you need so much money?' Aína asked, as though chiding a child for a whim.

Joaquín had already been to the bank. There had been seven thousand euros in the business account – money already earmarked to pay bills, but, even so, he emptied the account. Even then, he did not have nearly enough.

'I need it to find Lucía,' Joaquín said. 'You can hardly refuse to help me find your granddaughter?'

Joaquín had often fantasized about his parents dying. They were both over seventy. It would not be a shock if they were to pass away. His father's heart was starting to give him trouble, and his mother had problems with her blood sugar levels.

If he could just bury them, everything would be easier.

'One of these days, maybe you'll knock on our door and not ask for money,' Aína said, and looked at him reproachfully, but Joaquín did not care. He had spent several hours with Virginia. The journalist was waiting for him down in Val de Sacs. All he wanted was to take the cheque and leave as soon as possible.

The smell of manure suddenly became overpowering. The wind had shifted. Aína got up and laid the blanket that had been on her lap over the back of the chair. Beneath her dress, her legs were crisscrossed with varicose veins. As he watched her walk back to the house, Joaquín thought about the cesspool into which the glacial waters flowed. He saw it as a sewer; tourists saw it as a pure, fresh spring. As he got to his feet, he decided that the first thing he would do when his parents died was send that fucking mare to the knacker's yard.

Quim climbed out the window and crouched for a minute on the roof overlooking the back garden. He was only a few metres from Ana's bedroom. He thought about getting some pebbles and throwing them up at her window. He smiled at the thought that the window might be open and the pebbles might hit Ana on the head. But the smile froze before it could become a laugh. The naughty neighbour boy kills the girl who came back from the dead.

He was just about to jump down on to the lawn when he heard Ana's voice calling to him, almost making him lose his balance.

'Careful!' he heard her say.

He gripped the edge of the roof and looked down at the four metres separating him from the ground. He would have taken a serious knock. When he regained his balance, he looked up at Ana, leaning out of her window. She had a black baseball cap pulled down to her eyebrows.

'What's with the cap?' he said.

'My hair is starting to grow back, and it looks horrible,' she said, pulling the peak down until it touched her nose.

'You're blonde; I'm sure no one can even see it.'

'You remember?' Ana's eyes seemed to light up.

Quim was about to say, *How could I forget?* Her father had plastered her photograph all over the village: a gap-toothed girl with a fringe of blonde hair falling over her forehead, her eyes so dark it was difficult to distinguish the iris from the pupil. But he said nothing. He figured that Ana must be fed up of talking about the abduction and what had happened in Monteperdido while she was not around.

'What are you up to?' he asked instead.

Ana shrugged. 'I'm bored,' she said.

Quim smiled. She had spent five years trapped in a hole in the ground, but now she was bored.

'What would you like to do?' he asked, sitting on the roof of the porch.

Ana opened her mouth, but the words she wanted to say did not come. She changed her mind and looked at the pine forest behind the house, and, further still, at the mountains that ringed the horizon – the Accursed Mountains that rose into the heavens like a jagged saw.

'I'd like to learn to swim,' she said finally.

Víctor had several stitches in his forehead. Sara had emerged without a scratch, though she was still feeling lightheaded.

She followed Víctor down the corridor of the police station to the interview room, trailing her right hand along the wall for support.

An ambulance had met them at the scene. Gaizka had also escaped without serious injuries. One of his arms was in plaster, he had a cut on his face, but there was nothing that would prevent him from talking.

Víctor opened the door and waited for Sara to go in before closing it. She pulled up a chair and sat facing Gaizka. She could see his right leg twitching under the table, balanced on the ball of his foot. Sara studied his face before saying anything. His greyish complexion, like a shroud pulled over his bones, with none of the elasticity one might expect in a man his age, was something she had noticed when she had interviewed him in Posets. His arms were grubby, the left in a sling across his chest, the other resting on the table. He compulsively sucked in his lips and wet them with his tongue. He sniffed loudly, then rubbed his nose and sighed.

'You can't drive for shit, Gaizka,' she said.

He gave a little laugh, unable to think of a response to this comment.

This whole thing is absurd, Sara thought. She had no desire to be here, in the interview room. Gaizka's voice, and the smell of sweat and fear, made her want to retch.

She tried to focus. Get this over quickly.

'What did you throw into the canyon?'

'A rifle. It just fell; it went off and startled me.' He had clearly been thinking of this answer ever since his car crashed into Víctor's jeep. Given how much time he'd had, Sara thought the answer was pretty shit. She did not care. Did not press him.

'Last night, at about ten o'clock, you asked one of the truckers who works for Joaquín Castán to take some crates to a lock-up at La Portellada industrial estate in Barbastro.'

'It was the paintballing helmets,' Gaizka said. 'After what happened with the missing girls, it freaked me out just having them there in the storeroom. I wanted rid of them.'

'It was drugs,' Sara said without looking at him. 'How much did you pay Zacarías to move them to a different lock-up?'

Now she looked at him. She knew Gaizka had not been expecting to be found out so easily. Convinced that this part of his plan was airtight, he was now wondering, had Zacarías given the game away? Had he slipped up somehow?

'It doesn't matter.' Sara leaned back in her chair and looked around. 'You're an arsehole. And a pervert. Five years you spent living with Álvaro, and you never thought to mention that you'd seen him with Elisa.'

'You can't blame me for the fact that this shit-hole village turned on him,' Gaizka said defensively. He did not know whether it was because of the crash, but he was having trouble keeping pace with the assistant inspector.

'I'm not blaming you for anything,' Sara said, without changing her tone. 'I was just pointing out that you're an arsehole and a pervert.'

'Elisa is crazy. She was crazy back then. She was the one who made the moves, she got me into bed, and I was shit-scared – knowing her father was capable of accusing me of rape and I don't know what else. Víctor –' he turned to the sergeant for support – 'you know what Marcial is like.'

'And you didn't want to go back to jail,' Sara said, pushing a police record across the table. Gaizka did not even look at it. 'Eight months in Teixeiro Prison for drug trafficking. Was it really that bad?'

Gaizka gritted his teeth and turned a glassy stare on Sara. He had a slight scratch on one eye. The pupil seemed to float in a pool of blood.

'So what happened this time? Were you afraid we'd bust you for a couple of grams of coke?' Without waiting for an answer, Sara stood up and turned away from him. 'Could you open the door, please?' she said to Víctor.

Víctor opened the door and Sara sucked in the cool air. She walked over to the wall and gently banged her head against the plaster.

'Sara?'

She heard the concern in Víctor's voice, but still she went on banging her forehead against the wall. She needed to focus on the here and now.

'Do you know anything about the missing girls? Or do you have no fucking idea where Lucía might be?' Her words came out in an angry torrent.

'No, no . . .' Gaizka said nervously. 'You can't pin that shit on me. I was the one who found Ana. Someone around here should be thanking me.'

Sara strode across the room, grabbed Gaizka by the collar and roughly shoved him. The chair toppled and he tumbled backwards. He screamed as she put the weight of her knee on his broken arm, pressing it into his chest. Then she grabbed his throat.

'You're a fucking coward,' she muttered through clenched teeth.

Víctor tried to intervene, shouting for her to stop, but Sara would not let go. Her fingers dug into Gaizka's dirty, sweaty flesh. Finally, Telmo rushed in from the observation room, where he had been following the interview, and together the two policemen managed to pull Sara away.

On the floor, Gaizka vomited a thread of bile as he struggled to catch his breath. 'You still haven't charged me with anything,' he muttered. 'Why am I still in custody?'

'Do you really need us to tell you?' Víctor bellowed, lifting him off the floor. 'We have the drugs from the lock-up. Zacarías put the crates in number thirty-seven while the truck driver was there, but, after you phoned, he moved them to a different unit. We have the call logs. How do you know Zacarías? From back when he worked for Joaquín?'

Sara saw Gaizka mumble something unintelligible.

'Your guide managed to abseil down the canyon wall and recover the rifle,' Víctor said, still staring at Gaizka. 'It didn't fall very far before it got caught on the rocks. You don't have much luck. We know it will be a match when ballistics compare it to the bullet that killed Santiago Baín.'

Sara needed to get out of the interview room.

The whole thing seemed so ridiculous.

How many years had Santiago been on the force? How many cases had he dealt with?

And, in the end, he had crossed paths with a drug dealer.

A dealer who had killed him for no good reason other than blind panic.

As she walked down the corridor, she heard Gaizka whining, 'I didn't mean to do it . . . I'm a junkie . . . It's the coke . . . It fucks up my head . . . I need help.'

Sara clapped her hands over her ears. She could not bear to listen.

He would not get the help he needed in prison. Did she find this fact comforting? No.

When she reached the lobby, she saw Elisa arguing with Chief Sanmartín, from the Mountain Rescue Team, who was trying to tell her that she could not speak to Inspector Campos right now. Sara grabbed Elisa's arm and dragged her towards the exit. As they reached the door, Elisa's back brushed lightly against the frame and she jerked away, as if she'd had an electric shock. She howled in pain, her piercing wail echoing through the police station. Officer Rojas got up from his desk and marched over, threatening to call Elisa's father unless she calmed down.

Jesus fucking Christ, Sara thought. She took Elisa gently by the hand and led her into the bathroom. She ordered the officer washing her hands to get out. She did not want them to be disturbed.

'It was a lie,' Elisa said. 'All that stuff I told you about being with Álvaro – it was a lie. I didn't see him do it, but I know he's the one who kidnapped his daughter and that other girl. He's a fucking bastard.'

Elisa's clothes were dirty and crusted with dried mud. She seemed thinner and frailer than ever, hunched over, fluttering nervously like a frantic bird in a windowless room. She was beside herself.

'That's enough,' Sara said, gently gripping the girl's arms.

'You have to put him in jail,' Elisa begged.

Sara hugged her, hoping that the warmth of her body would calm the girl. She could feel Elisa trembling with cold and fear. 'That's enough,' Sara whispered in her ear. She ran her hands down Elisa's back to the hem of her T-shirt. Very carefully, she lifted it up, the dried mud cracking as she did so. Gradually, she saw Elisa's bare back in the bathroom mirror.

'Look at yourself,' Sara said.

Elisa shook her head vehemently. The screams and the protests had died away, and now there was only a ragged breathing that sounded like a whimper.

'He is the one who should be in jail,' Sara said, turning Elisa's head so she could see herself in the mirror. Her back was covered with the weals her father had inflicted, a grisly network of criss-crossed lines. Despite Elisa's fears, none of the wounds was bleeding. The girl's eyes followed the trail of scars, like a hamster in a maze, getting lost, starting over, yet never finding its way out.

'This is you,' Sara said.

It was the answer to the question Elisa was asking herself: Who is that woman in the mirror? The girl turned away, buried her face in Sara's shoulder and wept.

'I'm scared,' she said between sobs.

'You cannot stay with someone who treats you like this.'

Sara hugged her, and felt Elisa dissolve in her arms.

'Where did he take you last night?' Sara asked.

'We turned off the road at the Carretera de Francia and went to the old tunnel at the foot of Ixeia. He helped my grandmother inside . . . but then . . . we had a fight and I ran away.'

Sara managed to persuade Elisa to calm herself, to breathe in time with her. She went with Elisa as the girl remembered running through the forests on the slopes of Ixeia. She felt the girl's determination give way to fear. She slipped and slid as she forged her way through the darkness and the lashing rain, scratching herself on low branches, falling heavily into muddy puddles, until finally she came to a ravine and was forced to turn back. Not knowing which way to go, she had felt disorientated. Terrified that the Ésera would flood. The same river had carried her mother away seven years earlier. She had often had fantasies about sinking into the Ésera and disappearing forever. But not that night. She trusted Álvaro, believed the promises he had made her. She had only to summon the strength to get back to him. Back to the hotel room where they had made love.

By the time she'd seen her father, it was too late. Marcial had hunted her like an animal. He did not want explanations; he simply wanted to vent his impotent rage. He pulled off her T-shirt. Embarrassed, Elisa covered her breasts with her hands. Marcial took off his belt. This was not the first time. Elisa had come to think that he was somehow aroused by this form of punishment, and that simply made her feel worse, as though she were to blame for this warped attraction. Marcial whipped her with the belt. She screamed, but who would hear her? The rain drowned out her voice and washed away the blood that streamed down her back.

She curled into a ball and squeezed her eyes shut, clinging to the idea that, when this was over, she could go to Álvaro and begin to heal.

But Álvaro had lied to her.

He had used her.

Now, part of the blame for the slashes across her back lay with Álvaro.

'That's not true,' Sara said, still holding her. 'He is not the one who held the belt.'

Elisa lifted her head. Sara's T-shirt was wet with tears.

'He's my father. Why does he want to hurt me? Why doesn't he love me?' she whispered, though she did not expect an answer.

Sara had to bite her lip to stop herself from crying.

She knew that love was not something that could be demanded, like a plate of food. How many times had her own parents thrown it back in her face?

When the two women emerged from the bathroom, Sara ordered Rojas to take Elisa back to La Renclusa and get her a room there. He was not to leave the girl's side until further orders.

'Put a call out to whoever is on patrol,' Sara added. 'Tell them to arrest Marcial Nerín and bring him to the station. He can spend the night in the cells.'

Then, she went to find Víctor. She wanted to go to the spot where Marcial claimed to have spent the night: this unfinished tunnel on the slopes of Ixeia.

'Don't make me do it,' Virginia pleaded, after Joaquín had explained what he wanted her to publish.

He was sitting in a battered chair in her room in the Val de Sacs guest house, next to a window that overlooked a narrow street, and offered no glimpse of the surrounding landscape.

'I'm giving you a story that's going to make you a fortune. You have the police sketch of my daughter and Ana's account of her incarceration. You can't just turn me down,' Joaquín said, though his tone was not a plea but an order.

'Don't you think it's enough that I'm prepared to publish your offer of a reward?' Virginia tried to reason with him. 'I'll print your phone number. You'll have people calling you at all hours, but that's your problem. All I'm asking is that you don't force me to publish a lie.'

'Have you seen that assistant inspector? She's little more than a kid. And she's in no fit state to lead the investigation. The sooner they take her off the case, the better.'

'Who is going to confirm that she had a panic attack when she saw her murdered colleague? Or that she physically manhandled a suspect? They were friends; anyone can sympathize with how she felt. I don't know who told you this story, but I can tell you that they won't repeat it in public—'

'Do you want the money or not, Virginia?' Joaquín said.

'I don't recognize you anymore,' the journalist said, with a flicker of disappointment.

'People change.'

Joaquín got to his feet and stared out of the window at the blank stone wall. Virginia had seen him like this in other hotel rooms: a statue as cold and immovable as the stones he was staring at. Had she ever loved him? Or was it simply lust? She remembered a night they had spent in a hotel in Madrid after a protest march. Joaquín had been at the front, holding a placard whose slogan she had forgotten. Then they had had a drink or two in the hotel bar, probably too many, and she had invited him to her room for a nightcap. They had fucked. It had been clumsy and frustrating. Neither could get what they truly wanted from the other.

Virginia walked Joaquín to the door. Yes, she had loved him. She had come to love the man who had risen above the storm and demanded justice. But what was left of that Joaquín?

'If you won't publish it, I'll call some other journalist,' Joaquín said as he left.

'You know how much you are going to hurt that girl,' Virginia warned him. He had expected a different answer. 'But I need the money,' she said, admitting defeat.

'Thank you.' Joaquín walked off down the hall.

It's just one of those stories where there are no winners, Virginia thought. Lucía's father had survived it longer than anyone, but, in the end, like all those who were affected by the girls' disappearance, he had fallen apart. He was no longer a statue; he was just a pile of rubble, a ruin of the man he had once been.

As soon as the door closed, Virginia started packing her suitcase. She did not want to be in Monteperdido when the article was published.

★

The tunnel yawned like a mouth in the slopes of the mountain. There were wheelchair tracks still visible on the ground outside the entrance. There were also footprints that had been made by various different shoes. At least one of them was very small: no bigger than a size five.

Sara shone her torch into the tunnel. In the cavernous darkness, the slender beam of light looked ridiculous. Like a lone firefly.

They had made the journey in silence, weighed down by recent events. Just after they passed Fall Gorge, Víctor had turned on to the Carretera de Francia, which was actually little more than a rutted dirt track, half overgrown with moss that grew in the shade of the brambles. This, then, was the 'Highway to France'. Sara found it endearing, rather than absurd, that this narrow muddy lane might dream of crossing the Pyrenees.

Once past the brambles, Ixeia rose up before them. One of the mountains that rose to more than three thousand metres, it was capped by a jagged reddish peak – an impassable wall that the people of the valley had tried to tunnel through to end their isolation. The highway would have connected them to the far side of the mountain, to France and to the rest of the world, and would have given them hope at a time when the villages in the area had little hope and few prospects for the future.

The tunnel would have helped them survive, cutting a three-hour journey, along roads that were often impassable due to snow, to less than an hour. But the project had foundered almost as soon as it began, almost twenty years ago. The mouth carved into the rock face became a symbol of what never was.

The entrance to the tunnel was shored up by steel girders to prevent rockslides, Víctor explained. Sara could see a network embedded in the rock above the hole. What had seemed, at a distance, to be a perfect arch, proved crude and irregular as they approached. She shone the beam into the darkness again, then trained it on the ground. With every step, the oppressive silence grew. The void.

'About thirty metres,' she heard Víctor say. 'That's all they managed to excavate.'

Pointing her torch at the ground again, Sara spotted a trail of blood: a brownish stain mixed with soil. As though someone had spat, the thin line broke off and there were smaller blood spots a few centimetres away.

Her first thought was of Marcial's belt, but she immediately dismissed the idea. Given the driving rain and the distance from the place where he had caught up with Elisa, it seemed impossible. He could not have had much blood on him.

A blow. A punch.

'We need to get forensics here,' she said to Víctor, and heard her voice echo from the walls and die, deep in the tunnel.

Who exactly had spent the night here?

She re-emerged, blinking, into the light, shielding her eyes from the sun that blazed red as it began to set. She walked back to where the jeep was parked at the end of the Carretera de Francia. They were about a kilometre from the main road into the valley.

On her left, Sara saw a thicket. Were they beech trees? Valencian oak? She assumed that this was the way Elisa had run and that behind the trees was the ravine that had forced her to turn back. To her right was an expanse of flat ground carpeted with pink rhododendrons, which stretched all the way to the horizon and then dipped into a little valley. Behind the distant mountains on the edge of Ordesa National Park, the sun was sinking. The last rays, sharp as blades, stabbed into the ground all around her.

She heard a rustle of leaves and the sound of footsteps, and turned back towards the thicket. She saw a dark shape and, as it emerged from the shadows, the animal stopped as though frozen in place by the light.

'It's a chamois,' she heard Víctor say, but she could not tear her eyes from it. 'Must be old; the young bucks don't wander around alone.'

The rays of the setting sun made the animal's copper-coloured fur blaze crimson as blood, streaming through it, like gentle rivers of lava, as though light were spilling from the goat's pelt. An animal bathed in blood, Sara thought.

'He won't hurt you,' Víctor said.

The chamois tilted its head slightly – a childlike gesture – and the animal seemed suddenly innocent. It was not as large as it had appeared at first: a little bigger than a domestic goat. It took a couple of steps, moving out of the sunlight into the shadow of the mountain, then turned back towards the trees and the valley beyond, tossing its white head, as though it had smelled something interesting. Suddenly, it sprang into the thicket and all Sara could hear was the sound of hooves as it scampered away.

Sara looked again at the carpet of rhododendrons. What had the chamois goat smelled?

She wandered after it, paying little heed to the question that Víctor had been waiting to ask: what had she been looking for in the tunnel?

Suddenly, she saw it hanging on a bramble hedge on a raised embankment: a blue cardigan. She pulled on latex gloves before examining it. On the sleeve, near the wrist, there were smears of blood. Size: XS. On the label, the name of a French clothing chain: *Pimkie.*

When Víctor came to join her, Sara said, 'Do we have a sample of Lucía's D.N.A.?'

'Of course,' Víctor said, confused.

'I want it cross-checked with the smear, here, on the cardigan, and the blood spots in the tunnel. Call the forensics lab; there was a bloodstain on Marcial's mother's hand – I want it compared to that.'

'You really think it might be hers? Lucía's?'

Sara did not answer. She examined the label inside the cardigan closely. It was fabric, but inside there was a small magnetic tag. Was this a stroke of luck? She had seen these before. 'R.F.I.D. tags' was the technical term: tiny chips inserted into items of clothing that tracked everything about a garment from the moment it was manufactured to the moment it was sold. Days, times, places. And the identity of the buyer, if the payment had been made by credit card.

She was exhausted, but still she refused to close her eyes. It was dark now. Outside the car window, the mountain was a shapeless black blot. Her heavy eyelids drooped a little lower, as though weighed down by the silence. She did not seem to have the strength to keep them open.

But she did not want to sleep.

The whisper of the tyres on the tarmac road was a lullaby she found difficult to resist.

I don't want to sleep, she thought.

The yellow glow of the street lamps flickered as the jeep drove past.

'Talk to me about something, anything . . .' she said to Víctor.

He looked at her for a moment; she was curled up on the passenger seat, facing the other way. He looked back at the road and wondered what he could say. How he could comfort her.

Why doesn't he love me? Elisa had said to Sara, and the memory of the question was like the forgotten taste of a childhood sweet. Talk to me, Víctor, she thought.

'When I was little – I don't know . . . six, maybe seven – I got lost in the mountains.' Víctor's voice was like the hand that catches you before you fall.

'Go on,' Sara said.

'I had gone out with my brother, Román. You've met him. He loved climbing the mountains. You can't imagine how much he loved it. Me – I was . . . I was intimidated. I felt so small up there, compared to the rocks and the trees . . . Everything seemed gigantic, do you know what I mean? I felt as though I might simply vanish at any moment.'

Sara turned in her seat to look at Víctor as he talked. He gave her a sidelong glance and then continued.

'I don't remember exactly what happened. My brother went on ahead, or maybe I strayed off the path. All I know is that, suddenly, I was standing on the rocky cliff, completely alone. With Cajigal Canyon straight ahead and a beech forest behind me.'

The car drove on through Monteperdido, towards the junction where the side road turned down to the police station. The headlights traced a curve as Víctor turned on to the bridge over the Ésera.

'It wasn't cold – at least, I don't think so – I would remember if it had been winter. But it was starting to get dark. I knew that I should not move from where I was – my brother had told me that a million times – but, to tell the truth, I didn't know which way to go. I was completely silent, listening to hear if Román was calling me, but all I could hear was the wind and the animals moving among the trees. I don't know; I probably only imagined a herd of wild boar, but, at that moment, I thought I could *see* them.'

He pulled into the station car park, turned off the engine and took out the key. The inside of the car was lit by a small orange light.

'Who found you?'

'My brother, Román. I was crying, but he just laughed. He told me it was no big deal. That we had only been separated for an hour . . . I swear – to me, it felt like an eternity . . .'

Sara smiled and began gathering up her things.

'When I was up there, on my own, I don't know why, but I convinced myself that no one would come looking for me. It's stupid; why wouldn't they come looking for me? But I was a little kid . . . I suppose we all have insecurities . . . I felt like I had been left there deliberately. I peered down into Cajigal Canyon . . . and . . .'

Víctor turned towards Sara. He hesitated for a second before admitting to her that he had been on the verge of jumping. For a moment, it had seemed to him the only way out. In fact, a completely logical solution.

'You can never trust your own thoughts a hundred per cent,' Víctor said. 'Sometimes, we think really dumb things.'

'Would you have done it?' Sara asked. 'If your brother hadn't found you, if it had got dark, would you have jumped?'

'My brother was looking for me, Sara,' he said. Then, as he got out of the car, he added, 'There's always someone looking for you.'

★

313

In the squad room, they bumped into Burgos, who had come by to chat with colleagues after his shift at Ana's house. He had shown the girl a photograph of the blue cardigan and she'd confirmed that Lucía had one like it.

Now, they knew for certain that Lucía was still alive. And nearby.

It's her blood on the ground, Sara thought. The results of the D.N.A. analysis would take time, but she was convinced the blood was Lucía's.

'We've got data on the cardigan.' Rojas came to meet her when he saw she'd arrived. 'The company just sent it through. It was bought in a branch of Pimkie in Perpignan, France, but the buyer paid cash.'

'Have you asked for the C.C.T.V. footage?'

'Yeah, but there won't be anything. It was bought almost a year ago.'

'Do we know the date?'

'The eleventh of August, at 6.34 p.m.'

Víctor took the email printout from Rojas, looking disappointed. Lucía had once again disappeared into thin air.

'Do you want me to drop you back at the hotel?' Víctor asked, but Sara was already heading towards her office.

She closed the door before turning on the light. The moon reflected in the whiteboard next to her desk and, at first, she did not realize.

There was nothing for her to do.

Sara had spent all day hopping around, as though crossing a river on stepping stones.

Marcial, Gaizka, Elisa, Marcial again, Lucía.

There were no more stepping stones.

She did not have the strength to reach the other bank.

Looking at her desk, she felt as though she had fallen into the river and was being swept away by the current.

What you need to do is sort out this desk, Santiago had said, pointing to the paperwork piled up everywhere.

Now her desk was spotless. Every file and every report neatly labelled. The photographs of those implicated in the case were pinned to a corkboard pasted to the wall, next to the map of Monteperdido that she had hung up on her first day; the rest were in a box file. Markers and pens were no longer scattered over the desk but stowed in a chrome desk tidy. The flash drives with the recordings of every interview were in a case, each clearly marked and slipped into a plastic sleeve.

She could almost see Santiago in the shadows. Sitting in his chair, putting every piece of paper in its place, every photograph in its file. Working with that mixture of precision and satisfaction, like a father tidying his daughter's room.

What will you do when I'm not around? Santiago had asked her.

Sara felt tears scald her cheeks. Her legs gave out under her. Gradually, she let herself fall, until she was kneeling, her face pressed to the floor, sobbing.

'You want me to pray?' she raged furiously, to herself, to Santiago.

She hugged herself, and tried to pretend that the arms around her were not her own, but Santiago's. That same hug that woke her from a nightmare.

'Why couldn't you leave me some of your irrational faith?'

With Santiago dead, she was dying too.

Part of her life was in the morgue with his body. All the years she had lived with him and he had protected her. He was the only witness to the teenage girl who had ended up living on the streets, rejected by her parents, the only witness to Sara's life up to the moment when she had managed to take control. To study. To get a job.

Who could tell Sara's story now that Santiago was dead? She had existed only in his eyes, and now those eyes were lifeless.

There came a knock at the door and, stifling the urge to scream, she said she wanted to be left alone.

Sara looked at the desk that Santiago had tidied before he headed off to Transportes Castán.

She knew what he would have said: *The truth is, we don't weep for the dead. We weep for those still living.*

She got to her feet, picked up the case in which Santiago had filed the memory cards of the interviews, and looked for the most recent interview with Ana: the one where Sara had not been present.

She sat at her desk, slotted the flash drive into the laptop. An audio player appeared on the screen and she pressed *play*.

'*You're not afraid that he'll come for you?*' Santiago's voice was warm but deep.

'*I don't know; should I be?*' Ana said.

'*Of course not. That's why we're here — to protect you.*'

Sara leaned back in the chair and closed her eyes. She was barely listening to Ana's responses. She just wanted to hear Santiago's voice, warm and protective. She wanted to imagine that he was here, now, talking to her.

'*What else happened that night?*'

The sound had changed; he must have moved the recorder closer to Ana. Santiago's voice now sounded more distant. Sara felt a twinge of disappointment.

'. . . *I saw some shooting stars. Before . . . Papá and I used to lie out in the garden and stare up at the sky; he said, if we saw a shooting star, we could make a wish.*'

Sara pressed *pause*, and took the recording back a bit. Ana's voice rang out, and this time Sara listened carefully.

'*No, I couldn't see it from where I was . . . But I saw some shooting stars. Before . . . Papá and I used to lie out in the garden and stare up at the sky; he said, if we saw a shooting star, we could make a wish. I made a million wishes . . . but I never wished to get out of there. I didn't think that would ever happen.*'

Sara took the recording back again; this time, a little further.

'. . . *I remember a night, it was a while ago now . . . It wasn't cold. I was only wearing a cardigan, but I didn't feel cold. I was upstairs. He was down in the basement, with Lucía.*'

'*Was that the last time you felt warm?*'

'*Maybe.*'

Sara got up and left the office. Behind her, the interview was still playing. Most of the Guardia Civil officers had left. Víctor and Rojas were having a coffee.

'What day was the cardigan bought?' Sara asked as she walked towards them.

Víctor and Rojas looked at her, puzzled. 'The eleventh of August last year.'

Sara looked angry and disappointed. She stopped in the middle of the squad room, flailed around and, in a sudden burst of fury, swept everything off the nearest desk, sending it crashing to the floor. The computer monitor shattered as papers and case files rained all around.

'Shit!' she roared. 'We've had this all wrong from the beginning!'

Víctor ran over. 'What's going on?' he said, putting his hands on her shoulders.

'There are two of them,' she said. 'Don't you understand? There are two kidnappers . . .' Sara shrugged off Víctor, who was clearly wondering how she had reached this conclusion. 'The cardigan was bought in France on the eleventh of August last summer. That's the other side of the Pyrenees. How long would it take to get there from Monteperdido?'

'Perpignan is about six hours by car,' Rojas estimated.

'The eleventh of August is the date of the Perseids meteor shower. They call them the Tears of San Lorenzo. Shooting stars. Ana talked about them in the last interview. That would have been last summer,' Sara explained.

Víctor was beginning to piece things together. Now he realized how Sara had worked it out.

'Ana is up in the mountain hut, looking at the stars. One of the kidnappers is in the basement with Lucía. Meanwhile, the other is in Perpignan, buying clothes for the girls,' Sara said. 'If the cardigan was bought at 6.34 p.m., he wouldn't have got back to Monteperdido until the middle of the night . . . That's why Ana's descriptions of the kidnapper have been so contradictory. She's not trying to hide the truth. She doesn't realize it, but she's describing two different men.'

5

The Tarn

As the flames consumed the coffin, Sara closed her eyes and tried to find peace, the same peace she wished for Santiago as she imagined him transformed into ashes, quivering in the wind, the way a ballerina raises her arms, her hands fluttering like birds.

Few people attended the service: a distant relative, a few close friends from Madrid.

They treated her as though she were the widow.

Hugs and condolences.

As they left the crematorium, Miguel Ángel Figueroa came over to her.

'Fancy a quick coffee?' he said.

He gestured to a nearby bar. It did not look particularly welcoming, but it was probably better than the cafeteria in the crematorium.

'What would you like? Figueroa asked, but she just waved her hand as though even the thought of making a choice was impossible just now. He went up to the counter and ordered a whisky from the South American barmaid, who said she would bring it over.

He spared her his memories of Santiago Baín. There was no, *He was a decent man*, no anecdotes about when they were partners on the force. Figueroa had climbed the greasy pole all the way to the Jefatura de Policía. Sara did not know whether he was a political animal or had got there on his own merits; she barely knew the man.

It had been almost two weeks since Santiago's death.

Meanwhile, the investigation had become a wild animal she could not control. Perhaps it was not wild; perhaps she was simply weak.

The waitress brought the whisky, and Figueroa added a 'darling' to his thank you. The girl smiled and went back to the bar. Figueroa was a couple of years younger than Santiago. He was a chubby man, clearly uncomfortable in the suit he was required to wear. On the few occasions Sara had met him, the suit had always been creased, the shirt tails hanging out, and he constantly had to hike his trousers up over his paunch. He stank of aftershave.

'I want you to trust me, Sara,' he said. 'We're going to sort this out, you and me. No need for paperwork and politicians.'

He took off the suit jacket, slung it carelessly over the back of the chair and rolled up his sleeves.

'Who exactly was the fuckwit who leaked the police sketch and the interviews with Ana to the press?' he asked, as though he expected her to give him a name, so he could track the man down and give him a beating.

Sara had no doubts; Joaquín, Lucía's father, had been a problem ever since she started working on the investigation. He had never been satisfied with the statements or the methods of the police. It seemed clear that he had his own ideas, and, after a period of grace, had decided to put them into action. The journalist who had published the story, Virginia Bescos, had regularly worked with Joaquín in the past. Ana's parents denied that they had given Joaquín any of the information that had appeared in the article, but Sara did not believe them. She knew they felt indebted to Lucía's family and uncomfortable that they had been the lucky ones. There was little doubt that they had supplied the police sketch and Ana's statements.

But none of this seemed to matter to Figueroa. It was a shit-storm, there was no doubt about that. The portrait of Lucía had been on every television news bulletin and on the front page of every paper. Ana's account of her imprisonment had been analysed down to the last comma. Some days later, Virginia Bescos had published another article, announcing a reward of thirty thousand euros for information leading to Lucía's safe recovery. This time, Joaquín made no attempt to hide. It was he who was offering the reward, 'given the lack of action on the part of the police,' he added.

'I'd like to beat the shit out of him,' Figueroa growled. 'If his daughter ends up getting shot, we're the ones who'll be blamed.' He sipped his whisky and smiled at Sara. 'Lord deliver us from knaves and fools.'

Recent reports on the case had also mentioned Sara Campos. It was reported that the S.A.F. assistant inspector was having difficulty getting over the death of her colleague. In condescending terms, it was suggested that she was like an orphaned girl who should be taken into care by social services. At times, unable to act; at others, out of control. Gaizka alleged that he had been physically abused while in her custody in Monteperdido. More than anything, what bothered Sara was the journalist's phoney compassion, when what she was actually trying to do was bury her.

'What are the local Guardia Civil like?' Figueroa asked. 'Morons?'

Sara praised the local officers, particularly Víctor. They had done exemplary work since she had arrived. She had no complaints. Figueroa took it for granted that they would not corroborate this story of police brutality. An officer had just been murdered; what kind of people would use kid gloves with the culprit under such circumstances? This Gaizka had deserved the beating he got.

'He's just a drug dealer, right?' Figueroa asked. 'He's got nothing to do with the kidnappings . . .'

Sara did not think so, but there was little she could say for certain. The D.N.A. analyses had confirmed that the blood spots in the tunnel and on the sleeve of the cardigan were a match with Lucía. She had been in the cave in Ixeia on the night of the storm, probably with her kidnapper. He had hit her while she was standing facing Marcial's mother. Lucía must have touched the old woman, because there was a bloodstain on the palm of her hand. But that was all they could say. Whatever Marcial's mother had witnessed was forever locked in her brain by Alzheimer's.

Sara explained that they had changed their approach to the investigation: they now believed there were two perpetrators. One might be the dominant partner and the other weaker, easily led. They had checked with the weather services and the only night that shooting stars would have been visible over Monteperdido was 11th August.

'A madman and his lackey,' Figueroa summed up. 'This all came after what happened to Santiago?'

Sara nodded. This new approach forced them to reappraise the whole investigation. They had been ruling out suspects who had alibis for the two key moments in the case: the day of the kidnapping, and the day that Ana had reappeared. But if there were two perpetrators at work, this logic did not apply. One of them could have abducted the girls, and the other could have been in the stone hut when Ana escaped.

Álvaro, Marcial and even Gaizka were all still in the frame.

'What the fuck was Santiago doing down at the haulage company?' Figueroa said, draining his glass.

Sara did not have an answer. Maybe he had found out something about Gaizka and, thinking he was involved in the abduction, had gone to find him. Maybe it had something to do with Joaquín; there were times when she felt that Lucía's father was doing everything in his power to thwart the investigation. Sara had spoken to Montserrat, who admitted that her husband had not been home that night. Joaquín claimed he had been drinking in Val de Sacs. Maybe he had been to visit Virginia Bescos, though he refused to say as much.

'What about the girl? Is she touched in the head or what?'

This was more a complaint than a question. Figueroa had read the transcripts of Ana's interviews; he knew that she had told them almost nothing useful.

'You sure you don't want a drink?' he said, getting up to order another whisky.

Sara watched him wearily totter to the bar, as though unaccustomed to walking. He obviously said something funny to the waitress, because she laughed as she got the bottle down from the shelf. He gestured for her to give him a larger measure, then turned and glanced at Sara, his face grim. Though he did his best to hide it, Santiago's funeral had affected him.

He sat down again and said to Sara that she really should drink something. A tonic water, if she did not want alcohol. She did not even have a glass to drink to Santiago's memory, something he wanted to do with her.

'Which country is it where they smash the glasses on the floor? Or is it plates?'

'Greece,' Sara said.

'You can't imagine how much I want to smash things.' There was no humour in his voice now, only bitterness. 'A couple of days before . . . well . . . before that bastard shot him, Santiago sent me a memo.'

Figueroa searched the briefcase at his feet, then pushed the memo across the table.

'I'll sum it up,' he said, with a weary sigh; this was not a conversation he wanted to have. 'He wanted us to reassign you to a different unit. To take you off field work. A nice little office somewhere in the south, with lovely weather and lots of documents to stamp . . .'

Sara could not help but smile as she began to read the memo. She knew that Santiago had probably written it just after her interview with Ana. Bastard, she thought.

'He said that you are extremely clever and very well prepared, but that, if you keep getting involved in such cases, you'll end up a fucking basket case.'

'That was his psychological terminology? A fucking basket case?' Sara said, and smiled at Figueroa. Just how much credence did he give this memo?

'I'm not going to pull any punches, Sara,' Figueroa said, clearing his throat and trying to sound candid. 'I've spoken to the officers you've worked with on other cases, I've called Víctor Gamero at Monteperdido. Every one of them says you're amazing. The best. And I can think of no one better to lead this investigation. So why the hell did Santiago send me this letter?'

Sara was holding the letter and glanced at it again before she answered.

'Because he loved me,' she said. 'And he was afraid for me.'

'So what am I supposed to do? Toss the memo into the bin, or send you off to the Canaries to photocopy traffic reports?'

Sara thought for a moment.

'Can I give you my answer after I've found Lucía?'

Figueroa smiled; this was what he wanted to hear.

His phone had been ringing a dozen times a day since Virginia's article was published. Joaquín had begun to decline some of the calls, sick to death of opportunists and of lunatics who swore they had seen Lucía in their dreams. The one that had genuinely upset him was from a woman with an Eastern European accent who insisted she had met his daughter, who had asked her to give him a message. She did not want the reward money, she just wanted to pass on what Lucía had said: 'Stop looking for me.' Joaquín hadn't known what to say, and, after a moment's silence, he hung up.

But that *Stop looking for me* echoed in his mind like a haunting, harrowing refrain. What pushed these people to call him? Was it needless cruelty, or a desire to be famous? The police had advised him that offering a reward was a bad idea, that all he would get for his trouble was a load of bizarre stories that would only fuel his fears.

Stop looking for me. In his mind, he could hear Lucía saying the words. He had not mentioned this call to anyone, not even to

Montserrat. He could not bear to imagine her response, whether it turned out to be, *She's right,* or, *Can't you see what this is doing to you?*

He had arranged to meet Rafael in the offices of Transportes Castán. The car radio was on, with the volume so low that the presenter's voice was little more than background noise. As he passed the bridge nearest to the school, his mind wandered back to the terrible flood, seven years ago, to a time when he had been the man he'd decided to be.

The floodwaters had surprised them. It was a morning in early June, and the village was going about its business. The kids were in their classrooms, the adults at work.

The Ésera had not been dredged that year. Swollen with meltwater from the glacier and unseasonal torrential rains, the levels were rising dangerously. Joaquín was in his office when Montserrat phoned to say the river had burst its banks up near Posets. From that moment, he did not hesitate. His every action had been swift and decisive.

He phoned the school as he drove back towards the village and was told that his daughter's class had already been evacuated. The school was in a natural hollow and there were fears that it might flood. Pupils were being taken across the bridge to the highest point in the village. As Joaquín arrived, he saw the column of children trudging through the driving rain towards the bridge. Lucía was at the front, walking next to her teacher.

Water began to seep between the stones of the bridge, the raging torrent pounding at the pillars, and Joaquín suddenly realized that at any moment the whole structure might be swept away. He stopped his car at the far side of the bridge, leaped out and shouted to the teacher to turn back, but his voice was drowned out by the roar of the water. He watched as the teacher stepped on to the bridge, urging the children to run, aware there was danger but oblivious to the fact she was leading them to their deaths.

One of the bridge supports suddenly collapsed, as though hit by a mortar shell. Joaquín did not think twice. He dashed on to the bridge, which seemed to be swaying with the rushing current. The teacher grabbed two of the children and tried to go back, but Lucía stood, frozen. Joaquín ran to her, grabbed her around the waist and threw her over his shoulder. His daughter's breathing was ragged; she was sobbing. He quickly led the teacher and the other children back to the bank, just before the bridge crumbled.

He did not want to look back. The teacher and the children were hysterical. He shouted at them to get away from the riverbank, pointing to a house on a hill to the south. He knew that it was only a matter of time before the river burst its banks. He ran all the way to the house, carrying his daughter in his arms. Only when they were safely inside did he set her down again. He looked at Lucía's face, streaked with rain and tears.

It's OK now, darling, he had said, hugging her. She had been nine years old.

Stop looking for me, the woman on the phone had said. How could he stop looking for his daughter? Who could simply forget and move on?

He parked the car outside his office. The door of Transportes Castán was open. They hadn't worked since the body of the inspector had been found on the forecourt. In the hangar, the three Pegasos and the Volkswagen looked like terminally ill patients, staring out of a hospital window at a world they knew they would not set foot in again.

He tried not to think too much. Keep moving. He was aware that, if he stopped and looked in the mirror, he would not like what he saw. Sometimes, Joaquín felt as though he left his own body and could see himself from the outside; in those brief flashes, he had seemed like an aeroplane in flames, hurtling towards the ground, knowing that the crash was inevitable.

'I'm going to wind up the business,' he said to Rafael as he sat down at the desk. 'I'll sell off the trucks and use whatever I get to pay off my debts, and to pay you back, obviously.'

Rafael did not even look at him. Those first years of unconditional help and support had gradually turned to mute resentment about how Joaquín was running the business, how he was dragging Montserrat down with him, how he was turning his back on Quim.

'Whatever you think,' was all he said.

'I'm not going to do it overnight, and I should get some money for the land too. There's no way anyone can save the business now,' Joaquín said, as though he had to justify himself to his brother-in-law.

He knew this was not quite true. The money he had managed to raise for the reward could just as easily be used to refloat the business. The trucks were a symbol of an independence that had been hard won. His parents had been determined that he should take over the family farm, but Joaquín had fought to escape their shadow. And he had succeeded. He had set up a small haulage business that had grown into his own empire, with more than twenty trucks criss-crossing the Pyrenees. What was left of all that now?

What does it matter? he said to himself, trying to ignore thoughts that could only hurt him. His daughter had disappeared.

'What do you want me to do?' Rafael said. 'I can file the paper-work for the liquidation—'

'It's probably better if we get a lawyer to sort it out.'

How could he let Rafael deal with the paperwork when, in the five years he had been working here, he had never managed to file a tax return on time?

Rafael got up and grabbed his jacket. He glanced around and asked whether he should come in tomorrow.

'I'll let you know if I need anything,' Joaquín said.

Rafael simply nodded and walked out, as though he had only been looking after the business for a few hours while Joaquín was out on an errand. Was it possible to calculate the debt of gratitude he owed his brother-in-law? How often had Rafael meekly agreed to Joaquín's requests?

Can you look after Quim while Montserrat and I go on a protest march?

Can you drop by the house on Lucía's birthday? I don't want Montse to be on her own.

Can you give up driving and look after the business?

Can you put your life on hold for us?

And Rafael had accepted without a word of complaint.

Had Joaquín even asked, or had he simply demanded? He had treated Rafael like all those around him; it never occurred to him that anyone would say no. He expected everyone to be as commit-ted as he was to the search for his daughter.

Sooner or later, he would find himself completely alone.

Joaquín's mobile rang and it took him a moment to react. He fished it out of his pocket and looked at the screen: *Unknown num-ber*. He answered, mostly so he would not have to deal with the dark thoughts, circling like hyenas, waiting to pounce. He did not expect anything to come of the call.

'I've got information about your daughter.' It was a woman's voice, hoarse and cracked with age. The accent was local, possibly from the Catalan region of the Pyrenees. 'But first I want the money.'

Joaquín assumed it was just another opportunist who took him for a fool.

It was the first time that Montserrat had been to Barbastro shopping centre. It had opened three years earlier, but she had avoided coming, as though the pleasure of visiting the shopping centre was forbidden for her. She walked past rows of bustling shops whose lights and garish colours clamoured for her attention. She was carrying two large bags of clothes. Other than a few shirts for Quim, everything else was for her. She had been afraid that she might bump into a neighbour while she was choosing dresses and trousers from the racks.

What would she say to them?

She felt more comfortable now, as she elbowed her way through the throng of anonymous shoppers. She was just thinking about getting a coffee before heading back to Monteperdido when she came to the top of the escalator and saw a toy shop. She went inside, not stopping to wonder why or what she might be looking for. Almost without realizing, she found herself standing in front of a huge display: rows of dolls were lined up next to one other, in pristine boxes that Montserrat realized, with a shudder, reminded her of coffins. Seeing the Barbie dolls with their frozen smiles, their flower-print dresses and their bridal gowns, she felt the urge to cry. Was this what she had come for? A Barbie doll for Lucía?

'That one is pretty.'

Startled by the sound of a familiar voice, Montserrat turned around. Nicolás Souto was pointing to a doll in a black box: a limited-edition reproduction of a 1950s Barbie, with a red dress and a mane of dark hair that fell over her shoulders. Montserrat felt ashamed; she did not know what to say. Souto craned his neck, raised his eyebrows and nodded to the doll again. Montserrat smiled; Nicolás's expression as he peered over her shoulder and looked inquisitively at the dolls made her think of the marmots she sometimes saw scurrying around the mountains, peering over rocks with that same inquisitive expression, only to instantly run away again. But Nicolás was still standing behind her; he had not scurried away. He had grown a thin moustache that gave him a faintly ridiculous air, like a teenage boy who should have shaved as soon as the first downy hairs appeared on his upper lip.

'I called to you as you were coming in,' the vet said nervously, 'but, with the loud music, it's hardly surprising that you didn't hear me ...' Nicolás saw that Montserrat was staring and, like a nineteenth-century gentleman, he stroked his moustache and said, 'Do you like it?'

'Yes ... Well ... I don't know. It's the first time I've seen a moustache make someone look younger.'

Nicolás hid a scowl; this had obviously not been his intention when he decided to grow out the thin, straggly hairs he called a moustache. He jerked his hand away from his face and, not knowing what to do with it, picked up one of the dolls at random. Doctor Barbie wore a white lab coat and pink glasses that were obviously supposed to make her look intelligent, though Nicolás Souto thought they made her look like a porn star.

Montserrat said that she was not buying anything, that she did not really know why she had come into the shop.

The vet put the doll back on the shelf and picked up the first one he had pointed out: a doll that looked like a 1950s movie star. 'I prefer this one . . . Do you mind if I buy it?' he said.

Montserrat knew that he was not trying to make her feel uncomfortable, and gradually relaxed. She said that she had been looking at a different Barbie, with a swimsuit and blonde hair tied back in a ponytail. She liked the expression on the doll's face.

They decided to buy both, then Nicolás invited her to have a coffee on the roof terrace of the shopping centre. They sat at a table under a parasol, sheltered from the sweltering July sun. Summer promised to be very hot.

'Do you think it's silly of me to buy her a doll?' Montserrat asked, after they had been served.

'Why would I?' Nicolás said with a smile. His shirt was damp with sweat and he hunched over a little, hoping she would not notice the stains under his arms.

'It doesn't really make sense . . .' Montserrat said. 'Ana said that Lucía doesn't like dolls anymore. But . . .' She could not find the words to explain how she felt.

'It feels like having her close to you, doesn't it?' Nicolás said.

She smiled. He was right. They had known each other since childhood. At school, when Nicolás had been the shy, awkward boy everyone made fun of, Montserrat was the only girl he spoke to. She knew that he was falling in love with her. He gave her stories he had written that she felt obliged to read, although they were terribly boring. But this was Nicolás's way of declaring his intentions, and she felt that not reading them would be like closing the window while he was serenading her.

Montserrat knew that he had never really believed he had a chance with her. He had surrendered before the battle had even begun. As a boy, he had been as timid and self-effacing as he was now. When Montserrat had started dating Joaquín, Nicolás had accepted his defeat without demur. He had drifted away, and stopped giving her his stories to read.

'I'm writing another book,' Nicolás said. '*El follét del albarósa*. The Ken Follet of Monteperdido.' He laughed at his own joke – two loud chuckles that trailed off when he saw Montserrat look away. 'No, it's not about Ken Follet; it's about *los folléts* – you know, the woodland spirits,' he explained. 'It's sort of inspired by what's happening in the village right now . . . Except that, in my story, they find Lucía,' he added, as though this might reassure her.

Montserrat smiled. She knew that, in his clumsy way, Nicolás was simply trying to please. The past weeks had been difficult. Joaquín was more preoccupied than ever by his obsession and pushed her away any time she said something he did not like, as though she were abandoning him. Quim was a stranger; her son spent most of his time out, and, when he was at home, he barely said a word to her. She could hardly blame him. For too long, she had turned her back on him; she would have to earn his trust. And so she was flattered that Nicolás wanted to cheer her up without expecting anything in return.

'How far along are you?' Nicolás asked, rummaging in his pocket for change to pay the bill.

Montserrat smiled at him, embarrassed. How had he realized?

'I saw you the other day in the chemist, remember?' Nicolás said reassuringly, eager to let her know that the information would not leave the table. 'You were buying pills, and I thought it was strange, because Joaquín usually buys everything in bulk in Andorra . . . I noticed it was folic acid.'

Montserrat took a deep breath. 'Two months. At first, I just thought I was late . . . But I bought a pregnancy test, and it was positive.'

She wanted it to sound as though she was concerned, but she could not hide her smile. Nicolás was the first person she had told that she was pregnant.

'Congratulations.' Nicolás sat up and held out his arms. 'Can I . . .?'

She let him hug her, and it felt good. She wanted to celebrate. She wanted to enjoy this new life, and wanted everyone to know.

'Have you told Joaquín?'

'Not yet.'

How could she tell her husband they were going to have another child? She knew he would see it almost as a betrayal.

'If you need anything . . . Obviously, I'm not a doctor, but I've helped quite a few cows to calve . . .'

Montserrat laughed and thanked him. How could Nicolás ever be a good writer when he always chose the worst possible words?

Joaquín Castán had emptied the business account. He was selling up. Sara had got a warrant to put a tap on his phone. She knew Lucía's father would not share any information with her, though she also suspected that the reward he had offered would only attract calls from cranks. She did not really think of him as a suspect. Joaquín was so invested in the role of the brave, angry father, there was nothing she could do to stop him, even though his antics were wasting time and resources.

The police-sketch artist had gone back to visit Ana. Sara wanted to see whether it was possible to differentiate the traits that Ana had described, now that they were sure there were two perpetrators. The results were inconclusive: it was impossible to definitely assign any particular feature to one or the other of the kidnappers.

'How are things going with the big boss?' Víctor asked.

'No change,' Sara muttered.

She stared at the desk. It was beginning to get dark and most of the officers had already gone home. As he had done every night recently, Víctor suggested they have dinner together at the Hunting Society, and, as she had every night, Sara declined. She was still staring at the desk. She had not moved anything since she had found it like this after Santiago tidied it. What was on this desk that had prompted him to go to Transportes Castán?

Yet again, she picked up the case file and reread every memo and every report as night drew in. Outside, the pine forest changed colour in the twilight, the trees taking on a deep purple, turning the scene into something surreal, more like a painting than a place.

When dawn came, Sara was still sitting at the desk, feverishly reading and feeling she was getting nowhere. She had spent the night struggling to keep her eyes open, desperate to ward off sleep and the nightmares that had returned since Santiago's death. Featureless men, whose faces were blank but for a small hole, like a vortex, swallowing up their skin.

Sara wasn't sure when the dreams had started; for as long as she could remember, the nightmares had been there, lying in wait every night. The hallucinations were the result of a dysfunctional overlap between wakefulness and sleep, and, in Sara's case, they could last for hours. Sometimes, whole nights. The brain entered R.E.M. sleep, leaving her body paralysed, even though she was still awake; she could see, hear, feel. 'Sleep paralysis' was another term for it, the doctor had told her. He had prescribed antidepressants, but she found they dulled her senses during the day. She became a shadow of herself; her brain was foggy and refused to function. She stopped taking them.

The stability that Santiago provided had helped her to deal with the nightmares. Being away from her parents, living in an apartment that gradually came to feel like home, her studies and, later, her job had all helped to keep the hallucinations at bay.

But, a few years ago, they had started to come back, with the same terrifying intensity they had had when she was a little girl.

They had been working on a case involving a missing teenager, in a seaside village in Almería, close to where Sara had grown up. Santiago had seen Sara slowly falling apart, unable to relax, becoming fearful as night drew in and she knew she would have to go to sleep.

She had been determined to prove to Santiago that she could cope, and he had wanted to believe her, though he knew her efforts were doomed. This was why he had written the memo to Figueroa.

Sara tried to shut out these memories, to forget the memo Santiago had sent and focus on the case files in front of her. It was an avoidance strategy.

In the middle of the night, when she was rereading the witness statements taken five years earlier, just after the abduction, something caught her eye. Something she had not noticed until now. In his statement, José Alberto Mencía, who worked at the petrol station outside Monteperdido, had mentioned a co-worker, Fulgencio Heras. A footnote referred to Fulgencio Heras's interview, *Documents 24/10/09*. Sara searched every box, but found nothing. She went down to the records room. Perhaps the statement had been misfiled, so wasn't with the rest when Víctor gave her all the original paperwork. But there was no sign of it in the records room.

Burgos hung back about a hundred metres. This was the private space Álvaro had managed to secure for his daughter in negotiations with the police. Quim and Ana were walking up ahead. Engrossed in their conversation, they had left Ximena behind, almost without realizing.

'Are you on speed or something?' Ximena complained. 'You're walking at, like, a million miles an hour.'

Quim and Ana turned and saw Ximena planting a stick in the ground to help her climb the mountain slope. Further below, Burgos was a small blot on the landscape.

'You remember what you said to me?' Quim said, with a mischievous smile. 'About how you'd like to learn to swim? Do you trust the teacher?'

'If you trust him, you'll drown,' Ximena joked feebly, but Quim and Ana had already turned away again. Ana said she would love to learn, but there were no beaches nearby.

The day had dawned clear and bright. They had arranged to meet up early, outside Ana's house. 'So, what are we going to do?' Ximena said, breaking the awkward silence as they stood, shuffling, like strangers. Leaning on the railings outside the house, Burgos watched them. 'Why don't we go for a walk in the mountains?' Quim suggested. What else was there to do in Monteperdido? They headed out of the estate and crossed the bridge over the river. On the far side of Avenida de Posets, the lower slopes of Monte Ármos were ringed by a green belt of trembling aspens, above which the grey slopes of the mountain soared to almost two thousand metres, thrusting a rounded summit, like an animal's rump, into an indigo sky. Neither Quim nor Ximena noticed the effort Ana was having to make to stem her panic as they walked through the forest. She stared at the leaves of the trembling aspens, terrified that, sensing her presence, they might begin to quiver, to rustle. But the *trémols* remained silent. They did not make the pitter-patter like rain that she had heard so often in the five years in the hole. *Fibbers*, Ana remembered she used to call them. Now, they rose high above her, the dense tangle of branches blotting out the sky and the mountain.

'Careful of the wild-boar shit,' Quim warned, theatrically stepping off the path and pointing to the droppings.

'Do you know where we're going?' Ximena said, feeling as lost as Ana in the woods.

'You're going to get us all lost,' Burgos called from further down the slope, panting as he continued to climb.

But Quim knew the way by heart. From time to time, he would point towards places hidden behind the belt of trees – to the east, a gully called La Camera, where hunters stationed themselves during drives; to the west, the area where the wild boar built their nests – as he strode on, deeper into the forest. They had been walking among the *trémols* for almost an hour before they finally emerged from the woods on to a bare slope, where a path of rhododendrons led towards the summit. It was shortly afterwards that Quim had offered to teach Ana to swim. There might not be beaches on Monte Ármos, but there were lakes.

'There's a tarn at Tempestades – let's go there,' Quim said. 'Let's see whether our flat-footed cop friend can keep up.'

Quim broke into a run. Ana followed.

Ximena sighed, looking behind and seeing that Burgos was too far away to notice they had made a run for it. She trotted after them. 'We didn't even bring swimsuits,' she protested, but Quim and Ana did not seem to hear.

They scrambled up a rocky path. Ximena noticed Quim was constantly glancing at Ana, especially when the path was narrow. He held out his hand to help her up a particularly steep ridge. On their right, the ravine known as La Camera plunged ever steeper. Ximena stumbled on, though with every step she felt more like a gooseberry on this outing.

Tempestades was the first of four lakes on the slopes of Monte Ármos. After two hours trekking along a narrow path, dislodging showers of small stones, they came to a valley. They could see the lake, less than three hundred metres away, ringed by the Tempestades cirque, which seemed to embrace it with its rocky arms. How many times had Quim been here? When he was younger, his father had taken him into the mountains every weekend. Later, Lucía had gone with them too. La Camera, the cirque, the red snow, the groves of aspen and mountain pine. The roe deer, the marmots and the wild boar. The carpets of rhododendrons in summer. This was the only entertainment available in Monteperdido, and by the time he'd reached his teens, he was heartily sick of it. While others stood, wide-eyed and speechless in astonishment, Quim simply saw rocks, trees, water and timorous animals.

But now, taking Ana up to the tarn and seeing her amazement when they reached Tempestades, it was as though he were seeing it through her eyes, as she gazed up the sheer granite walls to the glacier above.

'Why is the snow red?' she asked.

'Apparently it's the wind from the Sahara. It sounds incredible, but it carries grains of red sand all the way here and they get trapped in the ice,' Quim explained.

In winter, the tarn was completely frozen over. In summer, it was filled with meltwater from the glacier. Fresh, crystal-clear water. A mirror that reflected the scarce mountain pines, the scarred rock face and the sky, forming a strange rainbow of indigo, green and red. An iridescent opal.

Ana walked to the edge of the lake and took off her black cap. Quim could see that her hair had begun to grow back, a fine duvet that glittered gold in the sunlight. She looked so perfect that he felt he could not touch her. He sat down next to the tarn. There was no wind and barely any sound. He filled his lungs with the pure air.

When Gaizka had been arrested, it had become impossible to find hash in the village and he'd been afraid of how he would cope without it. But all he had suffered were a few sleepless nights. He would climb out of his bedroom window, sit on the roof of the back porch and chat to Ana, who leaned out her window, until they both felt sleepy.

They never talked about the abduction. Or about Lucía. Not that these subjects felt taboo. Simply, whenever they saw each other, they ended up talking about other things. Mostly, plans for the future. He dreamed of travelling; she was in no hurry to leave. Her dreams were more ordinary: curling up under a blanket on the sofa, next to a log fire, while it snowed outside; learning to cook like her mother; learning to drive; going to the cinema; listening to music; getting a dog.

'Come on, let's get in the water,' Quim said, pulling off his T-shirt. 'Don't be scared. It's not deep around the edge . . .'

He threw off his shoes, shucked off his trousers and leaped into the water in his boxer shorts. As he broke the surface, the mirror images shattered into waves, gradually coming together again when he popped his head out of the water and shook his hair, a few metres from where he had landed.

'What are you waiting for?' he called to Ana.

She was nervous. She had a distant memory of her parents taking her to the seaside. How old would she have been then? Four? Five? The lake was both a temptation and a trap. She was convinced that, as soon as she stepped into it, she would sink.

Ximena had taken off her shoes and was dipping a toe in the water. 'Given how difficult it was to convince your parents to let you come out, they're not going to be happy when they find out about this!' Ximena shouted, not taking her eyes off Quim.

It was true that her mother had been reluctant. Álvaro had been encouraging when Ana had asked if she could go for a walk with Quim and Ximena someday. He understood her need for freedom better than anyone.

Quim was splashing noisily in the tarn. Ximena turned to Ana and took off her T-shirt. She was not wearing a bra, and Ana was embarrassed that she could see her breasts. Taut and brown, like her stomach. Then she peeled off her jeans and stood there in a thong.

Ana looked at the Colombian girl's perfect, bronzed body. She could not help but mentally compare it to her own: her skin was white as snow, her body lacked definition, she still had the puppy fat of childhood.

Ximena turned away again and plunged into the water, swimming towards Quim. Ana could see her mane of hair under the water, like the shadow of a fish.

'Come on, Ana,' Quim shouted. 'I thought you wanted to learn to swim.'

Ana squeezed her eyes shut, and hoped that a breeze would sweep away her shame. She stood with her back to the lake. If I can't see them, they can't see me, she thought. They were sheltered by the cirque, this granite crater eaten away by time, so battered and yet somehow so beautiful. Up above, the red snow. Her eye was caught by a dark shadow, some twenty metres away. It was lying at the base of a sheer wall, in the centre of the semicircle formed by the cirque. At first, Ana could not work out what it was, but she stepped closer and, as she did so, she froze.

'What's wrong?' she heard Quim call from the water.

Ana could not take her eyes off the animal. At first, she thought it was asleep, but decay had already begun to take its toll on the skin, the eyes. Black death emanated from the dead roe deer like a plague, although there was not a drop of blood. The stag's head was resting on the ground. One of the antlers was broken, but the other flaunted its three points, like a pennant planted on a battlefield where nothing remains but the dead. Why had she thought it was asleep? The legs, twisted at impossible angles, made it obvious that the animal had fallen from a great height. Ana looked up at the cirque wall, which soared some twelve metres above her head, and nature, which had seemed so beautiful, suddenly seemed cruel.

'It probably came down with an avalanche,' Quim called from the lake. He had come closer to the edge to see what Ana was staring at. 'It happens in winter. Deer get swept down the mountain and buried in the snow until the spring thaw. That's why it looks like that.'

The lines of a poem came back to Ana: *This quiet roof, where doles of doves assemble / Between the pines, the gravestones, seems to tremble.*

Suddenly, she turned around, trying to erase the image of the deer from her memory. She took off her jeans, but kept on her T-shirt. She walked to the edge of the tarn, the sharp gravel digging into her feet. Slowly, she waded in; the water was freezing, and the cold sent a shiver through her. The bottom of the lake was slippery, and she thought she could see tadpoles swimming around her legs. When she was waist deep, she froze, unable to take another step. Quim took her hand and led her out until the water came up to her throat. Ana lifted her chin and looked at the sky, trying to stay above water. Ximena watched them, then dived down and disappeared from view, probably to disguise her irritation.

'Push off the ground,' Quim said.

Ana did as she was told, and found herself floating. For a moment, she found the weightlessness frightening, and then she noticed that Quim had a hand on her stomach, supporting her.

'Turn over,' he said, helping her. 'Float on your back. It's not that easy, here, because it's not salt water.'

Ana could feel cold water trickling into her ears and over the scar on the back of her head. Quim's hand was now supporting her neck, stopping her from sinking. Then he placed his other hand on her shoulder, and she felt herself rocked, as though by invisible waves. She felt the warm sun on her face. She closed her eyes and the image of the dead deer reappeared, but she dismissed it. *Where doles of doves assemble / Between the pines, the gravestones*, she thought, and then she said, 'I'd like to stay like this forever.'

Ximena had got out of the water. She pretended to dry herself in the sun while she rummaged for something in the pockets of her jeans. She dialled the number for Officer Burgos. Quim had never looked at her like that. When Burgos answered, she told him that they were in Tempestades cirque.

Meanwhile, Ana and Quim carried on with their swimming lesson.

The woman with the hoarse voice called again, some days later. Joaquín Castán was getting dressed when the phone rang. His hair was still wet and he only had his trousers on.

'I want the money. Send it to me, and then we'll talk,' said the woman's voice on the other end of the line.

'How do I know that what you're going to tell me will help me find my daughter?'

'I can't promise anything about your daughter. But I can tell you where to find the man who took her.'

This time, Joaquín paid a little more attention. The woman sounded as though she was about seventy, her voice gravelly from years of smoking. In the background, he could hear a television. An ad break.

'Why don't you just tell me? I swear, I'll send you the money if it's a genuine lead . . .'

The woman was silent. He could hear the television more clearly.

'I don't trust you,' the woman said, and hung up.

Joaquín put down the phone. *Money Woman*, he wrote on the notepad. It was not the first caller he had believed. He had also given money to Whispering Man and Latin American Woman, but their information had led nowhere.

He looked in the mirror on the inside of the wardrobe door and saw himself, sitting on the bed, his shoulders bowed, his paunch falling over his belt. The skin on his arms had patches of white where he lacked pigmentation. The hair on his chest had begun to turn grey, a little tuft in the centre that sometimes peeked out of his shirt collar. He felt old, a caricature of himself. A lone animal in the mountains, abandoned by the herd, prowling the rocky crags, waiting for his time to come. What had happened to the body he had been so proud of? He felt as though, in the past two weeks, he had aged twenty years.

He got up, closed the wardrobe to hide his reflection, and pulled on a shirt. He was still doing up the buttons as he wandered into the kitchen. Rafael was having breakfast with Montserrat. His brother-in-law did not look at him as he said good morning. Montserrat was washing cups and asked if he wanted coffee. He thought he could see her smile, and it irked him, the way she moved, lightly, almost happily. He said he had things to do, that he would get coffee later, and he left.

After Joaquín left, Montserrat sat down with her brother, and Rafael laid his hand on hers.

'You won't have to do this alone,' he said.

Montserrat gave him a grateful smile. Rafael was the rock she relied on. Sturdy, unchanging, he had been with her through all the years, dealing with all the things they let slide – especially their son.

'Will you talk to Quim?' Montserrat asked. 'I know he's been a lot better since he's been hanging around with Ana . . . but . . . I don't know how to tell him . . .'

'This is good news,' Rafael said. 'It's easy to tell people good news.'

Rafael was right. Quim was never going to be the problem. The problem was her husband.

To Sara, it felt as though the days and nights were piling up, like useless junk in a drawer. Every tiny step forward in the investigation quickly proved to lead nowhere.

She told Víctor she had not been able to find Documents 24/10, the witness statement given by Fulgencio Heras. Víctor searched the records office in the basement to no avail. He could not remember what had been in the statement, but he did not think it was very important. Almost everyone in the village had given a statement at some point during the investigation.

Sara tracked down Fulgencio Heras. He had retired and was living in an old house in Val de Sacs, which he was renovating, now that he had time. Sara decided to stop off and talk to him on her way to Barbastro, where she had to give evidence at Gaizka's preliminary hearing.

Chief Sanmartín of the Mountain Rescue Team drove her there. It had been a quiet summer for him; he was used to dealing with dozens of emergencies a day as soon as the weather was fine, but the news from Monteperdido was hardly an invitation to come and holiday in the valley, and most people had cancelled their reservations. Despite the contemptuous way he talked about the tourists,

Chief Sanmartín seemed to miss them. Hoteliers and restaurant owners had also started to complain, but Sara turned them a deaf ear. What was happening was hardly her fault.

Fulgencio Heras's house was on the outskirts of the village. Val de Sacs was the poor relation in the valley – not so much a village as a trickle of houses along the roadside and scattered on the slopes of the mountain.

Sanmartín waited in the car while Sara went to talk to Fulgencio, a man of seventy-five, but still hale and hearty, he insisted. He told her that, when the girls disappeared, he had been working for José Alberto Mencía at the petrol station.

'A decent bloke, Mencía,' Fulgencio said, inviting Sara to take a tour of his memories. But she wanted to discuss the witness statement he had given. Fulgencio gave a brief smile and said that, in his original statement, he had told the Guardia Civil that, on the day of the abduction, he had seen a high-end black car – an Audi – passing by. It had driven towards the village at a hundred kilometres an hour, although the speed limit was fifty. Fulgencio was still indignant at the thought, even now: outsiders hurtling through Monteperdido at top speed, as though it were a desert, without a thought for the children or the pedestrians they might encounter. Sara asked if he remembered the registration of the Audi, but he could not. How could he be expected to remember a registration number after five years? 'But I gave it to the officers at the time,' he said. 'They're bound to have it written down somewhere.'

Sara thanked him for his help, wished him good luck with the renovation work on the house and went back to Sanmartín's car.

Fulgencio was just another dead end.

★

When it began to get dark, Sara locked herself in her office. In recent days, she had been back to the hotel only to shower and to change her clothes. She spent her nights in the station, avoiding the sleep she feared.

But too many sleepless nights were beginning to take their toll.

As soon as she sat down, her head fell back against the headrest and, thinking she would just close her eyes for a second, she fell asleep.

She looked around. The office had been transformed into a jigsaw puzzle of shadows. A harlequin pattern covered the walls, the floor, the shelves. Black and grey shapes. There was someone hiding in the shadows. Sara tried to get up, and it was then that she realized she was dreaming. The man materialized from the shadows, naked. When he sat down in the chair on the other side of the desk, she saw his featureless face: glossy and smooth, but for the little vortex in the centre, particles of his own skin being sucked in, like an eddy. Sara tried to scream, to get up and run, but she could not move.

She was awakened with a brutal jolt and heard herself scream. The light in the office was on, and she found herself standing next to her desk, frantically looking around, trying to work out what had happened. The faceless man had disappeared and, in his place, she saw Víctor, trying to hug her.

Shamefaced, she shook him off.

'You were screaming,' Víctor said. 'You scared me.'

Sara leaned against the wall and retched. She had woken from the dream too quickly and she still could not control her body. Her knees gave way and she was about to collapse, but stopped herself in time, tensing every muscle in her body.

348

'You can't carry on like this, Sara.' Víctor sounded genuinely concerned.

'I'm fine,' she managed to say. 'It was just a nightmare.'

Elisa took a swig from her glass and looked drunkenly around the bar. The dim lighting and the alcohol made people's faces look like blurred, colourless splotches. A song she did not know was playing, but it made her think of robots dancing mechanically. She wanted to press herself against someone. Feel someone's breath on her face.

Some days earlier, a group of boys from Valencia had arrived at the hotel. Three lads, who had come to Monteperdido to go rafting. Before winding up in this bar tonight, she had slept with all three of them, but she had not wanted to go home.

Everyone has somewhere to go back to, she thought resentfully. Had she said it aloud?

She felt a hand grab her arm and she turned to the man who had just stopped her falling off her stool.

'It's a trick,' Elisa said. 'And it always works, doesn't it, darling?'

'Do you want me to take you home, Elisa?'

The tone of his voice did not sound like it promised a night of unbridled passion. But, even so, she went with him. Outside the bar, the cold night air woke her up a little. He was lighting a cigarette and, now, she realized it was Ismael, the guy who worked with Ana's mother. She even remembered his surname: Calella. Ismael Calella. He had stayed at La Renclusa for a few weeks when he first arrived in Monteperdido. She had been working afternoon shifts at the time. He was cute. Too cute, maybe, but she liked his thick, black curly hair, tied back in a ponytail. Was he fucking Raquel? Not anymore, probably. Álvaro had taken his place.

'Hey, carpenter,' Elisa said.

Ismael sighed and did not answer.

'Did I say something rude?' Elisa asked.

'I won't hold it against you.'

'At least tell me what I said. That way, I won't make the same mistake again . . .'

Ismael put an arm around her waist and they set off down the hill. The bar was ten minutes from Elisa's house and, while they walked, she laid her head on Ismael's shoulder, as though they were a couple. She liked the way he held her, she liked the smell of him, she wanted to go to sleep and wake up beside him.

'Must have been something about Raquel,' Elisa muttered. 'What I said that made you angry. It was something about Raquel, right?'

Ismael pushed her away slightly, but she clung to his arm.

'I won't say anything else, I swear . . .'

When they came to Elisa's house, Ismael said goodnight. He suggested she take a couple of ibuprofen before going to bed, or she would wake up with the hangover from hell. Elisa stared at the empty house.

'They're all the same,' she said, as Ismael was walking away. 'Forget about her. Let her go back to that pig of a husband.'

'Elisa, you need to get a grip,' Ismael scolded. 'The whole village is talking about you.'

'Fuck the lot of them,' she said angrily. 'All they do is talk about other people.'

'Well, you're giving them every excuse.'

'No more than anyone else,' Elisa objected. 'Now everyone thinks my father is the devil and Álvaro is a saint. No one gives a shit that he fucked me as soon as he came back to the village . . . that he used me to get the police off his back. No one cares about that.'

'What do you mean, Álvaro used you to get the police off his back?' Ismael had retraced his steps and was standing a few inches from Elisa.

'You know what really happens in this village? They're eaten up with shame. They're all talk, but when it comes down to it, they're a bunch of shits . . .'

Ismael felt pity for Elisa as he watched her spinning out of control, staggering towards her house, screaming and insulting the neighbours. She shouted their names: 'Mariángeles! Nieus! Where were you?' she shrieked. 'That's right, you just close your fucking windows.' She accused them of turning a blind eye when her father was beating her.

Granted, Marcial was now being charged by the Guardia Civil, but Elisa had refused to report the abuse. As a precautionary measure, the judge had imposed a restraining order, and Marcial was not allowed to set foot in Monteperdido. Elisa had heard he was living in Barbastro with his mother.

She slumped down on the threshold of her house and sobbed.

'Why don't you try to start again from scratch?' Ismael tried to sound encouraging.

Elisa said nothing for a moment, then turned, retched and threw up at her feet. A pool of vomit as red as blood began to spread. Ismael helped her to move so that her clothes did not get stained. She was ice cold, but sweating. Elisa lifted her head and closed her eyes. A trickle of drool still hung from her lips. Ismael took out a tissue and wiped it away.

'Thanks,' she whispered, and when she opened her eyes, they

were filled with tears, yet expressionless – defeated. 'I'll go to Barbastro with my father,' she said.

Ismael helped her into the house, led her up to her room and laid her on the bed. Deep down, Elisa was still a little girl who simply wanted to be looked after, but he could not stay with her.

When he got home, Ismael realized that it would not be easy for him to start over either. He had moved to Monteperdido to be close to Raquel. His whole life had revolved around her: the renovation business, and the business of rebuilding Raquel herself. He felt jealous that Álvaro would get to enjoy the results of his hard work. What sense did it make to carry on living in the village? The past four years had disappeared in a puff of smoke because of a miracle: Ana had reappeared. He felt a sudden flash of rage; he wished he could put her back in that hole.

Doodles filled the margins of the reports. Sara Campos spent hours poring over them – reviewing the names of villagers, rereading Ana's statements – all the while unthinkingly drawing geometric shapes, one over the other. They spread like cobwebs. Triangles, hexagons, broken lines shaded to look like flights of stairs, straight lines that came to dead ends, and, next to them, rectangles that took over whole pages, enclosing text and photographs. It was a tic that had frustrated Santiago. How could they present these documents in a courtroom, or to their superiors? *It helps me think,* Sara always said.

As she wandered through the pine forest behind the houses at Los Corzos, Sara thought of these scribbles. The paths through the woods were as confusing as her doodles. Next to her, Ana was sniffing her hands; her fingers still smelled of beaten eggs, sugar and vanilla. When Sara had picked her up at the house, she had found her in the kitchen, making a sponge cake with her mother. Now, she was sniffing her hands as though the smell might transport her home.

'How are the swimming lessons going?' Sara asked.

'I can only doggy-paddle, but at least I don't sink anymore,' Ana said with a smile. This was probably the best thing that had happened to her since she escaped from the hole.

Burgos's screams had echoed around Monte Ármos the day that the teenagers had run off. He had called Víctor and was about to organize a search party to comb the aspen forest when he got the call from Ximena. Once Ana was home, Sara had asked her not to do anything like that again.

'All we want to do is protect you,' Sara said.

Since Santiago's death, Sara had been spending every afternoon at Ana's house, talking to her. At first, they sat in the living room or in the garden, going over the details of the abduction and talking about how Ana was adjusting to her new life. But they quickly stopped hanging around the house and had their conversations as they walked around Monteperdido. Sometimes, they would wander away from Los Corzos and head into the old town, cross the square in front of Santa María de Laude, or wander through the arcades outside the town hall. They usually avoided Avenida de Posets; although there were not many tourists that summer, the few who came tended to hang around the shops and bars along the main street.

Gradually, the journalists had left the village. It was already August, when many reporters took holidays and newspapers were short-staffed. The story of Ana's reappearance was no longer sufficiently interesting to keep them around. By 14th August, they had all left.

'When are we going up to see the stag?' Ana asked. She had told Sara about the dead stag they had found at the foot of Tempestades cirque.

Sara said no one was going to do anything about it. The people at SEPRONA had decided to let nature take its course.

During their walks around Monteperdido, Sara tried to retrace the years that Ana had spent in the hole. From the blind fear of the first weeks, to the surprising acceptance of this unnatural routine: two girls locked in a basement, eating out of Tupperware containers brought by their kidnapper, relieving themselves in buckets that often went unemptied for days, entertaining each other with absurd games, arguing over trivial things and, mostly, being bored. With a certain guilt, Ana admitted that the most intense feeling she had experienced in those five years was boredom. The boredom of time slipping past while they grew and their bodies became those of young women. Ana read every book that was tossed into the hole; she pleaded with Lucía to ask the kidnapper to bring more. But her friend was not growing at the same pace as she was. Lucía sought refuge in a childlike world, as though determined to preserve the innocence she had had when she first arrived. She was not interested in books, was uncomfortable at any mention of sex, and refused to explore her own body as Ana did. Lucía was interested only in dolls, and, when she grew bored of them, in clothes. The kidnapper brought catalogues and Lucía would choose outfits for her and for Ana, as though they were now the dolls she wanted to dress up.

As time passed, Ana seemed to put a certain distance between herself and her memories. She was trying to leave that part of her life behind, to dissociate the Ana walking around Monteperdido with Sara from the little girl locked up with Lucía. Two different people. Who would not try to create such a protective barrier?

Sara stopped next to the tree where Ana's schoolbag had been found.

'I was jealous of Lucía,' Ana said suddenly. 'No one took any notice of me. At least she got to spend the night with him. Talking. But I was just a burden. I would only be there until they got sick of me. I was scared when Lucía used to get angry and say that she didn't want me around . . .' Ana paused before confessing something she found it difficult to accept: 'I wanted him to love me just a little . . .'

Sara remembered the words that one of the kidnappers had said to Ana at the very beginning: *One day, I'll kill you.* Threats and taunts had followed her like a shadow every day of those five years.

It was beginning to get dark and they decided to head home. Ana had got her life back; in her parents' eyes and in Quim's eyes, she could see herself as someone – someone she wanted to be. These conversations unsettled her and there always came a moment when she needed to get back – to Raquel, to Álvaro, to Quim. Sara saw her sniff her hands again as they emerged from the forest, but perhaps they no longer had that smell of home.

Sara had come to the conclusion that the two men who had kept the girls captive had taken turns looking after them, but that one of them had had little contact with them. The man who had abducted them in the forest, who had threatened to kill Ana – he was the one who had brought Ana upstairs and left her tied to a beam while he was down in the basement with Lucía. The other man was the one who bought the clothes. He was the one who brought them food and looked after them when the first man was not around. The girls had assumed that the kidnapper was angry with Lucía, and this was why he did not come to see her, but Sara believed that, for some reason – work, maybe? – these were days when he could not visit the hut, and so the other man took care of them. And this other man was forbidden any contact with the girls.

They said their goodbyes outside Ana's house. The girl opened the garden gate, but then she did something that caught Sara's attention: Ana twisted her body so that she did not have to look at the Castáns' house. At first, Sara assumed it was simply embarrassment, since, at that moment, Quim had just come through the front door with Nicolás Souto. Sara knew that Ana and Quim had started some sort of relationship and assumed that the girl had turned away so that no one would notice their burgeoning romance. But what if it was the vet she was trying to avoid?

This was another of the reasons for their long walks around the village; Sara had not yet given up the idea that Ana was not telling the whole truth. Perhaps she did know the identity of her kidnappers, but said nothing out of fear. Fear and the proximity. If the two men lived in Monteperdido, Ana would have seen them – if not in the hospital, then certainly on the street – after she had come home.

Sara was constantly evaluating Ana's behaviour in the village. Which places did she avoid? Where did she seem most uncomfortable? It seemed logical that she would avoid places where the kidnappers might be – assuming that she did know who they were.

Until this afternoon, Sara had not noticed Ana acting strangely anywhere. Something was going on in Joaquín's house. Both Quim and the vet were looking serious, having a whispered conversation as the boy walked Nicolás to the gate, when the vet only lived across the road. The upstairs lights were on. Rafael's car was just drawing up outside. Meanwhile, Ana had her back turned to the Castán house and was hurrying to her own door, as though trying to get away from something. The street lights flickered on, scattering the twilight shadows. Rafael stopped for a moment to talk to Nicolás and Quim before going into the house. Through the windows overlooking the garden, Sara thought she could see Joaquín in the living room.

Ana was already inside her house and had shut the front door.

Montserrat was staring at the ceiling. The bedside lamp blinded her. There seemed to be a blurred halo around it, or was she crying? Nicolás had told her to stay in bed. Complete rest, for at least forty-eight hours, until the bleeding stopped.

What had she lost? A life? A future?

She had been startled that afternoon when, going to the toilet, she had noticed blood spotting on her underwear. She'd called Nicolás. The vet came and carefully examined her. She was in serious danger of miscarrying. It was not unusual in the first trimester, while the foetus was not fully implanted. Quim had found them together in the bedroom.

'I don't want to lose the baby,' she'd said to her son, when he realized what was going on.

'Don't worry; everything will be fine.' Quim's words sounded reassuring, grown-up. He took her hand and she smiled at him. 'I hope you're not going to treat this baby the way you treat me,' he said jokily.

'I'm sorry, darling,' was all that Montserrat could say.

Nicolás was downstairs in the living room when Joaquín arrived home.

'Phone Rafael,' Montserrat said to her son when she heard the front door. 'Ask him to come round.'

Quim understood his mother's need to feel protected. He went to his bedroom and called his uncle. From the living room came the sound of voices. Joaquín pounded up the stairs, as though trying to break them.

Montserrat took a deep breath and closed her eyes as Joaquín appeared at the bedroom door. She opened them again and saw him at the foot of the bed. His face was contorted, as though he had found her in bed with another man. She sat up, a knot in her stomach.

'I didn't plan it, honestly,' she said, then wondered why she was apologizing. 'But I want to have it.'

'So why didn't you say anything to me?' Joaquín tried to contain his fury.

'I was scared, Joaquín . . . I didn't want to tell you like this, but then I started bleeding and . . .'

Joaquín turned his back; he did not want to hear her excuses. He did not want to know the details that would make this pregnancy a reality.

'So you're done with searching for Lucía?' Joaquín's words were like daggers. 'What are you trying to do? Take over her room for the baby? Fill the gap?'

Montserrat struggled to find some way to answer Joaquín, but Quim was ahead of her: 'If Lucía is dead, that doesn't mean other people have to die,' he said evenly; he had accepted this reality long before them.

Joaquín looked at his son and, without thinking, lashed out, giving him a slap that made Quim stagger back. Nicolás ran up the stairs and told Joaquín to calm down.

'What the fuck are you even doing in my house? Get the hell out!' Joaquín roared.

Montserrat tried to get out of bed, but Nicolás pleaded with her not to.

'I'm going,' he said. 'But if you need anything . . . call me, please . . . You need to rest . . .'

Quim followed Nicolás downstairs. Joaquín heard the vet offering soothing advice: 'He'll feel differently about things tomorrow, you'll see. It's just a matter of time. No point trying to sort things out right now . . .' Then his voice trailed away.

Montserrat lay back on the bed and stared at the ceiling, the lamp still blinding her.

She knew that she was about to lose something: either her unborn child or her husband. One way or another, tomorrow, nothing would be the same.

Which would she find more painful? As she thought this, Montserrat realized that she had long since lost her husband. It was a grief to which she was accustomed.

Quim came back into the house with Rafael, who stopped in the doorway and watched Joaquín angrily prowling the living room, staring at the photos of Lucía that gazed down from every wall. Hearing Rafael come in, he whipped round.

'Who the fuck called you? Your sister, I suppose?' Joaquín made no bones about the fact that her did not want his brother-in-law there.

As ever, Rafael stoically bit his tongue and headed for the stairs.

Suddenly, Joaquín's rage exploded. Everyone is against me, he thought. He strode across the room and grabbed Rafael by his collar.

'Let go of him!' Quim yelled.

'This is my family,' Joaquín growled at Rafael, ignoring his son.

'You touch one hair on my sister's head, and I'll kill you,' Rafael said calmly. He took Joaquín's hand, prised it from his collar and pushed the man away.

'I'm the only one who really cares about Lucía . . .' Joaquín muttered angrily. 'The rest of you don't really give a damn.'

'You think you love Lucía?' Quim said, and ran upstairs.

Joaquín watched as Rafael followed. He was trying to persuade Quim to calm down, but the boy was not listening. Too many years had passed. Too many years dealing with his father's frustration. Quim knew that what hurt his father was not that his daughter was still missing, but that *he* had not been able to find her. He wandered into his sister's bedroom and, as he did, he remembered all the times his father had told him the story of how he had saved Lucía's life during the flood. His heroic feat.

Piled on the bed were the presents their parents had diligently bought for Lucía every Christmas and every birthday. The largest, heaviest box was wrapped in pink paper. Quim picked it up, staggered on to the landing and hurled it down the stairs.

'This is all that's left of Lucía!' he yelled.

Joaquín had to step aside to avoid being hit by the box, which exploded with a metallic clatter on the living-room floor, the contents spilling out like the inner workings of a robot. It was a computer tower. Joaquín remembered the day he had gone to the shop in Barbastro to buy it.

Quim reappeared on the landing with two more boxes and threw them down the stairs. His father screamed at him to stop what he was doing. Rafael tried to hold him, but Quim shook him off and went on throwing the presents, shattering them. One fell on the glass coffee table and burst.

'Give up with all this shit and let other people live their lives!' Quim wailed, exhausted, sobbing as his uncle took him in a bear hug.

Joaquín looked at the living-room floor, at the gifts he had bought in the hope that, one day, when Lucía came home, she would open them and realize that they had never stopped thinking about her. Seeing the computer games, the roller skates, the dolls strewn all over the floor, even he realized that they looked ridiculous.

But he could not admit this, even to himself. Lucía was his daughter. He had to find her, even if no one else would help.

He grabbed his car keys and stormed out of the house.

Joaquín drove aimlessly for a while, staring through the windscreen as the car ate up the ribbon of road. When he reached the tunnel at Fall Gorge, he pulled over. He took out his phone and searched his contacts: *Money Woman*. He was not going to wait for her to call again. He would give her as much money as she wanted to tell him what she knew.

Sara bought a bottle of wine on the way to Víctor's house. He had organized a barbecue, his brother and his family were going, and he had insisted that she join them.

As the door opened, she noticed that, behind Víctor, his dog, Nieve, was watching her from a wicker basket.

'The local plonk?' Víctor said, seeing the bottle she was carrying. Then he noticed that Sara could not take her eyes off Nieve. 'Come on, come in. He won't bite.'

'Are you sure? If someone shot me, I'd be just itching to get revenge.'

Víctor pulled her across the threshold and led her to the basket where Nieve was curled up.

The smell of a coal fire filled the house. There was a warmth that she found cosy, fluffy as a feather pillow. Sara half-heartedly followed an excited Víctor, who was telling her that Nieve had almost completely recovered from the accident. Nice of him to call it an accident, Sara thought. The dog would have a slight limp, but that was all.

Nieve lay in his basket, watching. His coat of long white hair rippled, like waves in a breeze.

'Go on, then – stroke him,' Víctor said, taking Sara's hand.

Still clutching the bottle of wine in one hand, she extended a trembling finger of the other, and Nieve growled and bared his fangs.

'See?' Sara said, jerking her hand away. 'He hates me.'

'It's not that,' Víctor explained. 'It's just that he can sense your fear.'

'I don't mind, honestly. This is your house and I'm a dog killer. He has every reason to hate me.'

'Why are you so tense?'

'Maybe because I've just seen him bare his fangs.'

'I told you, he won't bite.'

'How do you know?'

'Because I know him; he's my dog.'

'You know what you sound like?' Sara said. 'You sound like the neighbours when it turns out that some guy has murdered his family and eaten them: "He was such a lovely man."' She looked away from Nieve, holding up the bottle of wine. 'This needs to be chilled. Where's the kitchen?'

Víctor nodded and gave up on his attempt to reconcile Sara and Nieve. He led her into the kitchen, opened the freezer and put the bottle inside.

'We're having dinner in the back garden,' he reassured her. 'Do you think you'll be able to relax enough to eat, or should I chain up the ferocious hound?'

'Don't laugh at me, please,' Sara said with a sheepish smile, and glanced at the clock on the kitchen wall. It was ten o'clock and Víctor's brother had not shown up yet. For a moment, Sara thought Víctor had tricked her and it would just be the two of them for dinner. Almost without realizing, she began to try to come up with excuses to leave. She was not sure what they had to talk about, other than work.

'Román's always late,' Víctor said, as though he could read her mind. 'When you've got two kids, you have to move heaven and earth to get away for the night . . .'

He handed Sara a glass of wine. She was still glancing into the living room to make sure that Nieve had not moved from his basket.

'Animals just give back what you give them,' Víctor said. 'If you give them fear, they'll respond with fear.'

'I think humans are easier to understand,' Sara confessed.

She followed him into the back garden. It was not particularly big, about twenty square metres of lawn, with a wooden table in the centre, laid for dinner. The barbecue was already blazing. This was the source of the smell and the warmth she had noticed when she first arrived.

'Do you really think so?' Víctor said. 'Do you understand the vicious bastards you've had to deal with during your cases?'

'I think I do,' Sara said, taking a sip of wine. 'Are you not having a drink?'

'I'm the chef tonight. If I start drinking now, I'll set fire to the house . . .'

But Víctor's joke did nothing to hide the real reason he did not drink alcohol, and they both knew that. Sara was sorry she had asked the question. In the awkward silence, they heard Román's car pull into the drive and they both smiled, relieved they had company.

Román was slightly taller than Víctor; he was easy-going and – Sara was pleased to find – very chatty. As was his wife, Ondina, who confessed to Sara that she had just turned forty. Pale and smooth-skinned, she was clearly accustomed to playing the little wife to Román and was besotted with her children. Ondina was the sort of woman who could talk for hours, about everything and nothing – the weather, her children's latest exploits. It was a gift that Sara envied, since she was incapable of making small talk and assumed that anything she had to say was of no interest to anyone. But she enjoyed the company of people like Ondina, who used stories to create a common ground where strangers could meet.

While Víctor set about preparing the barbecue, and their children – two boys, aged seven and five – kicked a football around the garden, Román and Ondina monopolized the conversation. They chatted about the long summer holidays, how they coped when the children did not have school, and then talked about the forthcoming festivities in Monteperdido, in early September. They explained to Sara about the '*baile de los hombres*', a traditional dance performed by the guildsmen of the Cofradía in front of the statue of Santa María de Laude. They joked about the year Víctor had been one of the dancers. He had two left feet.

'In my defence, it was the morning after a particularly long night before.' Víctor smiled as he tended the barbecue.

'You've no idea how much people in the village drink at these things,' Ondina laughed.

Sara smiled, warily eyeing the two boys kicking the football, convinced that at any moment the ball would end up on the barbecue.

'So, are you coming to the Hunting Society tomorrow?' Román asked Víctor when they finally sat down to eat. 'We're drawing lots for the *battue*.'

'I don't think I'm up for it this year,' Víctor said. 'Are you handling the draw?'

'You mean, given that Marcial is . . .' Román let the word trail off, as though, by merely mentioning Marcial's name, he had stepped into quicksand.

Sara was looking at the table and eating a piece of grilled veal when she realized everyone was staring at her. 'I've never understood how you can love animals and love hunting at the same time,' she said.

'I thought you said you understood human beings?' Víctor quipped. 'Well, give it a try. Why do you think we like to hunt?'

Sara saw Víctor's half-smile. She knew this was a challenge.

'It's the only time when you get to behave like animals,' she said.

'You're surrounded by them all the time, here, in the mountains. Animals don't have to worry about mortgages, or about their kids getting good marks at school. All they have to do is eat and survive. When you go hunting, you get to feel like they do – like wild animals, roaming the forests of Monteperdido.'

Román chuckled riotously at Sara's description. 'Tell that to Rafael,' he said when he finally managed to stop laughing. 'We hunt because we love going up into the mountains. And, afterwards, we eat the game we've caught, at the Hunting Society ... That's our idea of entertainment around here. That's all. No need to get all Freudian.'

Sara held up her hands in surrender.

'Besides, there are no natural predators in the mountains,' Román went on, putting a forkful of beef into his mouth. 'How else can we control the population of wild boar or deer? There's no one else to hunt them. Only us.'

Román refilled the wine glasses and proposed a toast: to the ecological balance of Monteperdido. They drained their glasses – all except Víctor, who barely wet his lips.

The night was strangely warm. Normally, the village was kept cool by the stiff mountain breezes. Here, in Víctor's back garden, sheltered by high walls covered with vines, it was hot. On the barbecue, the last coals still glowed, casting a reddish glow on their faces. Sara watched Víctor relax as he listened to his brother's stories and played with his nephews, who insisted he be goalkeeper.

Sara drank another glass of wine and, almost without realizing, she began to drift. The combination of the wine and too many sleepless nights was beginning to take its toll. She thought about making her excuses and going back to the hotel, but she felt comfortable here. Protected.

The sound of a phone ringing brought her back to reality. Víctor went inside to answer it. Román offered her a little more wine and Sara did not have time to refuse before he filled her glass.

'You look tired,' Ondina said.

'There'll be time enough to sleep later,' Sara said, trying to sound self-assured.

She heard Víctor call from the living room. As she got to her feet, Sara worried that it would be obvious that she'd had too much to drink, so, as she walked, she stared at Víctor, using him as a fixed point.

It was the Barbastro police, he said. Marcial had called because his daughter had just shown up at his apartment and, given the injunction, he did not want to get into trouble. Elisa was insisting on staying with her father . . .

'What did you say?' Sara asked. She could picture Elisa begging Marcial for forgiveness. Kneeling before a cruel God.

'I told them I'd phone them back . . . I've no fucking idea what to say,' Víctor confessed.

We all need somewhere to go, Sara thought. Even if it is a place of pain and suffering.

'Tell them to station a squad car outside, but let her stay with him,' Sara said.

'Are you sure?' Víctor asked, but Sara had already turned away.

Who else could give Elisa what she needed, Sara was thinking. Although, since Marcial's exile, the village had tried to offer her a refuge, it was not enough.

As she passed Nieve, she remembered what Víctor had said: *Animals give back what you give them.* If only it were as simple with people. Give love, get love.

She did not even realize that she was crying until Víctor asked if she was OK. Sara brought her hands to her cheeks; she tried to blame the wine. Víctor sat her down in the kitchen and made a pot of coffee.

She heard him apologize to his brother's family as they bustled out of the house. The children's babbling died away as the engine started up and the car drove into the distance.

Sitting there in the kitchen, sobbing, Sara felt ridiculous; she wanted to leave before Víctor reappeared. The coffee pot began to bubble.

'You're not going anywhere tonight,' Víctor said, handing her a mug of coffee and leading her into the living room. He sat her on the sofa. 'Is this about Elisa?'

Sara shrugged. Grief had become a virus infecting everything. It was about Elisa and it was about Santiago. It was Joaquín's failure and Lucía's absence. It was about Ana's fear of the kidnappers, who were still moving around the village where Sara could not see them.

It was her whole life.

'Trust me,' Víctor said. 'I'd like to help.'

'Why?'

The question summed up all Sara's insecurities. Why would any-body worry about her? Víctor took the coffee cup and set it on the table. Then he sat down next to her, laying a hand on the nape of her neck. She could tell that, at every moment, he was expecting her to reject him, but the closer he came, the stronger she felt. As though Víctor was the armour she had always dreamed would protect her.

It was she who brought her lips to his. They tasted of damp earth, of wood burning in a fireplace. Then she fell into his arms. Víctor kissed her cheeks, tears that had dried on her skin.

They made love in his bedroom and, afterwards, enfolded in the sheets and the shadows, he whispered, 'I've been looking for you a long time. I never thought I'd find you.'

She settled back into his arms. She pictured the last doodle she had scrawled in the margin of a case file: the impossible maze. And, as she did, she saw a red line appear, weaving its way through the maze, finding a way out.

There's always someone looking for you, she remembered Víctor had said.

They stayed awake, talking. She told Víctor about Santiago, about her parents. About how the toxic relationships in her family had been much like what Elisa was going through. How her father had beaten her mother. How, as a little girl, she had lived with the constant tension, desperate for some sign of affection from parents who were so obsessed with their own relationship, they had no time for her. Then, at the age of sixteen, she had gone to a police station and reported her father's abusive behaviour. He had been arrested and charged, but, when it came to trial, Sara's mother testified that her daughter had made it all up, accused her of being a jealous little girl who had lied to try to break up her parents' marriage. Sara's father had been acquitted and returned home. Though she could not accept it, Sara knew she was not wanted. Then, one day, she had run away, intending to give them a fright. Later, when she went to the police station and met Santiago, she found out that her parents had made no attempt to find her.

You are no one if no one is looking at you, and no one had ever looked at Sara.

Víctor made no promises; he did not need to tell her that, from now on, she would always know someone was looking.

They finally fell asleep as dawn was breaking.

Sara woke to something gently stroking her hand, like a feather brushing against her fingertips. Opening her eyes, she saw that Nieve was walking back and forth beneath her arm, which was dangling off the side of the bed. Stroking himself against her hand.

Sara gently ran her fingers through the dog's soft coat and Nieve stopped.

'Do you forgive me, Nieve?' she whispered.

She pulled on a T-shirt and got up. Before leaving the room, she glanced at the bed, where Víctor still lay sleeping.

As she stepped into the living room, her mobile rang. It was a call from the police station. Sara tried to answer it, but the phone flickered off; the battery was dead.

She looked around for a charger, reluctant to wake Víctor. She opened drawers and cupboards at random, until she finally found a phone charger in the hallstand.

As she closed the drawer, something caught her eye: a case file. She lifted the corner to see the report number: *24/10/09*. It was the file she had been looking for – the file Víctor had said he knew nothing about.

She felt her stomach lurch and had to lean against the hallstand to keep her balance. Her brain was firing in a thousand different directions. What was she doing in his house, half naked? How real was it, this night they had spent together? Who exactly was Víctor?

Sara hid the report as she heard Víctor emerge from the bedroom. Still half asleep, he told her that the station had called.

'Something's come up from the intercept on Joaquín Castán's phone. He's been heard telling a woman that he is going to give her the reward money . . . Should we intervene?'

She had been at work by nine o'clock, as she was every day, though today she had woken hoping this would be her last time. She hoovered the living room and loaded the washing machine. There was no one home, so she sat by the kitchen window and lit a cigarette. She kicked off her shoes and looked at her feet; the summer heat always made them swell. They were black and blue. But still she had to carry on, for hours every day, cleaning other people's houses. Not that she earned much; certainly not enough to make ends meet. By now, her granddaughter was used to waking up alone and making her own breakfast. The girl would come home from school at four and make herself a snack. When she got home from work, she would find her granddaughter in her pyjamas, lying on the sofa, watching cartoons. She had left a Tupperware container of macaroni cheese on the counter. The night before, she had told her granddaughter that she would be a little late home, but that she would have a surprise.

Though she tried to ignore it, she felt nervous. She kept glancing at the clock, waiting for it to strike one so that she could leave. She had to be at the petrol station on the outskirts of the village by two o'clock. This was where Joaquín Castán had agreed to hand over the money. Then she would go to his office and tell him everything she knew.

She was not planning to con him out of his money; she just wanted to make sure that the reward was real, not a ruse to lure stupid people like her.

She had been surprised when Joaquín called, the night before.

She'd felt sure he was going to ask her to accept only part of the reward, but Joaquín was prepared to give her the whole sum. He accepted her conditions. She could tell that he was desperate.

She was supposed to clean the bathroom, but this morning she was too tired to kneel beside the toilet and scrub the porcelain. She knew the house would be empty all morning. Even now that Joaquín had closed Transportes Castán, Rafael did not like to be there while she was cleaning. On Fridays, he left money for her on the kitchen table and went out as soon as she arrived. Some days, she had to put up with Quim and Ximena lounging around the house, leaving ashtrays overflowing with cigarette butts and messing up everything she had just tidied.

This was the only work she could find. Ever since the timber merchants closed down, she had had no choice but to clean other people's houses. At first, she had earned enough to pay the bills, but now she could only manage a few clients. She had an eight-year-old granddaughter to look after, and every time she looked at the little girl, she wondered, Where did I go wrong with my own daughter?

All her life, she had been a hard worker, and she thought she had passed on to her daughter the importance of selflessness and family, but maybe her daughter thought she was a fool for working every hour of the day and night with nothing to show for it. And not a minute of the day to herself.

Who gives the cleaner a second thought? Who cares?

She turned on the television and sat watching a celebrity gossip programme until it was time to leave.

She did not have a car, so had to go on foot. As she walked, she thought that she would just carry on past if she saw Joaquín Castán prowling around when she got to the petrol station.

She wanted that money. She needed it. As she stood by the side of the road waiting to cross, she watched the stream of cars leaving Monteperdido and heading towards the tunnel at Fall Gorge. The first thing she would buy was a car, she thought. Drive through that tunnel. Living in the valley with no car was a nightmare. Walking for hours up steep hills to get from her house in the village to the houses she cleaned. And then she realized she wouldn't have to clean houses anymore. She had hoovered Rafael's living room for the last time.

She walked along the side of the road, her pulse racing as she came in sight of the petrol station.

Was what she had to tell him really so important that he would let her keep the money?

She glanced furtively at the petrol station. She had told Joaquín to leave the money behind the boxes at the back of the forecourt. The only people to go there were the garbage collectors, and they only came once a week. And, since the petrol station had installed a card payment system, there was no one working at the till.

She allowed several cars to pass before she decided to cross the road. She peered into the trees behind the petrol station, to see whether Joaquín was hiding there. She could not see anyone. She lit another cigarette and walked past the petrol pumps, completely forgetting that she was not allowed to smoke on the forecourt. She saw an S.U.V. drive up the hill, but it carried on towards the village. The only sound was the wind rustling the trees.

She walked over to the boxes and, behind one of them, she found a black rucksack. She picked it up and opened it; the money was inside. More money than she had ever seen in her life.

She wanted to whoop with joy. To go and collect her

granddaughter, take her to the shopping centre and let her buy all the toys she wanted. She steeled herself. She dropped her cigarette butt and ground it under her shoe.

Maybe she was not so stupid, after all.

What if she just walked away? What if she simply left, right now? She could tell Joaquín what she knew by phone; she could write him a letter. Why risk getting into any more trouble? What if he insisted that she go to the police and she ended up having to give back the money?

A wail of sirens startled her. She was tempted to run and made a brief jog to nowhere, but her feet hurt. Where had all the cars come from? Two jeeps swerved into the petrol station, blocking her escape. She looked around at the trees. And where exactly do you think you're going to hide, you old fool? she thought to herself.

She looked at the rucksack stuffed with banknotes and knew it would never be hers.

An officer carrying a gun walked towards her and told her not to move. She was under arrest.

'Put your hands where I can see them.'

This was something she had only ever heard on the afternoon TV.

Sara stayed inside the jeep while Víctor arrested the woman: Concepción Bartolomé, sixty-nine, born in Valls de Valira, a small village in Lérida. What did she have to tell Joaquín? The woman did not look like an opportunist trying to make money from someone else's tragedy. Then again, Sara was not convinced that whatever she had to tell them would prove useful.

She took out the report she had found in Víctor's house and

called the police station. In the witness statement, Fulgencio gave the full licence plate of the car he had seen speeding towards Monteperdido on the day the girls had disappeared – the number he could no longer remember. Sara asked the officer on the end of the line to run a check on the plate number; she needed to know who had owned that car.

When he heard the sirens, Joaquín feared the worst. He raced from his office at Transportes Castán, but, by the time he got to the main road, the police cars were already pulling into the petrol station. They had turned off the sirens, but the lights were whirling, flickering on the tarmac. He saw an officer holding the black rucksack he had left behind the rubbish bins. Víctor was gripping Concepción by the arm. Was this the woman he had been talking to? The woman who cleaned Rafael's house? What could she possibly know? But his doubts were quickly swept away by a wave of blind fury: the police had jumped the gun.

'Are you fucking idiots or what?' he screamed at them, terrified that now Concepción would never tell him what she claimed to know.

Lucía lay back on the mattress and stared at the small, narrow window on the far wall, just below the roof. A shaft of sunlight streamed in, lighting up motes of dust like tiny suspended snowflakes. It was hot, too hot. She felt hungry, but she was also sleepy. How many hours could she sleep in a day? She had asked him for a watch, but he had never brought one. He kept making ridiculous excuses that had begun to irritate her. Perhaps he was afraid that she would use it to calculate how much time she had left to live. In the past few days – or had they been weeks? – she had felt that time was running out. Since Ana had disappeared, nothing had been the same. He had changed. Or was it she who had become a different person? Now, whenever he brought her food and water, he scared her. She thought about Ana, about the sister who had slept next to her for the past five years, the girl who had always been pacing up and down in the basement. 'I don't hate you, Ana,' she whispered in the silence of the dingy little room.

6

The Hunt

'How long is it going to take? Two hours?' Sara spoke into the
phone and waited for an answer, then said to the officer she was
speaking to, 'I don't give a shit. Bring him here, to the village. I
need to talk to him.'

She was hanging up as Víctor appeared in the doorway of the
office.

'Concepción is ready. Shall I take her to the interview room?' he
asked, oblivious to what Sara had been doing behind his back.

Concepción found herself staring at a mirror that ran the length of
one wall, thinking that someone needed to give it a good wipe
down with Windolene. It was filthy with fingerprints and dust.
'See? You're no use for anything else, Concepción,' she said to herself. And then she remembered the thick wads of banknotes in the
rucksack that she would never get to touch.

'Concepción Bartolomé,' Sara said as she sat opposite the woman.
'Are you aware that withholding information relevant to an investigation is a crime?'

'Are you going to put me in prison?' Concepción said, though this was not what was really worrying her.

'I hope that's not going to be necessary. Because you are going to help us now, aren't you?'

'What about my granddaughter? She's all alone in the house and she's going to be scared when I don't come home.'

'There's a Guardia Civil officer with her.' Sara leaned back in her chair and studied the woman: calloused hands, wrinkled skin. The exhaustion of someone who had worked every single day of her life. The look of defeat and distrust. 'What exactly were you going to tell Joaquín Castán?'

Concepción glanced around the room before answering, at the one-way mirror through which Víctor was observing the interview. Her face was old and tired. Ugly.

'When I read the interview that Ana did in the newspaper, there was something that caught my eye. Them dolls she said he brought them . . . Them Barbie dolls that Lucía played with . . .' Concepción's eyes met Sara's and, with a sigh, she gave up on any possibility of making money from what she knew. 'My granddaughter's got them now.'

'What makes you think they're the same dolls?'

'In the newspaper it said that she drew all over them with red marker. My granddaughter's were just like that, until I cleaned them up.'

'How did your granddaughter end up with these dolls?'

'Someone gave them to me.'

'Who?'

Joaquín saw the Guardia Civil jeeps drive away from the police station at full speed. The sirens wailed, yowling like a whipped dog.

He started his car and followed. He was the one who had brought Concepción to them; they had no right to sideline him.

They drove up the school road and, when they came to Avenida de Posets, they turned right. Up the mountain. Where were they heading? Back to the village? To the Hotel La Guardia?

He felt his heart pound as the cars turned towards Los Corzos. Could the man who had abducted his daughter be living so close to him?

The police cars drove on, past the houses of his neighbours. Families who had come to the meetings of the Foundation, who had stood by him, were suddenly suspects. Until he saw the cars pull up outside his own house.

Víctor and Sara got out of a jeep; from another vehicle emerged several Guardia Civil officers carrying guns. The lights were still flashing, the sirens were probably wailing, but Joaquín was no longer listening. He was filled with an utter, complete silence.

Álvaro. Ana's house. Were they going to arrest him? At the thought that he had been right all along, he felt a bitter mixture of anger and pride.

He had no time to put on his trousers. He had just had a shower and was dressed only in boxer shorts and socks. He had been reaching to pull up his jeans when they crashed into the bedroom.

Nicolás Souto stood and stared; with his jeans up to his calves, he stumbled and fell. Víctor pounced on him and pinned him down. The vet tried to find an explanation for what was happening.

'What have I done?' he screamed at them. 'What's happening?'

'Keep calm, Nicolás. It's for the best,' Víctor said as he

handcuffed the man, hauling him to his feet and helping him pull up his jeans.

Sara glanced around the room: a double bed in the centre, flanked by two nightstands; a picture of a deer in the middle of a snowfield hanging above the headboard; white walls; a wardrobe with walnut doors. Minimalist, spotless, neat. A smell of detergent and steam came from the bathroom across the hall.

Beads of sweat trickled from Nicolás's armpits as Víctor led him to the door. Sara thought she saw a look of bewilderment on his face as his eyes darted nervously around his own bedroom, as though to make sure he had not left anything shocking lying around. As he was taken from the house, they passed Ximena, who was standing at the foot of the stairs. The look in her eyes was not fear, but embarrassment.

Lucía dragged the wooden crate she had been using as a dining table to the tiny window, climbed on to it and tried to peer outside, like a dog sniffing the wind. She could see only a patch of clear blue sky. She clambered down and furiously kicked at the door; it barely quivered. It was not the cramped conditions that made her anxious; it was the silence. 'Come back now,' she said aloud, more to break the silence closing in and choking her, like an invisible embrace, than because she really wanted him to come back. How long had it been since he had last come? She was hungry and thirsty. Her heart was pounding erratically in her chest. She had never been alone; Ana had been her shadow. Lucía could only make sense of being alone when Ana was there, as though they were two halves of one person, and now they had been ripped apart. Ana had hurt her with her accusations, her taunts, like a remorseless conscience, constantly judging her and finding her guilty. Lucía paced the small room, then sat, cowering, in a corner. She closed her eyes, trying to control her fear. She imagined that Ana was with her, pacing up and down, reciting those stupid poems of hers. But it was useless to imagine. She knew that she was alone now.

Raquel ran up the stairs of the Castán house. Quim was standing at the front door, staring out into the street. The police had left now; there was no shriek of sirens, only the sort of deafening silence that hangs in a room after a vicious argument.

Raquel found Montserrat sitting on the bed in her room, her head in her hands, sobbing.

'Do you think it could be him?' Montserrat asked fearfully, and Raquel knew that the answer she was hoping for was both *Yes* and *No*.

'You've got nothing to feel guilty about,' was all Raquel could say.

She crouched down beside Montserrat and hugged her. She knew exactly what Montserrat was thinking: had she placed her trust in the man who had abducted her daughter?

Nicolás Souto was a strange man. Raquel had never managed to work him out. He had his fair share of problems – the mocking taunts of the villagers, his own insecurities, a daughter who was out of control, to say nothing of his relationship with Ximena's mother – yet he seemed oblivious to them all.

'Are you feeling any better?' Raquel asked, patting Montserrat's belly. 'Quim told me,' she explained.

'I've stopped bleeding,' Montserrat said, wiping away her tears.

Raquel's phone buzzed in her pocket.

'Go ahead, answer it,' Montserrat said.

Raquel looked at the screen and saw the name *Ismael Calella*: the carpenter who had helped her launch her business, the guy who had brought her back to life, the man she had slept with, planned a future with. She had been putting off the moment when she would have to face him, but she knew she could not do so any longer.

Quim stepped out of the house. Standing in the garden, he glanced over at Ana's place. He could see her through the living-room window. He turned and glared at Nicolás's house. How had Ana been able to live so close to this monster? Or had she not recognized him? Ana disappeared behind the curtains and Quim crossed the street. Ximena needed him.

Sara strode out of the police station and found the officer from headquarters waiting in the car park. She opened the back door of his car and climbed in next to the man she had ordered the officer to bring to Monteperdido for questioning. He was the owner of a car-rental company. The licence plate of the car seen hurtling through the village five years earlier corresponded with an Audi 8 in his fleet.

'Sometimes we rent cars with drivers,' the man explained, clearly irked by how he was being treated by the police, being forced to come to this small village with little explanation.

'Who rented this particular car?' Sara asked.

'That information is confidential,' the man balked. 'We can't go giving out customer details—'

'You want me to get a search warrant?' Sara snarled. 'Do you really want me going through all your business papers?'

'I don't know who rented the car,' he said. 'And I don't think I kept the paperwork. It was a long time ago. And we do a lot of business, here, in Monteperdido.'

'Really? Why?'

The man bit his lower lip and heaved a sigh, avoiding Sara's eyes.

'We have a deal with the Hotel La Guardia,' he admitted, knowing he was opening a can of worms. 'We transfer guests. We don't ask for any details and all payments are off the books. Serna, the guy who owns the hotel, insisted on the terms.'

'Why is he so keen for them not to be traceable?'

The man shrugged, determined to distance himself from whatever happened after guests arrived at the hotel. 'Privacy, I suppose,' he said, weighing his words to try to satisfy the police without incriminating himself. 'He also insisted that all the cars have tinted windows.'

Joaquín went into his house, tossed his car keys on the hallstand and ran up the stairs. The bedroom door was open, but his wife was not in bed.

'Montse!' he shouted, but there was no answer.

Ever since they were children, Nicolás Souto had spent his life trailing after Montserrat like a lapdog. Whenever Joaquín had an argument with his wife, Nicolás was waiting for her with a word of encouragement and a shoulder to cry on. How had he not noticed this before – when he found out that they had once shared a kiss in school, when Nicolás bought a house right across the road, when Joaquín saw him watching Lucía playing in the garden . . .?

'I told you a million times that I didn't want that man in this house,' Joaquín snapped at Montserrat when he found her in the bathroom. 'But you kept on inviting him in. A couple of days ago, you spread your legs for him, for fuck's sake . . .'

Montserrat could think of no answer. She leaned against the washbasin, trembling at the memory of Nicolás coming into her home, examining her in her bed. She felt guilty and sullied.

'I'm sorry,' was all she could say.

Joaquín watched his wife tremble, trying to choke back her tears. He could have reassured her, told her it didn't matter now, that they needed to focus on the police finding Lucía before it was too late. Instead, he stood in the doorway, feeling suddenly powerful again, buoyed by the knowledge that he had been right all along. He had been right, and yet everyone had told him to let it go. Even his wife.

He turned on his heel and walked away.

Sara looked through the one-way mirror to the interview room. Nicolás Souto was sitting slumped in the chair, hands pressed between his knees, staring at the mirror, knowing he was being watched. He had a thin, straggly moustache, like a grey smudge under his nose.

'So you're still not going in yet?' Víctor asked as Sara sat down.

'I want you to conduct the interview,' she said, and Víctor noticed that she was avoiding his eyes. 'I'd rather stay out of it, this time.'

Víctor went to the door of the interview room and realized, as he laid a hand on the doorknob, that he was nervous. He was afraid Sara would not simply be scrutizing Nicolás's answers, but also his questions.

'Have you got a problem with me?' Víctor said to her before he opened the door.

For the first time, Sara looked at him. Víctor knew she had been avoiding him all day, putting a distance between them that, at first, he interpreted as embarrassment because they had slept together.

'Check out his alibis, for the day of the abduction five years ago and the day Ana reappeared,' Sara said. 'And don't handle him as though we've already made up our minds that he's guilty.'

What had happened to make her look at him as though he were a stranger? These eyes were not the ones he had stared into while they lay in his bed, while she confessed her deepest, darkest fears. Sara had changed. Last night, she had been someone he could protect. Now, she seemed like a threat.

Ximena picked up the porcelain vase and dashed it on the floor. Shards scattered in all directions. She stepped on one, and ground it under the heel of her boot.

'I wish he was dead!' she screamed.

Quim was trying to soothe her, but every time he got close, she pushed him away.

'You should take something to help you calm down,' he said.

'What I should do is leave this shit-hole village. I'm not even from here! Just look at me!' She spun around, showing off her dark skin. 'I don't belong in Monteperdido. That shitwank is not my father.'

As if she had made her decision, she raced upstairs and into her bedroom. Quim kept his distance as Ximena opened the closet, threw a suitcase on the bed and began filling it with clothes.

'What are you doing?' he said, watching as she shut the suitcase. 'Where are you going to go?'

'What the hell do you care? Go fuck Ana; at least you care about her—'

'You're talking rubbish, Ximena—'

'Am I?' Ximena faced him. 'Tell me you don't want to screw her. You feel sorry for her, don't you? Poor little thing deserves a good fuck, yeah?'

'This isn't the time to talk about Ana,' Quim said evasively.

'Why not? It's not like you and I are going to see each other again, Quim. Not that you care. You've never taken me seriously.' Ximena began to sob, unable to control herself any longer. Quim tried to put his arms around her, but she pulled away. She wanted to spew it all out, even if the words burned her throat.

'I was good enough for you when your life was a piece of shit . . . I listened to you bitch about the way your parents treated you, how you wished you were dead . . . About how they wished it was you and not Lucía who was abducted . . .'

'I wish things had turned out differently for us too,' Quim said apologetically.

'Don't lie to me! For fuck's sake, Quim . . . Just go . . . Leave me alone . . .'

She pushed him out of the bedroom and slammed the door. As soon as she was alone, Ximena slumped to the floor. She was scared. So petrified, she could not move. She had always known that, one day, Quim would turn his back on her. He had never really loved her. Not the way she loved him. And, almost without realizing it, she began to wish that Nicolás were here so he could comfort her. Hug her in that clumsy way of his, as though he didn't know where to put his hands, awkwardly reassuring her, telling her she was a good girl, that she was pretty, that she could do anything she wanted.

★

'Where were you on the day the girls were abducted?' Víctor said, not looking up from the witness statement Nicolás had given five years earlier.

'I was up in Linsoles, checking on some cattle at Cuéllar's farm ... I left there around four o'clock, and got back to Monteperdido after dark.'

'You were alone, up at the farm?'

'They always just leave me to get on with things, Víctor; you know that. I needed to take blood samples from the cattle; why would anybody have been standing around watching?'

'What about the day Ana reappeared?' Víctor changed the subject. He did not want Nicolás getting bogged down in endless explanations. He needed it to be concrete.

'I was on the plaza outside the church. We all were. At the meeting of the Foundation. You know as well as I do that Joaquín takes a roll-call at those meetings ...'

Víctor stopped listening as Nicolás rambled on, straying from that day outside the church, to Foundation meetings he hadn't been able to attend because he was working, and how Joaquín had bawled him out later, at the Hunting Society.

'What did you do that night?' Víctor interrupted.

'Which night are you talking about?' Nicolás said, bewildered.

'The day Ana reappeared. Where were you that night?'

'I was with you at your house, Víctor. Remember? I went to treat Nieve ... after that policewoman ...' Nicolás shot a look at the one-way mirror. He knew Sara was on the other side. He trailed off.

'I phoned you at about four fifteen a.m.' Víctor propped his elbows on the table. 'You didn't show up until five thirty. Over an hour is a long time to get from your house to mine.'

'I'd been asleep,' Nicolás muttered. 'What with having to get up, get dressed—'

'That's not true,' Víctor said categorically.

'Seriously, are you crazy or what . . .? I don't know why you've arrested me, but how could you think I would hurt those girls? I watched them grow up. They lived right across the road. You really think I'm capable of something like that?'

'Where were you when I phoned, Nicolás? Because I know I didn't get you out of bed.'

Nicolás nervously glanced at the mirror and then at Víctor. His shirt was dark with sweat stains. He stroked his thin moustache, then laid his handcuffed hands on the table. 'It's got nothing to do with the girls,' he blurted, admitting that Víctor's allegation was correct.

'I think I'll be the one to decide that,' Víctor said.

'I've got witnesses, Víctor.' Nicolás's words were a veiled threat: *Don't go there. You're wasting your time.*

'So you're not going to tell me?' Víctor pressed him.

'Some things are a bit embarrassing to talk about,' Nicolás whispered, looking Víctor in the eye.

In the observation room, Sara leaned forward. What exactly was Nicolás trying to say to Víctor? This was the first time he had looked the sergeant in the eye, and now Víctor was staring down at the statement on the table. The silence dragged on and Víctor seemed to struggle to resume the interview.

'I'm not going to say another word until you tell me exactly what you've got on me,' Nicolás said, offering Víctor a way out.

'You know Concepción, don't you?' the sergeant said casually.

'She used to help out around my house when Ximena was little,' Nicolás said.

'You gave her some toys for her granddaughter – Barbie dolls. Do you remember?'

Nicolás stammered, 'Um . . . yeah, sure . . .' But his eyes froze, and his mouth dropped open. Was it shock at realizing he had been found out? Or had he just realized something that had been staring him in the face?

'I've talked to Ana. The dolls you gave Concepción are the dolls Lucía used to play with in the mountain hut,' Víctor said, waiting for an explanation.

'How long ago was that? Three years? I'd completely forgotten, I swear to God . . . I found them up in the mountains; they were lying in a ditch. I knew that Concepción's granddaughter didn't have many toys . . . and Ximena was too old for them—'

'And, when Ana mentioned the dolls in the newspaper interview, you didn't think that they might be the same ones?'

'I'm a shitty writer . . .' Nicolás said with a nervous laugh. He seemed relieved to know that this was why he had been arrested.

'That won't be enough to keep you out of jail,' Víctor said evenly.

Sara waited for Víctor to ask again where Nicolás had been on the night of Ana's reappearance. For now, he allowed Nicolás to talk on about the day he had found the dolls. They had been in a muddy plastic bag in a ditch beside Barbastro Road, near the spot where Ana had reappeared. Some of them were undressed, others had been scrawled on. Nicolás had assumed someone had been clearing out their house and had thrown them away. After he gave them to Concepción, he had forgotten all about them.

Why are you dodging the real question, Víctor? Sara thought.

Come on, don't be a fucking idiot. Ask him! You know I'm sitting here watching you. Give me an explanation.

'There is no one who can confirm where you were on the day the girls disappeared,' Víctor recapitulated. 'In fact, it's not unusual for you to spend whole days away from the village.'

'That's only because of my job.'

'The reason doesn't matter, Nicolás; the fact is, you spend a lot of time away from the village. Most days, your daughter has dinner across the road, with Rafael and Quim . . .'

Nicolás looked down. He knew where this was heading.

'And on the night after Ana reappeared, you were not in the village then, either. Now, we know that whoever kidnapped the girls went up to the mountain hut that night. He got Lucía out of there, and torched the place.'

'You know how much I care about Montserrat,' Nicolás bleated. 'I'd never do anything to hurt her.'

'Where were you that night?'

Nicolás glanced at the mirror before he answered. Víctor's question had not been threatening, had only invited him to explain himself.

'I was at the Hotel La Guardia.' Nicolás sighed. 'I go up there two or three nights a week . . . You can ask any of the girls. Ask Elena – she'll tell you I was there . . .'

With that, Sara realized that the interview was over. Nicolás had fallen silent, a silence that could be construed as shame. Víctor had begun to gather up his files. She knew he wanted to get out of that room, out of the police station, without having to talk to her, but instead he turned and looked at her through the one-way mirror. Was he asking for forgiveness?

★

He had never thought about killing himself. Maybe he should have, back when all this had simply been a fantasy. He had thought this moment would never come. Idiot. He had spent five years living in a bubble. The daily routine had almost made it seem normal. He thought about Lucía – when was he not thinking about her? – and he could not help but worry. How long had he left her on her own? His little Lucía. His little wild animal.

He remembered staring out at the forest from the mountain hut. The trembling aspens, the pines, the oak trees, the mountains, glorious and verdant in the summer, the carpets of pink rhododendrons. He thought of all the things living beneath the branches, the leaves and the flowers: the wild boar, the chamois goats, the roe deer . . . He didn't like hunting with beaters. He preferred to hunt alone. To track the animal. To outsmart his prey. Of all the animals on the slopes of Monteperdido, his favourite was the roe deer: small, elusive, quick-footed, almost impossible to catch. The spirit of the forest, they called it.

Víctor tossed the keys of the jeep to Telmo. By the time he'd emerged from the interview, Sara had disappeared. Officer Pujante came and told him they were going up to the Hotel La Guardia in two cars. Sara would be riding with him, and Víctor was to drive up with Telmo.

'What the hell are we going up there for?' Telmo had said, puzzled.

Víctor had no answer.

When Raquel came into the café, Ismael was already sitting at a table by the window, waiting. They had changed the window frames — the dark mahogany had been Raquel's idea. Ismael had done a magnificent job on the coffered ceiling, and, on the beam over the bar, he had carved the head of a stag. The three-pointed antlers, like the branches of a tree in winter, cast a shadow on the ground. The café was called La Corza Blanca, and this carving by Ismael had become its emblem.

Refurbishing La Corza Blanca had been one of their first commissions. Raquel remembered how surprised she had been at Ismael's talent for sculpture, the way he could bring life to a lump of dead wood. At the time, Raquel had felt just like that — a piece of dead wood — and she had let Ismael carve her into a new woman.

He sat up slightly as she came to the table, and asked what she wanted. Raquel ordered a Coke, although she knew she would not drink it. She hoped this would be quick, clean, like a surgeon's incision.

'Don't worry; I'm not going to make a scene,' Ismael said quietly as she shifted uncomfortably in her chair. 'I know it's over.'

Although he was younger, Ismael had always seemed more mature than she was.

'I'm going to leave Monteperdido,' he said.

'Where will you go?'

'The south, maybe. Or Portugal. I haven't really decided.'

'We'll have to settle up. I still owe you money—' Raquel began, but Ismael interrupted her. He had not come to talk about money.

'Are you sure you know what you're doing?' he said. 'Taking Álvaro back, I mean . . . Do you really think you can trust him?'

Things had been moving so fast that Raquel had managed to avoid asking herself certain questions. Her daughter was back.

Her husband had come home. When she looked back on the time she had spent with Ismael, it seemed like someone else's life, not hers.

'I know how much I've hurt you—' Raquel started to apologize.

'I saw Elisa a couple of days ago,' Ismael interrupted her, raising a hand to show he was not looking for an apology. 'I know there's something not quite right about her, but . . . she told me something about Álvaro . . .'

Raquel felt herself blush, as though Ismael had just entered a dirty, untidy room she wished was neat and spotless. 'I know it's not fair on you,' she said, desperate to stop him from continuing. 'But Álvaro and I are going to try to forget the last five years. We're going to start again.'

Ismael leaned back in his chair; he had reconciled himself to walking away from Raquel, to accepting the inevitable, but he could not just leave without saying anything.

'Elisa told me he used her to get the police off his back. He slept with her—'

'He told me,' Raquel said, tersely. 'He's not the one who lied, it was Elisa . . . I don't care that her father beats the shit out of her. Have you any idea the damage she did to us?'

Raquel had tried to contain her anger, not to raise her voice. Yet still the words came as a shock: *the damage she did to us*. She and Álvaro were together again and there was no room for Ismael.

'I'm just worried about you, that's all,' Ismael said ruefully.

'I'll be fine. I know I will,' Raquel reassured him, trying to sound conciliatory.

There was an awkward silence. Raquel wanted to get up, to go home, to be with her family. She needed to leave behind the person she had been when Ana was missing. Ismael had revived the doubts she had hoped to lay to rest when she slept with Álvaro: the fear that she did not really know her husband at all, that she could not predict his actions, his decisions.

'When were you thinking of leaving?' Raquel said, desperate to break the silence, to dismiss these thoughts.

'After the hunt. I paid to go, so I don't want to waste the money,' Ismael said, with a smile that promised not to speak of Álvaro again.

He looked at the stag's head over the bar and thought that this would be the one mark he'd leave behind in Monteperdido. A mark that, over time, would fade. *Who carved the stag's head?* someone would ask one day, and no one would know. He told Raquel he would call round to say goodbye before he left the village. He could tell that she wanted to get out of the café.

As Raquel left and waved to Ismael through the window, she knew this would be the last time she'd ever see him. Who was this man with whom she had shared four years of her life? She had been so self-absorbed throughout that time, only now did she begin to wonder. Who was Ismael, really? How had he come to be in Monteperdido? What had drawn him to her? It was too late for answers.

Raquel headed home, walking along the almost deserted street, thinking that, as much as we like to pretend otherwise, we are all strangers, really. A long-forgotten image came back to her: sitting next to Montserrat in a snowy playground on a winter's morning, while Ana and Lucía threw snowballs at each other. A deer had walked past; she remembered the feel of its warm breath, and how it had made her feel as though she was part of something. A piece of the puzzle that was Monteperdido.

She wished she could feel that warm breath again.

They drove to the point where the road trailed off, the tarmac giving way to a dirt track that led to a patch of flat ground with a few parked cars. They were all expensive, Sara noticed: Mercedes, Audis, a Jaguar. The Hotel La Guardia was a rectangular two-storey building. Beneath the gabled roof of black slate was a row of small windows – attic rooms, Sara guessed. The hotel exuded a subtle, unostentatious opulence. Only the expensive cars clashed with the simple, rough stone walls, which seamlessly blended with the rock face. This was the closest she'd been to the summit of the mountains. It felt as though she could reach out and brush the sky with her fingers.

'What can you tell me about Serna?' Sara asked Pujante as they sat in the car.

'The guy who owns the place?' Pujante said as he turned off the engine and stared at the hotel for a moment, trying to think of an appropriate description. 'I think he's from Castellón. He comes and goes; nobody ever really sees him in Monteperdido. He's about fifty years old, single; I don't really know him personally.' Pujante thought he was managing to sound professional. 'People say he's loaded. A room in this place costs and arm and a leg. It's a four-star hotel, and there aren't many that have a better setting . . .'

As she got out of the jeep, Sara looked around. The last thickets of black pine forest ringed the hotel; the lush green of the mountain slope marked the boundaries of the valley; a few clouds scudded past the peaks beneath a vaulted sky that looked like a blue dome. A few hundred metres away there was a lookout tower, a mirador from where there was a breathtaking view of the River Ésera, a silver ribbon winding through villages, like the trail left by a toboggan in the snow. Though it rose to almost two thousand metres, from here Mount Ármos seemed smaller.

Víctor said nothing to Sara until they were inside the hotel. The lobby had the same atmosphere of understated luxury as the façade. Here, the carved stone was complemented by timber: parquet floors, exposed beams on the ceilings. They asked to see Serna, and it was a few minutes before he arrived. He extended a strong, confident hand to Sara and said, 'I just want to say how sorry I am about your partner.' The condolences sounded sincere.

They followed him into his office. Sara noticed Víctor's eyes were fixed on her, gauging her movements. Serna was dressed casually: jeans and a blue pinstriped shirt. Though his aim was to look just like anyone else, Sara knew that those clothes, that wristwatch, those shoes were things that hardly anyone could afford.

'We need to speak to Elena,' Víctor said. 'Nicolás claims he was with her on the night Ana reappeared. We need to confirm that.'

'Do you want me to call her?' Serna said solicitously. He had already picked up the phone on his desk.

'Please . . .'

'It's me,' Serna said into the receiver. 'Could you ask Elena to come by my office? Thank you.' He hung up.

Sara wandered over to the window. When would this farce be over? She heard Víctor and Serna exchange small talk about the lack of tourists in the valley this summer. The steady trickle of news about the girls' abduction had continued, and, together with the murder of a police officer and the cordon, had dissuaded tourists from coming to a place where they would usually hope to find peace and calm.

Elena was twenty-seven. Serna introduced her as the bar manager. She wore an elegant hotel uniform, and she was undeniably beautiful, with smooth skin, large brown eyes and bleached blonde hair tied back in a ponytail. She kept her hands clasped behind her back as she spoke, as if to emphasize the formality of the meeting.

'Yes, he was here,' she said, when asked about Nicolás. 'I remember we talked about the fact that Ana had been found.'

'I assume there are security cameras in the hotel that can corroborate your statement?' Sara said.

'Is that really necessary?' Serna sounded uncomfortable. 'There would have been other people in the bar that night – isn't that right, Elena? We can call them, and they can corroborate—'

'Do you have some sort of problem with giving us access to the C.C.T.V. footage?' Sara said, her tone increasingly strained.

'I'm just saying I don't think it's necessary,' Serna said defensively.

'Why don't you let me decide what's necessary?' Sara saw Víctor bow his head and stare at the floor. 'For example, I don't think that little pantomime with Elena is really necessary.'

'We are simply cooperating with your request,' Serna said, finding it difficult to contain his anger. He did not look like a man accustomed to being on the ropes.

'In that case, perhaps Elena wouldn't mind telling us how many girls work as prostitutes at the hotel. Was Nicolás a regular customer? He certainly has a thing about you.'

Elena looked away as Sara approached her, turning to Serna and babbling that she had no idea what Sara was talking about.

'How much does it cost to spend a night with one of your girls?'

Sara asked, turning to Serna. 'Elena, here, for example. Four hundred euros? More? It's not exactly a roadside whorehouse—'

'If you're going to accuse me of something, then get on with it.' Serna was no longer playing the cooperative citizen. He leaned back in his chair and crossed his legs. This was a man who expected others to do his bidding. 'I would have liked to have politely cooperated with your investigation, but it would appear that is impossible.'

'I don't care about the whores,' Sara said, looking at Elena. 'You can go now. I know Nicolás was with you.' She opened the office door and, with a nod from Serna, Elena left. Sara closed the door again and looked from Víctor to Serna before saying, 'I want a register of all customers over the past five years. And access to C.C.T.V. footage from every security camera. That is how you can politely cooperate.'

'I can't do that,' Serna said, adopting the cool professional tone of a hotel owner. 'It would violate my clients' privacy—'

'Then we will come back tomorrow with a search warrant,' Sara threatened.

'See you tomorrow, then,' Serna snapped.

Sara walked out of the room, leaving the door open. She was livid. She wanted to break every rule in the book, seize the computer in the lobby, search every room in the hotel. But she knew that, if she did so, it would only jeopardize any trial. Serna would have twenty-four hours: more than enough time to get rid of anything incriminating.

Morons, Sara thought. What the hell are they playing at? She went outside and walked to the mirador. The whole valley was spread before her feet. She wanted to scream in frustration. Why were they so determined to protect themselves? Did no one in this fucking village want to find Lucía?

She heard Víctor call her and, turning, she saw that he and Elena were walking towards her.

'She wants to talk to you,' Víctor said.

They would give her a little snack, Sara realized, as long as she did not ask for a full meal.

'The girls who work here do it because they like it,' Elena said simply. 'Serna's not some kind of pimp—'

'What else did he tell you to tell me?' Sara said sceptically.

'We get a room and board in exchange for a percentage of our profits. The men who come to La Guardia pay well,' Elena said, trying to ignore Sara's mocking sneer. 'Nicolás comes a couple of times a week, and, yes, he usually asks for me. The night that girl reappeared, for example. We were up in my room, but then someone phoned and he had to leave.'

'Perfect . . .' Sara said. 'Everything fits together perfectly — doesn't it, Víctor?'

Sara's eyes locked with his. Víctor had the feeling this was the first time she had looked at him all day and remembered, many weeks ago, when she had first come to Monteperdido, that he had had the same impression standing outside Ana's: Sara, looking at him, her eyes boring into him, searching his deepest recesses.

'Thank you, Elena,' Víctor said. 'Would you mind leaving us . . .?'

Elena turned and walked back to the hotel, the sound of her footsteps fading as the two officers stared at each other in silence.

'Well, are you going to spit it out?' Víctor said.

'You're an idiot.' Sara could not hide the sadness in her face. 'Did you really think I wouldn't find out?'

'It has nothing to do with the investigation,' Víctor said defensively.

'How do you know?! How can you be so sure?!' Sara raised her voice, her words echoing around the valley. *Dust, shade, nothingness,* she thought.

'Because I checked at the time,' Víctor said in a low voice.

'In case you haven't noticed, you're a fucking Guardia Civil in a one-horse village. Stick to what you know – cleaning up rivers, buying cakes, taking your dog for a walk – and leave me to do my job.'

'The reason you're pissed off with me is because you've got nothing, Sara.' Víctor managed to keep his tone even, but he was furious at her contempt. 'You're groping around wildly, and you're not going to find Lucía that way.'

'Is that what you think?' Sara took a deep breath, stepped closer to Víctor and, word by word, she buried him in shame. 'Stop me when I get this wrong. Serna is running a luxury brothel upstairs. The girls are pretty, young, available. We're not talking street whores. And it's not open to just anyone. You have to have a personal invitation from Serna. Most of the clients are well-heeled men from outside the valley. There is a dedicated shuttle service to bring them to the hotel: no details, no trace, no list of clients, no payments that can be traced. This is one of the advantages of the hotel: complete privacy. That's why it's so expensive. There are a few exceptions, like Nicolás. Five years ago, when the girls disappeared, a man working at the petrol station outside Monteperdido reported a car speeding through the village: an Audi 8. You conducted the interview yourself. And then you buried the report. I found it by accident, at your place. I guess Serna didn't want the search for the girls fucking up his business, right? He told you there was nothing here. That his customers were upstanding men. How much did he pay you? Enough to buy that house of yours? Or has he been paying you ever since?'

'I haven't taken a cent,' Víctor muttered.

'What am I supposed to think, then? That you're an idiot?'

'I tracked down the man who was in the car that night,' Víctor explained, though he could not bring himself to look at Sara. 'It was a businessman from Zaragoza. He had a wife and children. I kept him under observation for more than a month, and he didn't move from his house. I know he had nothing to do with the abduction.'

'For Christ's sake, Víctor – what about the rest of the people who've been coming and going from this place? How much do you know about them?' Sara tried to calm herself. She glanced at the jeeps; Pujante and Telmo were trying to pretend they weren't interested in their argument. 'This place is a fucking black hole. Do you know how much time we've wasted because of you?'

'I had to do it.'

'I do not care about your reasons,' Sara said sadly. Víctor knew those words marked an ending.

The mountain breeze whipped Sara's hair. She loosened her ponytail and retied it. She zipped up her sweatshirt. To Víctor, she seemed as distant as the night they had just spent together, naked in his bed; already it seemed to be lost in time, something that had happened so long ago it was only a vague memory, like a dream that fades when you wake.

'You're off the case,' Sara said, as she headed back to the jeep. 'I'll file a report requesting that you be suspended on full pay for obstructing an ongoing investigation.'

Víctor said nothing. He knew this was what Sara was obliged to do. He could not bring himself to look at her as she walked away, to see what he had lost. He leaned on the railings of the mirador. Before him was his valley, his home – the place that had saved him when he had lost the will to fight. Was that an excuse? Was a mistake justifiable simply because it was made in a moment of weakness? He thought of the families of the missing girls: what did they care what Víctor was going through when it happened? If he had not been so selfish, he would have stepped aside and said nothing. He would have accepted defeat and let someone else take his place.

At the same time, he felt a strange sense of freedom at the thought that he might never have to put on this uniform again.

The police car stopped outside his house. Nicolás knew that he would have been better off renting a hotel room for the night. But he owed Ximena an explanation. He did not want his daughter getting the wrong idea, after everything that had happened. My daughter, he thought. He only dared think the words. She had long since forbidden him from saying them aloud. *If you have to call me something, call me Ximena,* she had said after a particularly bitter argument.

'I'll be patrolling the area all night,' the officer who had driven him home said when he saw that Nicolás was reluctant to open the car door.

He had been released without charge and yet he still felt guilty. Dirty and vile. He could almost smell the stink of sex from all those nights spent at the hotel. He pictured himself, a pathetic fool, panting and moaning with someone who probably hated his guts.

He thanked the officer and got out of the car.

★

From the bathroom window, Joaquín saw the car draw up. He had showered, put on fresh clothes, and had convinced himself that this was the beginning of the end. As he was combing his hair, he looked at himself in the mirror, trying to decide which shirt to wear, which one Lucía would like best, as though he was getting ready for a date.

He had been avoiding his wife. Montserrat and Quim were cowering somewhere in the house. Regretting the fact that they had not supported him all along, Joaquín thought. Then he saw the police car pull up outside Nicolás's house. Saw the vet say goodbye to the officer. What was he doing there?

He ran down the stairs, through the living room and out into the street. As Nicolás was going up to his house, Joaquín screamed at him to stop. The vet tilted his head to one side, hunching his shoulders as though trying to make himself smaller. He fumbled clumsily for his keys.

'You son of a bitch!' Joaquín roared as he reached the garden gate. 'How dare you come back here?'

Though Joaquín did not realize it, Burgos had just come out of Ana's house. He had seen Joaquín striding across the street towards Nicolás. Burgos shouted for him to stop, not to do anything stupid, but Joaquín was not listening.

Nicolás frantically tried to fit his key into the lock, but his hands were shaking and the keys clattered to the ground. He bent down to pick them up. Why had Ximena not opened the door? He had rung the doorbell several times. Kneeling on the step, he just had time to see Joaquín running up the garden towards him. Burgos was still on the far side of the road. The patrol car that had brought him home had already turned around.

'I never did anything to your daughter,' was all Nicolás could think to say as he tried to get to his feet.

Joaquín felt his every muscle tense, the rage that had been building up for five long years finally bursting its banks, urging him on. Nicolás was still crouching and, as soon as Joaquín was close enough, he lashed out, kicking him in the jaw. The blow slammed Nicolás against his front door. Joaquín did not stop. He grabbed Nicolás by the hair and dragged him up.

'Where is Lucía?!' he bellowed, but did not wait for an answer. He slammed Nicolás's head against the door, leaving a dark blood-stain on the wood. 'If they can't fucking make you talk, I will,' Joaquín shouted. 'You know I'm not going to stop. Where's Lucía?'

Nicolás tried to stammer something, but managed only to open his mouth, revealing his bloodied teeth. Joaquín was about to slam his head into the door again, but, as he raised his arm, he felt someone grab him. He tried to shake them off and, when he could not, he let go of Nicolás; the vet slumped to the ground, semi-conscious.

'Are you out of your mind?' Burgos said, pinning Joaquin's arms behind his back. 'You'll kill him—'

'Let go of me!' Joaquín roared, viciously breaking free and almost knocking Burgos to the ground. 'I hand it to you on a fucking plate and still you can't do your fucking jobs.'

Joaquín was leaving Nicolás's garden as the squad car stopped in front of him. The officer driving got out and tried to restrain him, but Joaquín pushed him away. He felt capable of anything, like a giant stomping through a kindergarten. They were useless. All this time, and what had the police done for his daughter? Nothing. He was the only one who had really fought to get her back.

Resolute, he did not even look back to see Nicolás get up off the ground, to see Burgos coming to his aid and the other officer phoning for an ambulance.

He stormed into the living room, not hearing a word that Quim or Montserrat said.

You just carry on like that, he thought, believing someone else will bring your daughter back, your sister back. Do you even want her to come home?

He raced up the stairs and into his room, flinging open the wardrobe. He rummaged on the top shelf until he felt the rifle, and took it down. He sat on the bed and removed it from its holster.

No one is going to bring Lucía back unless we do something.

No one is going to bring her back.

He opened the breech, fumbled in the dresser drawer for ammunition and loaded the gun.

No one is going to bring Lucía back because she's dead, he thought. And he felt the adrenaline that had been surging through his body start to fade. He had never thought this before. He had not allowed himself to.

He looked across the road to where Burgos and the other officer were helping Nicolás to his feet.

He cocked the rifle. He was a good marksman, but this was not a sure hit. There was a chance he might wound one of the officers.

It had to be Nicolás. There was no alternative. Who else could have abducted the girls?

He felt doubt begin to writhe inside him, like a tapeworm growing and taking over his body. What if it wasn't Nicolás? Joaquín felt his strength drain away. What would he do tomorrow? And the day after tomorrow? Where would he look for her?

He lowered the rifle and stared into the black hole of the barrel. Give up, it seemed to say to him.

He felt his eyes well up, his muscles relaxing at the thought that this might be the end. The end of him.

He had given every last drop of sweat and blood. He was empty inside. He would rather be dead than have to wait for someone to come someday and tell him they had found Lucía's body.

He stepped back and sat on the edge of the bed, holding the rifle between his knees, the butt resting on the floor. He ran his hand down the smooth barrel until his finger found the trigger. Then he rested the muzzle under his chin.

The bullet would shatter his brain. He closed his eyes; tears stung as they streamed down his face, as though the dam that had been holding them back for years had finally burst.

'Joaquín, please . . .'

He heard Montserrat's voice, but did not open his eyes, did not take his finger off the trigger.

'Don't do it.'

What could he give the child that was growing in his wife's womb? What kind of parent would he be?

'You've got to live.'

'What for?' Joaquín managed to say. 'Go away. I don't want you to see this . . .'

But Montserrat did not leave. He could smell her scent as she came to him. He squeezed his eyes tighter. Come on, this is the last step, he thought. Just do it.

'You did everything you could for Lucía. You're not to blame for what's happened.'

'I should have done more to protect her,' Joaquín growled

between clenched teeth. You deserve to be punished, he thought. You deserve to lose your child.

'That's not true . . .'

Joaquín felt Montserrat's hand on his. Her warmth contrasted with the cold trigger against his finger.

'You've always taken care of us. Let us take care of you. This can't be fixed overnight. We'll take it slowly. But we'll get there, I promise . . .'

Was he a coward? Why not just pull the trigger?

'We've lost so much, Joaquín . . . Don't turn your back on what we still have,' Montserrat whispered as she eased his finger off the trigger.

Why did he let her do it? Joaquín wondered. And then he realized that there *was* something he dreamed of doing tomorrow. He wanted to wake up next to his wife, to take her in his arms. To shelter in her warmth. To let her put together the pieces of the man he had once been. He wanted to kiss Quim. How long had it been since he kissed his son?

He dropped the rifle and it clattered to the ground. Montserrat wrapped her arms around him. Their tears mingled. They became one.

'I'm sorry,' Joaquín sobbed.

'Come here.' Montserrat gently took his hand and slowly laid it against her belly, which was just beginning to swell under her clothes.

He felt her warmth, and knew there was the pulse of a new life inside her; it was still faint, timid, but growing stronger every day.

★

In summer, the deer's coat was reddish brown, a white patch on its rump the size of an asphodel; wild, it could be seen leaping through the dense forests. In July, during the rutting season, he could hear the stags grunting. The roe deer mate and, from August, the doe carries the seed of life suspended in her womb, like a secret, until winter comes. Only in December does it begin to grow, to be born in May. It is called gestational diapause. He liked to think that, just as the female deer suspend the development of their foetus, he is holding Lucía until conditions are ripe for her release. One day, he thought, she will go out into a meadow at twilight, as the sun behind Monte Albádes stains the grass like blood. Lucía would walk free, but, realizing that she was not safe, she would simply wet her lips in the waters of the Ésera, and return to the shelter of the forest, next to him. They would be the secret of the valley.

Nieve hungrily licked at his bowl, his eagerness sending it clattering across the floor. It had already been licked clean; there was not a scrap left of the stew Román had given him, but still the dog kept licking. Víctor looked at the animal and smiled.

'I'll be heading up at five o'clock,' his brother said, spreading a map out on the bar. 'Why don't you come with me? It's just me and the hounds.'

'I don't feel like going hunting,' Víctor apologized and took a sip of the soft drink he was holding.

The Hunting Society was closed by now; it was just Víctor and Román. The main lights had been turned off; Román was working by the glow of the bottle rack and the orange lampshades that hung over the bar. He had drawn a circle on the map in red marker, indicating where the battue would take place. The circle ran from the aspen grove on Mount Ármos to the ravine. The boars would be driven along the clearing between the forest and the gorge.

'What happened up at La Guardia?' Román asked. 'I saw Telmo earlier. He told me you and Sara had an argument . . .'

Víctor shrugged as if to say it was not important.

Sara had a point: he had been covering up a hole in the investigation. A hole, like a black tunnel, through which anyone could have slipped in or out of the village without being noticed. What if she was right? What if the girls had been abducted by one of the hotel guests?

It would mean the villagers, his family, were not to blame. At least not directly. The evil had come from beyond the valley. Yes, the kidnapper would still have needed the help of someone local, a man to take care of the girls on a daily basis. But he was just a jailer.

Román grabbed a sack of food and suggested that his brother come with him to feed the hounds. They left the Hunting Society and walked in silence along the cobbled streets. Román lived behind the town hall, a five-minute walk from the Society. The house lights were on and Víctor pictured Ondina scolding the children, telling them to put on their pyjamas and get to bed. Nieve trotted behind them, limping, barking in answer to the baying hounds, who could smell the food that Román was bringing. On the other side of the fence, they jumped up and down and ran in circles. Snow white and muscular, they surrounded Román as he walked over to fill their troughs. Román had fifteen hounds. The catch dogs were white so that the hunters would not mistake them for game and shoot them. Víctor remembered one of the dogs coming up to him one day after a hunt, spatters of blood like red plastic against its snow-white coat. The dog had faced a boar; there had still been clots of blood in its teeth.

Víctor thought of the cars with their tinted windows, ferrying people up and down the Posets Road to the Hotel La Guardia. One of them might have been carrying the man who had kidnapped the girls.

Víctor knew better than anyone what happened in the attic rooms of La Guardia. Serna had fed him snatches of information over the years. The more he knew, the more he was trapped: that was what Serna had thought. And, for a while, it had been true – when his job was all he had, and he clung to it for dear life. Things were different now.

'Do you know if El Negro is still living in the valley?' he asked his brother.

'He's working in a bar in Ordial, I think . . . I ran into him a few months ago, in the supermarket in Barbastro,' Román said as he padlocked the gate. 'What the fuck is going on, Víctor? I don't know whether you're going to find Lucía, but I do know that you're turning this village upside down . . .'

Víctor told him everything was fine. He knew his brother worried about him. This was precisely why he'd decided not to mention that he had been taken off the case, that he had been suspended. That he had no idea what was going to happen to him.

'Sara Campos!' She heard someone call her name from the shadows of the hotel lobby. 'Seems to me that lately you've not been getting any sleep.'

Sara was tempted to say goodnight to Caridad and go upstairs to her room. She thought she could see the woman smile at her from the table, though she was little more than a silhouette framed against the window.

'I don't get much sleep wherever I am,' Sara said, and decided to go over to her.

'So I've heard.' Caridad let out a raucous laugh and Sara turned away to hide her embarrassment, but there was no one around to overhear. 'I don't think I've had a fuck since 1982,' Caridad said when she managed to stop laughing. 'And don't go asking me how old I was back then.'

'Seems to me that, in this village, everyone knows everything, and no one knows anything,' Sara said, taking the seat opposite the older woman.

'People round here are pretty peculiar. I'm sure you've noticed, yourself. Very warm and welcoming, and complete hypocrites. Must be something in the water.'

The two faces of Monteperdido. Within a few weeks, this valley teeming with life would be frozen. Dead. Once the summer ended, the trees would lose their leaves, the river would freeze over, the animals would retreat into the mountains, the houses would be covered by a mantle of snow. Everything hibernating. And, buried beneath the snow, all the secrets people refused to bring out into the open.

'Can I tell you something?' Caridad said, drumming her stubby fingers on the table. 'A couple of nights ago, I slept like a stone. Woke up, must have been ten o'clock, sun streaming in on my face. *Deu*, can you imagine? I felt like screaming with joy . . .'

'Congratulations,' Sara said. 'I'm happy for you, honestly . . . Have you had a good night's sleep since?'

Caridad shook her head. 'I don't care. I could have a hundred sleepless nights; I'm never going to forget that night I slept like a baby . . .' She zipped up her tracksuit. 'What about you, Sara

Campos?' she asked. 'Don't tell me you don't have at least one fucking night that's worth remembering . . .'

'I'm not sure,' Sara confided. 'There are times when you think you have something – like a good night's sleep – but it turns into a nightmare. And you end up thinking to yourself, Maybe everything looks perfect and wonderful, but it's just a façade . . .'

'Things are never what you expect,' Caridad said, and she glanced out into the street, which was quiet and dark at this hour.

Sara tried to focus on the case, on the fragments that she had to piece together. She took a pen from her bag and picked up a paper napkin. She had been granted a search warrant for the Hotel La Guardia, although she assumed that, by the time they got there, Serna would have destroyed all the evidence on the computers and the C.C.T.V. system. Nicolás had been released without charge; Sara believed his account of where he had been on the night Ana reappeared, but that did not completely exonerate him. It was still possible that he was the man who had helped the kidnapper. He was eager to please, easily influenced. He fitted the profile. This was precisely why they had released him; now, he might make a mistake and lead them to the right place. Instinctively, Sara had already begun drawing geometrical figures on the napkin.

'Have you noticed that there are lots of places in the valley that have the same name?' Caridad said. 'La Corza Blanca, for example. Not exactly an original name, I'll grant you, but there's the café on Avenida de Posets, there's a house on the outskirts of the village, and a hotel in Ordial, if memory serves . . .'

Sara had noticed. The story of the white deer – 'La Corza Blanca' – was a legend in the Pyrenees. Santiago had told it to her.

'The valet fell in love with his master's daughter,' Caridad began.

'The girl was pretty, but very fickle – they always are in fairy tales. It doesn't matter; the point is, the boy wants to woo her. In the valley, there are rumours that there is a white deer, so he promises the girl that he will hunt it down and give it to her. The boy wanders around the mountains with his rifle, until he sees a herd of deer drinking from the River Ésera. Among them is a doe – a white doe. He takes up position with his rifle and, just as he's about to fire, the herd of deer is transformed into a group of naked girls bathing in the river . . . And one of the girls is his master's daughter, the one he fancies. No surprise there, then. The boy rubs his eyes and thinks to himself, This is bullshit. And, as he is thinking this, the girls change back into deer. But they sense his presence and they run off . . . All except the white doe, which is caught in a thicket . . . The boy picks up his rifle and puts a bullet in the doe's head. Then he runs over to take his prey, but, when he reaches the thicket, he sees that it is not a white deer but the girl he loves that he has killed. She is lying in a pool of blood . . .'

As Caridad finished recounting the legend, she took a swig from her bottle of red liquid and looked at Sara, who had been listening intently. Caridad burped loudly and the smell of blackcurrant floated in the air. She did not even apologize.

'I've never understood what the fuck that story means,' Caridad confessed. 'And I was born in this fucking valley. I've been listening to that story for as long as I can remember. No idea. Do you have any idea what the moral is?'

'That nothing is as it seems?' Sara guessed.

'Or that everyone around here is more than a little *llunéro*,' Caridad said, twirling a finger in circular motions next to her temple. 'And they go around shooting girls they want to fuck . . . Well, I suppose it's one way of getting her into bed.'

Sara leaned back in her chair. She let silence settle around them. She wondered why the girl in the legend didn't tell the boy that she was the white doe when he said he was going to hunt it. Maybe she wanted to test him. Or maybe she wanted him to hunt her. Sara looked at the doodle she had been drawing on the napkin and, as usual, it did not look like a maze in which she was lost, but a wall behind which she was hiding.

They did not speak again until Sara headed up to her room. Spending time with Caridad was almost better than sleep. It was more comforting, more relaxing.

'You'll find her,' Caridad said, seeing Sara get to her feet. 'You'll find your white doe, you'll see . . . Just be careful not to shoot her, Sara Campos.'

Caridad gave her a thumbs up and winked, like a teenager encouraging her friend. Sara wished she could believe her.

Nicolás was at the kitchen table, cleaning his hunting rifle. The ramrod, oil and cleaning rags were strewn around and he was worried he wouldn't be able to do it without damaging the gun. How long had it been since he last used it? He had googled how to clean a rifle and was now peering at the instructions on his laptop, but the gash on his head was still throbbing. He had patched himself up quickly: some antiseptic, a few sutures, a dressing to cover the wound.

The laptop went into sleep mode and Nicolás moved the mouse. On the screen was the manuscript of *El follét del albarósa*. Though he told everyone who would listen about his new novel, he had barely written a few paragraphs. He skimmed the sentences and felt ashamed. *Why do you insist on writing in* patués? Víctor had asked him. *So no one can read it,* Nicolás should have said, if he were being honest.

Ximena came downstairs, stopping on the last step and shooting him a look of contempt. If she were any closer, his daughter would have spat at him, Nicolás thought as he closed the Word file.

'Do you really think I'm so pathetic?' he said as he went back to the task of cleaning the rifle.

'I used to. Now, you sicken me.'

'Well, I suppose that's progress.' He picked up a bronze bore brush, inserted it into the muzzle and pumped it up and down the barrel. He had decided to join the boar hunt. He was not going to hide away.

'Is that how you met my mother? When you were whoring?' Ximena snarled. She was still standing on the last stair, as though she wanted to look down on him.

Only a few hours earlier – before the police arrested him, before Joaquín had pounded his head against his own front door – Nicolás would have felt anxious, he would have stuttered and stammered, *What makes you say that? Who's been telling you that drivel?* And he would have been sweating. But a lot had happened in the past few hours. Nicolás was sick and tired of hiding.

'What difference does it make, Ximena? She's not here. She left you with me. I'm the only family you've got. You can either deal with it, or you can walk out that door and disappear. I won't come running after you.' He withdrew the bore brush and inserted a cleaning rod with a petrol-soaked rag.

'The way you never ran after Montserrat?' Ximena's bitter joke masked a genuine pain.

Nicolás set the cleaning rod down on the table. He wiped his hands on a rag and looked at his daughter. He insisted on calling her that. He could not see her as just some girl.

'Falling in love with someone and having them love you back is like hitting the jackpot. We both know that . . . And, so far, our lottery numbers haven't come up, have they, Ximena?'

'So what do you do? Pay people to love you?'

Ximena went outside. She needed to breathe the pure night air. She felt like she was suffocating. In recent years, she had done her best to ignore Nicolás. If she did not look at him, did not speak to him, maybe one day he would simply disappear. But, even so, she had always been aware of the nights he did not come home. His constant travelling. His long absences. She had come to realize that everyone in the village treated him like dirt, and she could not help but wonder how he could bear it. Why was he still living in the valley? Where did he find the strength to keep smiling, to keep writing those stupid novels?

The night was clear and cloudless, the sky a calm ocean. Lying on her back lawn, Ana leaned her head on her father's chest, rocked by his breathing. It reminded her of floating in the waters of the tarn, the slow rise and fall of the swell. Her mother came out into the garden and lit a cigarette, then, seeing them lying on the grass, she knelt down next to Ana and stroked her hair. Ana saw her mother's face silhouetted against the dark sky. From where she was lying, she could see only a vast expanse of stars and she smiled at the thought of Raquel as an astronaut. 'Aren't you cold?' she said, and tugged at her mother's sleeve so she would lie down next to her. She felt her parents' hands meet across her stomach. She remembered the years she had spent in the hole, the nights spent staring up at the flittering stars through the hole where the roof had caved in. She had given the brightest stars names: Álvaro, Raquel and Lucía. Her childhood had been stolen from her, but no one could ever take away this moment. She laid her hand on top of her parents' hands.

This was home, not the travesty she had experienced in the hole. Here, people cared about her. This girl lying on the lawn between her parents, her eyes as black as the night sky that shrouded them like a blanket, this was the girl Ana wanted to be. A girl she had never seen reflected in Lucía's eyes.

Where are you, Ana? What are you doing right now? Lucía wondered. She tossed and turned on the mattress, too hungry to be able to sleep. She thought about Ana. She thought about him. Why had he left her alone for so long? Would he ever come back? She remembered the nights – or were they days? How could she tell, when the only light in the room had come from a narrow crack, a thin streak of yellow around the trapdoor in the ceiling? This had been the only thing to mark the passing time: sunlight trickling through a crack. Do you remember, Ana? Do you remember how you used to call me a slut, how you used to ask if I enjoyed it? I remember your poems. One verse: *The wind is rising . . . We must strive to live!* Isn't that what we did? I hated those fucking books. Your constant demands. And how I miss them.

A sudden noise startled her, but Lucía assumed it was an animal, a wild boar snuffling outside the cramped room in which she was locked. She sat up and, as she did so, she heard the metallic clack of a padlock. The door opened. She saw him framed in silhouette, his weary frame eclipsing the glow of the stars. He was carrying a bag;

as he set it down, there was a clatter of plastic. Then he closed the door and sat down on the floor next to her.

'I brought the cereal you like,' he said.

Lucía grabbed the box he was holding out to her. She was starving. 'Where have you been?' she said. It was then that she saw the rifle. He had propped it against the wall, next to the door.

Ximena wandered aimlessly, trying to understand her mixed emotions. The shame at what everyone in Monteperdido must be saying about Nicolás and his whores up at La Guardia. No one could keep a secret in this valley; Ximena was convinced that everyone had heard by now. Nicolás and his girls. The little sluts. But this shame was drowned out by something more palpable, more painful: the fear of Nicolás going to prison, of losing her father. Because, though she was reluctant to admit it, Nicolás was the only father she had.

She was wandering back towards her house when she was startled by the sound of footsteps behind her. When she turned, she saw Ana crossing the road towards her. Ximena thought she looked like one of the animals that lived in the mountains, a roe deer, leaving the shelter of the forest to graze in the meadow.

'It's late. What are you doing up?' Ximena said, trying to keep her distance, but Ana did not stop. She kept coming.

'I wanted to talk to you. I've been waiting for you to come back.' Ana's self-assured tone made her sound older.

'You can keep Quim. I'm over him,' Ximena said, but she did not sound as confident as Ana. She took two steps back; she found the other girl's presence intimidating.

Ana took a breath and looked around at the silent rows of semi-detached houses. 'It's about Nicolás,' she said, and, stepping closer, she pressed her lips to Ximena's ear and whispered, 'He's not the man who kidnapped us.'

Ximena heard the quiver of fear in her voice.

Nervously, Ana glanced around, as though someone other than Ximena might hear.

Ximena stood, rooted to the pavement, as Ana returned to her house and closed the door. The wave of relief she had felt when Ana admitted that Nicolás had nothing to do with the kidnapping gave way to a different fear: What exactly did Ana know? What was it that Ana was not saying?

Ana crept through the shadowy living room and climbed the stairs to her bedroom. Why had she told Ximena that Nicolás had nothing to do with the kidnapping? For some reason, she felt like she owed Ximena something. For taking Quim away from her, yes, but also because of how Ximena had been treated after the abduction. She had been the lucky one, everyone told her. The girl who had come within inches of hell itself, but escaped. What had Ximena got to complain about? All her problems seemed like the whims of a spoiled little brat. But loneliness was not a whim. Ana knew that.

Lucía nervously wolfed down the cereal. He got up and walked over to the door, where he had left the rifle. The shack smelled of piss and sweat. Of animal. Honey-coated sugar puffs were her favourite. She was as choosy as the spirit of the forest. The roe deer would walk for miles to find the tender shoots they liked best.

Sara watched wearily as officers trooped from the Hotel La Guardia carrying boxes of files, computer hard drives, C.C.T.V. tapes. She knew that the search would yield absolutely nothing. Serna was leaning on the veranda, smoking, and Sara itched to wipe the smug smile off his face. The hotel staff were gathered around a table under an awning on the terrace, chatting and giggling, like children given a day off school.

Sara had had another talk with Elena, the girl who had given Nicolás his alibi. Like the rest of the employees, she had nothing of interest to say; the truth was a far cry from the litany of clichés they were selling. If she did a lot of digging, and she was lucky, Sara might be able to nail Serna for tax avoidance, because all the money paid out by the guests was off the books. But simply identifying the guests was something that could take months.

Lucía could not wait that long.

Víctor's car pulled into the car park. Sara could not bring herself to look at him as he walked over to her.

'You can't be here,' she said. 'You're suspended.'

'No one here is going to tell you anything about Serna. Let me help you.'

'So now you want to help me?' Sara made no attempt to hide her bitterness.

'I've got someone here, in the car,' Víctor said. 'I'm just asking you to talk to him.'

Despite his name, Vincent – *El Negro* – was not black. At best, a little tanned. He was about fifty, paunchy and clean-shaven, which gave him a sort of boyish innocence. He was not prepared to talk anywhere near the hotel. He did not feel comfortable with Serna close by. Víctor drove the three of them back down to the outskirts of Posets. He pulled up at a junction, where Sara and El Negro got out. They wandered off towards the pine forest as they talked, leaving Víctor leaning on the bonnet of his car. He did not try to insist on going with them.

'Serna knows exactly what to do to keep people quiet,' said El Negro, shooting a glance at Víctor.

'Did Víctor ask you to talk to me so you could tell me his side of the story?' Sara said curtly. What else could this middle-aged waiter possibly have to tell her?

'He asked me to tell you how things work at the hotel, that's all.' El Negro was irked that Sara seemed to be treating him like a criminal.

'Fine,' Sara said. 'Tell me everything you know about La Guardia.'

El Negro had been a waiter there for seven years. He had joined the staff shortly after Serna opened the hotel. From the beginning, La Guardia had been extremely exclusive. It did not matter how many rooms stood empty for much of the year; what guests paid for a couple of nights more than compensated. The girls lived up in the attic rooms. Serna did not accept just any girls; most of them had university degrees. They had to know how to make intelligent conversation as well as how to fuck. There were contracts with two or three private taxi services. At the time El Negro took over as bar manager, most of the guests were from Zaragoza and the Basque Country – high-level businessmen, guys with serious money – but gradually people started coming from all over Spain, and even from France. They were collected in taxis from Zaragoza, from Barcelona, from Vitoria.

'These are influential people we're talking about; that's why Serna ensures that anyone who sets foot in the hotel says nothing,' El Negro said.

'What about people from the valley? Monteperdido, Posets . . . Did any of them ever come up to La Guardia?'

'Very few,' El Negro said. 'At the bar, we were charging thirty euros for a drink. Who's going to pay that for a gin and tonic? When he re-opened after the renovations, you'd sometimes get women coming up for day trips, but Serna hiked the prices so much they stopped coming.'

'What about the men? Nicolás was clearly a regular.'

'Serna made a few exceptions,' El Negro admitted. 'Nicolás was one of them. The poor bastard was mortified every time he came to the hotel; I think he hated the idea of sleeping with prostitutes, but he couldn't stop himself. He came back every week.' El Negro let out a bitter laugh that rolled around the forest.

Silence, Sara thought, and shame as a weapon for ensuring it.

'What about the others?' she said. 'How is it possible that no one ever mentioned what was going on?'

'The devil's in the detail. Serna's a smart bastard. He started get-ting the girls to sell a little cocaine on the side. Not that they did the dealing themselves – that was Gaizka's job – but it meant that Serna had something over them. With other people, he used whatever information he could get his hands on.'

El Negro paused and looked at Sara as though asking her permis-sion to talk about Víctor; Sara nodded.

'OK. So, Víctor was in a pretty bad way after his fiancée died in the flood. He'd come up to the hotel to drink; he didn't want people in the village seeing him shitfaced, and he was the police sergeant, so Serna wasn't going to make him pay full whack. One night, one of the clients got a little rough. It didn't usually happen, but this guy couldn't handle his blow. He slapped a girl in the bar. Víctor was there at the time, but he didn't notice anything. He was blind drunk. But the whole thing turned into a clusterfuck when the guest grabbed Víctor's gun and threatened to start shooting.'

Sara looked behind her. She could just see the road through the trees, and Víctor leaning on his car. He was dressed in jeans and a T-shirt, and it occurred to Sara that this was the only time – other than at his house – that she had seen him out of uniform.

El Negro explained how Serna had promised Víctor that he would not report the incident. He had been drunk on duty and had allowed someone to grab his service revolver; he would have been fired on the spot. And then Serna began to ask for small favours in return. He asked Víctor not to log the neighbours' occasional complaints about speeding taxis, not to look too closely at Serna's connection to Gaizka. He gradually reeled him in until, eventually, Víctor was his pet officer.

'So what's the deal with you?' Sara said. 'Seems to me that you're not scared of Serna.'

'I was dumb,' El Negro said with a smile that made him look even more boyish. 'I fell in love with one of the girls. Built the whole thing up in my head like a movie – how I'd get her out of there, all that shit . . . But she decided to stay with Serna. I was so fucking angry, I went to the cops and made a statement.'

'And Víctor buried it,' Sara said.

'To be honest, I'm grateful that he did,' El Negro admitted. 'It would have just made things worse.'

Sara looked up at the treetops, an almost perfect dome of dark emerald green. What was the connection between the Hotel La Guardia and the missing girls? Perhaps Víctor was right; perhaps there was none. Perhaps it was just one more of the valley's secrets. But something told Sara there was more to it than that.

She remembered one of Ana's interviews – the description she had given of her rape.

Sex.

Why the sudden brutal sex, when, after the abduction, everything had settled down into a familiar routine?

'Were there any underage girls working at the hotel?' Sara asked.

'Not while I was there. Serna sometimes introduced a girl and said she was sixteen, but that was bullshit. They were all over twenty.'

'What else went on at the hotel? Did the guests just choose a girl and spend the weekend with her?'

'Sometimes there were . . . you know . . . parties . . . in the first-floor salon. There were three, maybe four a year. That was when things really happened. The hotel would be booked solid for the weekend. You know the kind of thing: a little blow, some girls, some stage shows . . .'

Sara remembered what Ana had said: *It felt like lots of people were watching me . . . I knew this was something I would never be able to forget.*

'Porn flicks?' she said.

'Oh, yeah, sure.' El Negro nodded.

It felt like lots of people were watching.

'What kind of porn? Did you see it?'

'Home movies. P.O.V. porn. Hidden camera shit. That was mostly what they played.'

'And, in these movies, the girls were underage?'

El Negro stopped and tried to remember. Sara felt as though she was about to reach the end of a thread, though she still had no idea what she would find there.

'I don't think so . . .' El Negro said, but he sounded doubtful. 'I thought some of them looked pretty small . . . I remember, three years ago, some guy telling me there was no way the girls in these films were underage . . . That he knew, because he'd seen movies with real underage girls. But it's possible. Like I already told you, Serna lied about the ages of the girls at the hotel . . .'

Sara was no longer listening.

'Who was he? This guy who told you he'd seen "the real thing"?'

'I don't know . . .' El Negro racked his brain. 'I only saw him there a couple of times. He never stayed the night. He only came to watch.'

'Did he say anything else about these movies he said he'd seen?'

'To tell you the truth, I thought he was bullshitting. He claimed he'd seen one with a thirteen-year-old girl that was still playing with dolls . . .'

Sara felt her heart quicken. She was close. Very close.

'Would you recognize him if you saw a photograph?'

'Yeah, it's possible.' El Negro shrugged.

Quim had run into Álvaro in the doorway of the Hunting Society. He had come to sign up for the hunt. Álvaro had decided that, this year, he would join the rest of the village men in the mountains.

'They're inside,' Quim said. 'They're sorting out the shooting positions.'

'Are you going?' Álvaro asked.

'Yeah, with my uncle,' Quim said. 'We always go together.'

Quim had hardly ever fired a shot. He did not carry his own rifle. He signalled to Rafael when he saw movement in the under-growth, heard the boars' hooves, birds flying out of the treetops, Román's hounds barking.

Right now, the dogs were in the back of a pickup parked out-side the Hunting Society; Román was planning to take them up into the mountain for a walk through the woods before the battue, so they could catch the scent of the boars. In the back of the truck, the hounds yapped and jostled, eager to be let loose on Monte Ármos.

'I've never even been on a hunt before,' Álvaro confessed. 'I'll be happy if I manage not to shoot myself in the foot.'

Quim smiled. Ever since Ximena had come to his house the night before, he had been frantically worrying about what to think, what to do . . . He had let Ximena sleep in his room; she had not wanted to go home to Nicolás. When Quim had seen Nicolás in the Hunting Society a few moments earlier, Rafael had been telling him his shooting position was about a hundred metres from theirs, on the eastern edge of the aspen forest.

'Hang on a minute, Álvaro.' Quim stopped Lucía's father before he could go inside.

Maybe Ana just said that to reassure Ximena, Rafael had suggested. Yeah, or maybe she's afraid to tell people what she knows, was what Quim had thought. Why else would Ana tell Ximena that Nicolás was not the man who had abducted them?

'Look, I don't know if it's important, Álvaro,' Quim began. 'Last night, Ana told Ximena that Nicolás was definitely not the man who had been with them in the hole . . . Maybe you should talk to her. Just in case she knows more than she's letting on . . .'

After five years, a long-buried hope in Quim had suddenly flared to life again, rising from the tomb like Lazarus. What if there was still a chance to find Lucía alive?

★

Sara strode through the squad room of the station. El Negro and Víctor followed close behind. As soon as they were in her office, she gestured to the wall where Santiago had pasted the photographs of everyone with any connection to the investigation: the girls' fathers, Álvaro Montrell and Joaquín Castán; Nicolás Souto, Marcial Nerín, Ismael Calella and Gaizka . . . Víctor was surprised to see a photograph of himself, between one of his brother, Román, and one of Rafael Grau. What had he done to be included in this long list of suspects?

'Take a good look,' Sara said to El Negro. 'The guy who talked to you about seeing porn movies with underage girls . . . Could he be anyone here?'

El Negro stepped closer to the wall, scanning the sea of faces for that of a man who had said to him one night in the hotel bar, *I've seen the real thing.* And when El Negro had said he didn't believe him, the man had replied, *Just turned thirteen. Still plays with dolls.*

'It was him,' El Negro said, confidently jabbing at a photograph.

Sara felt a hole open in the pit of her stomach.

'Are you sure?' she said.

'Yeah, I remember him.'

He was pointing to a photograph of Simón Herrera. Ana's 'saviour'. The man who had died in the car wreck.

The phone rang, echoing through the house. Raquel was in the kitchen making food, and asked Ana to answer it. She searched for the cordless phone on the sofa, between the cushions, and found it on the third ring. Burgos was in the kitchen with her mother; he wanted to learn how to make Raquel's famous *recau*. Every time she had made it, Burgos had come back for second helpings.

Ana answered the call and walked a little further from the kitchen, to get away from the noise of the extractor fan. She asked
who it was, but heard only silence. Then she heard a ragged breathing she instantly recognized. She had spent five years feeling that
breath on her face, day and night.

'Ana . . .' Lucía pleaded. 'Don't tell them anything else. Please . . .
He'll kill me.'

Lucía's sobs were cut off by a disconnected tone. He had hung
up. He knew that Lucía had said all she needed to say.

New trousers, new shirt, freshly shaven. Why had she not noticed
these details at the time? Sara wondered. The wardrobe in Simón
Herrera's house had been filled with threadbare cast-offs. She should
have realized that, if he was wearing new clothes, it was because,
for him, this was a special day. He was going to get Ana out of the
hole. He was going to *save* her.

As Víctor drove in silence to Ana's house, he kept glancing across
at Sara's face, a rictus of guilt and rage.

'Stay in the car,' Sara said as she got out. 'You can't be involved
in this.'

Víctor did as he was told. Sara was right. Any breach of protocol
could scupper the prosecution's case. They could not afford another
mistake.

Sara knocked insistently until Burgos came to the door.

'What's happened?' he said.

'Where's Ana?' Sara asked, pushing past him.

Raquel appeared from the kitchen, looked around the living
room and, when she did not see her daughter, said, 'She's probably
up in her bedroom.'

Sara raced up the stairs, throwing open the door. The room was empty. Frustrated, she went back to the landing. She checked the bathroom. Raquel's bedroom. She called the girl's name.

Ana was not in the house.

She ran across Avenida de Posets. Hearing the sound of an engine – a car coming behind her – Ana turned towards the slopes of Monte Ármos, scrabbling up the steep embankment and plunging into the forest of trembling aspens. 'Don't say a word, fibbers,' she muttered. She was an animal that had spotted a hunter. And, like an animal, she was fleeing into the mountains. Anywhere. Far away from the man who would not stop hunting her.

How was he still able to track her every movement?

Sara's head was pounding. She squeezed her eyes shut and rubbed her temples, as though she could stop it from spreading through her brain, this jolting pain, like electric eels squirming inside her.

'Put a trace on the last number to call the phone at Ana's house,' she said to Pujante as she walked into the police station.

She called off the search at La Guardia. All available officers were to come back to the village and help with the search for Ana. 'Stay here, in the house,' she had said to Víctor when she left. 'I don't want you drawing attention to yourself, but I need you to coordinate your officers.' Within half a hour, Sanmartín and the officers of the Mountain Rescue Team had joined the search of the area around Los Corzos.

There were only two officers in the police station. Sara told them she wanted every scrap of evidence that had been gathered on Simón Herrera since the beginning of the investigation.

A man who had lived like a ghost, she remembered thinking at the time.

Stepping into her office, she looked at the desk. At the neat piles of papers that were exactly as Santiago had arranged them. Every report and every document that had been generated since his death was scattered somewhere on the floor. Small mountains of paperwork.

I think you're right. We've got something, Santiago had said.

Sara knew that that 'something' was somewhere in the files on her desk. Until now, she had not known what to look for. The folders had been staring at her silently, refusing to give up the secret that Santiago had taken to his grave.

What had made him go to Transportes Castán?

Simón Herrera, Sara thought. She called to the two officers still in the station. When they came into the office, she divided up the folders on the desk between the three of them.

'What exactly are we looking for?' one of them asked.

'Any connection between Simón Herrera and Joaquín Castán's haulage company.'

Sara thought back to the day she had searched Simón Herrera's house. In the bedroom, she had spotted a phone charger in the drawer of the nightstand. There had been no mobile phone found in the wrecked car.

It had been a stupid decision to stop investigating him.

'The last number to call Ana's house . . .' Pujante said, clearly puzzled by what he was about to say, ' . . . is registered in the name of Simón Herrera.'

Why, Ana? Why did you lie to me? Sara thought. The pounding in her head was getting worse.

'Are you OK?' Pujante asked.

Sara could just about bring herself to nod.

'Keep looking for a connection between Simón and the haulage company,' she said, and walked out of the office. It felt as though her brain was rattling inside her skull, slamming against the walls of bone, like a madman in a padded cell.

An image popped into her head: the Ésera, raging wildly, water rising, threatening to burst its banks. She stumbled out of the station, trying to calm herself, sucking in lungfuls of fresh air, feeling the tepid warmth of the August sun.

A stormy night.

Her brain had come adrift from its moorings. It was being tossed on an angry sea. She knew what was coming; she had been here many times before.

She found herself on her knees in the pine forest where the girls had disappeared. She sobbed with helplessness, with rage, for all the pain that ran beneath the surface of Monteperdido, like the diseased roots of this pine tree. She fell to the ground, utterly defeated.

She felt a cold hand grab her arm and haul her into a sitting position. She heard laboured breathing behind her as someone lifted her off the ground, hissing in her ear, 'What the fuck is wrong with you?'

Sara saw the figure fumble in a bag tied around its waist, but she could not make out the features; the skin looked greenish, reflecting the colour of the pine trees.

'Come on, open your mouth,' the figure said, and Sara felt fingers in her mouth trying to prise her teeth apart. The bitter taste of a pill under the tongue. 'Take a deep breath; you're going to be fine,' the voice said. 'It's just a panic attack.'

Sara sucked air into her lungs and felt herself gradually regaining control. She pushed away the hair plastered to her forehead with sweat. She opened her eyes and saw Caridad squatting in front of her, her head slightly tilted, like a curious cat.

'What did you give me?' Sara managed to say.

'Rat poison,' Caridad said. 'What do you think I gave you, woman? It's a tranquillizer. And, since I can't trust you not to do stupid things, I'm going to give you a bunch of them.'

Sara sat up a little and looked around, trying to get her bearings, to remember how she had come to be there.

'Sara Campos,' Caridad said, taking her chin and forcing the younger woman to look at her. 'You see me? Look very closely – look at my nose and my beautiful green eyes. Do you see them?'

Sara nodded.

'*Deu*, you can't keep scaring me like that. If you're determined to die, then don't do it anywhere around me; I've got a soft spot for you.'

'I'm not going to die.'

'Good. I'm glad.' Caridad fell silent, scanning Sara's face, gauging the effect of the tranquillizer.

Sara's jaw relaxed. She wiped her eyes and attempted a smile to convey that she felt calm. 'I have to get back to work, Caridad,' she said, but she would not meet the woman's eyes. 'I can't stay here . . .' She pushed herself to her feet.

'What will happen if you don't find the girls?'

Sara heard Caridad's knees creak as she stood up. The woman leaned against the tree and shook her stubby legs, which seemed to have fallen asleep. Sara looked down the path that had led her here.

'Listen, kid, you have to be prepared to make mistakes,' Caridad said softly. 'You have to be prepared to lose. I lose my battle with insomnia every night.'

'But sometimes you win.'

'Not often – you know that.' There was no trace of irony in Caridad's voice. 'Sometimes it takes an occasional sleepless night to enjoy a good sleep.'

'I'm trying, Caridad. I'm really trying,' Sara said.

'Then that's enough.'

Sara smiled gratefully as Caridad laid a pudgy hand on her shoulder.

'That's what life is: trying,' the older woman whispered, as if this was goodbye.

Keep running, Ana thought to herself. A rocky path along the edge of the ravine – what had Quim called it? La Camera? – was taking her from the forest of trembling aspens, spiralling upwards, towards the summit. The Tempestades cirque. However far you run, you can't run away from the shame, she thought, the fear.

'What do you want me to do, Lucía? What do you want me to do?' she screamed at the blank rock face of Monte Ármos.

He looked at the mountain, thrust against the clear August sky. At first light, he would go out hunting. He had had everything, and he would rather kill himself than lose it all, he thought. He was going to steal the spirit from the forest.

'We've got something here,' the officer said.

Pujante looked up from the paperwork he was reading as Sara reappeared at the door of the squad room. She looked pale; there was a yellowish shadow under her eyes. Her sweatshirt was stained and her jeans were smeared with dirt. She collapsed into a chair a little way from the officers, tugging her hair back into a ponytail. 'What have you got?' she asked.

'Zacarías Gutiérrez,' the officer said. 'This contract says he's still employed at Transportes Castán, but he hasn't worked there for more than a year. He used to work there as a security guard—'

'I know the guy,' Sara said. 'He works down in Barbastro now, on the industrial estate.'

'We pulled his police record, and look . . .'

Sara picked up the report on Zacarías. She had assumed Santiago had ordered it as a routine background check. A couple of arrests for petty theft. Three months for possession with intent to supply. She assumed this was his link to Gaizka. Then she saw the name of the prison where he had served his time: Martutene, San Sebastián. From 3rd May 1992 to 7th August of the same year. Still clutching the report, she reached for Simón Herrera's record. He had been convicted of possession of child pornography and served time from 1989 to 1993, also at Martutene Prison, San Sebastián.

Zacarías and Simón had met in prison.

This was what Santiago had noticed. This was what had prompted him to go to Transportes Castán.

Santiago could not have known that Zacarías was no longer working there. It was a mistake that had set him on the right track.

'We need to issue an arrest warrant for Zacarías Gutiérrez . Warn the Barbastro police; we can't let him get away.' Sara turned to Pujante. 'You, come with me.'

★

After checking that no one had seen Ana on the school road or the road into the village, Víctor restricted the search to the areas around the back of Los Corzos. A group of officers was searching the pine forest where the girls had first disappeared. All the others were combing the slopes of the mountain on the far side of Avenida de Posets. Monte Ármos was a difficult area to search; there was the density of the aspen forest, a thousand hiking trails that wound up among the oak trees, La Camera ravine and the stream that fed meltwater from the glacier into the tarn at Tempestades cirque: the natural amphitheatre carved by nature itself.

Víctor saw Quim racing towards the house.

'Where's Ana?' he shouted.

The sergeant told him to calm down; they would find her soon. But he felt a lump in his throat as he looked down the road and saw Raquel and Álvaro hugging each other. Raquel's face was buried in her husband's shoulder. Álvaro's blue eyes gazed up to the mountain, his grey hair shifting in the gentle breeze.

That same breeze also rustled the leaves of the trembling aspens, creating a sound that, at times, was almost like a giggle.

One day, I'll kill you, he had said. And the words were like a telescopic sight trained on the back of her neck. Ana was sweating, exhausted. Even the cool breeze was not enough to stem the heat. *One day, I'll kill you.* This was the gag, the thing that had kept her silent. When they had wheeled her down the hospital corridors to her room, she had seen him. What if he had allowed her to escape, so that he could hunt her down? What if he was looking at her right now? Just like that day in the hospital, when he had looked at her as if to say, *One day, I'll kill you.*

435

Until now, he had spared her life.

Until she had said too much.

'I'm sorry, Lucía,' she said over and over, as if her friend could hear her. She came to the cirque, to the edge of the lake, and saw herself reflected in the water, rippling gently in the wind. 'I hate you, Ana,' she said to her reflection.

Joaquín was getting ready for the boar hunt – his rifle, his hunting clothes, his ammunition belt – when the officer came to tell them that Ana had disappeared again. He heard the officer talking to Montserrat, heard her say, 'It's impossible; how could she have gone missing?' Ana had run away, the officer explained. Joaquín headed down the stairs, plagued with doubts. Why had Ana run away? What had made her run? Midway down the stairs, he stopped and the officer turned to him, clearly wary of how Joaquín would react. Montserrat was explaining that they had not seen Ana all day. What had happened before she vanished? What prompted her to leave? Joaquín did not ask these questions. He had lost the war, he knew that now. He was a soldier sent home, listening to the news from the front lines but unable to do anything.

'Do you know where Quim is?' Joaquín said, realizing that, for the first time in years, his son was the focus of his fears.

The Guardia Civil were searching the slopes of Monte Ármos. A villager had told them he thought he'd seen Ana crossing the road and heading into the undergrowth. The officers were twenty metres apart, moving up the slope, heading into the forest of aspens.

The noise of leaves flapping in the wind seemed to applaud their efforts.

Quim knew this mountain like the back of his hand. Trails ran through the aspens, leading up the mountain. They sloped gently at first, until they reached the area where the forest was dense and the trees rose up like a wall against intruders, a protective rampart. If you strayed off the hiking trails, it was easy to become lost or disorientated. Quim knew other paths, half-hidden by the branches and the leaves. Like the wild boars that lived on these slopes, Quim did not need trails and arrows to find his way through the forest.

If Ana had gone into the forest, it would not be easy to find her. Quim knew this, and he followed the Guardia Civil as they moved through the trees, keeping several metres apart, but close enough to maintain visual contact. The search moved slowly, careful not to overlook a single shadow.

Still, the leaves of the trembling aspens kept applauding, and the noise began to bore into him, like fingernails dragged along a blackboard.

Once they emerged from the forest, the climb became steeper. Some of the paths veered dangerously close to La Camera canyon, where there were sheer drops of twenty, a hundred, two hundred metres. Quim remembered grabbing Ana's hand so that she would not slip on the scree, how they had climbed together far beyond the oaks and the black pines to reach Tempestades cirque and the first of the four tarns on Monte Ármos. He remembered the cold, crystalline water, and trying to ease her fear. *I wish I could stay here forever,* Ana had said when he taught her to float.

He left the officers behind and ran between the trembling aspens. He might be wrong, but he wanted to believe that Ana was looking for somewhere safe, that she had gone to Tempestades cirque.

★

For Sara, Simón Herrera was a wound that would not stop bleeding. Unassuming, taciturn, living his life in the shadows, he'd had a marriage that seemed more like an alibi, and a wife who never doubted a word he said. A man tormented by his desires, his attraction to young girls. New trousers, new shirt. A mobile phone that had never been found. The rash on his feet and his ankles from brushing against bear's ear had not come from a single, chance contact. The weeds lined the path that he took to the mountain hut every day.

She imagined Simón Herrera in the bar at the Hotel La Guardia. Drinking too much and chatting to El Negro. In the first-floor salon at one of the parties, with porn movies playing of girls who were supposedly underage. Simón, arrogantly thinking he was better than all these rich people who paid a small fortune only to be conned. The girls they had their arms around, the girls they took up to their rooms were not girls.

Simón Herrera knew what a girl looked like. He had seen one.

It was this arrogance that had goaded him into saying too much: *Just turned thirteen. Still plays with dolls.* Remembering what he had said to El Negro, Sara thought about Lucía, about the Barbie dolls she spent hours playing with, drawing on their faces in red marker, those silent witnesses to what happened when she was alone with him.

Maybe this was why Lucía had stopped playing with them. The dolls had seen too much. Their glassy eyes reminded her of what happened those nights and she could not bear it.

But Simón did not seem like the kind of person who could mastermind a kidnapping. He could be a jailer, the man who bought them clothes in Perpignan and ran errands in exchange for being allowed to peep through a crack. But Simón was not the man who had built a basement in the derelict mountain hut. Not the man who could carry on leading a normal life, chatting with his neighbours in Monteperdido, while holding Ana and Lucía captive.

The features of the two men were intermingled in the descriptions that Ana had given.

Simón was on the short side, with curly hair, a little overweight, no visible hair on his arms. He had a pale complexion and was clumsy, even awkward in his movements: a man who could just about open the trapdoor to lower the food and water down to his captives.

The other man was taller than the girls. He was not thin, but powerfully built, tanned, and he had close-cropped hair. He was self-assured, confident in how he moved. This was the man who had pointed a rifle at Ana and said that one day he would kill her. This was the man walking free in Monteperdido – the man Sara had to find if she wanted to find Lucía.

As she arrived at Los Corzos, Sara looked at Lucía's house and remembered the odd way Ana had behaved that day as they came back from one of their walks around the village. The way she had turned her face away and hurried up the garden to her house. Who had been there? Who was it she had seen who had terrified her?

'Still no sign of Ana,' Víctor said as he saw her arrive. 'Do you have any news?'

Sara's mobile phone rang and she answered, hoping it was the Barbastro police.

'Zacarías Gutiérrez has been arrested,' said the officer on the other end of the line. 'They're bringing him here, to the station.'

The circle was closing.

'Let me come with you,' Víctor said when she explained Zacarías had been arrested, that he was the link between Simón Herrera and Transportes Castán, the reason Santiago had gone there that night.

'Why did you have to be so stupid?' Sara said angrily. 'I need you, but I can't have you working with me. You're off the case.'

'I don't have to be in the interview room; just let me observe. I know Zacarías. I can help.'

'What are we going to do? Maybe we should just call the whole thing off,' Román said. The white hounds were barking in the back of the pickup truck. He could see them jumping up, pressing their noses to the glass as if they could already smell their prey. He preferred to remain silent while he came up with solutions. He thought of the wild boars, sleeping in the woods right now while people discussed their fate. By this time tomorrow, many of them would be dead, skinned and hanging in the Hunting Society. He gripped the rifle between his thighs, carefully oiled and just waiting for a target. He could sense how difficult this would be, and it excited him. As if this was the best day's hunting he would ever see.

Víctor pressed the intercom switch so he could hear Sara and Zacarías on the other side of the two-way mirror. Zacarías was squirming in his seat, unable to get comfortable. He was not wearing the uniform they had seen him in at the Barbastro industrial estate, but jeans and a shirt spattered with paint and dirt. After Gaizka's arrest, when his involvement had come to light, Zacarías had been fired.

'Do you think he'll tell us anything?' asked Pujante, who was sitting behind Víctor.

Víctor turned to the rookie cop. He looked worn out, but it was an exhaustion born of frustration rather than physical exertion.

Before this summer, Pujante's greatest feat had been rescuing a few lost hikers, catching a few poachers. What was happening here was very different. The very men they had danced with in front of the statue of the Virgin on feast days, the men they had spent their lives with, drinking and hunting, who they had laughed and joked with while they spit-roasted wild boar, were showing their dark side, revealing their secrets. Víctor was no exception and he could see the disappointment in the eyes of his fellow officer. Everyone, it seemed, was hiding a secret behind a façade of normality.

'I still have no fucking idea why you brought me here,' Víctor heard Zacarías protest.

Sara looked up briefly from the reports on the table and smiled, but said nothing. She went on studying the documents that even Víctor knew were not worth reading. She was just trying to put Zacarías off his guard. And, watching him writhe and squirm, it seemed to be working.

'This whole thing is probably illegal,' Zacarías muttered.

'We have been reviewing Gaizka's case and we suspect that you did rather more than hide some merchandise for him in the lock-up,' Sara said, closing the folder, leaning back in her chair and staring at Zacarías. 'You helped him ship drugs into the village, didn't you? Back when you were working for Joaquín Castán's haulage company, and in the Barbastro industrial estate.'

'I don't know where you got that idea. It's not my business to know what's in the crates,' Zacarías said defensively, though there was a quaver in his voice.

'Maybe Gaizka told us,' Sara said, toying with him.

'And you're going to trust the word of a drug dealer?'

'If he has proof, we'd even take the word of a paedophile.'

Zacarías hid his hands under the table. He was not as dumb as he looked; he clearly realized exactly where Sara was heading. This was not about Gaizka. Or the cocaine. Or even the murder of the police officer.

'You remember Martutene Prison?' Sara asked.

'That was a long time ago.'

'Not so long that you wouldn't remember the friends you made there.'

'I was only banged up for three months. I didn't make any friends.'

'You seem like a nice guy, Zacarías. I can't imagine you sitting in a corner, not talking to anyone. You must remember who your cellmate was—'

'Listen, why don't you fucking ask me what you want to know straight out, b . . .?' Zacarías trailed off, as though he had intended to say something else.

'Bitch? Is that what you were going to call me, Zacarías?'

Realizing he had backed himself into a corner, Zacarías said nothing, but stared defiantly at Sara. She was not going to make him go anywhere he didn't want to go.

'Simón Herrera. Why don't we talk about him? He was your cellmate in Martutene.'

'What do you want me to tell you?' Zacarías said with a shrug. 'I've no idea where he is now.'

'Dead and buried,' Sara said tersely.

'Really? So what has that got to do with me?' Zacarías said, with a feeble attempt to sound surprised.

'You don't read the papers?'

'Only the sports pages.'

'Probably for the best. Anything for a quiet life,' Sara said, looking through the papers on the table. 'Well, let me explain a little. You see, Simón Herrera rescued Ana Montrell – one of the girls who disappeared five years ago in Monteperdido. Does that ring a bell?'

'I didn't know he was involved,' Zacarías said.

'I'll let you in on a little secret: we thought he was a hero. But it turns out he wasn't. Simón was one of the men who kept Ana and Lucía prisoner. From hero to zero,' Sara said, picking up the document she had been looking for. 'And, since I know you're not stupid, I'm guessing you have a very good idea—'

'If you're trying to frame me for this kidnapping shit, you've got it all wrong—'

'You see this form? It's an insurance form. About three years ago, you wrote off your car, up near Ordial. You called the insurance company, and who shows up with a tow truck? Simón Herrera. Your old cellmate.'

'And you're going to use that to say I knew about the girls?'

'Oh, we've got a lot more than that on you, Zacarías. There's Gaizka. All the little jobs you did for him while you were working for Joaquín Castán. Accessory after the fact, in the death of Inspector Santiago Baín. Because, maybe, you knew exactly what Gaizka had done and simply forgot to report it to the police. But we can forget all that if you tell us what we want to know about Simón.'

Zacarías gave a little smile. This was a fishing expedition; she was trying to see what she could scare up. Like a hunter releasing the hounds to flush out the game. But he had no intention of being prey. He knew that the less he said, the better were his chances of survival.

'Simón was a man of few words. When he came to tow the car, he told me he was living near Ordial and working with the tow truck . . . He dropped me off at the garage in Barbastro and I never saw him again. I don't know what else I can tell you.'

'Why don't you try telling me the truth? I might be a bit more convinced.'

'You might not like it, but that's what happened.'

Sara could see that Zacarías was shutting down, feeling increasingly confident in silence. More worried about being implicated in the kidnapping than in any charges that stemmed from his relationship with Gaizka. She could not keep him in custody, she knew that, and she knew that time was running out. Not so much for her as for Lucía. What had Ana done to force the kidnapper's hand? What had she said? Perhaps, without realizing, she had put the noose around Lucía's neck. Maybe this was why she had fled, unable to cope with the idea that, in saving herself, she had condemned Lucía to death.

Sara had to gamble with a lie.

'Simón's wife told us she often saw him with you, Zacarías.' She gauged his reaction. When you find yourself on quicksand, you have to walk quickly and surely, she thought, before adding, 'Obviously, he didn't tell her what you got up to: the whores and the parties, up at the Hotel La Guardia.'

Zacarías tried to stay calm, but his body betrayed him. He could not meet Sara's eyes, he kept his hands hidden under the table and was clearly making an effort to control his breathing. Hang in there, he said to himself.

'Would you like me to bring in one of the hotel staff to I.D. you? To tell us they saw you there with Simón?' Sara knew her intuition had been right; she had to keep pushing it.

'If you're going to accuse me of something, I'd rather you bring in my lawyer.'

Sara forced herself to relax. This was not what she wanted to happen: Zacarías clamming up, refusing to talk, waiting for his lawyer, dragging things out until they had to release him.

'There's a sixteen-year-old girl missing. Are you really going to screw up the only opportunity we have to save her life, Zacarías?' Sara begged him, though she knew it was a mistake. It was tantamount to surrender, but in that moment there was nothing else she could do.

'I can't help you – that's what you don't seem to understand.'

Víctor got up from the chair where he had been sitting, watching the interview. He left the observation room, throwing open the door so that it slammed against the table. He strode angrily across the squad room, sweeping everything off his desk; the reading lamp, the computer keyboard, files and folders crashed to the ground. He glanced behind him. Pujante had his head in his hands, as exhausted and depressed as Víctor was – sick and tired of the selfishness that meant everyone defending their own corner with no thought for the consequences.

Víctor saw Sara speak to Pujante before she went back to her office. He knew she was telling him to release Zacarías. He did not have the courage to talk to her. He had behaved appallingly.

He left the station and, out in the street, he saw the sun was beginning to sink behind the mountains. Monte Ármos glowed crimson in the sunset.

Time kept up its steady pace, indifferent to the fact that it was ticking by too quickly for them.

★

The surface of the tarn shimmered red and Ana imagined a lake of blood. Dusk moved across the expanse of water before dying in the west, behind Monte Albádes. Just being in this place brought her the peace she had been looking for. Behind her, the craggy, sheer rock face of Tempestades cirque greeted the last rays of sunlight like an old woman, sitting outside, eyes closed, letting the light fall on her scarred, wrinkled face. Above, on the glacier, the red snow glinted.

The dead roe deer at the foot of the cirque was little more than bone and entrails in the shadow of the few black pines growing around the lake. Soon it would be no more than a stain.

Ana heard a noise and thought of squirrels jumping from branch to branch, but, seeing a figure in the distance, she ducked behind the rocks, left the banks of the tarn and sought shelter between the pines.

'Don't hide!' Quim called to her, but Ana hid among the trees. Quim realized he was still running and forced himself to slow his pace. Was that what was frightening her? Instinctively, he adopted the behaviour of a hunter stalking his prey: taking small steps, studying the forest, trying to predict which way the prey might try to escape. Unwittingly, he was driving Ana in a direction that offered no way out.

Crouching behind the trees, Ana watched Quim's shadow lengthen as he approached. To her left, she saw a path leading down the mountain towards the river.

'It's just me, Ana,' Quim called. 'I don't know what's happened, but don't be afraid. I'm not going to hurt you.'

Quim did not really care what he was saying; all that mattered was that she could hear, that she knew exactly where he was and which way he was heading.

Ana stared at the trail that seemed to lead down to the river. Silently, she crept towards the only way out. She had seen herself in Quim's eyes; she had seen the woman she wanted to be, not the girl she had been. She broke into a run as the trees opened up into a clearing.

Quim sensed she was about to make a break for it when he saw the branches quiver. He knew he had no need to run. Ana did not know these mountains as well as he did. This path ran up an embankment that hid the fact that, on the far side, the trail came to a dead end.

Just when Ana thought she was free, the mountain fell away beneath her feet; the path was a mirage. Once past the embankment, it ceased to exist and there was a sheer drop that plummeted dozens of metres: La Camera canyon. At the bottom of the ravine was the stream that flowed from Monte Ármos – the river Ana had thought would be her escape. She looked back and saw Quim coming towards her quietly.

'You're like a roe deer. But I've tracked you,' he said.

'Leave me alone, Quim. I don't want to see anyone. Least of all, you.'

'What did I do?'

'You love me.' Ana choked back a sob; she resisted the temptation to gaze down into the abyss beneath her feet, to jump.

'And that's a bad thing?' Quim said as he took her hand in his. He pulled Ana to him and felt her quiver against his chest, wanting and not wanting to be held.

'I haven't told them everything I know . . .' Ana confessed, huddling against him.

'There are some things we have to forget in order to carry on living.'

'Lucía will never forget,' Ana said.

Then the words poured out in an angry torrent, wild and vicious, like knives raining down on herself.

'I hated her,' Ana said. 'I wanted to hurt her. Really hurt her. And . . . when she talked to me, I used to spit at her.' She clung tightly to Quim, imagining that at any moment he would push her away in horror. She was not trying to justify herself, only to confess everything she had kept hidden since she had escaped from the hole. The man who had kidnapped them loved only Lucía; he hated Ana – he treated her like dirt. Ana had watched as he gave in to every one of Lucía's smallest whims, while she had to take what pleasure she could in her books. Then, one day, tired of listening to her read aloud, Lucía had asked the man to take the books away. To burn them. Ana's deep hatred stemmed not from revenge, but jealousy. The man worshipped Lucía like a man prostrating himself before his God. Why did he not feel the same way about Ana? Why could he not even bring himself to talk to her, touch her? What was it about Ana that so disgusted him? She could not confront him, but she could take it out on Lucía. Ana knew Lucía needed her company just as much as she needed the love of their kidnapper.

'Living in that hole, I felt like I was dead,' she said to Quim. 'And I wanted to live.'

Lucía had become the focus of her rage; she mocked her, slapped her, forced her to face up to the idea of sex. She knew that Lucía was still a little girl and terrified of sex. Ana had become Lucía's tormentor in that dark hole, barely twenty metres square, where they were incarcerated for five years.

'I saw the fear in her eyes,' Ana confessed. 'Her fear of me. Lucía was terrified of me.'

What kind of person had she become?

Ana turned away to hide her tears. Quim's silence made every little sound more intense: the faint breeze, the quiver of the trembling aspens on the mountain slopes. Ana thought about the canyon, about ending this once and for all.

'I tried to forget my sister ever existed,' Quim said finally, in a small voice. 'I couldn't bear it, day after day after day ... Her absence. It was so painful that it was easier to think she was dead ... and that way ... I wouldn't feel ... bad ...'

Ana turned back and saw that Quim was crying. *Bad.* It was a childish word to describe how he had felt, but he was still trapped in a childhood that had been blighted by his sister's disappearance.

They had been too young to recognize the need for survival that lurks in everyone. Quim leaned towards Ana and kissed her. His lips, wet with tears, gently pressed against hers, and she thought of a line from a poem she had learned by heart: *Your heart pierced by an Angel's fiery spear / to the waters, run, Teresa, pale and dappled deer.*

If only she could forget.

She hugged Quim and whispered, 'Take me to the police station, Quim. I need to talk to them.'

Quim would have liked time to have stopped at that moment. So far from everything, so close to Ana. Alone on a mountaintop, like disembodied beings floating above the world. The sun was barely a faint glow behind Monte Albádes now. Once night fell, they would be trapped there in the mountains.

'Who is holding Lucía?' Quim asked.

'Don't make me tell you,' Ana pleaded.

Once he knew, there would be nothing she could do to spare him the pain, but she did not want to be the one to have to tell him. She looked up at the sky and thought, *pale and dappled deer / for there the fount of life that thee awaits / is fire, too.*

As they walked back to Monteperdido, she would teach Quim that poem.

Zacarías pulled into the car park of a bar just outside Val de Sacs. He got out of the car and lit a cigarette. The street lights were already on, but looked faint against the glow of sunset. He did not see Víctor pull up, a hundred metres behind, just as he had not seen him following all the way from Monteperdido.

'You think you're smarter than everyone else?' Víctor had muttered through gritted teeth as he drove, gripping the wheel, his knuckles white.

'Hey, Zacarías!' Víctor called to get his attention, and he smiled as Zacarías turned, the cigarette dangling from his lips, and stared at him. 'It's Víctor. You remember me.'

Zacarías looked around; the car park was almost empty – there were only four or five cars parked. The lights in the bar were on, advertising a lunch menu for only seven euros. Hands in his pockets, Víctor was walking towards him. He was wearing jeans and a white shirt with the emblem of the Cofradía de Santa María de Laude embroidered on the breast. What was he doing here? Zacarías had heard the sergeant had been suspended. He had not seen him in the long hours he had spent in Monteperdido police station. He thought about running, then changed his mind; there was no way Víctor could know what had happened with the police.

'How are things, Víctor?' he said, exhaling a plume of smoke. 'The boar hunt is tomorrow morning, yeah? Are you going?'

'I'm thinking about it,' Víctor said, still walking towards him. 'Let's hope Ana shows up; that way, we can all go.'

'She's only just reappeared, and she's running away.' Zacarías tried not to laugh, though he thought that Víctor could see the funny side of the situation; he was nodding and smiling.

Víctor asked no questions, wasted no time. As soon as he reached Zacarías, he pulled his right hand from his pocket. It was balled into a fist. He drew back his arm, arched his whole body, summoning all the power of his tensed muscles, and smashed it into Zacarías's jaw.

The punch had been unexpected and Zacarías was limp, unresisting. His head whipped round and he fell back, a dead weight. He still didn't realize what was happening as he felt Víctor's knees digging into his chest, felt him grab fistfuls of hair and jerk his head off the ground. Zacarías could just make out the dim shadow of Víctor.

'Now, you're going to tell me everything you know about Simón Herrera,' he heard him say.

Víctor pounded Zacarías's head against the concrete.

'What do you know about Simón?'

Zacarías tried to say something, but his voice was an unintelligible mumble. He felt the wound on his head throb, felt a trickle of blood dripping on the concrete. Víctor eased the pressure of his knees, then got to his feet, and at last Zacarías could breathe, roll on to his side and curl up in a foetal position.

'You want me to keep going?' Víctor panted.

'I didn't believe him ... I thought ... I thought he was bullshitting—'

Víctor kicked him in the stomach and Zacarías curled up tighter still.

'I don't give a shit what you thought. What did he tell you? Who was with him?'

'I don't know. I swear to God, I don't know . . .'

'Keep talking!'

Zacarías was choking on his own drool; bloody spittle foamed at the corners of his mouth. He spat, and then started to sob with the pain.

'He told me he had a video . . . of this girl—'

'Where?'

'Down the valley . . . just before you get to Barbastro . . . But I never actually saw it.'

Víctor took out his phone and dialled Sara's number. He saw Zacarías's eyes close and knelt down beside him. He turned him over and shook him.

'Don't go falling asleep on me, now. You're going to take us to visit this place, you hear me?'

Zacarías tried to shield his head, terrified Víctor would lash out again. He mumbled a faint, 'Yes.'

The roe deer is by nature a curious animal. The spirit of the forest, it is difficult to track, but can make excellent prey for the patient hunter. When it senses a predator nearby, it flees. Elusive and agile, it hides in the dense forest. It has to be guided to a place where it feels safe; only then will the roe deer offer the hunter an opportunity. It is pointless to shoot while it is flashing through the trees; the hunter is almost certain to miss his shot. Only when the animal emerges in the open country, in the moment before it races down the valley, does the roe deer offer a decent target. It pauses for a second, glances back to see the invader, to see its pursuer. The roe deer's curiosity offers the skilled hunter one last chance. If he has been patient, if he has waited until this moment, the hunter will still have a cartridge in his rifle.

The headlights illuminated a dirt track to the right of the main road. Zacarías told them he thought this was the place Simón had told him about. Víctor turned on to the track. It was potholed and overgrown with weeds. There were no wheel ruts. No car had come down this road in a long time.

On either side were vast stretches of wasteland. Once, they had served to graze cattle, but there were no cattle now.

Sara had called the station and asked Telmo to give her all the data he could find on the farm to which Zacarías was taking them. Telmo said he would call her back as soon as he had it.

The cloudless sky meant that the night was not entirely dark. A waning moon, studded around with small stars, was enough to cast a bluish glow.

Sara turned in her seat and saw Zacarías, sprawled in the back, cradling his head in his hands, as though to staunch the pain. When she had arrived at the car park and seen Víctor's bloody hands, she'd thought that he had done something crazy. That he had lost control. Víctor had led her to the car where Zacarías was propped up, and told her what he had said: a barn on a derelict farm, off the Barbastro Road.

'Let me go with you,' Víctor had said.

'You do realize you've just fucked your whole career as a Guardia Civil?' Sara said, looking at Zacarías's wounds.

'You can turn me in later. After we find Lucía.'

Víctor had not lost control. He had made a decision. Zacarías had the information he needed, and, in exchange, Víctor had given up his career. If they had waited for Zacarías to get a lawyer, and haggled while he tried to cut a deal, it would have been too late.

Sara looked at Víctor as he drove along the deserted track, past hectares of fallow land. She knew he would not regret his decision, whether they found Lucía or not. He had paid his debt. Not only to her, but to the whole valley – to these people he considered his family, the people he felt he had failed by letting Serna get the better of him.

Víctor rolled down the window, overwhelmed by the stench of blood and sweat from Zacarías.

'We'll call a doctor as soon as we get there,' Sara said as she scanned the horizon for the farm he had told them about.

'What if you can't find the place? Are you just going to let me bleed to death?' Zacarías whimpered. 'I need to get to a hospital . . .'

Sara and Víctor said nothing.

The only sound was the engine, the wind that whipped through the window and Zacarías's anguished groans.

Acres and acres of wasteland.

Sara's phone rang. It was Telmo. The farm belonged to Joaquín Castán's parents. Once, they had used the land to grow cabbage and raise livestock, but it had fallen into disuse years ago.

On the left of the dirt road, in the middle of a field, they saw a black silhouette that seemed to rise out of the earth as they approached. Sara hung up the phone. Víctor slowed the car and turned off the headlights.

They were on their own.

All the other officers were back in Monteperdido; they'd used every last minute of daylight searching for Ana, and were only now heading home. Sara had considered calling the Barbastro police, but she had not wanted to delay things.

'Have you got a gun?' she asked Víctor as she opened the door.

'A hunting rifle. In the boot,' he said.

'Get it.'

Sara got out and looked around, trying to decide the best way to approach the building. Víctor got the rifle, closed the doors and set the central locking so that Zacarías could not escape. He turned on a torch so he could pick his way through the shadows.

At a signal from Sara, they set off. The barn was a small stone building, with a corrugated-iron roof. A padlock hung on the metal door. It had been built to store farm machinery – there was no water, no electricity. Just four walls and a roof to protect the tools from rain and snow.

They kept their heads down as they ran, although there was no sign that anyone was inside. High on one wall there was a small window, the glass broken.

Víctor flattened himself against the wall next to the door.

'Someone's been using the place,' he said, nodding to the track left in the dirt from the door being opened.

Sara tried the door, but the lock clanged.

'Step back,' Víctor said.

He fired at the lock, which shattered into a thousand pieces, and threw open the door of the shack. He shone the torch inside: nobody was there. In one corner was a dirty mattress. The floor was littered with empty cans of food, and the whole place stank of excrement. Sara stepped inside and looked around the cramped space. Even now, the air was still stale from the life that had been there.

'Shit,' she muttered. 'She was here . . .'

Víctor picked up one of the boxes piled in a corner of the room. He opened it and pulled out a black paintball helmet.

'We've got him, Sara,' Víctor said. 'There's bound to be finger-prints and traces of D.N.A. all over this shit. He's ours.'

Sara said nothing. She walked over, pulled on a pair of latex gloves and began opening the boxes, wondering where Ana and Lucía were now. Would they come back? Right here, she had all the evidence she needed; with this, they would be able to identify the kidnapper. But Sara would have been happy to leave Monteperdido without ever knowing his name, if the girls could just be returned to their parents.

Alive.

In the crate was a mobile phone; she knew immediately it was Simón Herrera's. The one that had been used to call Ana's house.

Now, they were both missing.

Opening another box, she found a video camera. An old model. She turned it on and pressed *eject*; the camera spat out a tape.

Burgos had called the officers back as night began to draw in; this was dangerous terrain and it was not safe to carry on searching in the failing light.

The officers trudged back, disappointed and frustrated, glancing now and again at the shadowy mountain slopes. The two jeeps were parked on an area of level ground at the foot of the mountain, engines idling, headlights dipped as the officers gathered up their equipment. Román had just arrived in his pickup; the dogs were in the back. He wanted to take the hounds into the mountains to track Ana's scent.

But, just then, Quim and Ana appeared out of the darkness, shielding their eyes, dazzled by the headlights.

'Jesus fuck,' was Burgos's spontaneous greeting when he spotted them. 'Raquel! Álvaro! She's here! Ana's here!' He turned to the officers standing around Ana's parents, explaining that they had to call the search off for the night and offering to take them home. 'Ana's here!' he shouted again.

The roe deer's curiosity offers the skilled hunter one last chance.

Sara put the tape back into the camcorder. As the ambulance taking Zacarías to hospital sped away, its lights still flickered on the car windows, flashes of red and yellow lighting up the inside. She pressed *play*, and turned up the volume. At first, the image was blurred, grey, then it began to take shape: the basement of the mountain hut where the girls had been held. The hole, as Ana called it. Bare stone walls and, in the centre, a mattress fitted with pink sheets on a metal bed frame. The camera panned right, to a girl standing next to the bed. She hugged herself, her tousled, dirty blonde hair covering her face. The background noise suddenly cut out — someone had erased the audio track. From that moment, it was a silent film. The girl looked into the lens with her deep, black eyes. It was Ana. She was smiling. She was staring provocatively into the camera. Then she looked at the bed next to her and, swaying her hips, she walked over and knelt on the pink sheets. Why did she look as though she was enjoying this? Sara wondered. On the monitor, she saw Ana begin to take off her clothes.

First her cardigan, then her blouse. Kneeling on the bed, she stroked her small breasts, still looking into the camera. She wet her lips with the tip of her tongue.

The silence of the tape made it feel even more brutal.

There was a terrible sadness to this parody of sensuality, this little girl mimicking the gestures of a woman. Sara could see it in her eyes. On her lips. With every gesture, Ana was pleading, *Love me.*

She could not hold back her tears. Who could bear to endure such solitude? To never see themselves reflected in someone's eyes? Even the eyes of a monster.

Víctor opened the door of the car. 'Are you OK?' he said, leaning inside to talk to Sara.

Sara wiped her eyes and summoned the strength to nod. 'Ana knows who he is,' she said. 'She's known from the start.' She pointed to the bottom corner of the camera monitor, a patch of floor next to the legs of the bed. In the shadows, there was a black paintball helmet.

'He wasn't wearing it,' Víctor said.

Ana was still staring at the camera. Sara suddenly felt that she was on the other side of this unreal window. She could picture the bare bulb hanging from the ceiling, which gave the scene its dull yellow glow. Ana brought a finger to her lips and let it slide down over her chin, her throat, her breasts. She was forcing herself to smile. Her lips were moving, forming words that Sara could not hear. She was talking to the man holding the camera. She seemed to be inviting him to join her on the pink sheets.

What was Ana saying?

The soundtrack had been erased.

Sara stopped the tape, rewound and pressed *play*. She watched Ana's lips as she mouthed three words. The first two could be *Come here,* and the third . . . Could it be a name?

Sara looked at the long dark road that wound its way up to Fall Gorge tunnel, and to Monteperdido, lurking beyond.

'They've found Ana,' Víctor said, getting into the car and starting the engine. Sanmartín had called. 'She just came down from the mountain with Quim.'

In the glare of the headlights, they looked like fluttering moths. Ana squinted, shielding her eyes. Who was there? She thought she recognized some of the villagers, and officers from the Guardia Civil. Was he there? She gripped Quim's hand tighter, looked into his face and saw his reassuring smile.

She took a deep breath of clean, cold air. Night had closed over Monteperdido.

Behind her stretched the forest of trembling aspens, the mocking laughter of their leaves drowned out by the whoops of joy at the foot of Monte Ármos.

She could make out her parents among the silhouettes: Raquel in front and Álvaro a few paces behind. They were running towards her. Burgos stepped out of the way so they could greet their daughter. Ana did not need to see their faces to know they were crying tears of joy; she wanted to feel the warmth of her parents, to immerse herself in her mother's unconditional love, her father's blue eyes. This family was her shelter, it was where she found the Ana she wanted to be.

She felt Quim gently let go of her hand, his fingertips brushing hers for a second longer, then leaving her free to run to them. She took a first faltering step, but, before breaking into a run, she looked behind her at the forest of aspens from which she had just emerged, as though looking into her past, as though expecting to see herself. The little girl who had lived in the hole. The Ana who had been threatened and despised, who seethed with jealousy and bitterness. The Ana she was leaving behind in the shadows of the trembling aspens.

An Ana who was fading. *To Earth. To Smoke. To Dust. To Shade. To Nothingness.*

She could not help it; she was curious to see that Ana disappear into this forest as black as her eyes.

The flash was the last thing she saw clearly. The spark of a gunshot from somewhere between the dark trees, and then the searing heat as the bullet pierced her forehead and mushroomed inside her skull.

The impact threw her backwards; rather than falling, she felt as though she were diving – diving into the waters of the tarn, up at Tempestades cirque. Her eyes saw strange flickering images that faded as she sank into the depths. Through the dark waters, she thought she could see the star-speckled sky she had always gazed at longingly, the stars she had named after those she loved most: Lucía, Raquel, Álvaro . . . And a waning moon that she named Quim, and even as she felt herself falling, she felt him close to her, ready to catch her.

She heard voices screaming, but she thought it was the wind in the aspens. Or the sound of raindrops breaking the surface of the lake.

She wanted to tell them not to worry, that she did not feel any pain, only the boundless love of all these stars that surrounded her, gently catching her as she fell, gathering her into a net of light and then lifting her. Carrying her up to that quiet roof, where dove-sails saunter by, that dome of air and water. Between the pines, the tombs.

With Raquel, Álvaro, Lucía, Quim . . .

She could not tell whether she had dreamed them, or if they had dreamed Ana.

Until her consciousness melted into the skies of Monteperdido.

Run, he thought, racing between dark aspens. He did not wait to see the result of his shot. Mingle with the crowd before they have time to cordon off the mountain. His laboured breathing, his sweaty fear would not be noticed in the general panic.

The gunshots sounded somehow ridiculous, here, in the forest. Bullets splintered the tree trunks, ripped at the leaves, a flurry of flashes. In the back of the pickup truck, Román's dogs were barking frantically.

Raquel wailed uncontrollably as she knelt by her daughter's body, cradling the ruined head in her lap, stroking the lifeless skin as it grew cold. Joaquín elbowed his way through the crowd, searching for his son; Quim stood, paralyzed, a few metres from the body; his face was spattered with Ana's blood, but he did not notice it trickle down his cheek. Perhaps he thought it was his own tears.

Ismael screamed at the officers to do something. They poured into the woods after the man who had fired the shot. Burgos stood, looking from Ana's body on the ground to Álvaro's eyes, which were no longer blue, but grey. Álvaro was staring at the forest. Leaving his wife and his dead daughter, he grabbed Burgos's service pistol. Rafael ran to stop him – there was no point adding to the chaos; it would only make it easier for the shooter to get away. Álvaro roughly shoved him aside and, aiming the gun into the shadows, he fired again and again. Angrily. Furiously. Helplessly. Knowing that every bullet was useless; nothing would bring Ana back.

Nicolás led Montserrat away from the milling crowd gathered around Ana's body. The jeeps moved, the headlights scanning the woods for some sign of the killer, creating a play of light and shadow, shifting, flaring, meaningless. Caridad ran to Raquel and, seeing there was nothing she could do for Ana now, she hugged the girl's mother, who was still cradling her daughter's head on her lap.

Voices calling ambulances mingled with bursts of gunfire triggered by the slightest noise from the forest. Quim was pale and fragile, like a sheet whipped by a hurricane. Joaquín took his son in his arms, wiped the blood from his face, but Quim did not react. He was staring down at Ana, lying dead on the ground. As they'd walked down from the tarn, she had recited that poem to him, over and over. He knew it by heart, now: *to the waters, run, Teresa, pale and dappled deer / for there a fount of life doth thee await / a fire, too, whose blaze doth not abate.*

Víctor's car pulled up next to the police jeeps. Tragedy, like a black river, had spilled out, flooding the streets of Monteperdido. Sara knew something had happened before Pujante phoned her in tears.

While Víctor was trying to bring order to the chaos, shouting for everyone other than the police officers to clear the space, Sara moved slowly through the crowd. She saw Ana's body on the ground; her eyes were still open, staring up at the sky, as though pleading to be allowed to join the stars. Her mouth was slightly open; between her blood-red lips was a deep, black hole, filled with all the words that Ana would never say. Like the videotape, the soundtrack had been erased.

But not completely.

Álvaro emptied the cartridge and fell to his knees in front of the aspens, as though surrendering to a savage god. Sanmartín tried to gently help him to his feet.

Joaquín left his son with Ximena. Quim walked unsteadily, as though he could barely stand. Ximena took his arm and whispered something into his ear. Perhaps she suggested they should go. What more could they do?

This was the last defeat: a shot through the heart of Monteperdido.

Nicolás walked Montserrat down to the side of the road and told her to stay there. Then he turned back up the path, heading up the slopes of Monte Ármos.

Sara closed her eyes and pictured Ana's lips as she talked to the camera: *Come here.* She was sure these were the first two words.

Quim reeled, about to fall, as Ximena struggled to support him.

Rafael raced to help his nephew. 'We should go. There's nothing we can do here,' he said.

Joaquín went over to Burgos, who was barely able to control his panic; his heart was hammering in his chest, blood pounded in his temples. He was unable to calm himself.

'Tell us what to do,' Joaquín said. 'What if we let Román's dogs loose?'

Somewhere in the shadows was the man who had shot Ana, but it was madness to start a search; with no light, they would simply panic and end up firing at each other.

Ismael went over to Raquel and hugged her. 'I'm so sorry,' he said.

She shuddered as she felt his skin touch hers. 'Get away!' she screamed. 'I don't want you anywhere near my daughter!'

Everyone turned to look at Ismael, who struggled to his feet, embarrassed. People were staring at him contemptuously, and he looked at this family to which he had never belonged. They saw him as an interloper, someone who had tried to steal one of them away: Raquel. Where had Ismael come from? Who was he really?

Hearing Raquel scream, Álvaro pushed his way through the crowd around his daughter's body. He raised the gun and pointed it at Ismael.

'You're making a mistake, Álvaro! This is insane!' Ismael shouted, raising his hands and taking a step back.

But Álvaro was not listening to Ismael, or to Víctor, who was also pleading with him to put down the gun. He pulled the trigger. The hammer rang against the empty chamber. He had already fired all the bullets into the forest.

Ismael fell to his knees, sobbing.

'*To the waters, run, Teresa, pale and dappled deer . . .*' Quim whispered, standing over Ana's body, but he could not remember the rest of the poem she had taught him while they were coming down the mountain. And the words were stuck, repeating again and again: ' *. . . for there a fount . . .*'

Rafael grabbed his nephew and tried to turn him away from the girl, from the lifeless black eyes, as Quim whispered, ' . . . for there a fount . . .'

'Forget the fucking poem,' Rafael said.

Quim could not suppress a sudden hoarse laugh, almost a scream. But he said nothing else, as though he had emptied all the air out of his lungs and there was no room, now that they were filled with hate and fear and bitterness.

Sara stood, motionless, in the midst of the crowd. She tried to distance herself from the tears and the howls, from the visceral pain that rippled through them, so tangible she could almost touch it.

She closed her eyes and pictured Ana's lips on the videotape: *Come here,* she said, and then a name.

Víctor turned away from the forest. Pujante tried to explain what had happened: how Ana had reappeared, the shot from the shadows, the chaos. The confusion. A good hunter, Víctor thought. Someone who knows how to move quickly, how to wait for exactly the right moment. The moment when chaos erupted, when everyone turned away from the forest to see Ana crumple. In that split second, he would have run. Not up the mountain – at night the terrain was too dangerous, even for an experienced hunter – but down. He would have hidden among them, as he had been doing all along.

Víctor looked around. Joaquín. Nicolás. Álvaro. Ismael. Rafael.

Come here. Ana's lips moving soundlessly. 'I can hear you,' Sara whispered. 'Tell me who he is, Ana.' She saw the lips parted just a little at first, a brief flicker, then form a circle, an open vowel, then close again, leaving a narrow gap between them. Three syllables.

'How did you know it was a poem?' Quim said, and, glancing at his uncle, he saw the rage in his eyes.

Rafael pushed Quim towards the road. He was trying to look casual, but his every gesture was as jagged as a sheet of metal. Seeing Quim try to move away from him, he grabbed the rifle that was slung over his shoulder and placed his finger on the trigger. Quim wanted to scream, but no words came. Without thinking, he backed away, looking for somewhere to shelter; he was behind one of the neighbours' cars. He was all alone.

No one can see us, Rafael seemed to be saying, and he stepped towards Quim and pushed him. The boy collapsed on the ground, paralysed by fear. Rafael shouldered the rifle.

Come here, Rafael, Ana's lips mouthed. Sara opened her eyes.

She scanned the crowd; Víctor was walking towards her, the officers shepherding the villagers away: Álvaro, Joaquín, Nicolás. She took a step, looking around for him. Ana, lying on the ground, her head in Raquel's lap. Caridad, next to Raquel, comforting her. Ismael had already reached the main road, and was walking away from the circle of shadows. Ximena was sitting on the ground, her face in her hands.

Sara drew her gun as she saw the shadow behind a car parked at the side of the road. Rafael had his rifle shouldered. Quim was crawling on the ground, then she heard him scream: a cry of fear that rang out at the same moment as Sara's gunshot.

The bullet pierced Rafael's right shoulder, and he dropped the rifle and pitched forward on to the ground next to Quim, who lashed out, kicking him in the face until Víctor ran over and pulled him off.

Sara looked behind her – at Ana's body, resting on her mother's lap; at Álvaro, as he kissed the lifeless face.

7

The White Deer

'Lucía is dead,' were the first words Rafael said in the interview room.

Then he looked in the mirror that separated them from the observation room where the other officers were listening. Though he knew they were there, Rafael was not looking at them; he was staring at his own reflection, and, seeing his eyes were filled with tears, he gave something like a half-smile. He seemed happy to see that he was crying.

Blood seeped from the bandage on his right shoulder, where Sara had shot him. The ambulance would arrive soon, and the Barbastro police, and probably top brass. He would be taken to hospital and, from there, Rafael would drip-feed them his story.

'Where is the body?'

'In Cajigal Canyon.' Only now did Rafael finally look at Sara. 'Do you know where that is?'

'About two kilometres from the shack where you had her locked up.'

Rafael nodded as if to congratulate her. But he could not help but correct her: 'I didn't lock her up; we were in hiding.'

In the observation room, Víctor turned and sent two officers to go and search the canyon. Although he was suspended, the officers obeyed his orders as if he were still in charge. Cajigal was a narrow ravine with a sheer drop of more than a hundred metres; the bottom of the canyon was inaccessible. If Lucía's body was there, it would be weeks before they found it, assuming they did so before the first snowfall.

'Who were you hiding from?' Sara asked.

'From you,' he said, then gestured to the two-way mirror, at those watching. 'From all of them. No one understood about us.'

'Not even Ana?'

'She, least of all.' His voice dripped with contempt.

Sara took a deep breath. Who needs to understand a psychopath? Who wants to slip inside his skin? And then she remembered something that Santiago had said: *Our job rarely means saving the innocent. Most of the time, all we can do is understand the monster.* Rafael had just turned forty-five. Sara could still remember the birthday cake — chocolate, with a thin layer of jam in the middle — and his chapped lips as he casually blew out the candles as if to say that age was just a number. To those people standing around, clapping and cheering, those people who were supposed to be his family, he was a stranger. Perhaps that casual air was his way of hiding his alien nature.

An island within an island: Rafael within Monteperdido.

'How did Lucía die?' Sara remembered the smell of damp earth that had hung over the village the day after Santiago was murdered: the gritty taste in the air, the penetrating smell of pine trees and fresh water. As though nature did not surround Monteperdido, it *was* Monteperdido. In flesh and blood.

'I'd rather not talk about that,' Rafael said. 'It just happened. It had to happen.'

'You can try to fool me, Rafael,' Sara said. 'But you can't get away from the guilt.'

'If Ana had kept her mouth shut, none of this would have happened.' His rage was so fierce, Sara could almost see him pulling the trigger in the forest on the slopes of Monte Ármos.

'Why don't you talk me through it from the beginning?'

'Don't try to pretend you want to understand . . .' he sneered.

'I don't need to pretend. I do understand. You were alone. Everyone in the village had found their little niche. For some, it was comfortable; for others, not so much. Some of them had suffered or would suffer because of the role they had been assigned. But, then again, that's the wheel of life, of everyday life in Monteperdido: everyone is a cog in the machine. They know what they will be doing today, tomorrow. But not you. You were on the outside. You were not a cog in the machine; the wheel didn't need you to keep turning. In fact, you were a spanner in the works. All you did was get in the way. Somehow, you needed to make yourself indispensable. Everyone needs to feel that. Not indispensable to everyone; one person is enough: a wife, a daughter. Which was Lucía to you?'

Rafael had been listening, unconsciously nodding at Sara's logic. He had never thought of wheels and cogs. He had never used the word 'need' to define what had led him to Lucía. He preferred to call it love.

'My wife,' Rafael said, and the words were a badge of pride.

Five years ago. Even before that. Seven years ago. Rafael had heard about the flood in Monteperdido on the television. At the time, he had been working in Latin America. In his hotel room, just before he fell asleep, he would watch the international news, looking for stories that reminded him of home. But reports about tourism in southern Spain, or heat waves in the north were no more familiar to him than what he saw on the news about Argentina or Uruguay.

In that soulless hotel room, on the side of a road that began nowhere and trailed off somewhere in Patagonia, he heard the newsreader talking about the victims of the flood in Monteperdido. He recognized the images, saw the frantic looks on the faces of people who had been his neighbours, and he knew that, if he had been one of those who had drowned in the Ésera, there would not have been so much grief, so many tears.

What would the newsreader have said? Who would have remembered him the next morning?

He tossed and turned in his hotel bed, unable to sleep. His truck was outside in the hotel car park. If he had a heart attack tonight and woke up dead, it would simply be a problem for the kid who had given him the keys to the room, a delay for the Jewish guy he was working for in Buenos Aires. It would be weeks before the news reached Monteperdido and, by then, his body would have been cremated to save on storage costs.

He imagined a set of scales, with his lonely death on one side, and, on the other, the seven victims of the flood.

All those victims had left holes in the lives of people who lived on, whereas he would leave no hole.

How had he become this solitary creature? This was a question for which he had no answer. There was no specific moment when he had begun to disappear, fading until he was little more than a memory.

He told Sara that his parents had died young. He and Montserrat had been orphaned when they were in their early twenties. But he could not say that either the loss of his mother to cancer, or his father's heart attack had been particularly traumatic. By then, Rafael was already working on the road. He had never owned his own truck, but, since his first job in Barbastro, he had been working behind the wheel. His father had died suddenly; Rafael had been in Oporto when he heard the news. Montserrat phoned to tell him, but, though he heard his sister sobbing on the phone, he had hardly shed a tear.

He mourned these losses because, with the death of his parents, a part of his life also vanished. He described his childhood as normal, even boring: trips into the mountains around Monteperdido, his father telling him about the animals – the roe deer, the boars, the chamois goats.

'If you're hoping I'm going to say that my father abused me, you're going to be disappointed,' Rafael said, feeling awkward at having to talk about a time that was so distant it hardly seemed to relate to him.

'When did you come back to Monteperdido?'

'Three or four months after the flood. That same winter.'

Rafael fell silent for a moment as he remembered coming back. He was looking past Sara, picturing the snow-covered streets and the houses. The bitter cold, the people wrapped up in their dark coats, the way he had to keep his head bowed against the wind as he walked to his sister's place. Montserrat had ushered him inside. The feeling of warmth as he stepped into the house and his sister closed the door. Montserrat had hugged him and reeled off a string of reproaches that were her way of showing affection: Why had he not warned them he was coming back to the village? She could have made up the spare room. Had he seen the state of the bridge by the school? Still not rebuilt.

Rafael had phoned his sister from Argentina the day after he'd seen the flood on the news. She'd told him how terrible it had been, how Joaquín had saved Lucía from falling into the Ésera. For Rafael, it had just been a polite phone call.

But still, he had gone home.

Montserrat asked if he wanted a drink and showed him into the living room. There was a rug in front of the hearth, a deerskin, and, kneeling on the rug, lit by the flickering glow of the fire, was Lucía. She went on playing with her dolls and did not even look up until her mother told her to say hello to her uncle. Lucía had looked up and mumbled a half-hearted 'Hello' before going back to her game. The dolls. Montserrat did not scold her or tell her to get up; she was already in the kitchen making coffee, while Rafael stood in the living room, hands stuffed in his pockets. He was starting to sweat from the heat and did not know why he hadn't taken off his coat. Lucía made up little voices as she moved the dolls around on the floor, her back to him. She lay down on the ground, staring at the face of one of her dolls, and Rafael found his eyes tracing the arc of her neck, the bare shoulder peeking from her tattered T-shirt, her back as it curved to her buttocks, her legs drawn up under her, gently hugged inside sheer tights.

He'd felt ashamed when he realized he was aroused, and was startled when his sister told him to take off his coat and throw it anywhere.

He could not do it. He was terrified that she would see his erection.

He had hurried out of the room, telling his sister he had booked himself into La Renclusa, that he did not want to be a bother. In fact, he needed to get out of the house as fast as possible, to forget the image of Lucía in the glow of the fire. She was nine years old. It was wrong.

But he could not bring himself to leave Monteperdido.

Joaquín gave him a job at Transportes Castán and he rented a house, south of the river, away from the centre of the village. When he was not driving trucks, he would go up into the mountains to watch the animals and to hunt. He loved the roe deer best – so delicate, so elusive, so curious.

He went on seeing Lucía. In the village, in the park, at his sister's house.

He was brusque with the girl, but in fact he felt embarrassed. Awkward. Bashful.

He found himself studying her hands, her mischievous eyes, her laugh. He listened to her talking to her mother, to her friend Ana, and gradually he began to find the justification he needed to look, to listen, to touch without feeling ashamed.

He loved Lucía. He loved her more than anything in the world and he wanted her for himself.

But he wanted her to want him too.

As far as she was concerned, he scarcely existed. He decided to change that.

At first, it was little more than a daydream. Then it took up every idle moment. How to take Lucía, to have her by his side, always.

Even when he started to build the basement in the mountain hut, he thought he would never live out his fantasy. When he took the truck away on trips, he would postpone coming home and spend a day, two days, up at the *refugio*. Digging, putting up the beams that would support the roof.

Among the things he had ferried for Transportes Castán was the equipment for Gaizka's tour company. Abseiling ropes, rafts, paintball helmets. Rafael kept one of the helmets; he thought it might be useful. His fantasy was slowly impinging on reality.

He often drove into Monteperdido just to see Lucía. He would sit in his car at the junction of Avenida de Posets and watch her walk home from school, chatting and laughing with Ana. Sometimes Ximena was with them.

He waited until early autumn. October seemed like a good month. Only then did he realize that he was actually going to do this.

'Ana wasn't supposed to be there,' Rafael admitted. As he said it, he seemed to blame her for everything that had happened later. 'It was a Monday. Ana and Ximena had piano lessons. Lucía always walked home through the forest alone on Mondays, even though her mother told her not to take the shortcut when she wasn't with her friends. I found out later, she'd had an argument with Ximena ... I was only expecting Lucía. I had some tranquillizer darts from the Hunting Society ... She never even saw me coming. I put my hand over her mouth and injected the tranquillizer ...'

Rafael explained how he'd carried her to his car, which was parked at the edge of the forest. No one had seen him arrive. Then, suddenly, Ana had appeared and, terrified of being discovered, he'd sedated her too and put her into the car.

Rafael was staring at the palm of his left hand; he could still feel the touch of Lucía's lips that first time in the forest. His first kiss.

'I'm not a murderer,' he said, when Sara asked about the drive he had taken Ana on, just after they'd arrived at the hut. 'I should have killed her. That's what a murderer would have done, but I'm not a killer. I couldn't bring myself to shoot her. I treated her as well as I treated Lucía, although every day I wished she wasn't there. She was always being horrible to Lucía, telling her she was crazy, that she was sick. That was the real problem with Ana: she was jealous. Of what Lucía and I had. And she was always on the outside. Lucía loved her and did everything she could to make Ana happy, but Ana couldn't bear the thought that she was not wanted.'

Sara could not help but picture Ana in the shelter, tied to a beam, staring through the hole in the ceiling at the stars over Monteperdido. Constantly despised, humiliated, rejected.

Thinking about this, Sara understood why Ana had never betrayed Simón.

'Zacarías mentioned him to me,' Raphael said. 'Told me he lived up near Ordial, that they had met while they were in prison in Martutene. That Simón had been beaten up, there, because he was a paedophile.'

At first, everything had been easier than he'd expected. Kidnapping the girls, going up to the shelter to bring them food and make sure they were all right. He had to be careful that the Guardia Civil would not find his movements suspicious, but since he worked at the haulage company and Joaquín was no longer around to check on his comings and goings, he had the alibi he needed.

While the whole village was in shock, Rafael had been delighted with how perfectly his plan had worked. Sitting in his sister's kitchen, while Montserrat was having a nervous breakdown and her husband was howling like an animal, Rafael pretended to be sympathetic. He hugged his sister, did everything he could to support Joaquín. Quim was the only one in the house with any sense. Soon, Lucía's brother was trying to rebuild a life that his parents were determined to thwart.

Rafael felt sorry for his nephew. Lucía had taken up all the space in his parents' lives and there was no space left for him. This was why Rafael had invited him into his own home, talked to him about school, given him money he knew Quim would spend partying or buying hash from Gaizka.

Deep down, it suited Rafael to play all these roles – a friend and mentor to Quim, a shoulder to cry on for Montserrat, a self-sacrificing worker for Joaquín. They offered more and more layers to hide the real Rafael: the man who had two girls captive in a basement in the mountains.

The Guardia Civil investigation had been fruitless: the searches, the sniffer dogs, the helicopters looking for some evidence.

During the first weeks, Rafael had worn the paintball helmet when he went down into the basement with the girls. He'd barely spoken to them – just enough to feed their fears.

'I never even thought about how long it would last,' Rafael said with a half-smile. 'I never really planned that far ahead. It just started, and . . .' The words hung in the air, as though he still could not say, *and now it's over*.

As the months passed, the search eased off. Rafael no longer had to watch his every step. He got through the first winter, the first summer. It was at this point that he realized he could not keep things going by himself.

So he befriended Simón Herrera. He worked slowly, and never met him anywhere near the village, where someone might recognize them. They met in Barbastro, and even further south, in Monzón. He took him drinking. They talked about women. They talked about girls.

Rafael toyed with Simón, told him he could get him somewhere where he could see two naked girls. That nothing would happen. No one would ever know he had been there. Then, one day, Rafael took him to the mountain shelter.

Kneeling on the floor, Simón peered through the narrow slit around the trapdoor. Down in the hole, Simón could see Ana and Lucía. He could watch them play, see them dress and, sometimes, since they did not know they were being watched, they would wander around naked because the basement was sweltering during the summer months.

'You're the one in the video with Ana, not Simón,' Sara snapped.

Images from the tape flickered in her mind as Sara tried to turn the interview to the circumstances that led to the making of the video.

Why had Rafael crossed that line?

At first, Simón had accepted the rules, Rafael explained. But then, just looking through the crack or bringing their food was not enough. He wanted more.

'Simón wasn't able to touch the girls,' Rafael said. He clearly did not feel comfortable talking about what he had done to Ana. 'But he wanted to watch. He was like a kid who had done something naughty, saying, "I never touched Lucía. I couldn't have. I wanted to, of course, but I couldn't have forced her . . ."'

Sara felt sullied, dirty, as though she were wearing Rafael's skin over her own. She wanted to scream at him, call him a pervert, a sick bastard, but she needed to get to the end of the story.

She closed her eyes and tried to think of a calming image: Ana, learning to swim with Quim in the tarn, surrounded by the crystal-clear water of the lake, washing away her memories, turning back into the girl she had always been.

'Do you want me to go on?' she heard Rafael say.

She looked at him and he bowed his head. Though he had been prepared to justify what he had done with Lucía, he was ashamed to remember the video with Ana.

'I have to try to understand, Rafael; that's my job,' Sara said. 'But don't expect me to forgive you.'

'I can't forgive myself.'

But Rafael's remorse seemed to have nothing to do with what he had inflicted on Ana; instead, it stemmed from the betrayal he thought it represented in the relationship he imagined he had with Lucía.

The video was the point at which the situation began to unravel.

Simón watched the video compulsively and became obsessed with Ana. Perhaps he had been before, but Rafael had not noticed. Simón talked endlessly about Ana; when he was their jailer, he gave her preferential treatment, bringing food that Ana liked, agreeing to the few things that she asked of him, Lucía had told Rafael.

Rafael was also beginning to wonder whether he could trust Simón to keep his mouth shut; he felt that the pleasure Simón took in watching the video was multiplied when he could boast about it, as he had done to Rafael. He could remember every single frame. Rafael hated listening to him, but was worried that, if he did not, Simón might find someone else to talk to.

He should have done something, but instead he let time pass, and Simón built up the same fantasy about Ana as Rafael had built around Lucía. He wanted to protect her, to save her from Rafael's cruelty.

'What would have happened if the car had not crashed into the ravine when they were driving away?' Sara asked.

'I don't know,' Rafael said, though it was clear that he was also saying, *I do not care.*

Sara could understand why Ana had not wanted to implicate Simón in what had happened. She might not have had a clear idea who he was or what role he had played in her captivity, but also, in getting her out of there, he had been her saviour.

Pujante knocked on the door of the interview room. He came in and whispered something to Sara.

'They've found a pink scarf, like a muslin, next to Cajigal Canyon,' Sara said, after Pujante left. 'I assume it belongs to Lucía.'

Ana had survived the crash. When she was in the hospital, Rafael made sure she saw him, made sure she remembered his threat: *One day, I'll kill you.* He prayed that this would be enough to keep her silent.

Fear.

When he realized they would find the shelter, he decided to torch it. He had taken Lucía, but the roads were cordoned off, so he could not take her far. For a few days, they had hidden out in the tunnel in Ixeia.

Then came the night of the storm, when Marcial showed up with his mother. Rafael had been in a blind panic. From the moment he saw the headlights, he froze, became a block of ice about to shatter into a million pieces. It was this that had led him to hit Lucía; it was something he had never done before – he had never lost control.

But he had been lucky. They had been able to leave the tunnel without Marcial seeing them. They went across the fields and

Rafael discovered that the roadblock had been lifted. He took the car and drove to Joaquín's parents' farm. He had used the tool shed before, to meet Simón, to show him the videotape. He knew no one used the outbuildings. This was where he had kept Lucía ever since. After Santiago's death, and the newspaper articles about Sara, he had hoped perhaps the investigation would grind to a halt.

'Once things had calmed down, I'd take Lucía out of the valley in one of the trucks,' Rafael said.

But it was not like that. Sara was moving, slowly but inexorably, towards him. There was the discovery that two people had been involved in the kidnapping, the dolls Nicolás had found, Simón's involvement.

And then, Ana had stopped being afraid and she had talked. It was Quim who had told him. If Ana started talking, nothing could stop her. Lucía had made the phone call. Ana disappeared and Rafael hoped that the mountain would swallow her forever.

But, sooner or later, he knew Ana would come down from the slopes of Monte Ármos and tell everyone who he was.

It was over. He went to the tool shed, drove Lucía to Cajigal Canyon and killed her.

Then he mingled with the villagers searching for Ana. Biding his time, waiting for the moment when she reappeared.

'Then I just had to die and that would have been the end of the story,' Rafael said. 'You should have shot me in the head.'

Sara got up and left the interview room.

It was dawn by the time the ambulance drove up the school road and turned on to Avenida de Posets. Rafael was in the back, lying on the stretcher. The red cross on the window cast a shadow over his face. There was nobody on the streets. In every house, the blinds were drawn, the doors were closed. Hours earlier, the shuttered houses had watched as the ambulance drove past carrying Ana's body. It was as though the order had been reversed.

First death, then life.

Víctor found Sara leaning against the wall of her office. He could see she was trembling and he wanted to go and hug her. He wanted to tell her that this was just a nightmare, but there was nothing to wake up to. This was the real world.

Sara saw him in the doorway. Víctor did not know whether to come in or turn and leave. His knuckles and his shirt were still bloody from his altercation with Zacarías. His cheeks were streaked with tears.

'Would you mind being my driver one last time?' Sara said.

Víctor stepped aside and gestured, inviting her to leave the office.

Sara could not bring herself to look at the other officers in the squad room and she assumed that they did not want anyone to look at them. Only those closest to them could share their defeat, and though she felt she had carved a small place for herself in the station, she was not one of them.

Nieve barked as Sara got into the car. He stared at her encouragingly from under his white fringe and licked her hand.

Víctor started the car, and only then did he ask, 'Where are we going?'

'How about the place where we first met?'

'The petrol station?'

'A car is coming to pick me up from Barbastro. I don't need you to drive me all the way.'

They pulled away from the police station, engrossed in their own thoughts, leaving behind the ringing telephones, like echoes of another world, phone calls that had nothing to do with Sara and Víctor. Senior officers demanding explanations.

Víctor would be disciplined and almost certainly thrown off the force, after what had happened with Zacarías.

And Sara ... What about Sara? It was hardly likely that she would be congratulated for arresting Rafael ...

They drove past the pine forest where Ana and Lucía had disappeared five years earlier. The trees formed a dense wall that made it impossible to see into the woods; somewhere in there was the tree where Caridad had spoken to Sara, the diseased roots of which snaked underground. This land had given it protection, kept it standing and apparently healthy. Only the roots and the soil that fed it knew the tree was diseased, but they cared for it, loved it nonetheless.

The rising sun illuminated the slopes of Monte Albádes to the west, Monte Perdido and La Kregüeña to the north-east, the peaks of Los Montes Malditos to the south, copper-coloured and proud, as though victorious.

As they passed the bridge near the school and the junction with Avenida de Posets, Sara could not help looking to the right, to where Monte Ármos rose up to Tempestades cirque and the tarn where Ana had learned to swim. On the far side of the bridge was the road leading to Los Corzos, to the semi-detached houses of Ana and Lucía, at the end of the street.

Sara did not have the courage to say goodbye to the girls' parents.

'Don't drive so slowly,' she said to Víctor.

He turned left and Sara saw the Hotel La Renclusa. Her suitcase was still up in her room and she thought that she would send someone for it, or perhaps she would not bother. Was there anything in that suitcase that she wanted to keep? She remembered Elisa's words when she stepped into the room and looked out of the window at the mountain: *The sunrises are spectacular.*

The jeep's headlights traced a cone of light on the tarmac. They passed La Corza Blanca. *I've never understood the moral of that story,* Caridad had said, that night she had told Sara the legend about the woman who was a white deer.

I believe in God, not men, Santiago had joked as they left the church of Santa María de Laude, which stood on the plaza next to the café. This was a walled village, built to protect itself from outsiders. Self-sufficient. Sara thought about the Cofradía and its emblem, the eight-pointed star that was embroidered on the breast of Víctor's shirt, now smeared with blood and dirt.

On the right, behind the maze of twisting alleyways, was the plaza and the town hall with its colonnade, the Hunting Society and Nerín's Gunsmith's. Neither he nor his daughter would ever come back to the village.

Sara had mixed feelings, leaving Monteperdido. She would miss the cobbled streets and the people, but, at the same time, she knew that she would have never fitted in here.

The village needed to forget what had happened and she would make it impossible to do that.

'Where will you go?' Víctor asked as he saw the petrol station up ahead.

'I don't know,' Sara said. 'Back home, I suppose.' Although she knew there was no home for her to go back to.

Víctor pulled up at the petrol station and, before switching off the engine, he turned to Sara.

'Can I come with you? It doesn't matter where,' he said in a breathless rush of words. 'We could try.'

That's what life is: trying, Sara remembered Caridad telling her, but she did not answer.

Víctor wished he could have explained it better, found the words to describe the feeling that had been welling in him ever since Sara had left Rafael in the interview room and, sobbing, walked back through the station to her office. Víctor did not want to leave Monteperdido; this was his place, his family. He did not want to run away, but he did not want to lose Sara. Maybe it was selfish, but he liked the man he saw reflected in her eyes. He wanted to be that man: the Víctor next to whom Sara had slept soundly.

Sara felt lightheaded. She could not bring her herself to look at Víctor, sitting next to her, waiting for an answer, and instead she stared out at the pine forest, at the petrol station, and high above the rocky crags. The dawn sky was like a red sea, rolling on the horizon, between the peaks. Sara thought she saw a white deer emerge from the shadows and stop in a small clearing in the first rays of sunlight. The doe turned her head and, from far away, her deep, dark eyes stared at Sara, and then, with a bound, she disappeared into the thicket.

'Turn back,' she said to Víctor, and, urged on by her hunch, she said, 'Come on, come on – turn round. Back to the village.'

Víctor made a U-turn and headed back towards Monteperdido.

I'm not a murderer, Rafael had said.

'Is this about what I just said?' Víctor asked, keeping his eyes on the road.

'He dropped Lucía down the ravine and then came into the village and killed Ana. That's what he told us,' Sara said. 'Why? Why would he do that?'

'I'm not interested in his reasons,' Víctor said.

'He didn't kill Simón when he started to be a problem. He didn't kill Ana when she came home . . . There's something that doesn't add up. I don't believe the story that he was desperate. If what he's saying is true, he would have shot himself. He would have committed suicide. But he still had hope.'

'What hope?'

'Lucía . . . Stop the car!' Sara screamed as they were about to pass Transportes Castán. 'Drive in there.' She grabbed the door handle. She wanted to jump out. She wanted to get there as soon as possible.

Lucía was my wife.

He had kept her in the tool shed. He had forced her to make the call to Ana, and he knew that sooner or later they would trace Simón's phone. So he had moved her and hidden her somewhere else.

Once things had calmed down, I'd take Lucía out of the valley in one of the trucks.

'He was planning to kill Ana and then escape with Lucía,' she said to Víctor.

They pulled up on the forecourt of the hangar; in front of them were the few trucks Joaquín Castán still owned. Sara got out and ran towards them.

I wanted her just for myself.

'The son of a bitch would be happier for us to find her dead than for her to have a chance of a life without him,' Sara said. 'Look in the truck!'

Víctor opened the doors of the truck. It was empty. He heard Sara's voice: 'Víctor!' Before he could turn, he heard the gunshot as Sara blasted the padlock on the trailer and flung open the doors.

Víctor ran towards her and, from the look on her face, he could tell that she had found Lucía.

He was afraid they were too late.

He was afraid to find out what was in the trailer.

'It's all right,' he heard Sara whisper. 'Let's get you home to your family.'

Sara climbed into the back of the trailer and walked slowly to the corner where Lucía was cowering. Sitting on the floor, hugging her knees against her chest, the girl was trembling. Whether it was from fear or relief was impossible to say.

'Are you OK, honey?' Sara said softly, brushing the girl's hair from her face. And then she hugged her.

Sara felt Lucía's breathing gradually calm. When she looked around, she saw Víctor standing in the doorway of the trailer; the dawn light behind framed him with a golden glow. Although she could not see his face, she knew he was smiling.

Lucía shivered in the arms of this stranger, even though she knew she was safe. For five years, she had felt only the cold touch of Rafael, the rough, calloused hands she had tried to avoid, and Ana, whose skin was her skin. Her sister, holding her every night, stroking her hair, telling her to be strong, telling her she could survive.

'We didn't just hate each other,' Lucía remembered. 'We loved each other more than anyone.'

Lucía had saved Ana's life on their first day in the *refugio*; she had told Rafael she would kill herself if he hurt Ana. And although Ana could not have known it, she had saved Lucía every other day of their captivity – being in her bed, being her family, her conscience. Hate and love: two sides of the same coin.

Lucía did not need anyone to tell her. She could sense that Ana was dead.

Or perhaps she was not dead. Perhaps she had been transformed into something else – into one of the stars that peered down through the hole in the roof. A small light in the sky over Monteperdido.

Lucía thought of the winters and the snow. She remembered when they were little girls, jumping and laughing and throwing snowballs in the frozen playground. She remembered how cold she had felt, even wearing gloves, as she packed a snowball to throw at Ana, who was standing at the top of the slide, wearing her pink woolly hat. She remembered the snowball exploding and falling back to the ground, returning to snow. But Ana had not moved. She was staring at something behind Lucía, and, when Lucía turned, she too stood frozen, watching the deer.

It was standing next to Raquel, its breath a cloud of mist that dissolved in the air as the doe turned and carried on up the mountain.

All those memories of Ana's face, every gesture – they were safe within Lucía. Ana's voice, reciting the same poem over and over as she walked around in circles in the hole, so close it was as though she were whispering in Lucía's ear:

Your heart pierced by an Angel's fiery spear
to the waters, run, Teresa, pale and dappled deer
for there a fount of life doth thee await,
a fire, too, whose blaze doth not abate.

Acknowledgements

Village of the Lost Girls would not exist without Jorge Diaz, Carlos Montero, Angela Armero and Antonio Mercero. The idea for this story was born while we were working together at Magnolia TV in Barcelona. Thank you for letting me lose myself in these mountains.

Moreover, without the advice of Jorge and Carlos, this novel would not have been the same.

To Mireia Acosta, my imaginative agent, who crossed my path and plucked this story from me. It is thanks to his enthusiasm that it became a reality. To Lars Neubert, Alberto Marcos and David Trias, for believing in *Village of the Lost Girls* from the very first page.

To Felix J. Velando and Jose Oscar Lopez, thank you for reading this and many, many other stories that have never been printed.

For my mother, who has always made everything easier, and Dario and Laura, children I hope I'll never lose – thank you for accepting my absences while I was frantically writing with as much hope as despair.